The Curse of the Redhead

by

Nicki Pascarella

A Miranda Albright, Ph.D. Mystery
Book 2

The Curse of the Redhead

Cover Art by *Diana Carlile*

The Wild Rose Press, Inc.
PO Box 708
Adams Basin, NY 14410-0708
Visit us at www.thewildrosepress.com

Publishing History
First Edition, 2022
Trade Paperback ISBN 978-1-5092-4666-3
Digital ISBN 978-1-5092-4667-0

A Miranda Albright, Ph.D. Mystery Book 2
Published in the United States of America

Dedication

To my handsome husband, Hans. Thanks for putting up
with me for the past thirty-three years.

Chapter 1

Four days before bleeding out in a snow-covered parking lot, I sat across from a Himalayan-sized man with an intricately inked arm. His index finger slid under letters, he furrowed his brow in concentration, and sweat drenched his forehead. The snarling bulldog decorating his arm followed along as he repeated the words on the page.

While he read the book, I interpreted his arm— *celer silens mortalis*—Swift. Silent. Deadly.

The imposing man laid his palm on the page. "The end."

"Awesome, Wochowska. I'm impressed. You've been doing your homework."

"Yep." He smiled. "I practice every night. It's way more rewarding than bludgeoning dead beats."

When Wochowska grinned, his non-existent front tooth gave him an off-putting visage that terrified even the bravest of souls. Even though he had frightened me the first time I met him, he had become my star pupil and friend.

A few months earlier, we had become acquainted when I visited the loan shark and bookie Alexander Lowalski during the investigation of a murdered co-ed. Lowalski, a Godfather-like character for the Polish mob, and his assistant, Lester Wochowska, occasionally had to break bad clients' fingers.

That may have been something I shied away from before my recent move to Bellmount. However, almost three months of habitation in the small town had changed me. My cousin Liam insisted I had become impatient and reckless since moving into my aunt's inn. I blamed my new personality traits on a curse.

Wochowska and I packed up our belongings and headed for the exit of the magnificent three-story 1875 Colonial building that sat in the main quad of bucolic Bellmount College.

"Have a good night, Betsy," I called to the librarian as we passed her desk.

She waved. "Good night, Dr. Albright."

Woschowska stopped in front of her, blushed, and looked down at his feet. "Bye, Betsy, thank you for the books."

The mousy librarian beamed. "You have a good Thanksgiving." She tapped a finger on top of the pile. "*The Old Man and The Sea* is my favorite."

Wochowska's cheeks turned a deep crimson. "See you next Tuesday, Betsy."

She removed her rhinestone-studded cateye glasses, peered up at him, and fluttered her lashes. "See you next week, Lester."

Once we were in the parking lot, I tickled my giant. "You like Betsy."

"Doctor Miranda, please stop," Wowchowska said between giggles.

"Not until you admit you like Betsy."

If Wochowska wanted to make me stop teasing him, all he had to do was press on me with his thumb. I was five feet, three inches tall, and he was six, two. I weighed one hundred twenty pounds, and his scale read two hundred-ninety. I was twenty-five with long red hair and emerald eyes. He was pushing forty, had black hair and black eyes. I was a college professor, and he was an ex-Marine. My biceps were non-existent. His were the circumference of a beer keg.

"She's pretty," he admitted.

"She likes you too. I think she even got fancy new glasses for you. You should ask her out." I gave him a two-second tickle under his chin.

He giggled. "Really?"

"Really."

"Maybe I'll ask her next week after our lesson. Should I give her flowers?"

"I think she would love flowers. Bring something that she can sit on the circulation desk. She'll be the envy of all her librarian friends, having a big handsome man like you."

He grimaced. "I'm not handsome."

I wrapped my palm halfway around his forearm. "Of course you are. You're big and strong, and you have that cool bulldog tattoo. Women love those things."

The gargantuan man frowned. "You don't think she'll be upset about my job?"

Although his job working as a debt collector and bodyguard for the Polish Mob was questionable, I suspected that the smitten librarian might find it titillating.

"I think she will like you for who you are."

"Thanks, Doctor Miranda. You're driving straight home, right?"

"Yep."

He looked down at me and waggled his finger.

"You better not get yourself into trouble."

Having a criminal advise me to stay away from trouble had become the norm. Over the past three months, I had found a corpse, and angered most of the important people in town.

Although I had accidently put a bullet in West Westinghouse's well-formed derriere, I was not responsible for Greg Grainey's death. Still, most of the town's inhabitants blamed me. Maybe God did too, because I had been saddled with the gun peddler's obsessed ghostly form until I feathered my nest in the hereafter.

"I promise. I'm heading straight home." I yawned and wiped a sleep tear from my eye.

"Happy Thanksgiving," Wochowka called as he opened the door of his two-toned, four-doored 1980 monstrosity.

"You too, Wowchoska. Have a great time reading to your nieces." I climbed into my even uglier automobile.

I put my key into the ignition, pumped my pedal a few times, and then turned the key. *Bra bra bra bra*, my engine banged. I glared at the dashboard, willing the gas gauge to move from red to green.

"Come on. You can do it."

Even though the little pointer stayed close to the big red *E*, my car lurched forward in search of his next meal.

I had named the 1971 brown abomination that my father had given me following my doctoral dissertation defense, The Tank. Not a spot of rust. Old Mrs. White had kept him in the garage for eighteen years. Dad got a deal. He only had to pay three hundred dollars.

Lucky me! I drove the ugliest car in all of Bear County, and a good portion of my paycheck went to keeping my hideous automobile nourished.

My fingers remained crossed on the steering wheel for the four-minute drive to the Stevens Speed-mart. After pulling into the parking lot and hooking the beast to the paycheck-stealing gas pump, I sighed in relief. While the numbers on the pump increased, I petted the hood and cooed. "I'm sorry I'm so negative, buddy, but you're insatiable, and I'm trying to buy us a few things. Wouldn't you like to have one of those Radio World TC-1 Mobile Cellular Phones inside you? Tell you what, if you go on a diet, I might also be able to buy you a CD player. One more thing, I need to buy a briefcase. You need to cut me a break because a college professor carrying a blood-stained backpack is embarrassing."

I grabbed my wallet and entered the store. After fixing a cup of hot chocolate, I grabbed a long caramel candy, and headed for the cash register.

"Hi, Doctor Albright," the young man waiting on me said. "I think they're calling for snow tonight."

"It's a cold one, Mason."

"Brrr." He wrapped his arms around his torso and dramatically shivered. "That reading assignment was tough. Do you think I could have some extra time to write the paper?"

Good thing Mason Bitz had a charming smile because he was one of the few kids at Bellmount who didn't come from money. I considered his circumstances, and decided not to respond with a resounding *No*!

"Your last paper was dog doody. I wanted you to

have the assignment to me before the Thanksgiving holiday, but I'll give you the vacation to work on it. You need to type and proofread. If not, you'll have to redo it. And, it needs to be turned in first thing Tuesday morning."

"Deal! You're the best."

I switched on my stern face. "I know you're working long hours, but you need to take your time on this paper and do a better job if you want to pass the class."

"I promise."

I waved to him. "Have a great break." I unwrapped my candy, stuck it into my mouth, grabbed my hot chocolate, and headed toward the exit.

Bang! Bang! Bang!

I sprinted to the door.

"That sounded like gunshots," Mason said, coming up alongside me.

Car tires squealed as Mason and I pressed our faces against the glass.

After gawking for a second, I bounded out the door. A long caramel hung from my mouth; hot chocolate splashed onto my glove, and a nineteen-year-old Mason Bitz scrambled at my heels.

"I didn't see the vehicle. Did you?" Mason asked.

"No," I said before tripping over a pile of red and white fluff lying in front of my car. I bent to check the fur's pulse—no cheek, no left arm, no heartbeat. "Oh my God."

"Holy shit," said Mason.

"Hey, Crimson. I think someone shot Santa," declared the ghost peeking over my shoulder.

****

Greg the ghost stayed outside, looking for clues, while Mason and I stood by the counter, steadying our nerves and warming our frozen limbs.

"Dr. Albright, shouldn't we call the police?"

I bounced about, trying to get my blood pumping. "Yes, where's the phone?"

"Here." He ushered me behind the counter.

After dialing, I said, "Hi, Mrs. Little. It's Randa Albright." Then I waited an eternity for Tommy's mother to track him down.

As soon as he said hello, my speech tripled in speed. "Tommy, it's Randa. You have to get to the Stevens Speed-mart on Elm right away. I'm here with one of my students and a corpse. Are you leaving now? We have to call 911, and Shultz will be the first one here. Hurry!"

I pinned my gaze on Mason. "Call 911. I'm going to wait outside for Tommy Little." In truth, I wanted to touch the corpse without my student asking questions.

"Dr. Albright, should we have dialed 911 before we called your friend?" Mason asked.

"Yes. That's what we would have done if our sheriff wasn't a halfwit."

The door closed on Mason's wide-mouthed gape.

I had discovered firsthand that dispatch would send the coroner and the state police homicide detective. But, before they arrived, Edgar Shultz, the Bellmount municipal sheriff, would show up and make a mess of the crime scene. I would not let it happen again. Tommy Little, the local park ranger, had some legal authority over certain jurisdictions, and even though we weren't in the state forest, I needed him as backup.

Although I'm a reluctant telepath who can read

minds and find energy footprints, the Stevens Speed-mart didn't give off any psychic energy. I tip-toed cautiously, careful not to disturb anything. It was a waste of time since the sheriff was the kind of imbecile that waltzed around with dead bodies. Okay, I'm exaggerating a tiny bit. But I'm one hundred percent serious when I say the no-good cop would show up and inappropriately touch me right before his klutzy body fell face-first on the corpse.

It wasn't messing with evidence if I checked for a pulse, so I bent, steadied my breathing, placed my fingers on the dead man's carotid artery, and closed my eyes.

Electric current traveled from the man's neck through my arm, then to my core. There was a jolt and a staticky image. Santa pointed a gun at me, and the vision disappeared. Like the small amount of current that surges through an electrical appliance right before it breaks for good, I had experienced the last of this man's energy.

I struggled to decipher the incomplete vision. Had another Santa shot the dead Santa? There had been three gunshots, but the parking lot didn't have a recent psychic footprint. Had the murder happened in another location?

"Dr. Albright, are you okay? You look strange. Your hair is all spiky," Mason said from behind me.

"I'm fine. The wind wreaks havoc on my locks, and I'm double-checking for a pulse." While patting my electrically charged frizz, I cringed at the two lies.

Mason nodded and shuffled his weight from side to side. "I called 911. The state police and ambulance will be here soon. The owner of the store is also on his way."

I perused the lot. "Are there security cameras?"

"The one focused on the gas pump isn't working, but the one inside is okay. Guess that's no help." Mason frowned.

Greg reappeared and tapped at the corpse with his spanking new designer snow boot. Disgusted on many levels, I blew out a puff of air so strong it scattered the fresh flurries falling near my face.

Then we waited.

Finally, a white pickup truck with the Pennsylvania Park's Service logo pulled in behind my car. An adorable freckle-faced man with big ears and a buzz cut emerged.

"Tommy, thank goodness. Help me protect the scene," I said two seconds before muttering, "Fudge! Shultz is here."

"Shit," Tommy and Greg said.

A police car, siren blaring, pulled into the parking lot.

I pulled my shoulders back and prepared for battle.

****

Beside the big number two on my enemy list I had written: Shultz.

I took immense pleasure in planning his death. As he climbed from his cruiser, I immersed myself in a fantasy in which I used Princess, the bejeweled gun I carried in my backpack, to shoot a round into his gut. First, I'd flatten his skull with the gas pump. After that, I'd hop into The Tank and run him over. I'd back up and crash into him, again and again, until his body and the macadam were one.

Tommy and I did our best to contain the Shultz-damage until the coroner arrived. Eventually, an unmarked state police car pulled into the lot. The useless homicide cop, Detective Miller, climbed out of the passenger side.

A brown boot stepped from the driver's side. The boot was attached to a jeaned calf and the calf led to a muscular thigh. The owner of the well-formed quadricep wore a brown suede jacket. I may have hissed at his full disclosure because he looked to be in his mid-thirties, had a chiseled jawline, blue eyes, an alluring five o'clock shadow, and strawberry blonde hair.

"Oh, my," I accidentally said.

My utterance earned me a glare from Tommy and a snort from Greg.

"Dr. Albright, What are the chances?" said a sarcastic Detective Miller as he approached. He lifted his chin a fraction of an inch. "Mr. Little."

Removing my gloves, I checked out the circle clustered together. A palpable tension swathed us as the men grunted their greetings.

I detested the akin-to-devil-vomit sheriff. He loved my D cups and hair but hated everything else about me.

The park ranger had about as much respect for the sheriff as he had for a river troll hunting wildlife out of season.

The sheriff wanted the park ranger fired for the fun of it.

Detective Miller needed to retire then nap.

Mason Bitz craved a cherry Slurpicy mixed with Vodka.

Mike Stevens, the Speed-mart owner, wanted the entire thing moved from his parking lot.

Larry Watkins, the coroner, wanted to go home to his wife and baby.

Greg Grainey appeared and disappeared with the wind.

Then there was the man in the soft leather jacket.

Miller thumbed toward the Adonis beside him. "This is Sergeant Sean O'Sullivan. He'll be taking the lead on this case."

The magnificent cop shook hands with all of the men before grasping mine. A man after my own heart, he planned to solve a murder.

"Dr. Albright, with the long red ringlets?"

"You know me?"

O'Sullivan chuckled. "I got an earful from Miller on the way here."

"Anything you hear from Dweedledum and Dweedledee is a lie." I gave Miller and Shultz a big cheesy grin.

The insulted parties bristled, and the strawberry blonde man with the perfect teeth continued to smile.

"Let's start at the beginning. Tell me what happened, Dr. Albright," Detective Gorgeous said.

****

By the time the inquisition ceased and the coroner finished his preliminary investigation, the clock struck midnight. The temperature had risen to thirty-three degrees, and the snow mixed with sleet. A sheet of fresh ice coated the parking lot.

"The mountains are going to be treacherous tonight," Miller said.

Sean O'Sullivan tested his boot on a slick patch and frowned. "Maybe we should get a room."

"We have room at the inn," I offered.

"Room at the inn?" asked O'Sullivan.

Tommy shook his head. "I'm sure they don't want to stay at the inn."

Ignoring Tommy, I focused on my new cop friend.

"My aunt owns the Bellmount Inn, and I live with her. We have a third-floor room available. It's tiny but lovely and has two twins if you guys want it. Breakfast is included."

"We'll check into a motel on the way out of town," Miller said.

"Hell no. I want a homemade breakfast at a fancy inn," said O'Sullivan. "Dr. Albright, why don't you head home and get us checked in? We have a few things to finish up here."

I directed a "See you in a bit" to O'Sullivan and a "Hope I don't see you ever again, Shultz," to my enemy. "Bye, Mason, you earned yourself time on top of your extension. Take until next Thursday," I called over the wind.

"Thanks, Dr. Albright. You're the best!" Mason called back.

I waived to Mike Stevens and walked Tommy to his truck. "Thanks, Tommy," I said.

My friend's words were kind, but his furrowed brow betrayed his concern. "Sure, Randa. You know I'm always here for you."

"I know. What's wrong?"

"I worry because trouble seems to follow you."

I kissed Tommy on the cheek. I shouldn't have taken advantage of the moment to spy on his thoughts. It was a low-down thing to do since I had recently improved my ability to block out others' observations. Tommy Little exuded disappointment because I had asked him for help and was going home with another man.

I placed my hand on Tommy's forearm. "Please forgive me. I'm sorry I drag you into my messes. I won't do it anymore."

"No worries. I like helping you." He kissed me on the forehead. "Good night, Randa."

I waved then headed to The Tank, where a grinning Greg waited in the passenger seat.

"That was fun," he said.

I needed sleep, and my ghost needed a new hobby.

Chapter 2

Buzz, buzz, buzz went my alarm clock.

Lick, lick, lick went my Shetland Sheepdog.

Squeak, squeak, squeak went my brat of a rat on his wheel.

"Rise and shine, Crimson," said my ghost.

I rubbed my eyes and muttered, "Fudge." It was six-thirty a.m., and after four hours of sleep, it was time to start my day.

I was not to be outdone by a fairy tale princess. I had a tiny turtle named Princess Pickles—FYI, he happened to be a princess with a boy part, Simon, a lazy rat with an attitude problem, and Spot, a hyperactive Shetland Sheepdog. I also had my very own specter, the over-sexed ex-gun peddler.

My pretend castle was on the third floor of my aunt's Victorian. The magnificent structure was built in 1889 and had a romantic wrap-around porch adorned with decorative lattice work. Turn-of-the-century antiques decorated every room.

My Grandma Zoey and Grandpa Lucas bought the Bellmount Inn in 1942. My grandpa, a radio operator on a B-17, was shot down over Germany and declared MIA in the Great War. My grandma spent years attempting to use her psychic abilities to search for him. After two decades of dead ends, she had eventually "gone crazy," her telepathic skills adding another level

14

to her eccentricities. When Grandma Zoey passed, my Aunt Edith and her caretaker boyfriend, Russ Jenkins, took over the inn. I spent my first eighteen summers in western Pennsylvania with my aunt, who was a second mother to me.

My turret was decorated in various blue and white patterns and had a bay window with a large upholstered window seat that had served as my throne when I was a child. From my tower, I could look out over the town to the west branch of the Susquehanna River.

Greg appeared, interrupting my morning ritual of overseeing my kingdom.

"Crimson, I don't trust that guy at the Stevens Speed-mart."

"Mason? He's a terrible student but a super nice kid."

Greg sat beside me. "Not the kid, the store owner, Mike Stevens."

"Why do you say that?"

"I'm not sure. I caught him making a secretive call."

"Do you know who he called?" I asked.

"Missed the name, but I caught him saying, "Did you meet with the Santa guy? Cause there is a dead Santa in my parking lot."

"Those were his exact words?"

"Yep," Greg said. "Suspicious. Don't you think?"

"Did he say anything else?"

"Nope, nothing. I don't trust that cop either. Too much machismo."

"O'Sullivan? He seems like the first decent detective I've met since I moved here. Why don't you trust him?"

"Cause that detective has his sleazy eyeballs all over you," said my ghost, ogling me like I was his last meal.

"Greg, I can't believe you have the guts to say that. You're the slimeball. So far, he has behaved like a gentleman, and it's time for you to go. I need to get dressed."

"Fine, but I'm watching that sergeant detective. He tries anything funny with my girl, and I'll haunt the shit out of him."

I rolled my eyes and gave my ghost a mini finger wave. "Bye."

"Kiss for the road?" Greg puckered up and leaned in close.

I swatted at the air as I shooed him away. "Goodbye, Greg!"

He disappeared.

I undressed and climbed into my clawfoot tub shower.

****

Aunt Edith found etiquette to be non-negotiable. She was old school in her manners but hell on wheels liberal in her politics. According to my aunt, the conservative oligarchy in Bellmount needed to be kept on their toes. The town council was despicable, and Aunt Edith was outvoted four to two on every issue.

The first of my aunt's council adversaries was Ian Patterson. Ian was a wealthy coal mogul who refused to follow the environmental regulations. He had molded himself into a local hero and was running for Congress.

Next was Pastor Smith. Smith was a cruel Bible-banging man who wanted to play God and control the curriculum taught in schools. He had even covered up important details in his daughter Suzy's murder to protect his lily-white, holier-than-thou reputation.

There was Mayor Reynolds, who was more a cleaner than a mayor. He liked to sweep up anything he thought reflected poorly on him, and his handling of finances was beyond reprehensible.

The fourth member had been my shadow, Greg Grainey, the arrogant womanizing owner of Grainey's Gun Shop. His business thrived since Bear County was a sportsman's paradise. Jessica, Greg's beautiful daughter—and *numero uno* on my enemy list—was filling his seat since his death. Jessica was long and lean, with dark hair that shined like polished obsidian. She was so frigid that ice formed under her designer shoes, and frozen shards exploded from her cold blue eyes. Jessica had married then tormented the sweet Dr. Bradley Gordon.

Dr. Gordan was the fifth seat on the council and was my aunt's only ally and her best friend. He was thirty-three, six feet two inches of masculine perfection, and his eyes were the color of sapphires. The town consensus was that Bradley resembled a movie star. I thought him a cross between Bronte's Heathcliff and a fairy tale prince.

Finally, there was Aunt Edith—the champion of the little guy, the protector of the environment, the savior of the world.

When my saint of an aunt asked me to be polite and start every morning by introducing myself to the inn's guests, I obeyed. I did almost everything Aunt Edith asked of me. Although, despite her warnings, I couldn't stay away from Weston Westinghouse. It wasn't that she didn't adore Weston; she did. West and

Tommy Little were my cousin Liam's best friends and were like sons to her. However, she knew that West was my Achilles' heel and that he had been leading me astray since I was a toddler.

The defining moment had been a day nineteen years earlier when Liam took me home, my brand new pink dress and patent leather shoes soaked and muddy. Two years my senior, West, had dared me to leap across a non-jumpable creek, and I had tried. Staying away from West tested my limits, and I failed miserably at it.

However, greeting the guests at breakfast was something I could do. I grabbed my coffee from the sideboard.

"Hello, I'm Miranda, Edith's niece. What year is your daughter in?" I asked a middle-aged couple picking their daughter up from college for the Thanksgiving holiday.

"Hello. Nice to meet you. I hope you're enjoying your stay in Bellmount?" I said to a young couple visiting family.

Next, I greeted the wizened-faced man whose entire appearance could be described as light gray, dark gray, and gray. "Good morning, Detective Miller. Much nicer than the Holiday Inn, right?"

"Well, your aunt isn't quite the pain in the ass you are," Miller said.

There was no need to mince words with Miller since his evasion of detective work had led to Greg's death.

"Only because you haven't yet angered her. As soon as she understands how lazy you are, you will feel her wrath. Then you will pine for my company," I warned him.

O'Sullivan chuckled.

"Hi, Sergeant O'Sullivan," I said sweetly.

"Call me, Sean," said the handsome man whose reddish-gold scruff was taking over his jaw.

"Are you enjoying your western omelet and coffee cake, Sean?"

"Damn good breakfast."

"Told you." I smiled. "And, isn't the view of the town to die for?"

"Yeah." His fiery gaze pierced through me. "Breathtaking view."

Tearing myself from his perusal, I revisited the sideboard and topped off my coffee.

"Hey, Red," Sean called to me. "We'll be at the crime scene for the day. I'm planning to stay at the inn tonight, and I might need to interview you again."

Miller looked to the ceiling and shook his head.

"I get off work early for Thanksgiving break," I said.

Sean nodded. "See you then."

I continued to our combination kitchen, the swinging door bobbling behind me.

"Good morning, Aunt Edith."

Aunt Edith stood at her stove, preparing omelets. Russ wasn't back from his daily trip to the town center to pick up *The Bellmount Gazette*.

My aunt handed me a plate. "Good morning, honey."

"Thank you. Looks delicious. Where's Winona?"

Winona Westinghouse, West's older cousin, frequently helped my aunt prepare breakfast and bake treats for the guests.

Aunt Edith wiped her hands on her apron. "I gave her the morning off so she could help Polly get ready for Thanksgiving."

Polly was Winona's mom and West's aunt. The Westinghouse clan was numerous, and holidays at Polly's home were pure chaos.

Although Winona drove me looney, she was my confidant and friend. She was eight years my senior and looked out for me. She was clueless that I was crazy for her Casanova of a cousin. To be fair, Winona was clueless about a lot. We had something in common, though. She loved snooping in police matters as much as I did. Winona was living out a fantasy in which we were private investigators.

"Fudge. I wanted to talk to her." I chewed my omelet without tasting it.

My aunt broke into my sleuthing daydream. "Miranda, have you tried calling Bradley lately?"

I pushed a piece of omelet around my plate. "I called again a few days ago. I know you think he still has feelings for me, but he can't forgive me for the things I did to him, and I don't blame him."

"You didn't do anything to him," Aunt Edith said. "Greg Grainey was a dishonest rat and he sealed his own fate. It wasn't your fault, and this town needs to get over it. I assure you, Bradley doesn't blame you."

I cringed and searched for Greg, hoping he hadn't heard my aunt's insult. I didn't want him to hide her eyeglasses in the raw egg bowl.

No Greg complaining in my face, no flying utensils, no flickering lights. Thank goodness. The unfriendly ghost was probably checking on his gun store.

"And I know Bradley is crazy about you, Miranda. I don't know why he hasn't called. Don't give up."

My aunt wasn't privy to all of my secrets. Maybe Brad was crazy about me. Perhaps he didn't think I was responsible for Greg's death, but I had made unforgivable mistakes.

The kitchen door flew open and smashed into the wall.

"Oops. Sorry." Winona grimaced then charged toward me, carrying a newspaper.

Russ followed a few feet behind.

She waved the paper in the air. "Miranda, oh my God! I had to stop in to tell you. George Stiles was murdered at the Stevens Speed-mart last night. Grimwood is calling it The Santa Murder."

I grabbed the newspaper and scanned the short article. Thank goodness my name didn't appear in print. I sighed with relief, chugged the rest of my coffee, and packed my backpack.

Chapter 3

My best friend, Keisha Brown, the assistant to the dean, worked with me on the third floor of Sutton Hall. Her desk had been plopped between the stairs to the front and a questionably safe elevator to the back.

Keisha was beautiful, efficient, and had a mouth like an angry trucker. Her to-the-point demeanor was justified since her work area afforded her no privacy. Her day was occupied with annoying professors and demanding students. Since there were no walls to protect her, people didn't feel the need to respect her personal space. I recommended she construct duct tape barriers to keep out the riff-raff.

I pulled up a chair. "It was crazy. George Stiles' corpse was in front of my car, and he was in a Santa suit. Of course, Shultz showed up before the state police."

"No fucking way!" Keisha's colorful hair beads and dangling gold earrings swung about her face. "George? That's terrible. He was a good guy. He was a Little League coach, and he had grandkids."

"How terrible," I said.

"He was one of the Santas at Lightsingers Department Store. Did it for years." Keisha's full lips turned down at the edges, and her emotion-filled brown eyes betrayed her sadness.

The dean exited his office at the end of the hallway

and barged toward us.

"Good morning," he said

Although Johnson's abrupt manner and suspicious eyes intimidated the bejesus out of me, I gave him a cordial, "Good morning."

"Dean Johnson, I have that agenda for you." Keisha handed him a paper from her outbox.

"Thank you, Ms. Brown. Your immediate attention to this is appreciated. Enjoy the holiday." Johnson stomped down the hall, slamming the door behind him.

Keisha scowled at his back. "You would think that with all his fancy titles, the man could learn to close the door like a normal person."

"A Santa at Lightsingers?" I asked.

Keisha stared into my soul."I know that look. What is that scheming mind of yours up to

The elevator screeched into place, the ground shook, a bell donged, and the five-foot-four Professor Michaelson stepped into our sphere.

"Good morning, ladies, what's the word?"

I cringed.

Dr. Niles Michaelson was an odd little man. He obsessed over World War Two, taught his class in his bare feet, and had developed a personal code for social norms and hygiene.

"Christ, Michaelson, put your shoes on. What if your dream comes true, a bomb drops, and you have to go into your shelter without shoes? You'll be looking at your hairy ass toes until you're liberated," Keisha said.

Michaelson looked at his feet, smiled, and whistled to his office.

"That man needs help." Keisha rubbed her temples. "And back to my question. What are you up to?"

"I'm thinking."

"They send that disinterested homicide detective again?"

"Yes, but they sent another guy with him. His name is Sean O'Sullivan, and he seems to be on the ball."

Keisha rolled her eyes.

"What was that for?" I asked.

A door down the hall opened, and Dr. Lincoln Harrison strolled our way. The sixty-something Lincoln was my mentor, friend, and one of three people who knew that I was telepathic. Brad Gordon and West Westinghouse were the other two.

The psychology professor was not an expert in psychic matters. He hadn't even believed in them until he met me. He had been willing to suspend his skepticism for the sake of research, and over time had come to accept my strange abilities. Through trial and error, he had devised a method he called "putting up a shield." It protected me from others' unwanted thoughts and saved them from having me snoop around in their brains. It wasn't full-proof. I had occasional slip-ups with stressful moments and the divining of things I didn't want to know. Still, I had learned to block out about eighty percent of unwanted information.

Lincoln sat on the corner of Keisha's desk. "What's up, ladies?"

"You look quite Santa-ish," I said.

Keisha chortled. "Run for the hills, sucker. Our girl is up to one of her schemes."

Lincoln's blue eyes twinkled. "Fill me in."

"I don't know what you two are talking about. I'm not planning anything." I peered over my shoulder at the wall clock above the elevator. "Are you guys free after work?"

****

Bellmount boasted the historic turn-of-the-century Lightsingers department store. When we were children, Liam and I begged Aunt Edith to purchase items so that we could watch the sales clerk send notes through the magical pneumatic tubes. We were fascinated with the ladders leading to the eight-foot-high shelves that held the shoeboxes. Much to Liam's horror, we routinely visited the third floor to see the newest styles of fancy ladies' hats. We always ended our visits with a trip to the first-floor candy department.

Nineteen eighty-nine was the first time I experienced the nostalgic store during the holidays. The open ceiling allowed me to stand on the first floor and see up to the fifth story. A Santa in his sleigh display hung suspended below the skylight, and elves greeted children at each of the stairwells. The store Santa had set up shop on the second floor North Pole.

Keisha, Lincoln, and I bamboozled a poor secretary with confusing stories then barged into the store manager's office. Uninvited, we made ourselves comfortable as manager Lucas Timberlane glared at us.

"Look, I'm swamped. Some damn real estate company just bought the property and is talking about raising the rent. I think it's because they want to bring in a cheesy-ass mall. The owner of the store is threatening layoffs. I have a psychotic elf telling me how to run things and a Santa that didn't show up for his shift. The holidays make me so mad I want to kill someone." Timberlane checked his watch. "So what do you want?"

"Kill people? Damn, you have a bad attitude," Keisha said.

Timberlane's gaze cut from Lincoln to Keisha, and a grin spread across his previously tense face.

"We are here to apply for the Santa job," Lincoln said.

Timberlane stared at Keisha's lips. "We hire four Santas and a rotating staff of twelve elves every holiday. We already hired our full staff for this season."

Lincoln cleared his throat "But you are one Santa down."

"What are you talking about? I'm not ready to fire the guy who didn't show—yet."

If the depraved Lucas liked breathing, he needed to lift his gawking peepers from Keisha's legs before he earned himself a bloody nose.

"Your Santa didn't show because someone murdered him," said the no-nonsense Keisha.

Timberlane gaped.

"George Stiles was murdered last night. It was in the papers this morning," Lincoln said. "And since I have always wanted to be a department store Santa, and it looks like you require one, I thought, why not?"

Timberlane's brow lifted.

"Haven't the police been here asking questions?" I asked.

Timberlane looked from Keisha to Lincoln to me. "Oh, I get it. This is some sort of prank. That's why they sent a Santa-look alike with a redhead and a goddess. Who put you up to it? If it was Dinky—the bastard—tell him to go to hell. It isn't funny. Tell him—"

A knock interrupted.

The white-haired secretary leaned into the office. "Mr. Timberlane. There are two homicide cops here. They say they need to talk to you right away."

O'Sullivan and Miller pushed past the woman.

"Now, this is taking the joke a bit too far." Timberlane held out his hands. "Cuff me Officer Shit For Brains and Officer Pecker. Lock me up and throw away the key."

Miller scowled at me and huffed. "Damn it."

I forced a smile for the sergeant detective. "Hi, Sean."

My new cop friend looked me in the eyes, elongated his handsome features, and *tsk*ed.

"Mr. Timberlane, they really are cops. We are going to head out now," I said.

"Yep," Sean said. "I'm Officer Pecker, also known as Sergeant Sean O'Sullivan, Homicide Division with the state police." He held up his badge. "And this is Officer Shit for Brains, but you can call him Detective Miller."

Lincoln choked back a chortle. "I accept the job. Here is my contact information." He handed Timberlane a card.

Lincoln stood. Keisha and I followed.

Timberlane's mouth formed a big O. "Wait. I didn't offer you the job."

"That sucks. I guess my elf costume won't be getting any use this year." Keisha performed an award-winning dramatic sigh.

"You an elf?" Timberlane asked her.

I pointed to Lincoln. "He comes with three elves, and you can use our paychecks to purchase gifts for needy children."

O'Sullivan herded us to the exit. His hand lingered on my shoulder before the door closed behind us, shutting us out and locking away the befuddled manager with Officer Shit for Brains and Officer Pecker.

"Do you think we got the Santa job?" I asked.

Lincoln shrugged. "Not sure."

Keisha put her hands on her hips. "Three elves?"

I grimaced. "Sorry."

"Not only am I gonna have to fend off Timberlane the pervert, but I'm gonna have to put up with her moronic ass. Her IQ is ten points minus five dozen."

"It would break Winona's heart to be left out," I said.

Lincoln finally let his chortle rip.

Keisha bobbed her head, stirring up some serious attitude. "You owe me, Miranda Albright. And for the record, I'm going to be a sexy elf. None of that nerdy, pointy ear shit that I suspect her spazzy-ness will insist on wearing."

I sighed.

"And you wanna tell me why you didn't mention that the strawberry cop and you have a little spark?" she asked.

"No spark. I'm off men for the time being. Maybe forever."

My comment earned me stereo snorts.

"I'm serious," I called over my shoulder as I clonked down the department store stairs.

I one hundred percent meant it.

Chapter 4

My boycott of the opposite sex lasted less than six hours due to The Bear Claw Pub's proximity. The restaurant/bar sat five hundred feet downhill from the inn. Five members of the Westinghouse clan ran the establishment, and it was the best place in Bear County to get a burger, fries, and a draft beer. I didn't drink alcohol, but I was partial to the mozzarella sticks and the bartender's tongue.

Following my mini reprimand for showing up at a department store that I had every right to be at, Sergeant Sean O'Sullivan and I sat at the end of the bar. West Westinghouse dried a spot for us.

"Hiya, Doctor Shortcake. How goes it?" West asked.

"I'm good." I thumbed toward the newcomer by my side. "This is Sergeant O'Sullivan. He's the lead detective on the Santa Murder. He's staying at the inn for a couple of days."

West greeted him with a nod. "Shortcake doesn't drink—unless she's in a mood, then she's a lush. What can I get you?"

I flashed West the nastiest look I could muster. I had imbibed one time in my twenty-five years, and West never failed to use it against me.

I stared into West's eyes and grumbled, "I'd like a cup of coffee." Then I smirked, relishing in his annoyance at having to make a fresh pot.

West scowled.

"Irish Red on tap?" Sean asked.

"Nope. Bottle," West said.

"Perfect." Sean handed West a ten.

West crumpled the bill in his palm. "Hey, Shortcake. Have you heard from your doctor boyfriend?" He flashed me a smug grin.

"Hey, West, you bought any T-shirts that fit you lately?" Contorting my face, I made a dramatic show, acting as if his tight, shirts weren't unbelievably sexy.

Before taking his leave to fix our drinks, West shot me a look that could have singed my eyebrows.

"Yikes! Bad blood between you two?" Sean asked.

"He's my friend, but he can be a jerk. He's mad because I accidentally shot him in the butt."

West had forgiven me for the klutzy mishap and considered it his "Shortcake love tap." The truth was, I didn't understand why West and I were often cantankerous with each other.

"You shot him?" Sean asked.

"He and Tom Little were teaching me how to use my gun, and West stepped in front of my target." I left out the part where I wasn't paying attention because I was distracted by West's perfect posterior.

"What kind of gun do you have?"

"A second-hand 1969 22 caliber semi-automatic. The sheriff hasn't signed my paperwork to carry it yet. Shultz and I hate each other." I didn't think it necessary to mention that pink rhinestones covered my gun's barrel.

"A vintage weapon, to go with your vintage car. Very cool," Sean said. "I didn't know you had a boyfriend? And Shultz, well…"

"Ex-boyfriend. I'm sure Miller filled you in on the Grainey debacle?"

"Yes. Horrible that you had to witness it."

"Dr. Gordon was there. He was my boyfriend at the time, but he has refused to talk to me since that night."

"That's ridiculous." Sean shook his head. "The lieutenant thinks Miller bumbled the shit out of the investigation. That's why she assigned me to tag along this time. Bellmount isn't usually my jurisdiction."

"I'm glad they sent you. Our sheriff is a criminal, and Miller is incompetent."

"Hey, Red, if you tell anyone, I bad-mouthed a fellow cop, I'll deny it."

I stuck out my pinky. "I won't tell a soul. Although, I think everyone with half a brain knows Miller's a joke."

Sean stared at my little finger and chuckled.

Winona joined us, and I introduced her to the detective. West returned with a condensation-coated bottle a moment before Sean's pager went off.

"Hey, man. Can I use the house phone?" Sean asked.

"Yeah." A frowning West showed him to the storeroom, returning in time to hear his cousin gush.

"No fair, Miranda," Winona said. "How come you get to find all the dead bodies and have all the handsome men?"

West grunted.

"What's your problem tonight?" I asked.

"I don't have a problem. Just seems you like to collect corpses."

"West is jealous cause he isn't the most handsome

man in the bar tonight," said Winona.

Sean O'Sullivan was fine on a million levels. He was gorgeous, and he had a rugged scar that ran through his right eyebrow. He looked and smelled like he belonged in an Irish soap commercial. Still, Weston Westinghouse, the Third was no slouch. He had long lashes and hair that changed from light brown in the winter to golden in the summer. His jeans fit his derriere perfectly, and I could discern his well-formed pectorals through his cheap t-shirts. The kicker was West's country boy drawl made me gooey.

The first problem with him was, he was as smug as a Greek god was beautiful. The second problem was, West and I had a secret. He had recently taken my virginity. Town rumors were that West knew how to please a woman, and a night with him would ruin her desire to be with another man. I learned firsthand they were indeed hard facts. We'd done our best to keep the indiscretion a secret, since it would cause a rift between West and Liam. The only person who knew about us was Dr. Brad Gordon, my ex-boyfriend, who refused to return my calls.

"I'm still the sexiest guy in this bar, right, Shortcake?" West smirked and sat a cup of coffee in front of me.

"Umm." I wasn't about to admit that I thought West was the sexiest man in the solar system.

"I can get any girl I want," West assured Winona.

"You're so full of yourself. I bet you our tips that you strike out tonight," Winona said.

West snorted. "That's nuts. Why would you think that? I never strike out, and you want to bet? You can kiss your hard-earned cash goodbye."

"You seem weird. Your face is all angry looking, and you're super gross and sweaty right now. No girl in her right mind would think you're sexy. They're all gonna want the detective. He's dreamy, and he smells good, not like your stinky body odor."

Winona was wrong. There was at least one woman who found the sweaty, frustrated Weston the Third quite desirable.

"You're full of shit, Winona, and you're on. Do I need a full-out shag?"

I gasped.

Winona scrunched up her face. "Maybe not. I don't want some poor girl to be the victim of your piggishness. How about second base?"

I sipped my coffee and hissed as the hot liquid burned my digestive tract.

"A little boob action." West clicked his tongue. "You're on."

They sealed their deal with a fist bump.

West tapped my shoulder. "Shortcake, you pick my chick."

"Why me? No way. I don't want any part of this."

I would have rather eaten baboon brain or had a baboon eat my brain than pick a girl for West to "shag." Unless, of course, I picked myself, and the jerk knew it. As usual, he was messing with me.

West's tongue tapped a tooth at the side of his mouth, and he looked to the corner. Then he licked his top lip as he stared into my eyes. The mongrel!

"How about her?" Winona pointed to a cute blonde surrounded by friends.

"She goes to the college," I said

West looked her over from head to toe. "She isn't

jailbait. I carded her earlier."

"West," I pleaded. "Don't. She's too young."

"Go card her, Winona, to double-check. I don't remember her name. Get it for me, and we're on," he said.

Winona, the airhead, agreed. She left me alone with West while she rechecked IDs.

West leaned across the bar. "Hey, beautiful."

My insides flip-flopped.

"What?" I stared into space because if I looked into his eyes, I was a goner, and I'd agree to whatever he was concocting.

"I'm not interested in that girl. I pick you. What do you say? I promise I'll kiss you senseless. Then we can fuck and roll around in Winona's tips." He boinked my nose with his index finger and grinned.

I looked into his hazel beauties, remaining speechless as my teeth gouged my lip.

West's smart alec expression disappeared as he focused on someone behind me.

"Sorry, Red," Sean said. "Had to take that call."

Winona returned at the same moment. "The blonde is twenty-one, and her name is Amy."

"Never mind about her. I picked a different girl. Shortcake is the judge, and she'll be impartial, won't you?" West lifted a questioning eyebrow.

"Umm," I said.

"It's settled. Let the games begin," West sang out.

"What did I miss?" Sean asked.

West prepared a pretty pink drink while Winona embodied the wide-legged stance of an orator.

"West and I bet our tips. He's weird tonight, and I think he's gonna strike out. Come to think of it, he's been acting weird a lot lately." She thought for a second, shrugged off whatever had occurred to her, then kept rambling. "Miranda is going to be the judge since she's impartial. I picked that girl over there, although I shouldn't encourage his behavior." She lifted her tray off the counter and held it to her chest. "West might pick a different girl. It doesn't matter who he picks since I'm gonna win his tips. I don't think he even put on his deodorant today." She took one hand off her tray to pinch her nostrils.

For the record, at that moment, I couldn't smell West over Sean's aftershave.

West squirted whipped cream on top of the sex drink. "Watch this."

He walked that girly drink over to the pretty blonde and presented it to her with a flourish.

She touched her cheek and smiled.

West said something, and she giggled. Finally, he leaned forward and whispered into her ear.

She caressed his arm.

He faced us and lifted his chin to the ceiling in triumph. The co-eds' gaze tracked his backside as he strutted towards us.

My body recoiled in jealous indignation.

"Got my backup chick." West's gaze pinned me to the wall. "Not my first choice, but she's willing to go all the way."

Then he had the nerve to wink at me! Weston Westinghouse the Third was an impossible scoundrel!

****

I threw myself onto my mattress and rolled around. My dog joined me in bed.

"Oh, Spot, what am I going to do? West is such a

jerk."

Spot's *woof woof* and slapping paw meant, Play with me, and you will feel better.

"Simon, any words of advice?" He sent me a message in annoyed rodent squeaks that I translated as, Leave me alone. You're annoying. Then he gnawed on a carrot—typical Simon.

"What about you, Princess Pickles? Any advice?" My turtle pulled his head into his shell. He wasn't into communicating.

"Greg, aren't you going to stick your big fat nose in and give me advice?"

Greg didn't answer. He was probably visiting the psychic Madame Alina. He got all doughy-eyed when he talked about their late-night visits.

I wrestled with Spot a little longer before closing my eyes and thinking about West. He made me laugh when he wasn't making me angry. Since I was addicted to the sound of his voice, I wanted to listen to him whisper my name in between kisses. Although West was crazy about me, he would never admit it. He was terrible at committing and expressing feelings. However, he was spectacular at kissing and making love.

"Hey guys," I called to my gang. "I know this is stupid, but it's a holiday, so I should enjoy myself. Right? I'm going to help West win his bet, and when I get my share of the money, I'll go to Romano's Pet store and it's toys all around."

Spot barked. Princess Pickles finally woke up and stuck his chin into the air, and Simon didn't squeak-swear at me. I brushed my teeth, put on fresh deodorant and perfume, applied the ruby lipstick West liked and fluffed up my ringlets.

"West Westinghouse the Third is going to score a home run with a college professor," I announced to my reflection. Then I clomped down three flights of stairs, charged out the front door, and crashed headfirst into Sergeant O'Sullivan.

"I'm sorry, Sean," I gasped out, as his arms steadied me.

"Where are you headed?"

"I think I left my gloves at the pub."

"No. I'm sure you had them on when we came home." He tapped his forehead. "Details are my specialty."

My plan foiled, I temporarily conceded defeat. "What are you doing out here? It's cold."

"Getting some fresh air and thinking. A few things about this case don't make sense."

"I agree."

"I would kill for a cup of hot chocolate and one of your aunt's cookies." He tilted his head and dramatically fluttered his lashes. Obviously, he had a thing for my aunts baking. "And, maybe we could talk about a few inconsistencies in the case."

Kisses from Weston Westinghouse the Third or hot chocolate, cookies, and murder talk with Officer Hunky?

Easy decision! I had a man I needed to see and a contest to settle. "I have to run to the pub to tell Winona something," I lied.

"I'm sure it can wait."

"No. I have to go now." I bit my lip and looked down the hill.

"Let's have a snack and talk. I'm leaving first thing

in the morning to head to my mother's for Thanksgiving." Sean nudged me back inside and rerouted me toward the kitchen.

Since I wasn't going to visit West, I needed to dismiss the images of him wrapping the young Amy in his arms.

Forget about West! my common sense said.

Never. He is under your skin, my heart responded.

Sean sat at the table and stretched out his massive body.

I gathered the milk, syrup, and spoon.

"I don't think the murder happened at the convenience store. I think someone moved the body," he said.

Thank goodness he had figured it out without me having to tell him. I lit the gas burner under the pot.

"You said you heard three shots, right?" he asked.

"Correct."

He leaned back in the chair until the front legs lifted off the floor. Then he confidently hovered his mass on two stick-like spindles. "There were two bullets in the deceased, and we found three bullets in that parking lot. So, you should have heard five shots."

I stirred the warming milk as I carefully chose my words. "I think you're correct about the body being moved." I considered telling him I was pretty sure a Santa had killed a Santa, but there was no way to do it without sounding insane.

Chair legs *clonk*ed on the floor.

Within seconds, he stood behind me, peering over my shoulder "It seems like an odd coincidence that the video camera was out where the murder took place."

"I know. So, whoever left the body may have

known about the broken camera."

The chocolate syrup mixed with the milk and a strand of my hair moved with his breath.

"Can you ask around about the convenience store manager, Mike Stevens? You can learn a lot by sifting through the small-town gossip."

I poured the cocoa into foam cups, backed away a half a step, and handed him one. "I'm not into small-town gossip. However, I'm totally up for a stake-out."

****

As Detective O'Sullivan parked his police-issued 1986 nondescript car under an oak beside the Susquehanna River, he felt the need to remind me that a civilian engaging in official police work and spying on Bellmountians was unethical. He pointed out that it was merely a crazy coincidence that we had a perfect view of the Stevens Speed-mart from our scenic rest stop. I assured him that I would never presume to be a cop or spy on citizens. I simply enjoyed having a late-night snack by the water. Then I traded him a chocolate chip cookie for his night binoculars.

We started our non-investigation watching inebriated college students chow down on junk food. Eventually, someone over the age of twenty-one showed up.

"It's Shultz," I said. "I'm telling you the guy is a menace."

I had a clear view of his beady eyes since the Optimum Optics worked way better than the toy Spyfinders Liam and I played with when we were kids. The ape galumphed into the store.

"Damn! Your aunt makes good cookies," Sean said.

I desperately willed warmth to my limbs as I stared at the convenience store entrance.

"I wonder if the kid's working tonight," Sean said.

"Mason? No. He went home for the holidays."

Shultz shuffled out of the store, shoving the end of a tinfoil-wrapped sandwich into his mouth.

Sean reached for his binoculars. "Let me see."

I ignored him.

Shultz dropped a chunk of something down his front then climbed into his cruiser. A car pulled into the lot. The sheriff paused while a woman stepped out of the driver's side of a powder blue two-door.

Sean grabbed the binoculars.

"Hey," I grumbled.

"Interesting," Sean said.

"What's interesting? Let me see."

"Hold on a second."

"Is Shultz touching her?" I asked.

"Hold on."

I held out my palm. "Let me see."

He swished my hand away. "She's pissed."

"Who is she? Did he touch her breasts?" Shultz and a pissed-off woman signaled a repulsive grouping in my minds-eye.

"What?" Sean gaped at me before peering into and adjusting the lenses. "No, she has on a coat."

I grabbed them back. Shultz clambered onto his front seat, the woman strode into the store, and Sean again confiscated his optics.

"Binocular hog," I said.

He laughed. "I'm the cop, and they are mine."

"We aren't on official police business, and I'm the one with the cookies," I reminded him.

"Speaking of cookies." He held out his hand.

I placed one in his outstretched fingers. "Who is she? I couldn't see her face."

"Freida."

"Does she have a last name?"

He crunched, swallowed, and held the contraption to his eyeballs. "Freida is her last name. Madame is her first name."

"Madame Freida?"

"Yep. I wonder what she's doing in Bellmount at this time of night," he said.

"I'm missing details. Fill me in."

"She manages a brothel in Greenport."

"She's a prostitute?"

"Yep."

"There's a brothel in Bear County?"

Sean stopped spying to gawk at me. "You are a bit sheltered, aren't you?"

I crossed my arms over my chest. "Just because I don't know a lot about brothels doesn't mean I'm sheltered."

It was more that I had lived my life with my nose stuck in books. My knowledge of prostitutes came from what I had learned from Dickens and Steinbeck.

"Sorry. And yes, there is more than one in the county. Pretty much every town in the world has its share. Here she comes."

The door to the Stevens Speed-mart opened, and the woman exited.

"Let me see," I begged.

Sean handed them to me, and I watched her magnified form and pink teased hair slide into the car then drive away.

"Is she pretty?" I asked.

He shrugged. "Well kept and exotic looking, I suppose."

"How do you know her?"

"I worked on a dead john case a few years back."

"A dead john?"

"A john is a prostitute's client," he said.

"I know that," I snapped. "Was she innocent of the murder?"

"Yeah." He clamped his lips tight.

"She has a way better car than me."

Sean chuckled. "No way, your beast is cool. She's driving a girly powder puff."

I *harrumph*ed because I would have loved a small light-colored car.

I fiddled with Sean's police radio. Then I ran my fingers over a round magnetic car top strobe light. Sean stared out the window, and eventually, I dozed off.

He tapped my shoulder. "The store's closed for the night. It's time to head home."

I shook off my grogginess and stretched.

Sean started the car. "What the hell?" He turned the engine off and grabbed the binoculars. "Why is the mayor of Bellmount at the Stevens Speed-mart after closing?"

I rubbed my eyes and sat up. "What's going on?"

"Stevens, the store manager, was locking up, and Reynolds showed up. Reynolds looks pissed."

"Let me see."

Sean batted my hand away. "Hold on."

I popped forward and plastered my face against the windshield. "What's going on?"

"Reynolds just got into his car and left. Stevens is

still standing there. He's looking around the parking lot. Shit! I think he sees us."

"Fudge!" I ducked under the dashboard.

"He's on his way over."

"Drive away," I yelled.

"Sit up, quick."

Terrified, I sat straight.

Sean tossed the binoculars under the dashboard and cornered me against the passenger side window.

"Kiss me," he demanded.

"What? No!"

"Damn it. Hurry up and kiss me!"

I didn't kiss Sean O'Sullivan because he was masculine and smelled like a living, breathing soap advertisement. And, I didn't kiss him because he tasted like Christmas cookies. I one hundred percent kissed him for the sake of sleuthing and keeping our cover. That, and I was freezing and in desperate need of body heat.

Confused, I broke from our embrace and pulled away.

"Shit. That was close." Sean stared straight ahead as Stevens got into his pick-up truck and drove away. "Red, remember, we weren't here," Sergeant O'Sullivan said as he turned the key in the ignition.

No need to remind me. As far as I was concerned, I had spent the evening in my warm, safe, man-free turret.

Chapter 5

Since the Bellmount Inn was on the National Register of Historic Hotels, Aunt Edith felt it necessary to showcase a holiday display that put the White House to shame. Thanksgiving morning was not a time of respite for Edith's kin. As soon as we finished our pumpkin French toast and sausage links, she put us to work.

Our first chore was to festoon a garland of greens, red poinsettia, white roses, and gold bows up the winding staircase. Lucky Liam was the ladder climber who adorned the doorways with a matching poinsettia and rose spray. The three of us spent over two hours setting up the Victorian Christmas village in the front window. It was my job to create red and white floral bouquets for each of the guest rooms. While I played horticulturist, Liam and Russ anchored the nine-foot-high, five-foot-wide live Christmas tree standing in the foyer. Finally, Spot and I sat on the floor, sorting through the vintage Victorian ornaments, while Russ handed the colorful tree lights to Liam.

Aunt Edith spent the morning in the kitchen cooking. When she finally strolled into the foyer, sweat dripped down her cheeks. She hugged Liam. "How was your trip to Pittsburg?"

Liam, the newest accountant for the prestigious Lancaster firm, grunted. "Not great, Mom. I wasn't able to get E.R. Development to move their account to us. I wasn't even able to meet with the owner because he sent his attorney. Mr. Lancaster is disappointed."

"E.R. Development? I didn't realize that was who you were meeting with. They bid on the plot of land right outside of town," Aunt Edith said.

"What the hell?" Russ said. "What do they want with it?"

Aunt Edith's face contorted into a jumble of sharp stressed lines. "The company sent an attorney to meet with Reynolds. They made an offer. Two days later, Lesser Inc. offered more. Reynolds is determined to sell the property to this E.R. for a lower bid. He said they want to put in a mall that will improve the economy of the area. Tom Little told me the property is a watershed for the town reservoir and building there could affect our water quality. Reynolds says this isn't true. Bradley and I want more information."

"*Pfft*. Little is probably correct. The entire thing sounds iffy to me," Russ said.

"Hmm," I said. "Timberlane, the manager of Lightsingers, said that the store's rent increased and mentioned something about building a mall."

"Well, we haven't sold the land," Aunt Edith said. "Patterson is voting against the sale along with Bradley and me. So, for now, there's nothing to worry about."

"As long as the two biding companies don't buy off Patterson with the promise of campaign funding or votes," Russ said.

"I believe Patterson is holding off because he thinks we should be accepting the higher bid from Lesser Inc." Aunt Edith looked to the ceiling and sighed.

"What does Lesser Inc. want to do with the land?" Liam asked.

Over the past few months, the dark crescent shapes under my aunt's eyes had doubled in size and currently her limp arms hung by her side. "Reynolds's hasn't told us the specifics, but they have promised it won't pollute the reservoir. I'm not sure I believe them. They offered a lot of money, but since the council can't agree on anything, it remains a green space for now." She wiped the sweat from her brow. "Let's focus on the holiday. I could use some stress-free family time."

I popped from the floor to kiss her cheek. "It's going to be the best Thanksgiving ever, Aunt Edith."

Liam hugged her. "No more talking about politics today."

"You kids are awesome." She studied the tree, and for a moment, her weary eyes brightened. "Russ, could you help me get the silver serving platter from above the stove?"

Aunt Edith and Russ excused themselves, I settled on the floor, and Liam stepped back to eye the tree. He fussed with the placement of a few of the ceramic bulbs before breaking the bad news.

"Hey, little cuz, I have to tell you something, and you aren't going to like it."

I cringed in anticipation. "What?"

Liam wavered. One day he was my fun-loving cousin, and the next, he was a stick-in-the-mud accountant, carrying the responsibilities of the world on his shoulders. I assumed Liam was in nagging mode since I had a growing list of indiscretions. I had visited Lightsingers department store during a police investigation, stumbled upon another corpse, and eaten cookies with a handsome cop. Or, perhaps he discovered I had slept with West. Sometimes a discussion with Liam felt a lot like getting called to the principal's office. Not that I had ever gotten into trouble at school, but I suspected the two were similar.

He stared at the tree. "Gina's coming for dinner today."

Gina Schuster was number five on my enemy list. Liam's girlfriend was a beautiful old money debutante. She was also one of the nasty, notorious Bellmount Bitches.

"Oh, Liam. Does your mom know?"

"Of course Mom knows. She's thrilled. Please be nice to Gina. I want you two to be friends."

The ornament in my fingers hung midair swinging to and fro. "*Me*, be nice to *her*? I think you need to tell her to be nice to me."

Liam joined me on the floor. He tugged on a ringlet and then used his index fingers to push the ends of my lips into a smile. The next thing I knew, he pinned me to the ground. He held me down and playfully pulled at my hair while I punched his chest. Spot barked and jumped on top of our pile. Doing our darndest, not to smash antique decorations, we tussled, and giggled.

The front door opened, and Gina Schuster, the brown-eyed devil, interrupted our fun.

"Good God, Liam," Gina called out in her affected voice.

Liam crawled off of me and strolled to her. "Hi, darling." He wrapped her in his arms and kissed her on the lips.

Yuck!

Gina was too busy glowering at me to appreciate

my cousin's attentions.

"Mom's been working us to death, so Miranda and I were taking a break."

"You are wrestling like children," she said.

"Hi, Gina." I forced a smile. "Welcome to our family holiday."

Gina fried me with the fire spewing from her pupils.

"You know how it is when you're around cousins," Liam said. "It makes you act like you're a kid again."

Gina balked. "I don't know about that. I don't roll around on the floor with my grown male cousins."

"Too bad. You should try it. It's kind of fun." I gave her a big toothy grin.

It was no use. I appalled Gina Schuster, and she made me feel like a smelly infant diaper. My Thanksgiving was doomed.

"Gina, darling," Liam said. "Remember what we talked about?" His arms remained wrapped around her, and he pulled her tight.

Gina frowned and peeked out around him. "Happy Thanksgiving, Miranda."

Liam rewarded her with another kiss, and she clutched him close.

"You too, Gina," I said.

Double yuck!

As the lovebirds stared into each other's eyes, I excused myself and headed to the kitchen to help Aunt Edith.

My aunt had every pot and pan she owned spread out on the counter. Food boiled, baked, and fried. Thick steam hung over the room, and condensation coated the bay window in front of our family dining table. Russ passed by me on his way back to Liam and the tree.

"Can I help you?" I asked her.

"Aren't you helping Liam with the decorations?"

"Nah, Gina's assisting him." I failed at keeping the pouty from my voice.

"Miranda, I know how you feel about her, but this is important to Liam. We are both going to be gracious." Aunt Edith emitted a funny little noise.

Thrilled, my behind.

"You can set the table in the guest parlor. Use the good silver and the pink and yellow china, and set the table for six."

"Six? You mean five?"

She plunked a wooden spoon into the gravy and stirred. "Bradley is joining us."

I stared at her.

"Put Russ and me at the ends of the table. Put Gina beside Liam and Bradley beside you."

My shoulders slumped as I padded to the parlor to unload the antique British china from the cupboard. I had difficulty concentrating because my guilt, frustration, and excitement all mingled together. A few weeks ago, I thought I was in love with Brad. That feeling had faded and had become more of a nagging ache that I wanted to go away. Our relationship hadn't worked, and I could no longer take the pain.

Winona clomped into the parlor carrying a basket adorned with a big orange bow. "Happy Thanksgiving, Miranda. My mom sent one of her pumpkin logs." She held up the gift.

"Happy Thanksgiving, Winona. Aunt Edith is in the kitchen."

"Are you okay? You look funny."

I exhaled a ginormous sigh. "I'm fine."

"You're a big fat fibber, Miranda Albright. I saw Gina. I feel sorry for you. Is she being nasty?"

"Shh." I leaned close. "I know she's hideous, but Liam adores her, so I have to be a good hostess. And, get this—Brad is coming."

"Don't you wanna see Bradley?" When I didn't answer, she asked, "Do you wanna come to my house?"

I would have gladly joined the Westinghouse clan if I didn't think it would crush Aunt Edith. Or I could have had an elegant meal of Cornish game hen with Lincoln and his wife, Alice. Keisha's grandmother had invited me to ride with them to Pittsburgh. For the sake of my aunt, I had declined the invitations. The truth was, I missed my mom since her passing, and I wanted to be with my father for the holiday. He suggested I stay with Aunt Edith since he planned to spend the holiday with his new girlfriend.

"Thanks. I'd love to, but Aunt Edith has been cooking all day." I fiddled with a fork. "Timberlane called. We start our elf gig Saturday. We have the six to nine shift."

Winona's face lit up, and she clapped. "This is so exciting. I found these adorable pointy ears."

I smiled, recalling Keisha's on-the-nose ear comment.

"Keisha's doing the sexy elf thing," I said.

Winona frowned. "For Pete's sake Miranda, elves aren't sexy. What is Keisha thinking?"

"Did West win all of your tips last night?" I held my breath and waited.

"No. I won his tips. He told me he wasn't feeling well and handed me all his money."

"What?"

Winona shrugged and lifted her palms to the ceiling. "I know. That girl was all over him, and she was pretty."

"I don't understand."

Winona's brow furrowed. "I'm kind of worried about him. He doesn't seem like himself. I think he has blown off a lot of girls lately. He says he's too busy and not interested. Since when, right? Then last night, he said he didn't feel well. I knew he was going to strike out." She tapped her forehead. "I'm a pretty good detective."

Aunt Edith entered the parlor, halting our critically important discussion. "I thought I heard you, Winona. Happy Thanksgiving, dear."

Aunt Edith and Winona hugged. My aunt retrieved a basket from the pine sideboard, and the women traded goods.

Aunt Edith lifted the napkin covering her package. "Pumpkin log. Delicious. Please thank your mom."

Winona peeked into her parcel.

"Wild elderberry jam and scones. I know how much your dad and uncle love elderberries."

"Thanks, Edith." Winona grabbed my hand. "Wanna come to the pub tonight and hang for a bit? I thought I'd make you a special pumpkin hot chocolate. It's delicious."

"Are you open on Thanksgiving?" I asked.

"Three-hundred-sixty-four days a year. We only close for our family holiday party. She thought for a moment. "And during big blizzards."

"Sure. Sounds fun. See you tonight."

She waved and left me alone to finish setting the

table. As I worked, I fantasized about Winona's handsome cousin. I hoped that he was healthy and simply suffering from a case of redhead-itis because if that was his affliction, I had the cure.

****

Most of my wardrobe was quite schoolmarmish and unappealing to Weston Westinghouse the Third, the expert on all things sexy. Combing through my clothes, I searched for something he might find attractive. Soon I was dressed in a lavender shirt, a short skirt, and black tights. I coated my eyes with purple eyeshadow, layers of mascara, and thick black eyeliner. I added silk panties, high heels, ruby lipstick, and my Obsessive Love perfume.

As I studied my reflection in the bathroom mirror, Greg's face appeared beside mine. He let out a resounding, "Fuck, Crimson!"

"Greg, out! You know this room is off-limits to you."

He ignored me. "Where are you going? You look sexy as hell."

"I'm hanging with Winona. Then I might spend the night with Keisha." I had told Aunt Edith the same lie. Keisha and Nanna Brown were still in Pittsburgh. "It's girls' night, and you're not invited."

Greg shot me a raspberry in the glass. "Fine by me. Winona's a pinhead, and Keisha's hot, but she has an attitude problem."

I glared at his wispy reflection. "That's a mean thing to say. Winona was crazy about you."

"She was?" He ran a hand along his jaw as he studied himself. "I am good-looking, and she does have sexy hips." He licked his lips. "If I recall correctly,

Winona tasted sweet."

"Augh! Too much information. Go away. You aren't supposed to be in my bathroom."

"I'm going," he said. "I'm looking in on Jessica since she's having a tough time this holiday without Gordon and me. I wish she knew I was with her." His face fell and he exhaled. "Then I'm spending the night with Alina. How's about my Thanksgiving kiss?"

I waved to the mirror. "Bye, Greg."

He blew a kiss into the glass before fading.

After returning to my bedroom, I squatted to rub Spot's belly. I gave Princess Pickles the last of his turtle pellets and filled Simon's water bottle, saying, "Up yours too, Simon." I grabbed the book I was reading and shoved it into my backpack. Then I changed from my heels into sensible shoes because, once again, it was snowing, and the sidewalk leading to the pub was treacherous.

****

Since I stayed upright as I trudged down the hill I patted myself on the back for changing into rubber-soled shoes, and took a seat at the end of the bar.

Winona approached, wearing a big smile. "You made it. How did things go with Bradley?"

"He never showed. He called Aunt Edith from the hospital to apologize. They were short-staffed, so he helped out in the emergency room."

"Bradley's so heroic." Winona put a hand on her heart and sighed.

Brad was heroic, handsome, a gentleman, and the most perfect man in the world. Unfortunately, he avoided me like plague-infected fleas covered my flesh.

"Where's West? Is he feeling better tonight?" I

asked.

"He's in the storeroom. He ate four plates of turkey and stuffing at dinner, so I think he feels better. I'm going to make you your special holiday drink. Be back soon." Winona disappeared into the kitchen.

Greg had informed me that enthusiastic hunters would overrun the town after the holiday, but the pub was quiet on Thanksgiving eve. The college students were home with their families, and most Bellmountians watched football from their living rooms. The only people present were the locals who indiscriminately imbibed. I read *Beloved* by Toni Morrison until Winona returned, carrying a steaming cup, the whipped cream piled high. Her eyes wide with anticipation, she stared at me.

"It's too hot for me to drink."

She frowned. "Oh."

"I'm sure it's delicious," I assured her.

Pop, West's father, peeked at us from the kitchen. "Hiya, kiddo. Thank Edith for the jam."

"Hi, Pop," I said.

He looked at my cup and laughed. "Winona forcin' her 'holiday drink' on ya?"

I waited until Winona was distracted to crinkle my nose and cringe.

He chuckled.

"Winona," Pop called. "When West comes in from the storeroom, I need your help in the kitchen for a minute." Pop caught my gaze. "Only the three of us working tonight. I hate Thanksgiving." Then he headed back to his dishwasher and stove.

Pop had hated the holidays since Connie Westinghouse had left him with a toddler in 1964. As far as I knew, West still loved the season. He never mentioned his mother, and he pretty much enjoyed every day of life, unless it was one of those times he was annoyed with me.

West appeared, carrying a large cardboard box that he shoved into a corner.

Since my drink had cooled, I gulped.

West planted himself in front of me. "Hiya, Shortcake. Winona forcing her shitty drinks on ya?"

He touched my mouth, and my insides flip-flopped. Holding his whipped cream-coated finger in the air, he glanced around the bar then licked at the sweet topping that had seconds before been on my lips.

I gasped.

A mischievous grin spread across his face. "Where's your cop boyfriend?"

"Sean isn't my boyfriend. There isn't anything going on between us. He stayed at the inn, that's all. Plus, unlike Shutz and Miller, he's a decent cop."

West snorted. "Where's your doctor boyfriend?"

"Ex-boyfriend. And Brad is with his patients—like he always is." I sipped then licked the foam from my lips before West could taunt me.

He leaned across the bar, and I fought the urge to touch his cheek and read his mind.

"I like the new look. It's hot," he said.

Inwardly I was pleased. However, I rolled my eyes.

"Why did you purposely lose your bet last night?" I asked.

He dramatically lifted his hands into the air. "What do you mean?"

"You need acting lessons. You know what I'm talking about. Winona told me you said you didn't feel well. I don't believe that for a second. I think you let Winona win."

He stared into my eyes. "You reading my mind again, Shortcake?"

"No, West. I know you well enough to realize you threw that bet, and I want to know why."

"Well, there were so many chicks—"

"West, stop! Tell me the truth."

He rubbed his chin. "Fine. I just wasn't into her. I told you already; you were the one I wanted. You're the only one I want these days."

"Really?" I bit my lip and peered up at him from beneath fluttering eyelashes. "West, you are the only one I want."

West's frustrated expression changed into one of his smart-alec grins. "I think I'm feeling sick again." He rubbed his stomach. "Winona," he called into the kitchen before a curling finger motioned me close. "Give me fifteen minutes."

Winona peaked out from around the swinging door. "What do you want?"

"I'm sick again." He clutched at his abdomen. "Can you cover?"

Winona surveyed the room. "Yeah. Get out of here."

West kissed her on the cheek.

She swatted him away. "For Pete's sake, I don't want to catch what you have. You probably have that flu that's going around. Get out of here."

"Thanks, cuz." He distorted his face in an attempt to look sick and pathetic.

Winona shook her head before making her way to a beckoning customer.

West winked and leaped over the bar. His agile body popped at least four feet into the air. He landed beside me and clicked his tongue. "I practice in case I have to stop a bar fight or save a Harvest Princess."

The Harvest Princess crack was to goad me about the humiliating day I was officially named a Bellmount Princess and got so drunk he had to carry me home.

He grabbed his belly again. "Oh, it hurts." Then he whispered in my ear, "My place." Before heading towards the pub exit, the fake-belly-aching West pinched my behind.

I watched his backside retreat, and my girl parts sang out a joyful Hallelujah.

Chapter 6

Five minutes later, I climbed the stairs that ran along the left side of the pub, opened the weatherbeaten screen, and tapped on the wooden door. When no one answered, I peeked inside.

"Hello," I called into West's rustic studio apartment.

Nothing.

I stepped inside and listened. West's terrible crooning voice was audible over his running shower as he loudly belted out lyrics to a country love song.

I cradled my face in my hands and smiled because his off-key singing filled me with joy. I took off my mucky boots, set them by the door, sat on the shredded yellow seat cushion, and surveyed his bachelor pad. Someone had tidied West's pigsty.

The shower stopped, and his tune morphed into a cheerful tweet. Although West couldn't sing or act, he whistled like a champ. A few moments later, the bathroom doorknob clicked.

I stood.

"Shortcake?" West perused me from head to toe. "Anxious to be alone with me?"

A burning sensation overtook my cheeks. Although I should have exhibited patience and given West his fifteen minutes, I was excited to see him.

My early arrival meant he was naked except for the

towel wrapped around his waist. His wet hair formed seductive curly Qs that framed his cleanly shaven face, and a glow from the antique floor lamp lit up his eyes.

"I'm teasing you, beautiful. I'm happy you're here, but I wanted to change. I have a new sweater. I thought you might like it better than my t-shirts."

I stepped toward him. "West, I love your t-shirts. I'm sorry I teased you."

"Okay, but I look damn fine in my sweater." He grinned.

"I bet you do," I said.

He puffed out a guttural sound, and we both took another step toward the center of the room.

I inhaled his soapy scent. "You smell heavenly."

West's eyes softened. "I didn't want to smell like fried bar food tonight."

"I like that you always smell like mozzarella sticks. It makes you extra yummy." I licked my lips.

"Christ." His hands swept the length of his torso. "So, I did all this for nothing."

"I like this smell too." Since we were now within arms' reach, I considered lapping up his scent. "West," I said, my voice raspy and needy.

"What, beautiful?"

"The way you look right now is how you looked when we were teenagers, and we swam at the river. When you're wet, your hair curls, and your muscles..." I searched for my adjective. "Glisten." My gaze traveled from his face to his chest.

He twirled a strand of my hair between his thumb and forefinger. "You looked like a mermaid in the water. I especially liked the summer you wore the light blue bathing suit."

"But that was the summer you ignored me."

"Ignored you? No way. I got tired of fighting Little for your attention, and I didn't want Liam to know I was into you. Liam was such a bastard when it came to you." He grunted. "Still is a bastard when it comes to you."

"But, that summer, you were all over Mary Long and Sheila Rokowski."

West thought for a moment, threw his head back, and chuckled. "That's right. Now Mary is toothless, and Sheila is on her fifth rug rat." He took one last step. "Come here." He wrapped an arm around my waist and pulled me to him. "If I ever ignored you, I was a fool."

I ran my palms over his smooth pectorals before looking into his eyes. "I haven't stopped thinking about you since the night we made love."

West peered down at me. I stood tall and lifted my chin, and our lips met. I fought my desire to intrude on his thoughts and concentrated on his tongue as it tangled with mine.

He stopped kissing me to whisper, "Shortcake, that night when I didn't walk you home, and you got attacked, it almost killed me. I won't ever let anyone hurt you again."

Since West rarely communicated his feelings, a rush of warmth consumed me.

His lips traveled from my ear to my mouth, and his towel dropped to the ground.

****

I rarely thought of Weston Westinghouse the Third as vulnerable, but I suppose he had his moments. I stood before him fully dressed, and he sat naked on the couch. My red lipstick decorated his mouth and smeared across his cheek. His muscles were tense, his legs were splayed open, and his man-part stood at full attention. I'm not sure I had ever felt so powerful or that West had looked so unguarded.

I slid onto my knees and lodged myself between his thighs. "West?"

He seemed to have lost his ability to speak.

"I don't know what I'm doing, and I want to make you feel good."

His breath came heavy, and he nodded.

"Is it okay to read your mind?"

His "Ohh, yeah," was so guttural it landed in my core.

I ran my index finger over the tiny hole at his tip and wiped away a splash of silky fluid. I bent forward and licked where the liquid had been.

"Mmm." *Fuck.*

I gently used my fingers to explore. I started at the tip and ended at the base, where the appendage attached to his body. "It feels so strong."

His chuckle turned into a moan. "The word is hardddd."

"Hard," I muttered as I wrapped my hand around the length of him and gently squeezed. I looked up to meet his gaze.

I want to be in her mouth.

Our gazes locked as I leaned forward and guided his pink tip between my lips.

"Fuck," he said.

I broke eye contact to fully immerse myself in the taste, feel, and scent of the man making me dizzy. I licked at him. Since he tasted like sweet sin, I settled in and enjoyed. He uttered low reverberating sounds as I ran the length of my tongue over every inch of him.

Shortcake, please suck.

First, I sucked on the nib. Then feeling voracious, I pulled him in as far as I could.

God, yes. "Don't stop."

He gathered my hair, pulled it to the side, and held it out of our way.

As my hand, lips, and tongue worked in sync, I found the rhythm of my ravenous symphony. My body hungered as I dragged him deeper. My throat pulled him in and my tongue and hand guided him out, as West cooed soft sexy sounds.

Stop! I'm going to come.

So immersed in my task that an exploding nuclear missile head couldn't have torn me away, I ignored his mental message,

He pulled my face from his lap. "Shortcake, stop."

Feeling drugged, I wiped my lips and looked up at him. "What's wrong?"

"Nothing. You're sexy as hell, and I want to fuck you."

"Please, West."

He moaned. "There are condoms in my nightstand drawer."

I rummaged around, and grabbed a handful of the wrapped prophylactics. I padded back to West and shyly handed him what I had retrieved. The truth was, I had no idea what I was supposed to do with them. I understood the general concept, but I wasn't sure of the exact mechanics.

West chuckled. "This is a shitload of condoms. Is it a hint?"

My cheeks grew hot.

His intense stare penetrated my soul. "Are you still reading my mind?"

"No."

One eyebrow lifted. "Then you missed the part where I told you to get naked."

West watched with an intensity that singed my skin as I stepped away from the couch and pushed down my tights.

I unbuttoned my blouse.

He hissed.

I took off my bra.

"Christ, they're beautiful," he said.

I slid my panties off, and my skirt followed. I stepped over my pile of discarded clothing and gave a smile of triumph because I had gracefully undressed in front of West.

"Come here," he demanded.

I obeyed and stood before him. He leaned forward, reached for my waist, and pulled me close. He gently kissed under my belly button. His other hand danced over my hip and then dragged down my pelvis. My back arched and I whimpered as two fingers parted me. My mouth opened, my thighs parted, and my insides expanded.

"So wet," West growled.

Minutes later, his fingers abandoned their explanation, leaving me aching. He slid into a condom and reached for me.

I climbed onto his lap and straddled him.

West slipped into me as if we were matching puzzle pieces. My hands cradled the back of his neck, and I forced him to kiss me as I rode him. While one hand clutched my waist, the other gently tugged on my hair. Occasionally he stopped kissing me to rid himself of a groan. In one swift motion, he tossed me, back first, onto the couch.

He climbed on top of me, buried his face into the crook of my neck, and his flexible body molded to mine. Taking over our game of enter and retreat, he chose both the pace and the intensity.

Not wanting space between us, I wrapped my arms and legs around him and held him close. It wasn't enough. I craved to have West's entire body inside of me, and I missed his salty metallic taste. I seized a mouthful of his neck and latched onto his collarbone as if my life depended on it. One especially forceful thrust forced me to let go of his flesh.

"Oh, West!" A moment later, I held his neck between my lips. I was no better than an insatiable wild beast.

"I'm going to come, love," he rasped.

I stopped devouring him so that I could beg. "Please, West. Deep inside me."

He grew larger and harder. "Fuck, Miranda," he called as he exploded.

"West," I cried as my insides grasped for the liquid they craved.

West stayed on top of me long after our orgasms faded. His fingers gently brushed my hair from our sweaty bodies.

"Stay with me tonight," he whispered.

I wasn't going anywhere. Weston Westinghouse the Third was stuck with my stubborn, obsessed, freckled face until the end of time.

****

The sun shone through the lone window in West's

apartment, casting a ray over his sweaty body. He crashed onto the mattress, then deposited a wadded-up rubber on his nightstand with two others. The hideous bruises that covered his neck and shoulders did nothing to detract from his physical perfection.

I rubbed a finger over the marbled marks. "Do they hurt?"

"Does what hurt?"

"I'm sorry. I'm so embarrassed."

His eyes narrowed. "What ya talking about?"

I cringed. "I gave you bruises where I sucked on you."

West's face lit up, and he tickled me under the chin. "No shit. I have Shortcake hickeys?"

"Oh, West. They're awful. So trashy."

"Not trashy." He flashed me a lopsided grin. "Sexy." He grabbed the pile of our discarded protection from his nightstand and headed across the room.

I sat up and pulled the blanket to my neck. His well-formed backside disappeared into the bathroom. Left alone, I studied his surprisingly neat apartment. I contemplated a copy of *A Clockwork Orange* that sat beside his box of tissues. I hadn't pegged West as an Anthony Burgess kind of guy.

"Shit!" he hollered.

An all-consuming shame burned my cheeks before traveling downward and landing in my core.

West reappeared and leaned his god-like naked body against the frame of the bathroom door. His rumpled hair resembled a dilapidated bird's nest, and the skin discoloration was visible from across the room.

He wore a grave expression. "You know I can't let you get away with this." He pointed to his neck. "I look like I fucked a vacuum cleaner."

I bit my lip.

He stalked across the room, jumped into bed, landed on me, and held me down. "My turn." His mouth closed around the spot where my ear and neck met.

I pushed him away. "No. Please don't."

He clamped tighter.

I shoved at his chest. "West, seriously. You can't. Aunt Edith, Liam, Winona, my students…"

West's drawl took on a coercive tone. "How about where no one will see them?"

With an exhale, my willpower turned into a pile of pulsating flesh.

West strung kisses along my neck, down my stomach, and across my hip. When he reached my inner thigh, he stopped, drew my flesh into his mouth, and pulled. He worked the spot until I begged him to move higher. Ignoring my plea, he targeted his sensual assault on the inside of my opposite leg.

"Higher, please," I begged again.

"Later," he promised, hell-bent on marking me. "Roll over."

I plopped my face onto the pillow.

His hands traveled over my hips and buttocks, his hair tickling me the entire time. His mouth took hold of the small of my back and tugged.

It was settled. Since West Westinghouse knew how to make love to every inch of a woman, I required an eternity with his lips and tongue.

"There." Wearing an impish grin, he joined me at the top of the bed and nibbled on my ear. "Now, we're even. Everyone will think I was with some tramp, and you will still appear to be a lady. Our reputations remain intact."

I rolled to face him, and ran my hand along his cheek. "I'm hungry. Do you have anything mold-free I can eat?"

"One of my Aunt Polly's pumpkin logs is on the counter."

I popped to a seated position, grabbed the crocheted afghan, and formed it into a dress. Then I padded across the room to forage for food. With his hands behind his heads, West leaned against the headboard as I searched for a knife.

I sliced off a piece of the treat and shoved it into my mouth. Polly's pumpkin logs were to die for under normal circumstances. After a night of lovemaking, they were cream-filled slices of heaven.

"You need a coffee pot and a stove so that…"

I lost my train of thought because I was in awe of how West's contracted biceps framed his chiseled jaw-line, and the faraway look in his eyes stole my breath.

"I've got both downstairs in the pub."

I nodded and filled a glass with tap water. I guzzled the contents in four gulps, then looked out the window so that I could think. "I have to walk to the pet store this morning. Princess Pickles is out of his turtle pellets, and I refuse to chop up bugs."

West chuckled.

"It must have snowed all night. It's beautiful," I said.

"Do I have to plow the parking lot again?"

While I marveled at the picturesque undisturbed snow, West came up behind me and rested his chin on my shoulder. He wrapped his arms around me, and I relaxed into his embrace.

"I want to go downstairs and make you breakfast, but I have to clear the parking lot before my dad and uncle show up."

"Make me breakfast?"

Our bodies gently swayed.

"Yes." He nuzzled my ear. "Eggs, bacon, toast, pancakes, hash browns, and an entire pot of coffee just for you." A typical diner breakfast was all seduction, when whispered in West's drawl.

"That sounds delicious."

He nuzzled my neck. "Come back tonight. Tomorrow morning we'll have the entire pub to ourselves."

"Ahh, yes. I didn't know you cooked?"

"Of course I cook." He kissed my neck. "Who do you think will take over the grill when Pop retires?"

"Mmm," I responded to both his breath on my shoulder and the thought of food.

"It's a date," he said. "I finish up at two tonight. You can come anytime you want and wait under the covers for me. We'll go downstairs in the morning, and I'll make you the best breakfast you've ever had. Then I'm going to lay you out on the bar and fuck you for hours."

"West!" I attempted to sound offended. The truth was, I loved when West said filthy things to me because his words held a taunting playfulness that enticed me to no end.

He untied the knot holding the afghan in place, and the mass of colorful yarn dropped to the ground. My naked backside leaned against West's bare front. I pressed into him, resting messy ringlets on his chest. He caressed the length of my torso, lingering on my breasts.

"Mmm," and "Yes," we took turns muttering as his fingers gently pinched my nipples.

He bent me forward and positioned my elbows on his make-shift counter. His hands squeezed my hips as he slid inside. I braced myself as he began his forceful thrusts.

I considered reminding him that we had decided to use condoms, but a second later, West's body distracted me. "Harder," I cried.

He pounded on me with a force that shook a chunk of plaster from the wall. Something cracked. My arms buckled, and his counter gave way, sending me crashing onto the floor. West grabbed for me, but it was too late. I landed face first on his kitchen floor. A flimsy counter, a pumpkin log, a knife, a shattered glass, and an old afghan littered the ground.

West knelt beside me. "Shit. Are you okay?"

I was uninjured and still affiliated with an overactive libido, so I rolled over and pulled him on top of me. My lids closed, and my hips crashed against his. When I opened my eyes, a furious-looking, wispy form watched us.

I hissed and shooed Greg Grainey away. He dissolved moments before my insides exploded, and West followed me into bliss.

"Shortcake?"

"Yes?" I considered reading his mind.

Instead, we cuddled on his kitchen floor. All of our sweating and panting had us too exhausted to think. Of course, I was way too spent to walk into town to buy turtle food.

And I certainly didn't have the energy to deal with a jealous dead man.

Chapter 7

An eating-ice-cream-naked-in-the-Arctic kind of cold settled over Bellmount on Black Friday, as I performed the walk of shame clad in the short skirt and tights I donned on Thanksgiving Eve.

The outfit may have enticed Weston Westinghouse the Third into writhing with me for hours, but it clashed with my boots. At least I didn't slip as the snow crunched beneath the rubber soles, the wind whipped at my ringlets, and a pain in the patootie phantasm jabbered at my heels.

"The bartender? Seriously, Crimson. I was too much of a womanizer for you, but you are sleeping with the bartender? Why am I just finding this out now?" asked Greg Grainey.

I greeted and passed by Mrs. Silva—the town's busy body—before I responded.

"Who I sleep with is none of your business, Greg. And stop barging in on me."

"How is it not my business? You're my girl," he said.

I waited for the elderly Mr. Clifton to pass us. "For the trillionth time, I am not your girl. Remember the boundaries."

Greg snorted. *"Where are we headed first?"*

I didn't answer until we finished shuffling through the crowd. The small town of Bellmount, Pennsylvania, thought me at least one hundred fifty-seven scandals too much. I didn't need she-is-so-crazy-she-talks-to-herself-in-public added to the list.

I slipped into Nicole's Bakery for a cup of coffee. I had a severe case of caffeine withdrawal, and ice crystals formed in my veins. Greg peeked over my shoulder and stared into the dessert case.

"Hi, Nicole," I said.

"Hi, Dr. Albright. Did you have a good Thanksgiving?"

"I want a danish," Greg said.

"Aunt Edith prepared a feast fit for a king. It was wonderful. How about you, Nicole?"

"I don't know; maybe I want a chocolate chip muffin," Greg said at the same time that Nicole replied, "Thanksgiving dinner was awesome. What can I get for you?"

"A snickerdoodle. Get me a snickerdoodle," Greg said.

I did an internal eye roll. "I'll take a large coffee with cream and sugar and a pumpkin donut to go."

As the baker filled my order, a cookie rose from the case and hovered in mid-air. I grabbed it and shoved it behind my back. Then I perused the restaurant, ensuring nobody had witnessed the mysterious floating treat.

"Give me my cookie," Greg demanded.

I faced his wispy form and mouthed shut-up.

Oblivious that an incorrigible ghost had purloined a sweet from her case, Nicole pushed a few numbers into her cash register. "That will be one dollar and seventy-six cents."

I retrieved my wallet from the front pocket of my

backpack and handed Nicole three dollars. I told her to keep the change since I wanted to make reparations for the stolen snickerdoodle I shoved into my bag.

Greg followed me out of the store, begging for his cookie and chattering about how he missed cheeseburgers, beer, and eating pussy.

I stopped short, took the snickerdoodle out of my bag, and took a big bite. "Yum! Mmm, mmm, mmm." I dangled the cookie in front of the dirty talking specter.

The corners of his lips turned downward, and his filmy eyes lost what little spark his otherworldly existence had maintained.

I winced. "Sorry, Greg. I'm a complete jerk. Let's go get Princess Pickles his food."

Before strolling into the pet store, I stared wistfully at a sign that read Dr. Bradley Gordon, MD. Although my heart belonged to Weston, I wanted closure with Brad. I wanted to say I'm sorry. I wanted him to know how much he had meant to me. I wanted to say goodbye.

Lou Romano, the odd man who owned the pet store, stood behind the counter. He grinned and held two plastic turtles inches from my nose.

I cocked my ear toward him so that I could decipher his Philly Italian accent. "Yo, Albright, These are my friends, Cuff and Link."

Greg laughed. *"That SOB is funny."*

"That's nice, Lou," I said hesitantly. "Just getting my turtle some food."

Greg chortled as he followed me to the back of the store.

"Why is that funny?" I whispered.

"Pet store flirtation. I'd be pissed the SOB is

hitting on you, but he doesn't stand a chance."

I stared at the grinning ghost.

"Guess you aren't a fan of the greatest movie ever made?"

I continued to glare.

"Anyway, it's about this down-and-out boxer who owns turtles and does this chick on the floor of his dirty apartment. That was my favorite part."

Even dead, Greg was a cad. Frustrated, because I still didn't get the humor, I threw my hands into the air. Of course, I rarely understood pop culture references. Television and movies weren't my things. Give me a book, and I shone with self-assurance.

I paid for the turtle food, a tiny elf hat for my rat—he would hate it—and a smiling pumpkin squeaky toy for my pup. I shoved my purchase into my backpack, and Greg and I headed back into the frigid wind. Since my dress coat and gloves were useless against the elements, I chose a shortcut and headed down an alley. Not only would I get home faster, but the lack of crowds afforded me a chance to grovel to my ghost as I again asked for forgiveness for my cruel cookie taunt. An eternity without baked goods wasn't something I wished on my worst enemy. And, I confess, I had developed a soft spot for my perverted poltergeist.

A few feet into the alley, I stopped. A magnetic force pulled me in the opposite direction. "Greg, something's wrong. We have to turn around."

Greg followed behind me, chattering away as I dodged in and out of side streets trying to find the source of my disquiet. My search ended in the parking lot behind Brad Gordon's office. A pile of red and white fluff lay about seven yards away. Blood stained the surrounding snow, creating a gruesome red snow cone effect.

"Greg, I can't believe it! It's another dead Santa. That makes two in one week." I trudged to the body with my ghost in tow. Being careful not to spill my coffee, I knelt to check Santa's pulse. "He's alive."

Although the injured man looked familiar, I couldn't place him.

He reached his hand toward my face and uttered something that sounded like, "Help the girls."

Thinking Greg stood in front of me, I looked up. Instead, a different Santa pointed a revolver in my direction.

I gasped.

Santa number two lowered his revolver and aimed at bloody supine Santa one.

Bang!

The bullet hit the body that lay in front of me. Santa number two lined up his second shot.

Bang!

A millisecond later, something pierced my chest.

What happened next was insane. Santa number two's gun flew into the air and landed at his feet. When he bent to retrieve the weapon, it mysteriously popped into the air and settled a foot away from him.

The scene became increasingly blurry. Number two tracked down his gun, picked it up, and ran off. My sharp pain turned into a burning sensation.

I fell, and everything went black.

****

When I came to, a dark-haired man leaned over me. Even though the sunlight in my eyes kept me from discerning his features, I recognized him. Greg stood behind him, and a small crowd of people had gathered.

My coat was unbuttoned, and my purple shirt lay wide open, exposing my torso. The man's hands pressed on my bloody chest.

"I've got you, sweetheart. You're going to be okay. Close your eyes and relax." *God, please give me strength. Please let her live.*

"God damn it, Gordon, do something," Greg yelled.

"It doesn't hurt anymore," I whispered. "Am I dying?"

"Shhh, sweetheart. Close your eyes and relax," Brad repeated.

Chapter 8
Fourteen hours later...

When I awoke to a disconcerting *beep*, it took my pupils time to adjust to the dark. Once I gained my night vision, I saw that Bradley Gordon slept in the chair beside my bed. His body was much too large for the scanty furniture, and his head hung forward. Greg Grainey's translucent form lay next to me, and he stared at the ceiling, drumming his fingers on his chest.

At first, I had no idea why I was hooked to a monitor in a hospital room. All at once, I remembered the cookie hovering in Nicole's bakery, an odd Italian man clutching two plastic turtles, blood staining the snow, and a Santa pointing a gun at me... I gasped, and my body heaved as I recalled the painful gunshot I received after leaving West's apartment. My sudden jolt alerted Greg that I was awake.

He sat up. "Crimson, it's about time. You've been asleep forever."

"Greg, you attacked the shooter and saved my life," I croaked.

Brad stirred from his seat beside the bed. "Miranda?" He switched the light on, before settling back into the chair and grasping my hand.

Greg reached for my other hand but passed through it.

I had not yet tried to touch Greg's intangible form.

In fact, I had done everything to push him away. His pained eyes made me want to comfort him, so I grasped his fingers, making contact. Who would have guessed that touching Greg Grainey would cause me to grin from ear to ear?

"I feel your hand."

Greg smiled back at me. "I feel you, too."

"Miranda, you can see and feel Grainey?" Brad asked.

"Yep," Greg answered for me. "Only three people in this God-forsaken county know I'm around. Lucky me, Gordon, you're one of them."

Brad rubbed his eyes. "Jesus, Miranda, can you see Grainey right now?"

I pushed my sore body to a seated position. "Yes."

"So, I'm not seeing things?" Brad asked.

Every time I developed a soft spot for the ex-weapons dealer, he did something to remind me of the hideous man he had been.

I groaned. "Greg, you promised you weren't messing with Brad."

Brad's jaw tensed. "I've spent the last few weeks thinking I'd gone off the deep end."

Greg chuckled.

"You aren't crazy, Brad. Greg is haunting you and messing with your mind. And I told him weeks ago not to do it."

"What can I say, Gordon? All's fair in love and war. Go back to Jessica and leave my Crimson alone," Greg hissed, his tone menacing.

Brad wasn't a man who fought dirty, called people names, or kicked a man when he was down. Dr. Bradley Gordon was all class. He brushed Greg's aggressive taunt to the side. "Miranda, when Grainey showed up and told me you were hurt, I almost ignored him. I thought he was a figment of my imagination. God, what if I hadn't come?"

"I wouldn't have given up until I convinced you she needed help," Greg said.

I squeezed Brad's hand. "You saved my life. You helped me heal."

Brad sucked on the side of his jaw.

"Oh, no. Have you locked yourself away, thinking you were going crazy? Is that why you haven't returned my calls, and why you isolated yourself?"

His sigh was so painful and heavy that he was lucky he didn't crash straight through the floor. "Miranda, I was ready to close my practice and commit myself to the state hospital. Please tell me what's going on."

"I think it has something to do with our energy. Mine to read minds, and yours to heal. There is also a psychic in Greenport named Madame Alina who can communicate with the dead. I can't see any other ghosts, only Greg. Can you see others?" I asked.

"Only Grainey," Brad said. "He's been showing up daily, accusing me of everything under the sun and telling me to go back to Jessica. I thought I was seeing things."

"Oh, Greg. That was a horrible thing to do." Once again, I successfully made contact when I slapped his shoulder. "Can you at least tell us what else you know?"

Greg scowled as he dramatically rubbed his fake injury. "I don't have any idea what's going on. I think I'm stuck in this damn county for eternity. Maybe you two have been sentenced to accompany me in my hell."

"I tried to save your life, and this is how you repay me? By making me think I'm insane. I almost gave up my practice. I may have lost the woman I love."

"You haven't lost Jessica. She still loves you," Greg said.

Despite his new ethereal form, Greg's paternal instinct was as strong as ever. He hadn't given up hope that his ex-son-in-law might forgive his daughter for her marital indiscretions. However, Jessica Grainey's infidelity was not the reason for their divorce. Brad was a man who forgave quickly and loved with all of his heart. Simply put, the kind-hearted man disapproved of how spoiled and cruel his ex-wife was.

"Miranda, I'm sorry. Have I lost you?" Brad asked.

Greg's laugh started as a tinkling giggle. Then it became a haunting, eerie sound that increased in volume until it exploded like a devilish howl from an old gothic horror movie. He shot Brad an all-knowing evil glare. "Way too late, Gordon."

Knock. Knock.

The three of us jumped.

A middle-aged woman attired in green scrubs entered the room. An attractive blonde wearing a white coat and carrying a clipboard followed her.

"Hi, Bradley," the younger woman said. "Hello, Miranda. I'm Dr. Baker. We thought someone screamed. Is everything okay?"

Greg and his gosh darn malevolent howl!

"Everything's fine," Brad said.

Dr. Baker hung the clipboard at the end of my bed and checked my monitor. She stretched out her arm to shake my hand.

I was too overwhelmed to worry about my shield, so her thoughts traveled straight into me. *She should be dead. How did he save her?*

I assumed the injury had been life-threatening, the "he" was Brad, and his ability to heal using energy confused Dr. Baker.

The woman in green wore a name tag that read Theresa. Her tight gray bun tugged at the corner of her eyes, and her pinched expression made her sharp features especially harsh. The sourpuss stomped to my side, shoved my torso forward, and rearranged the pillows.

"My dear," Dr. Baker said. "You are one lucky woman. Your injury is healing quickly. You must have magic in your blood."

I sucked in a breath. If she only knew!

"I'm going to have you transferred from critical care to the second floor. If you continue to heal at this speed, I don't see why I can't release you into Dr. Gordon's care. I want to caution you, once you're downstairs, there is going to be a relentless cop in your face."

"Edgar Shultz?" Brad asked.

Brad and I glared at a snorting Greg.

Dr. Baker's gaze followed ours. Her blank expression indicated she saw a typical hospital room instead of a handsome ghost wearing a smart alec gleam.

She refocused her attention on me. "I don't think that was the detective's name."

"Sergeant O'Sullivan?" I asked.

If it was possible for a ghost to bust a gut with cruel laughter, Greg Grainey would need to be glued back together.

"O'Sullivan might be his name, and he is adamant that he talk to you. Once you leave my unit, it will be easier for him to get to you. Cops can be relentless in situations like this. They put their investigations before a patient's well-being."

"It's okay," I said. "We are working on a case together."

"Working on a case?" the physicians asked in unison.

I nodded.

"You're a detective?" Dr. Baker asked. "I thought you were a professor at the college."

"I am a professor. It's a long story."

Dr. Baker picked up my chart and wrote something.

The vexed nurse's voice was as sharp and spear-like as her appearance. "Your aunt visited. Then a reporter, a couple of large dishonest Polish men claiming they are your uncles, an angry woman with a head full of braids, and some distraught man all rudely demanded to see you."

"With Miranda, that sounds like par for the course." Brad's dimples deepened with his taunting grin.

The nurse grunted. "I know a lie when I hear one. Your fake uncles couldn't even agree on which side of the family they were from." She pounded on my pillow, then force-fed me a sip of water.

I studied the Nazi-like nurse, deciding it wise to hide my amusement as I pictured my friends Wochowska and Lowalski going to war with her. It was no use. I smirked as I imagined her trying to bar Aunt

Edith, Grimwood, and Keisha from charging into my room.

Was the worried man Russ, Lincoln, Liam, Tommy, or—fingers crossed—West?

"Sounds like you're a popular girl," Dr. Baker said.

At first, I scrunched up my face since "popular" wasn't the correct word. Then I beamed because being loved trumped popularity.

"Be back in a minute." Brad escorted Dr. Baker and Nurse Nasty from the room.

Left alone with my ghost, I let loose. "Greg? How could you do that to Brad?" I waggled my finger in his translucent face. "You better keep your mouth shut. I want to be the one to tell him about West. You keep your trouble making nose out of it. Do you understand?"

Greg's jaw clenched. "I hate Gordon. I wish I had shot him before the two of you killed me."

"You need a therapist. Is there such a thing as a ghost therapist because you seriously need help."

The door opened, and Brad strolled to my side. "All good news. You're healing beautifully."

"Brad, thank you. I would have died without you."

Greg cleared his throat.

"I would have died if it wasn't for both of you."

Greg's chest expanded like an inflating ballon.

"Greg, could you please excuse us? Maybe visit Alina and discuss the issue we just talked about."

The spectre put a hand on his hip and tapped a foot.

I glowered.

Finally, he disappeared.

Brad shook his head, sighed, then sat on the edge of my bed.

I took in a breath of courage before clasping Brad's hand and explaining to him that Weston Westinghouse the Third had stolen my heart.

****

Twenty-eight hours later, my unrelenting monitor continued its torturous song. Brad was again asleep in the chair beside my bed, and Greg stared at the ceiling from his spot beside me.

However, there were a few differences this time. First of all, I could see because sunlight was streaming in through the window. Secondly, I was no longer in the critical care unit. Finally, instead of wondering where I was, I thought about the dead Santa in the alley and his cryptic message. Why had he looked familiar? Who were the girls? Why was I supposed to help them? Why had two Santas been murdered? Who was the man who had shot me? Were Reynolds, Shultz, and Steven's up to something? As if that wasn't a lot to process, why did I keep stumbling over corpses? Even stranger, why were men suddenly paying attention to me? It had to be a curse or spell. I had a lot of questions and not a single answer.

Brad was still sleeping when Greg kissed me on the forehead. "I'll be back tonight. It's a big day at the shop. Buck season starts in two days."

"Have a good day, Greg," I whispered right before he vanished.

I propped myself against the headboard.

Although Brad's mussed hair stood in the air, the black stubble on his chin had filled in overnight, and he looked exhausted—he remained movie-star handsome. I was crazy about Weston Westinghouse, but it didn't detract from my knowledge that Brad Gordon was an incredible man.

Since entering the hospital, Brad had splayed his hands on my chest at least three times to send healing vibrations into my body. The problem was, I sucked all of his energy. Brad's wonderful qualities—that he was selfless, caring, and consumed with saving lives—were the same traits that caused him to ignore taking care of himself and exhausted him. They were also the reason he struggled devoting time to his romantic interest.

Still, Brad deserved to find someone as saintly as himself. Maybe a glamorous social worker or a loving Red Cross Nurse would make his perfect match. He didn't need a mess of a college professor who kept finding corpses and was obsessed with Weston Westinghouse's lips.

Brad blinked, lifted his arms to the ceiling, stretched out his long legs, and cleared his throat. "Good morning, Miranda."

I returned the greeting.

He rubbed the sleep from his eyes. "Let me check your wound."

"You've already done too much for me. I'm fine, and you are draining yourself."

"I'm certain you are doing great, but I'd like to make sure," he said.

I held up a palm. "No. I'm fine. Please take care of yourself. You're exhausted. I'm not taking any more of your energy."

"Miranda, I think—"

"Absolutely not, Dr. Gordon. The hospital staff is getting paid to take care of me."

"I am tired. I have to drive back to Bellmount, and I have a full day of appointments." He rubbed at the stubble on his chin. "I'll be back tonight, and then I'm going to check your injury."

"Fine. We can compromise," I said.

Although Brad smiled, his eyes were red-rimmed and didn't have their usual sparkle.

"Brad, thank you. You are amazing."

"I'm glad you think so because you're an amazing woman."

I didn't want to remind him of my foibles, so I focused on him. "When did you know you could heal with your touch?"

He settled against the back of his too-tiny chair. "I suppose when I was about eight, I saved a puppy that had been hit by a car. I didn't know for sure, but I started to suspect. Then there was the string of guinea pigs I kept reviving. My parents acted like it was no big deal and normal for a kid to touch an ill animal and have it get a burst of energy."

"Wow," I muttered.

"When I was in high school, a kid on my football team broke his back. It was awful. The worst part was the stadium was silent, except for his mother's prayers. I tried to comfort him while the paramedics loaded him onto a stretcher. The next thing I knew, I woke up on his stretcher, and he was walking beside me. The athletic trainer said the back injury diagnosis was an error and that I had collapsed from heatstroke and dehydration."

"That poor trainer probably thought he was losing his mind." I huffed at the bitter irony. "Was there someone in your family you inherited your ability from?"

"My grandfather was a field surgeon in World War

Two, and the rumors were he was an excellent doctor that knew how to ease pain and could heal the very sick. So, maybe him. How about you? When did you know you could read minds?"

"I guess I realized it when I was about six. Liam and I played cards a lot. If I touched his hand, I knew exactly where the Old Maid was. Sometimes he accused me of cheating."

Brad chuckled.

"I never told anyone because I didn't want people to think I was crazy. I convinced myself it was intuition and an overactive imagination until I moved into town."

"I can't imagine going most of your life, not understanding. The past few weeks of questioning my sanity were unbearable."

"Brad, do you think it's cheating if you are six, and without even trying, you know what cards a person is holding when playing games?"

He looked thoughtful, then shook his head. "Not cheating in the least. It's an incredible blessing. I have been given this gift to take away pain and heal others. I used to question it. Not anymore. I combine my unexplainable ability with traditional medicine and do my best to help someone if it's within my power. I wake up every day and proudly accept my mission."

"Even now, after everything we've been through, you still say the perfect thing I need to hear."

We laughed at the meaningful moment and my heart warmed. For years I had wanted someone with whom to commiserate. I had prayed for someone to come along who understood the loneliness of being different.

"You have a purpose for your abilities. I feel like a

freak," I said.

"You aren't a freak, and you'll find your purpose. Maybe you already have. Maybe you are supposed to educate people and solve crimes, and maybe I'm supposed to keep you safe." His dimples deepened. "I hate how dangerous your sleuthing is, but I will put bandages on your boo-boos. Just don't get yourself killed. I can't fix that. And promise me you'll do your best not to get injured."

I squeezed his palm.

His gaze intense he said, "I swear, if Westinghouse hurts you, he'll answer to me

When the door swung wide and banged into the wall, he dropped my hand. He sighed before waving goodbye and leaving me alone with my breakfast tray and an overworked snarky nurse.

****

After a dull morning spent surfing the four channels on the television set, I needed something to read so I finished *Beloved*. I also needed the ripe-urine-mixed-with-antiseptic odor to stop tainting the taste of my food. Nurse Nasty was a masochist who took delight in tormenting me. Every time I dozed off, she woke me with a poking or prodding. At least I was excited about visiting hours.

After an evening of friends and family, loads of new books, fancy wrapped chocolates, and a promise from two mobsters that they would get to the bottom of things, Detectives O'Sullivan and Miller showed up and began their interrogation. I had pushed my embarrassment over the undercover kiss to the back of my mind because some things couldn't be helped when it came to murder investigations. Telling a few lies, breaking a minor law or two, and kissing handsome men when undercover were all forgivable ethical violations when trying to solve a murder. Right?

Sean crossed one booted foot over the other and leaned against the wall. "Start at the beginning, Red."

I recounted almost every detail I could remember. The detectives didn't need to know that a ghost had attacked the shooter and that Brad had stopped my bleeding using only his mind and body.

Miller sat on the edge of the chair beside me. "The guy in the alley was Joe Morrow."

"I don't recognize the name. He looked familiar, but I can't place him," I said.

"Joe's name hasn't been released to the press or the public yet. The mayor wants things kept quiet until we know more because he doesn't want mass panic with all the hunters coming into town. Fine by me. It allows us to do the investigation without drama," Sean said.

"The mayor is dishonest. He covers up anything he thinks makes him look bad," I said.

Miller bristled.

I stared Miller down. "Be careful, Sean. Your partner likes to lick the mayor's boots."

Miller slapped his palm on his leg. "I've had enough of her insults."

Sean rolled his eyes. "Red, can you try not to piss off my partner? Consider it a personal favor. I'll owe you."

Since having a handsome homicide detective owe me a favor might prove to be a valuable asset, I acquiesced with a nod.

"Good girl," Sean said. "Stiles was a Santa at Lightsingers, and Morrow volunteered as a Santa at a few places around town. Both men are Bellmount natives. Both are middle-aged. Stiles was married with kids and grandkids. Morrow was single. They don't seem to have traveled in the same social circles."

"The last thing Joe Morrow said sounded like, 'Help the girls,'" I said.

Sean took a tablet and a pen out of his pocket. "Did he say anything else?"

"Nothing. But I still find it odd that there were five bullets found and only three gun shots. Why would they move the body?"

Miller shrugged.

Sean tapped the pen on his pad. "We're waiting for ballistics to come back, but it looks like the same gun was used for both murders. And, I agree. George's murder happened somewhere else, and the body was moved."

"Hmm," I murmured.

"You didn't recognize the guy who shot you?" Sean asked.

"No."

"Can you describe him?"

"No. All I can tell you is he had on a Santa suit and wire-rimmed glasses."

"Were the glasses real or fake?" Sean asked.

"I don't know."

"Real beard?"

"Fake, I think."

"Age? Height?"

"No, Sean. Nothing. I think I was too scared. He looked like Santa to me."

Our conversation halted when Winona peeked into the room.

She sprinted to my bed and clasped me in her arms. "Thank goodness. We didn't know if you were going to live. Edith told us someone shot you in the chest, and the rumors in the pub were that a man and woman died."

"I'm going to be okay, Winona. Brad was there to stop the bleeding, and Dr. Baker—"

West peered around the door.

"West!" I called.

He shoved his hands into the pockets of his blue ski jacket and hesitated before entering. His usually confident shoulders slumped forward, and his eyes were red. Instead of his t-shirt, he wore a blue and green zigzag patterned sweater. He locked gazes with Sean while Winona chattered away. I had no idea what she clattered on about. I didn't care about anything at that moment but comforting West. His energy was all wrong, and it was apparent he hadn't slept in days.

Sean peeled himself from the wall. "Hey, Red. We're going to let you visit with your friends. See you tomorrow."

I waved goodbye to the detectives as Winona sat on the edge of my bed.

"West, come sit." I pointed to the chair.

He stared at his feet before joining us.

Like a concerned mother, Winona ran her fingers through my hair. Unfortunately, her nails snagged in my knots.

"I told West he better not give you that flu he had. I even tried to talk him out of coming, but he insisted." Then, in typical Winona fashion, she asked me a string of questions. "Tell us what happened. All we know is you got shot. What did Sergeant O'Sullivan have to say? Does he know who shot you? Was it a Santa? Is it connected to the Santa murder? I think Officer Hunky has the hots for you. You're so lucky."

"Christ, Winona," West said. "Give it a rest. Give the girl a chance to answer."

Winona scowled at him before turning her worried expression back on me. "I overheard them asking you questions about what the Santa looked like, so I assume it's attached to the Santa murder. Ignore West. He's been a jerk since he got the flu. He probably needs an antibiotic."

"Christ, Winona," West said again. He slipped out of his coat, and a few beads of sweat dripped down his forehead.

"Winona, can you go down to the cafeteria and get me an iced tea and a butterscotch cake?" I asked.

"West can go. I want to talk to you."

"Can you go, Winona? West will mess up my order and bring me something like root beer and pork rinds."

West sent me a secret wink. "You don't want those overly sweet cakes. Pork rinds and beef jerky, now there's a snack."

I forced my eyes to squint and my brow to furrow. "See, what I mean, Winona?"

"Fine." She grunted. "West, why do you have to be impossible?" She stomped off to track down my snack.

West rolled his eyes, and I laughed.

"She means well," I said.

He cracked a smile. "I know."

"We missed our breakfast date." I fluttered my lashes.

"Damn! We thought you died. I've been—" He closed his eyes and exhaled.

I grabbed his hand and squeezed. "Are you hot?"

His other hand swept the length of his body. "Hot as hell."

I giggled. "That's not what I meant. You're sweating."

"I just spent thirty minutes in a car listening to Winona; hospitals suck, and this damn sweater is itchy."

Goosebumps traveled over my entire body. "Is that your new sweater?"

"This wasn't the occasion I bought it for." He frowned.

"I love it. Will you wear it on our next date? Of course, you can wear your t-shirt if you want. Or go naked." I bit my lip as my absurd blush took over. After everything that West and I had done, why did I still struggle with flirty, dirty talk?

West sighed and laughed at the same time. "So, Officer Hunky is back in town and has the hots for you?" He wiped his glistening brow on his sleeve.

"Are you jealous?"

"*Pfft.*"

I metaphorically crossed my fingers. "Did you come to see me last night?"

"Stayed here all night. That damn nurse wouldn't let me in. Of course, my family is all over my ass because they think I blew off work to bang some bimbo. Gotta keep my image intact."

I aimed for a sexy lip pucker. "Get over here and kiss me, Mr. Westinghouse. Or I will crawl out of this hospital bed and climb onto your lap."

West gently slid to my side and had wrapped an arm around me when Brad strolled in with a book tucked under his arm.

West pulled away just in time because a second later, Winona tramped in carrying an iced tea and a packaged baked good.

"Look who I found." Winona pointed at Brad, then held up the snack. "They didn't have butterscotch, so I got you peanut butter."

The ensuing awkwardness ripped me wide open.

"Westinghouse," Brad said sternly.

A sweat bead dripped down West's cheek. "Doc."

The clueless Winona blurted out, "Miranda, Bradley brought your favorite book so he can read to you. Isn't that romantic? It's so cool that he's a doctor and can stay and take care of you all night. West, I guess we have to go now because visiting hours are over."

West slung his coat over his arm, disappearing into the hallway. Winona continued blabbering while she hugged me, batted her eyelashes at Brad, then followed her cousin.

Greg stood at the foot of my bed, his vicious laugh so uncontrollable, it turned into a gargled choking.

Chapter 9

Despite my insistence that I could walk, Nurse Nasty shoved me into a wheelchair and pushed me to the front portico, where I waited for Aunt Edith. Theresa was a stickler for rules. She waited until I was in my aunt's care before turning the chair around and heading back into the hospital. I'd have bet all of my get-well chocolates that the masochistic attendant lived to manhandle the infirmed with rough baths, sharp needles, and cosmic scowls.

Aunt Edith and I had just pulled away from the curb when a pint-sized man strode toward us. He was dressed in yellow polyester bellbottoms, a palm tree patterned button-down shirt and a green corduroy jacket.

"Aunt Edith, hold on a second. It's Pat. I think he's here to see me," I said.

My aunt put her car into park, and I stepped onto the pavement to call to him. He waved back, and his already brisk pace quickened. Pat Grimwood, my journalist friend, did everything in double-time. He also ingested entirely too much caffeine, inhaled too much tobacco, and dressed as if he lived in a Seventies' disco. He beat me to the sidewalk.

"Hello, Professor." Pat had mastered speaking while a cigarette hung from the corner of his mouth.

"I've wanted to call you, but things have been a bit

crazy. My nurse told me you came to see me two days ago," I said.

The cigarette teetered precariously. "Nurse Bitchy wouldn't let me in."

I chuckled.

"What happened? No one's talking. Can't get any information. Just you were shot, and a man died in the alley behind Pine Street," Pat said.

"The detectives on the case have been to see me. They said the mayor is trying to keep the story quiet."

"Reynolds told me to stay far away from this one. Practically threatened me," Pat said.

I'm not sure why I asked, "Why would he do that?" since I already knew the answer. The mayor didn't want any more bad publicity or murder talk in his town. I had experienced enough notoriety with Suzy Smith's murder and Greg Grainey's death, so I didn't want my name in the papers, either. My desire for anonymity seemed reasonable. Reynolds's reasons seemed suspect.

"Gave some rigmarole about not wanting to scare the hunters during buck season. Said it hurts the tourism revenue." Pat sputtered before plucking his cancer stick from his mouth and flicking ashes onto the sidewalk. "Let's talk about the details of your brush with death, Professor."

"I was walking down the alley when I saw another dead Santa."

He inhaled toxic fumes. "Another dead Santa?"

"Yes, and the crazy thing was, it was a Santa that shot him. I think I interrupted the murder, so he tried to kill me too."

Pat blew out a cloud of smoke. "A Santa killing another Santa?"

I waved Pat's smelly exhale from my nostrils. "Yes, but unlike the first shooting, this one was in broad daylight. How bold is that?"

"Who's the second dead Santa?" Pat asked.

"Joe Morrow. Do you know him?"

"Drank. Gambled. Liked nefarious women. Recently found religion. Was straightening out his life," he chirped in his clipped speech. "Even volunteering at the community center and church."

"That's so sad. So, someone killed two Santas? One volunteering and one employed by Lightsingers?" I tapped a finger on my cheek as if the gesture might help me think clearly.

Pat sighed. "Morrow, the poor fool. Guess the devil caught back up to him."

Neither of us laughed at his bad joke.

"Are you going to run the story despite Mayor Reynolds?" I asked.

"Yep."

I used my best pleading voice. "Would you consider leaving my name out of it?"

"You got it, Professor. Just a woman was shot. No need to provide a name."

"Thank you. You're a good friend." I patted him on the shoulder.

We said our goodbyes, and I was about to climb into the car when I almost walked through my ghost. I don't know why I hadn't seen him right away because he wore a bright orange vest over his brown camouflage suit. A matching brown cap sat on his head.

"What the hell is the world coming to? Grown men with guns afraid of Santa," Greg said.

I couldn't resist. "Hiya, Elmer."

Years ago, Liam had forced me to watch Saturday morning shows with him, and the silly hunter had stuck with me.

Greg snorted. I supposed his vanity didn't appreciate the comparison to a goofy cartoon character.

I tapped the absurd hat. Could ghosts shoot animals? And why did he feel the need to protect himself with a neon garment when nobody could see it. It wasn't like a bullet could hurt him since he was already dead. I chose not to say anything at that moment because Aunt Edith was peering out the windshield, and I didn't want her to see me talking to the breeze.

As usual, Greg ignored my silence and continued chattering. *"Hell, if Reynolds is worried about economics, he should've put a bounty on that murdering SOB Santa's head. Every hunter with balls would show up and hunt him down. If I find out who he is, I'm going to blow the mother fucker to smithereens. That'll teach him to mess with my girl."*

I smiled at my ghost's overprotective machismo, then climbed into the car.

Greg appeared in the backseat and continued blabbing. *"Bellmount is full of pussies. Not the yummy kind. The chicken-shit kind. Reynolds is the biggest..."* Blah and blah. Blah blah, but blah. Then blah, blah.

Boy, could my ghost rant.

Aunt Edith called out, "Bellmount or bust!" as we drove out of the hospital parking lot.

****

Aunt Edith served a three-tiered almond cake oozing with tart cherry filling at my surprise party. Nicole from the bakery had created confectionary art.

Decadent pink, purple, and cream-colored buttercream rosettes covered the sides. *Welcome Home, Miranda* was spelled out in ornate purple script across the top, and a light dusting of pink sugar had been sprinkled over the entire tower, making the platter sparkle under the chandelier.

My friends and family packed the inn. Liam, Tommy, Keisha, Winona, Pat, Lincoln, his wife Alice, Wowchowska, Lowalski, Brad, and West were all present. Sean was once again staying with us, so he also joined the party.

My Polish friends gave my Irish friend a wide berth. I supposed the entire cops and bad guys eating cold cuts together wasn't the best laid plan. Lowalski and Wowchowska didn't stay long because they had business they needed to attend to. Still, they attended, had a few sandwiches, and let me know there was some "scumbag" in Greenport they were keeping an eye on.

Although not officially invited—because he didn't exist in a skin and bone form—Greg popped in. My special surprise was that my dad had driven from Harrisburg and planned to sleep on a cot in my turret for a few days.

I spent most of the evening curled up on the red velvet settee in the library. Grandma Zoey's watchful eyes peered at me from her portrait above the mantle. Spot sat at my feet, accepting ear scratches and nibbles of food from our guests. Every time I attempted to make the rounds to socialize, Spot herded me back to my seat, or Winona tracked me down and insisted someone wait on me.

I managed to escape to the turret once. Tommy wanted to say hi to Princess Pickles, and Lincoln wanted to check on the rat. After one three-floor journey that thoroughly upset a Sheltie and a waitress, it became easier to stay put and let people come to me.

West leaned against a bookshelf holding a can of cola. A flannel shirt hung open, revealing his form-fitting t-shirt. His hair was seductively disheveled; he was clean-shaven; his eyelashes appeared exceptionally long, and his hazel eyes looked almost golden in the well-lit library. His attention focused on me as he sipped. I stifled a moan when his lips curled around the rim of the can.

"West," I called. "Come say hi to my dad."

West gulped before walking to the settee. As he strolled across the room, my girl parts tingled.

"Hello, Weston." My father extended his hand in greeting. "Miranda tells me all about your adventures. I hear you let her use your backside for target practice."

I shook my head, letting West know I hadn't filled my dad in on everything. My father wasn't a violent man, but if he had any inkling just how torrid my "adventures" with West were, he would shoot West in the other buttock, then lock me into a chastity belt.

West seemed to understand my frantic gesture because he grinned. "Hi, Mr. Albright. Your daughter may be smart, but she can't tell a beer can from a man's can."

My dad threw his head back and chuckled. Although I had inherited my Grandma Zoey's eyes, nose, stature, and coloring, I had my father and Grandma Albright's wide, face-consuming smile. At that moment, my father's beam was all-encompassing.

"How are your dad and uncle? I thought Miranda and I might come to the pub for dinner tomorrow night so I can catch up with them," my dad said.

"They'd love that," West said.

As my father and West reminisced, I realized that I wanted to shout to the world that I was crazy about West. The time had come to look my bartender in the eyes and tell him the truth. Even if he teased me or told me he didn't feel the same way, I would be courageous. He was in awe of my bravery, after all. Once my dad headed home, I could be alone with West and prove to him just how brave I was. Afterward, I would declare my feelings for the world to hear.

Sean strolled our way. He acknowledged West with a nod.

West returned the greeting with a subtle chin lift, then turned to walk away.

I grabbed his flannel encased arm, holding him in place. "Dad, this is Sergeant O'Sullivan. He is the lead detective on the Santa case."

West tried to step away, so I gripped harder.

My father got up from the couch to shake hands with Sean, and they exchanged first names.

"You have quite the daughter, William," Sean said.

"I sure do. Sharp, beautiful, and gutsy as hell," my dad bragged.

Sean nodded. "Miranda, after the party, I have a couple of things about the case I want to discuss."

"Okay," I said.

Although West turned away from our conversation, he failed to conceal his eye roll.

"It was nice meeting you," Sean said. "Please excuse me. I need another beer."

"I'm empty, too." My dad held up his cup. I'll join you, detective." The two of them headed out of the library together.

Lincoln, Russ, and Pat were across the room, discussing the best way to grill a steak, so they weren't paying attention to us.

"Please, sit." I patted the seat beside me.

West hesitated for a moment, then sat.

Leaning close, I whispered, "I might not be able to visit you much while my dad is in town."

West didn't have time to respond because Brad approached. Greg blabbed away from beside him.

Brad expertly ignored Greg's incessant chatter. "Hi, Westinghouse."

"Doc," West said.

"Miranda, I'm heading home. I have an early morning appointment. Are you sure you are feeling up to returning to campus tomorrow? I can give you a doctor's note," Brad said.

Greg bent forward and pantomimed immature faces inches from the unsuspecting West's nose.

"No, I'm fine. I want to work tomorrow," I said.

"Do you need any painkillers?" Brad asked.

"Nope, I feel great. Just a bit tired." I swatted at Greg, who was still sticking his tongue out at West.

Brad cut his gaze to West, and in a firm tone said, "Westinghouse, Miranda can't be running all over the place, skiing and snowmobiling. Don't *hurt* her. She needs to heal."

West's eyes narrowed, and the smile he had plastered on his face morphed into a grimace. "I have no intention of doing anything to hurt her."

An awkward semi-silence enveloped us.

"Gordon and Westinghouse, you two are fools. You can stand here, having your little pissing match over

our girl all day long. That damn detective is the real problem. He needs to go."

I gasped.

Brad stared at Greg.

Although West wasn't aware of Greg's comment, he also appeared perturbed.

We were distracted from our uncomfortable conversation because Winona dragged Keisha into the library.

"Oh my God, Miranda! Sergeant O'Sullivan just told us. That guy that got shot in the alley was Joe Morrow!"

"Yes, I know. I still don't know who he is, though."

"Yes, you do." Keisha's voice boomed. "Remember, the guy who testified at Smith's church? The one with crabs who screwed a bunch of whores in one day?"

The party members' light chatter came to a screeching halt at Keisha's shocking proclamation. My friends and family looked as though an evil magician had frozen them in time.

I palmed my forehead as memories flooded in. "Wow, that's who he is."

When Keisha, Winona, and I had been searching for clues to who had murdered Suzy Smith, we had attended a church service and listened as Joe testified to Pastor Smith's rapt congregation. He provided details of his debased life of drinking, sleeping around, and consequently catching creepy crawlies in his briefs. The resolution of his disturbing tale was that he had kicked the devil from his life and found Jesus.

"Joe's funeral is at Konicki's, and Pastor Smith is

performing the service," Winona said.

"Fudge. We'll have to see Smith again."

Pastor Smith was number three on my enemy list, and we completely and thoroughly detested each other.

Winona's face lit up as she bounced on her toes. "Plus we get to work as elves. This is going to be so awesome!"

"Damn straight." Keisha cracked her knuckles." I'm going to kick some wimpy man-ass."

I wasn't as excited as my sleuthing assistants, and I seriously needed sleep.

I dug the heel of my hand into a newly forming headache. "Guys, no! It's a funeral!"

Chapter 10

I stood at the front of my classroom, pining for a magic genie to grant me three wishes. My first wish involved a two-foot-high thermos of hot coffee. It was only ten a.m., and I couldn't wait for bedtime.

Over the past week, my life had careened out of control. I had discovered two dead Santas, ignited the relationship with my childhood obsession, suffered a severe gunshot wound, spent three days in the hospital, and experienced emotional closure with my ex-boyfriend. If that wasn't enough, hunting season was afoot in Bellmount, the *No Vacancy* sign hung in front of the inn, and a dizzying energy had settled over the town.

The previous evening had done me in. I had stayed up late, eating sandwiches, chips, and potato salad. A sugar hangover from scarfing down two huge pieces of cake at the party and an even bigger one for breakfast left me queasy.

After the party, Sean cornered me and did his best to aid me in recalling my near death experience. It was pointless. Much to his disappointment, I repeated, "The guy who shot me looked like Santa" at least five times.

Since my dad snored, I didn't get much sleep. Think a howler monkey and a sperm whale singing a duet on a vibrating freight train. That is an evening in the turret with my dad.

For the first time in forever, I didn't feel unloved or lonely. My party with friends and family proved how fortunate I was. Unfortunately, I also felt fat, overstimulated, and exhausted. So, when Mason Bitz pushed his completed paper across my podium before class started, I may have worn a blank expression.

Mason smiled. "Dr. Albright, I finished two days early."

"Thanks," I said.

He stared into my eyes. Eventually, it dawned on me that he was waiting for positive reinforcement.

"Awesome, Mason. I'll correct it and have feedback to you in a few days."

"Thanks. I think I did a good job." He stuck his thumb in the air then strutted to the back of the classroom.

The little hand on the clock landed on the X, so I shook the fog from my brain. "Good morning, people. I hope everyone had a wonderful break."

There was a chorus of greetings. Then my students quieted, waiting for my first directive.

"Today we will discuss our final pivotal selection of the semester, a contemporary piece written by Toni Morrison—"

"Dr. Albright, before we start our lesson, could I tell the class what happened at the Stevens Speed-mart?" asked Mason.

Perhaps it was wise to address the situation. Then we could get back to class. I loved my job, but I knew I was off my game.

The sooner the workday was over, the sooner I could take a nap.

"Sure, Mason. Go ahead."

He sauntered to the front of the classroom and cleared his throat. "So, I was at work. You all know I work part-time at the Stevens Speed-mart on Elm. Right?"

"Of course we know, nimrod. You're always trying to pick up chicks by offering them a Slurpicy." John Gibbons lowered his voice a few octaves. "Wanna free slushy, babe?"

"Wanna sip on my cherry juice, sweetheart?" Dante Santiago called out while making kissing noises on his wrist.

Mason started to raise a middle finger, looked my way, and dropped his hand to his side. "I've never called it cherry juice, spazweed. So anyway, I was restocking the potato chips—"

John let out a dramatic yawn. "You're boring me, Bitz. Get to the good part."

Mason shot his buddy a good-humored warning glance. "So, I was stocking chips, and Dr. Albright walked in."

"Uh oh, Albright showed up? I predict a corpse somewhere in this story," said John.

I raised an eyebrow. "Keep in mind that I am responsible for your grade, John."

There were a few chuckles from the peanut gallery.

"So, Dr. Albright bought candy and hot chocolate and gave me an extension on my paper," Mason said.

Crap monsters! Why hadn't I warned Mason to keep the extension to himself? A can of worms was about to create a disgusting mess in the middle of my lecture.

"Hey! Can I have an extension on my paper, too?" John asked.

I ignored the request, and Mason said, "Then we heard three gunshots, and we ran outside. You won't believe what we saw."

"A dead Santa," called out Missy Helmuth from the front row.

"Yeah. He was lying in front of Dr. Albright's old car. How'd you know?" Mason asked.

"Everyone knows about the dead Saint Nick. It was in the paper, wartbreath," John said.

"Oh, yeah," Mason said. "Anyway, we called the park ranger."

"Why did you call the park ranger?" Missy asked.

Mason shrugged. "I guess Dr. Albright's dating him."

"Oh, no. What happened to the gorgeous doctor?" Shelly Byers asked.

"What happened to the bartender you shot in the ass?" asked John.

"Good grief. Tom Little, the park ranger, has been one of my best friends since I was a child. He has some law enforcement training."

The explanation seemed to placate my class's curiosity.

"So, anyway, after the park ranger showed up, that asshole sheriff that is always breaking up our parties showed up. Then the state police homicide squad showed up. We had to wait forever for the coroner to arrive. I had to close the Stevens Speed-mart until they all left. It was pretty cool." Seeming satisfied, Mason smiled. "Any questions?"

"Dr. Albright, I heard you were dressed like an elf and were delivering presents to an orphanage, and someone shot you in an alley on Black Friday. Is that true?" Missy asked.

Since thirty-three percent of the statement was factual, it felt like someone had just punched me in the chest. How could they know? Pat had kept my name from the morning edition, and Keisha and Lincoln wouldn't have told my students.

"Missy, where did you hear that I got shot?" I asked.

"I think my dorm RA?"

"I heard it, too," said Dante. "But I heard you had on that polka dot bikini, and a guy in a ghost outfit shot you."

I vehemently shook my head. "That's insane." The ghost had accidentally shot himself a few weeks prior.

"Well, obviously, it's all a bunch of gossip because you're standing here in front of us," Missy said.

"But the Stevens Speed-mart part is true. I was there," Mason assured everyone. "And it is extra crazy because someone robbed the store in early September. I didn't work there then, but the owner told me all about it."

"You're kidding," I said.

"Armed robbery," Mason said.

"What did they steal?" I asked.

"Everything in the cash register and a bag of chips," he said.

"Wow," I murmured.

"They caught the kid who did it," Mason said. "They didn't get it on camera, but a friend turned him in. Probably just a weird coincidence that there were two crimes at the same place."

Although I knew about the broken camera, I wanted details. "Why isn't it on camera?"

"The camera broke a couple of months ago, and the guy who's supposed to fix it didn't show."

"Do you know who was supposed to fix it?" I asked.

"No idea," Mason said.

Missy raised her hand and waited for me to call on her. "Dr. Albright, my friend Trixie says that her friend Amy saw you at the pub on a date with a super handsome international spy."

Four words ran through my mind. Homicide detective. So tired!

"Dr. Albright, you need to do something about always being the center of gossip," John said.

I cleared my throat. "Let's get back to class. I hope everyone was able to pick up their copy of *Song of Solomon* at the bookstore."

"Dr. Albright, can we talk about these extensions you're giving out?" John asked.

"That is some crazy rumor. Craziest one yet! There are no extensions in this class." I sent Mason a hairy eyeball.

John Gibbons frowned. "Fucking fudge!"

"Language, mister," I reminded him. "Now, back to our selection by the amazing Ms. Morrison."

****

I metaphorically rubbed my hands on my make-believe genie lamp and tried for wish number two—an afternoon nap. I dragged my carcass down the stairs of Sutton Hall and across the walkway that led to the parking lot. Set against the grayish-blue mountains, two figures perched against my poop-brown monstrosity.

As I got closer, I saw that one was Sean. He was leaning against my car, writing notes on his tablet. The collar of a white fisherman knit sweater peeked out from under his brown bomber jacket. He wore a red, brown, and gray tweed Irish flat cap. A matching scarf hung around his neck. Greg Grainey was sitting on the hood of my car. He wore a similar get-up in shades of blue and gray. Sean looked handsome. Greg was playing some sort of imbecilic dress-up game and looked like an arrogant jerk.

"Hey, Red," Sean said as I approached my car.

"Hi, Crimson," Greg said.

I ignored Greg. "Sean, what are you doing here?"

"I wanted to catch you right away. I have to talk to George Stiles' widow, and I could use a compassionate assistant, so I thought I'd take you with me."

"Where's your partner?" I asked.

"Miller's hardly compassionate. And, he's working on another case this afternoon."

For no reason whatsoever, Greg grabbed Sean's hat and chucked it across the parking lot. It looked like it might fall to the ground but caught in the breeze and traveled another foot. Sean watched it land before retrieving it.

I leaned close to Greg. "Aren't you supposed to be wearing a long flowy gown and chains around your neck?"

"Bite me, Crimson." He pointed at Sean. *"I don't trust him. Why would a detective take a college professor with him?"* He snapped his fingers beside my forehead. *"Oh, I know. So he can grab her rack and get her in the sack."*

"If you aren't going to behave, then leave," I whispered.

"What did you say?" Sean asked, coming alongside

111

me.

"Sometimes I talk to my car. I tell him to behave and stop eating so much gas."

Sean chuckled. "V8?"

"Yes."

"Can I drive 'er?" he asked.

"Sure." I scowled at Greg then tossed Sean my keys. "But she is a he. And his name is The Tank."

****

George Stiles' wife was a kind grandmotherly woman with grey pin curls. She lived in a cozy 1950's yellow Cape Cod that sat inside a white picket fence. Both of her daughters sat on the oversized living room furniture, one cradled an infant on her lap. Two little boys played with matchbox cars in the attached dining room.

Sean wore a soft expression as he sat beside the widow. "I know you have answered all of my questions before, Joyce. But sometimes, I hear something a second time that helps. Plus, today, I have Dr. Albright with me. She's a whiz at picking up clues."

Not to play the semantic game, but I was a "whiz" at reading minds, not picking up clues. Furthermore, I didn't plan to intrude on a grieving widow and her heartbroken daughters. Instead, I listened intently as George Stiles' family reminisced.

George had been a loving family man. His grandchildren were adorable; his daughters were pretty, and Joyce was a sweetheart. George had retired from Kutz Brothers, where he sold paper supplies to schools for forty years. For ten of those, he held the coveted salesman of the year award. The softball team he coached adored him, and he had played Santa at

Lightsingers since 1959.

I requested a photo of George in his Santa suit, and his wife obliged.

"Could I keep it for a few days?" I asked.

"Of course, dear," Joyce Stiles said. "And please give my best to your aunt. The flowers she sent were lovely."

****

After leaving the Stiles home, I dropped Sean off at his car. Unfortunately, my next task scared me to death. I drove to the center of town and parked The Tank in the lot where I had been shot. I exited my car and stood where I had passed out. Closing my eyes, I searched for the psychic footprint.

It took less than ten seconds for the nightmarish images to take hold. There were so many that they swirled around, slapping at me like sharp electric punches. Heat from inside my body seared my skin. Joe saw his killer, felt excruciating pain, then reached for me. I saw the bloody body and Santa holding a gun. Stabbing pain pierced my chest. Brad Gordon unbuttoned my coat and blouse and panicked. Images from the three separate imprints filled me, and my aching head forced me to flee the scene.

I charged toward The Tank and leaped inside. I drove from the spot, pulled to the side of the road, and breathed. I hadn't learned anything from my nightmarish adventure other than Joe had definitely said, "Help the girls." The Santa disguise concealed the killer's identity, and both Joe and I were too far away to distinguish features.

Once home, I sat in my turret and ran my fingers over George's photo. I wasn't able to divine information from images, but it helped me connect with victims. "I'm sorry, George."

A knock startled me. I set the photo on my dresser and opened the door. Sean's aftershave filled the landing.

"Miller's been in touch. I have to head to the state college to help him with that new case."

"Related to the Santa murders?" I asked.

"Doesn't look like it."

"When will you be back in Bellmount?"

"Not sure. I'm going to head home for a day or two, so probably Thursday."

"After talking to his family, I'm positive George Stiles was accidentally murdered. I can't figure out why anyone would want to hurt him," I said.

"It's my theory." Sean stepped into my room. "I think it was a case of mistaken identity, and the intended target was Morrow."

"I was talking to Mason Bitz, my student who works at the Stevens Speed-mart, and he told me someone robbed the convenience store a few months ago."

"Yeah," Sean said. "We're aware. Shultz never mentioned it, and there was no record at the police station, but an eighteen-year-old went to jail for it."

"No record? How does that happen?"

Sean grunted. "You've met Shultz."

"Jerk," I muttered. "But if a kid went to jail, then there is a court record somewhere? Right?"

Sean tapped his finger to his nose. "Bingo!"

"Who is in charge of fixing the camera?"

"Security company out of Pittsburgh." He took another step into my room.

I backed up half a step. "Why haven't they fixed it?"

"I called and talked to the receptionist. She says they were supposed to, and Stevens called and canceled. Stevens says he never canceled. They just didn't show up."

I rubbed my temple. Maybe after some sleep, I could think clearly. I sensed the detective wanted to talk, but my synapses weren't firing. If I took a short nap, I could get ready for dinner at the pub, and maybe when I next saw him, I could form coherent thoughts.

"I'm sorry. I'm so tired. This isn't like me." I clued him that it was time to leave by staring at the landing.

His hand landed on my shoulder. "Hey, Red. Are you and the bartender an item?"

Not knowing how to respond to the question, I bit my lip and looked at the ground. When the answer hit me, I met his gaze. "I think we will be an item after tonight."

Sean's blue eyes focused on mine, and he rolled a ringlet between his thumb and index finger. "Damn. That's too bad. That was one hell of a kiss you gave me."

My face caught fire, and heat spread over my entire body. "We were undercover, Sean."

"Yeah. You're the cutest damn partner I've ever had. Best kisser, too."

I fought an urge to run my finger over the scar that cut through his eyebrow.

"Good night, Sean. See you Thursday." I nudged him into the hall, closed my door, and leaned against it. I breathed in his lingering masculine scent.

What the heck was up with men the second they

stepped into Bellmount? Had they all lost their minds? Or had the curse that caused me to stumble over corpses increased in power to the point desirable men thought they liked me? Although the latter part wasn't a hideous burden on me, it seemed unfair to the poor unsuspecting men.

I rubbed my sleepy eyes and wondered if Lincoln knew how to get rid of curses. Then I crawled under my covers for a nap.

Unfortunately, ten minutes after my head hit the pillow, my alarm beeped.

****

Although my first two wishes hadn't panned out, I remained hopeful that wish number three would come to fruition. It was the most important, after all. I wanted a kiss from Weston Westinghouse the Third more than I wanted to breathe.

After squeezing into my favorite jeans, I considered passing on Aunt Edith's decadent desserts for a week or two. I distracted myself from that hideous prospect by slipping into my emerald mohair sweater with its swooping cowl neck. Keisha once told me that the color matched my eyes and complimented my hair. Succumbing to vanity, I put on my brown high heels. They were absurd shoes to wear in Western Pennsylvania in December, but they looked nice with my outfit, and made me taller. I'd lean on my dad for our downhill trek. I added a pair of matching green gloves. I no longer required them to muffle my psychic abilities; they kept my hands warm.

My dad and I sat at a table in the back corner of the pub. Since I usually hung out at the end of the bar, my new seat gave me a different perspective.

Unfortunately, it also meant I was further from West. I chose a chair facing him so that I could watch as he waited on customers. Goosebumps traveled over my body every time he sent a smile my way. Winona served the mozzarella sticks; Pop and Uncle Will brought us cheeseburgers and fries, and the Westinghouse family took turns keeping my dad's beer mug full as they chatted with us. Although I hadn't ordered it, West brought me a post-dinner cup of coffee and we engaged in small talk.

After a few minutes, West excused himself and called, "Winona, keep an eye on the bar. I need to put salt down in the parking lot." He shook hands with my dad. "It was good to see you again, Mr. Albright." He smiled at me. "Be careful in those heels, Shortcake. The melt is refreezing." After tossing wink in my direction, he headed outside.

I waited for a few minutes before excusing myself to the restroom. I navigated the hallway that ran from the main room to the back of the building.

Bypassing the bathrooms, the poolroom, and the storeroom, I headed out the back door. I crept to the side of the building, past the stairs that led to West's apartment, and peeked around the corner to the front parking lot.

West whistled as he sprinkled salt on the concrete. He hadn't bothered to don a coat over his flimsy t-shirt.

"Psst," I called.

He looked up from his task and grinned.

I stood on one heel while the other pressed into the brick wall. I wrapped my arms around my chest to keep warm and waited in the unlit eaves for him to finish his chore.

A few minutes later, he rounded the corner. "Shortcake," he said in his sexy drawl.

"I miss you, West."

"You look sexy. I love the shoes, but you'll break your neck in this weather."

"I'll be careful."

"Mmm." With one hand on either side of me, he caged me against the wall.

My insides got gooey.

"West, let's tell everyone about us. I don't want our relationship to be a secret anymore."

He nuzzled my neck. "Kiss me, and we'll discuss it."

Greg appeared over West's shoulder. West's lips brushed mine. Greg grabbed the keys that hung from West's back pocket and chucked them across the parking lot. They clanged on the pavement, and West stepped back.

"What was that?"

"Umm, I think you dropped your keys."

West's expression contorted in confusion. Understandably so, since his keys were four feet from where we were standing. I clicked across the parking lot to pick them up. As I passed Greg, I growled. His life, or lack of life, was not my fault, and I was tired of the guilt trip. Enough was enough! He needed a new human to haunt.

I was mid world's most evil eye when my foot slid out from under me. I tried to balance, but it was no use. I went down hard. A sharp pain shot through my buttocks. There was a pop, then my head hit the ground, bounced up, and slammed into the concrete again. Everything traveled far away and faded out.

West's face slowly reformed. His voice was soft at first but got louder as he repeated, "Shortcake, talk to me."

I whimpered. "West, my back and leg hurt."

"Christ. You got knocked out. Can you move your legs?"

I bent both of my knees and wriggled my toes. "Yes, I think so. Are they moving?"

West studied my feet. "Yeah."

"My head hurts, too."

He gently stroked my cheek. "Hey, beautiful, that thing about telling people about us. I hope you meant it because everyone is going to want to know what you were doing with me in the parking lot."

"I meant it." With all my heart.

"Good." He gently lifted my head off the ground and helped me to sit up. "Can you walk?"

"I don't know." I pressed my weight into my heels. A sharp pain shot from my foot up the back of my leg, landing in my hip. "I think something's wrong."

West bent low and slid one arm around my waist and the other under my thighs. I wrapped my arms around his neck. Even though I had been overeating of late, he lifted me like I weighed nothing. He carried me into the pub and sat me on a chair close to the door. My father, Polly, Winona, and Will all gathered around.

"Miranda," Winona asked. "What happened?"

Besides being carried like some helpless damsel in a British PBS drama, muddy slush covered my backside.

Pop came running from the kitchen. "Kiddo, you okay?"

Every inch of my body ached, and my ego had

taken one heck of a beating.

"I slipped on the ice."

"What the hell, West?" Pop said. "I told you thirty minutes ago to spread the salt."

"I did. I finished the order I was working on, made a pot of coffee, said hi to Mr. Albright, and then took care of it."

"It wasn't West's fault." It was the ghost's fault. "I was the dummy who wore heels."

"Winona could have made the coffee, and obviously, you missed a spot." Pop walloped West on the back of the head.

I cringed. West was being scolded because he had taken care of me, and I was the one who sidetracked him from the salt sprinkling.

"Can you walk?" my dad asked.

I attempted to put weight on my foot and winced. "I'm dizzy, and my leg and back hurt." I gingerly lowered my body back into the chair.

"Concussion?" Dad asked.

"Oh, no. Another concussion," Polly said.

A few weeks prior, I had suffered a severe concussion when two goons had attacked me in an attempt to scare me into moving back to Harrisburg.

"Miranda, what were you doing in the parking lot?" Winona asked.

"I wanted to see West."

Uncle Will backhanded West's shoulder.

"Ouch," West said.

"It wasn't his fault," I reiterated.

The pub door flew open, and Doctor Brad barged in carrying his medical bag. Greg followed at his heels.

"Please give me some room," Brad said to the

concerned crowd.

"I went for help," Greg told me.

I hope he didn't think that made his shenanigans okay. I would never forgive the dead man for this one.

The crowd backed up just enough to let Brad commence his poking and prodding.

After a thorough once over, Brad broke the news. "William, I'm going to take her to the hospital for an MRI. She may have herniated a disk. I also want the neurologist to check her out since this might be her second concussion in the past month. Do you want to ride with us?"

"Yes." My dad gathered our belongings. "Weston, could you let Edith know we're headed to the hospital?"

"Okay," West said.

"No need. We can call from my cellular phone," Brad said.

The doctor slid my arm around his shoulder and lifted me. I gestured to West, indicating I wanted him to help. Brad and West snipped at each other as they carried me to the car.

"Westinghouse, what was she doing in an icy parking lot?"

"Brad, it wasn't West's fault," I said.

"Whenever you get hurt, Westinghouse is lurking around somewhere, not paying attention and being irresponsible," Brad said.

West halted mid-step. "What the hell, Doc?"

"Brad, that isn't true," I said.

The men grumbled as they assisted me into the back seat.

I rested my head on my dad's shoulder and joined

in on the pout-fest. I had an entire twenty-five-mile drive to the hospital to immerse myself in misery and pity and obsess over Brad and West's out-of-character fight. Then it hit me.

"Stupid ghost," I muttered.

"What?" Dad asked.

"Nothing," I said.

I was zero for three. Not one of my wishes had come true. No thermos of coffee. No afternoon nap. No kisses from West. The men in Bellmount were definitely being affected by my stupid curse.

My genie was fired, and so was my troublemaking manipulative ghost. Never again would Greg Grainey throw West Westinghouse under the bus or convince the saintly Brad Gordon to behave like a jerk!

Maybe Greg was also responsible for Sean's hormonal-ness. On second thought, the Curse of the Redhead was probably the cause of all of their strange behaviors.

Whatever the catalyst, it didn't matter, because my ghost was dead to me!

Chapter 11

After only four days under Doctor Brad's attentive care, my back miraculously healed, the pain running the length of my leg disappeared, and my headaches ceased. By Saturday morning, other than feeling a little run down, I was as good as new.

Brad, on the other hand, was exhausted. I have no idea how he could stand to be near me. I had become one injury-prone energy-sucking woman. Although I was akin to a parasite, Brad remained compassionate. He spent any time he wasn't with his other patients administering his energy medicine to me. That afternoon, I was ready to tackle a costume project.

Aunt Edith sewed pockets resembling old-fashioned ribbon candy onto a green tunic. I created white fur cuffs for my wrists and neck. My aunt sewed a jingle bell at the tip of each of my curly-toed felt shoes, and one on the point of my hat. I added red tights and smiled at the adorable elf in the mirror. Spot chased my jingle feet as I shuffled around my room. And since I had booted Greg Grainey from my life, by insisting that he leave me alone, I didn't have to listen to his perverted commentary on my cute costume.

I drove The Tank down the hill to pick up Winona. After fifteen minutes of taping on my steering wheel, I went in search of my friend. Not wanting to get my homemade shoes muddy, I avoided the wet patches on the pavement and tip-toed into the pub.

West was behind the bar. He took in my faux fur, velveteen, and felt costume and lit up.

I jangled toward him.

"Hiya, Doctor Shortcake. Where are the crutches?"

"I don't need them anymore. I healed quickly," I said.

His eyes narrowed. "Wow. That was fast."

I shrugged. "I guess the injury seemed worse than it was."

West leaned across the bar and tapped the jingle bell at the tip of my hat. It tinkled, and he grinned.

"You look like a candy cane that needs to be licked. Why don't you crawl your adorable elf-self under my covers tonight, and I'll make you breakfast in the morning." He licked his lips.

"Yum! I'm feeling chocolate chip pancakes with lots of whipped cream."

"Mmm. Whipped cream. Are you making a pass at me, Jingles?"

A hot poker stabbed me in the girl parts as his meaning took hold, and the heat from my blush scorched my cheeks. He chuckled.

I pushed aside my embarrassment to shamelessly flirt. "Lots of whipped cream?"

"Yeah," he muttered.

My desire to diet had lasted less than four days. "And lots of chocolate chips."

"You got it. It's a date," he said.

"Where's Winona? We're late for work."

"I have no idea." West inclined his chin toward the backrooms. "Last time I saw her, she was getting into her costume."

I headed back the hallway in search of a tall elf. Every time my feet slapped the floor, I rang like a mini bell.

An elf-eared Winona sat on a box in the storeroom. She wore a long red t-shirt, with green pants shoved into red and white striped socks. An oversized Santa hat sat cockeyed on her head, giving her a deranged appearance.

I stopped short. "Winona, have you been crying?"

She dabbed at her eyes with a tissue. "I had an eyelash incident."

A long sparkly eyelash dangled from her eyebrow, and mascara ran down her cheeks.

I winced. "What happened?"

She held up false eyelash packaging. "Since Keisha is going to dress sexy, and you always look beautiful, I tried to make myself fancy. I don't know why I bothered." Torrential tears poured like a waterfall over a mountain of red velvet.

"Oh, Winona." I hugged her tight.

She clung to me for a minute before backing away. I plucked the eyelash from her brow and knelt in front of her.

She sniffled. "I accidentally glued my eye shut."

"It's open now." I flashed her a smile. "Although, unless you were going for the Picasso look, you got it wrong because the lashes weren't in the correct place."

I rooted through the supplies in her makeup bag. Once I found the cold cream, I dipped a cotton swab into the container and wiped the black streaks under her eyes. "You want to tell me what's really going on? I know my happy Winona Westinghouse would never cry over a little eyelash glue."

"It's a man," she said.

"A man?" I asked. "Who?"

"You're going to laugh."

I patted her hand. "Never. I might laugh at your eyelashes on your eyebrows, but I won't laugh about your hurting heart. Tell me."

"Tom Little."

"Ah." I nodded.

"I asked him to be my date for the holiday party we're having here. He hasn't answered me yet. I think there's someone else he wants to ask."

Unfortunately, I had a feeling I might be that "someone else." Still, I asked, "What makes you say that?"

She gurgled and choked out, "I don't know."

"Winona, no crying. I almost have your makeup fixed."

She swallowed. "Probably Doctor Handsome and Detective Hunky are going to fight over you. You'll have your choice of men, and I bet the manager at Lightsingers asks Keisha out, and I won't have a date."

I affixed Winona's eyelash. "There. Beautiful. Now, don't cry, or it will look like you have spiders drowning in your lap."

I handed Winona her make-up mirror.

She turned her head from side to side, studying her new look. Although her face remained puffy, she had the same spectacular eyes as her sexy cousin.

"Winona, I'm not dating Brad or Sean. In fact—" I exhaled. "I'm crazy about West."

Winona gawked like her lashes were crawling out of my ears. "West?"

I nodded.

She shook her head back and forth, her big ears threatening to slap her cheeks. "But he's all wrong for you."

Her comment stung more than any of the warnings I had received from Aunt Edith, Liam, Tommy, or Greg. "Why do you think that?"

"Miranda, I love West. He's like my baby brother, and you're like my little sister, but West sleeps around. He won't be a good boyfriend to you. I'm sorry." She patted my shoulder. "He even slept with some bimbo when he had the flu. He was covered in hickeys the day we came to see you at the hospital. He wore a sweater to cover them up. He had the stomach flu, and he was still messing around."

"*Pfft.*" I forced my face into a grimace. If I told Winona I was the "bimbo," West didn't have the flu, and that he had spent the night in the hospital worrying about me, I would also need to confess that he had lied to her. "We better go. We're running late."

"Wait a minute. Is that why you were in the parking lot with him the night you fell? Because you like him?"

"Yes. And West likes me, too."

Winona twisted her lips in skepticism However, her mood lifted as she packed up her cosmetics. "I think we should ask if anyone knew George and if he had any enemies. I think we should ask if he knew Joe Morrow. And, I think we should try to find connections between the two of them."

Although I was pretty sure George was not the intended target, I agreed, and we headed to the main room.

West watched as Winona and I walked to the exit.

"See ya later, wing nut," he called to Winona and her silly ears.

When I reached the door, I stopped, turned around, walked to the bar, grabbed West Westinghouse's face between my hands, and marked my territory by planting the world's biggest kiss on his lips. Winona, Polly, and Will all gawked in wide-eyed wonder.

Aunt Polly bopped West on the side of his head.

"Ouch." West rubbed at a tiny red splotch. Then he winked. "See ya later, Jingles."

****

By the time Winona and I arrived at Lightsingers, Keisha and Lincoln were already hard at work. The department store set designers had earned their pay. A gold Welcome to the North Pole sign hung on a green pole. In the center of the display, an oversized throne swallowed Lincoln, and the happy child perched on his lap. A twenty-foot Christmas tree towered right next to the chair. Thousands of colored lights twinkled, and wrapped boxes, some waist-high, sat every which way.

Keisha stood a couple of feet back, handling the line of children waiting their turn. Her shapely legs stretched from the bottom of her thigh-length red dress to her knee-high boots. Silver ribbons adorned her hair, and her lipstick was the same color as her soft dress. Unlike Lincoln, she wasn't smiling.

Timberlane eyed her lovely stilts as he talked at her. His gaze followed her fluttering hand as she waved to us.

He frowned and stomped our way. "You're late. I was just asking the sexy elf where you two were."

"I'm not sure her legs had the answer," I said.

He perused the room, his gaze settling on Keisha—

perhaps to double-check what answer her legs might hold?

"I had an eyelash incident," Winona confessed.

He grumbled something under his breath about "pain in the ass amateurs" and assigned me to first-floor candy duty.

Winona headed to the fourth-floor coloring page activity.

I grabbed a fistful of candy canes and arranged them so they peeked out of my pockets. Then I picked up a sack of treats and headed down the stairs to my post.

An elf with one red leg and one green leg worked at the bottom of the first-floor stairwell. She had the same pointy ears as Winona, although hers looked like they were growing out of her head.

I smiled. "Hi. I'm Miranda."

Her lips, nose, and forehead drew together and formed a huffy circle in the middle of her face. "What kind of name is Miranda? Sounds like a human name."

I was taken aback by her abrupt manner but remained cordial. "What do you think I should call myself?"

"I could care less. You're a fraud."

I contemplated her accusation. "I thought it would be nice to volunteer this season."

"Taking jobs from us real elves is a rotten thing to do." A blob of spittle flew from her mouth, barely missing my cheek. "I'm working here. Find your own corner. I don't need your kind giving me a bad name."

"Aren't elves supposed to be friendly?"

"Yes," she snapped. With an affable smile, she handed a boy a candy cane. "Merry Christmas. Have you been to see Santa yet?"

He took the treat and pulled on his haggard mother. "Mommy, I wanna see Santa."

"In a few more minutes, pooh bear," his mother said.

The edges of Angry Elf's lips turned up to form a quirky smile.

Hoping an explanation would smooth my path I said, "Mr. Timberlane assigned me here. I'm supposed to help you."

"Whatever." She rolled her eyes.

A little girl approached, and I handed her a candy cane. Her blue eyes lit up, and she smiled. "Thank you. You're pretty."

"Thank you, honey. Don't forget to see Santa." My voice was as sugary as the sweets I offered.

As the girl skipped away, I studied my peculiar partner's squished nose and heavy eyebrows, then tried again to be amicable. "What's your name?"

She refused to look at me. "Peppermint."

"I'll be Jingles. I'm from Harrisburg. Where are you from?"

A little boy holding his father's hand approached. The man eyed the candy in my pocket. Daddy looked like he might have a sweet tooth so I handed both father and son a candy cane.

Once the family rounded the corner, Peppermint reprimanded me. "The candy is for the children."

I captured my response in my puffed-up cheeks.

"Harrisburg?" She shook her head, and her green hat wobbled. "Knew you were a fraud. I'm from the North Pole."

I put a hand on my hip and glowered. "You know

you aren't an elf, don't you?"

Her eyes went wide. She covered her open mouth with the palm of her hand and cried out, "Infidel!" Then she leaned over and motioned for two boys that were watching to come close. She held up her hand and pretended to whisper behind it as she loudly announced, "Be careful. There are fake Santas and elves all around us."

"I saw a fake Santa once," one of the boys said. "He had his stick out and was peeing in front of the pet store. My mom says he was a fake. My dad said he was drunk."

I have no idea why I covered my mouth with both hands. Perhaps I was afraid my clenched lips were no longer sufficient to stop the commentary threatening to flow.

"Told you. Imposters everywhere," Peppermint said. "If you guys see any fakes in the store, besides her—" the insane woman pointed at me. "I already know she is a fake. Let me know because I need to alert Santa. He will make sure you get extra presents."

"Yay!" one boy cried out.

"Cool," the other boy said.

The boys skipped off to begin their zealous witch hunt. They oozed excitement over reaping the rewards each time they found a North Pole imposter.

"What's your problem?" I asked the sour Peppermint.

"First, they send a fake Santa who doesn't like kids. He shows up one time and quits. Then they hire a Santa who thinks it's more important to work at the Community Center than be here. Then they hire your pathetic-ness." She set her pointed shoe beside my adorable felt foot. Like one of my ringlets, her toe spiraled in on itself. "Pathetic," she sputtered as the lunatic compared our feet.

"A Santa who only worked one time?" I asked. "What day was that?"

"The day after I arrived from the North Pole."

"When did you arrive?"

She thought this over. "I arrived thirty-six days before the big night."

"The big night? You mean Christmas Eve?" I handed candy canes to a set of twins in red dresses.

"Of course. What kind of ninny are you?"

"What day did Santa leave early?" I asked

"Thirty-five days from the big night."

I performed the mental math. "So he left three days before Turkey Day." I pulled my shoulders back, proud that in my brief encounter with the loon, I had developed the hang of elf-speak.

Holding up fingers, she counted to three. "Yes."

"Peppermint, you are correct. I'll let the big guy know that you did a great job. I'll tell you a secret, but you can't tell anyone." I crooked my finger, motioning for her to come closer.

The crazy nut leaned in. Her eyes were as wide as her toes were curly. "I won't tell."

"I'm not an elf. I'm a detective. Santa hired me to be part of his Sleuthing Squad. We are the North Pole's equivalent of the FBI."

"I knew it!" She hopped and jangled.

"Tell me everything you can remember about the fake Santa who only showed up once, the Santa who left early to work at the Community Center, and what Santa did thirty-five days before the big night."

Peppermint may have been borderline psychotic, but she had a memory like a steel trap.

****

Every hour the elves rotated posts. At seven, I reported to fourth-floor craft duty. My partner was a normal elf. Ned was his human name and elf name, and he hailed from Bellmount, not the North Pole. We engaged in small talk as we babysat a table of children coloring Santa's sleigh pictures. During his non-elf hours, Ned worked as a cashier at the local hardware store. He was a nice guy, but void of Santa murder gossip. Although fourth-floor duty didn't provide a single clue, it was enjoyable.

At seven fifty-five, I received my order to report to Santa's workshop. During the five-minute transition, I briefly communicated with my crew.

Lincoln explained that little kids loved to pull Santa's hair. Keisha declared that dressing as a sexy elf wasn't her smartest move. Winona insisted that the infamous practical jokester, Dinky, was a nice guy.

My job for the last shift of the evening was to walk the kids to the throne.

I escorted a little girl with bouncing curls to Lincoln. "How's it going?"

"Ho, ho, ho. Santa thinks Wipey Diapeys need reinforcing," declared Santa Harrison.

I grimaced at the green towel protecting Lincoln's lap. "Eww." I counted my blessings that elves didn't have to put toddlers on their laps.

"Ho. Ho. Ho. What's your name?" Lincoln asked the cutie-pie.

"Allie."

"Were you a good girl this year?"

"Yes, Santa," Allie said.

"What would you like for Christmas?"

Allie scraped her fingers through Lincoln's authentic beard. "A pink pony and a kitten."

I left Allie with Santa since it was Keisha's job to escort her back to her parents. I headed to my line, where the Brat Brothers from the witch hunt were sucker punching each other. In my experience, absent parents signified horrid offspring. And, it seemed the two beasts had been orphaned for the evening.

"Santa's watching. You better be good," I told the boys.

"We don't have to listen to you. You're that fake elf," said the bigger of the two.

"I'm Detective Jingles. I'm part of Santa's detective squad."

"You're a big fake liar," said Big Brat. "There's no such thing."

"Yeah," said Little Brat, "You're a big fat liar!"

I cringed at the candy cane gunk covering the younger boy's hands and face. "If you don't believe me, ask the big guy." I thumbed toward Lincoln.

"I'm telling Santa on you," said Little Brat as he used his thumb and index finger to shoot a fake gun at me.

I bent forward and stuck my chin a few inches from his sticky nose. I didn't say a word; I simply stared. If a department store elf had been inches from my face when I was eight years old, it would have intimidated the bejesus out of me. Not Little Brat. He stuck his tongue out, gave me a candy cane-infused raspberry, and then continued to shoot me with his fake gun.

I'd like to say I was bold enough to grab the heathens by their ears and yank them to Santa. Instead, I asked, "Do you two have an uncle named Shultz?"

"No. You're stupid," Little Brat said.

"Lady, you're a big fat liar," Big Brat said.

"Humph," I said. "That's odd. Thought you were related because there's an uncanny resemblance."

Sandwiched between the little monsters, I walked them to the throne. They squabbled and slapped each other, occasionally nailing me in the process. We waited as Lincoln fashioned a fresh pee towel across his lap. Meanwhile, Big Brat punched Little Brat in the shoulder while Little Brat bawled his eyes out.

The disgruntled store manager clapped. "Boys!"

Ignoring Timberlane, Big Brat wound up and punched Little Brat in the shoulder—again.

Timberlane glared at me. "Part of your job is dealing with the kids. Get them under control."

The red-faced Little Brat screamed at the top of his lungs. Tears flowed down his round cheeks as he thrashed his hands hysterically. He backed up, bent low, growled, and ran headfirst into Big Brat.

I tried to step in between the boys and absorbed a hit that threw me backward, setting a chain reaction into place. I temporarily balanced, but a millisecond later, I tripped over a box. I righted myself, but my jingle toe caught, and I tumbled to the side, landing on my hip.

I got back onto my feet to find that Big Brat meant to head butt his little brother, or maybe Little Brat meant to head butt his big brother. Or, perhaps they both meant to head butt me because two angry children body slammed me.

Timberlane grabbed for me, but the velocity from

the roly poly children was too much, and I knocked Timberlane over. A crash so deafening it sounded like a bomb exploded in the middle of the store, echoed and echoed and echoed.

I lay flat-backed on top of a "fuck" spewing Timberlane. To his credit, he used the F-bomb as every part of speech. A twenty-foot Christmas tree lay under us. Broken bulbs and smashed ornaments littered the area. Dozens of shoppers and petrified employees came running to witness the North Pole war zone. Holiday characters with too-large eyes, long chins, and distorted grimaces stared down at me nightmarishly.

After a moment of chaos, followed by one of absolute silence, Keisha's "Holy fuck, Miranda" rang out. I'm unsure if the ensuing choir of gasps was directed at the tree catastrophe or the foul-mouthed elf.

"Are you okay?" Lincoln asked.

"Ouch." I moaned.

"I knew she was an infidel!" Peppermint hollered.

"Fake. Fake!" The Brat Brothers called out as they hopped about shooting me with their fake guns. Their bitty brains failed to appreciate the irony.

"You're fucking fired!" Timberlane groaned from beneath me.

I rolled off my ex-boss and sat up. Brushing a sliver of broken ornament from my cheek, I used the sleeve of my tunic to wipe away blood. I tried to untangle blue spruce from my ringlets but gave up, placing my elf hat on the top of my branch-head. Exasperated, I considered the possibility that I had shards of glass buried in my nether regions.

I sputtered an uncouth, "Friggin' fudge," as Santa pulled me to my feet.

It took the big guy himself—and a pair of horrified elves— to carry me to The Tank.

Chapter 12

Lincoln and Winona lowered me onto the settee in the library and covered me with a blanket. I lay on my belly, lamenting my situation. I had bonked my head on something—perhaps Timberlane's chin. I had bruised my hip the first time I fell, and bloody scratches covered my body. Some of my wounds stemmed from tree branches. Others came from the sharp corners of wrapped boxes. Timberlane's fingernails had marked up my forearms. Shards from the ornaments had done quite a bit of damage to my face and backside.

"You're Miranda Albright. Even glass in your ass can't keep you down," Keisha declared.

I didn't want to prove her wrong, so despite the pain, I discussed murder theories. "I was assigned to work with this whack-a-doodle named Peppermint, who thinks she is a real elf."

Winona knelt on the floor beside me and picked greenery from my locks. "You know there are real elves."

"*Pfft.*" Keisha stretched out in the wingback. "They hang out with the Tooth Fairy and the Easter Bunny."

Winona frowned. "Keisha, everyone knows the Easter Bunny and Tooth Fairy aren't real."

"Winona, elves are made up too," said the psychic with a ghost. I rubbed my forehead. "Anyway, the nutty elf told me that a fake Santa showed up once and never came back. She said that she was the only one paying attention and nobody else even noticed him. According to Peppermint, the guy said his name was Kris Krimple."

Lincoln arranged an oak chair so that he sat in front of me. "You think someone also murdered this Kris Krimple?"

"Perhaps, but I bet he is our murderer. Also, Stiles was supposed to be working at Lightsingers that night but left early to volunteer at a party for underprivileged children at the Community Center."

"That is where Morrow normally volunteered," said Keisha.

"Exactly, so what if Stiles was a case of mistaken identity and the murderer meant to kill Morrow? That would mean that for some reason, Morrow was somewhere else that night. Stiles was an upstanding man. I can't imagine who would want to hurt him. So, it would make sense that his death was an accident. Sean thinks the same thing," I said.

Keisha furrowed her brow. "We need to figure out where Morrow was. Maybe he was playing Santa somewhere else."

"Maybe. It seems that wherever he ended up had to be a bigger deal than the party for needy children. What would take precedence over that?" I asked.

"If he were still on the straight and narrow, it would have to be something more pressing than poor children. Maybe sick children?" Lincoln said.

I rested my chin on my hands. "Maybe."

With the removal of a floppy red hat, Lincoln morphed from jolly old Saint Nick into an experienced psychologist. "A lot of times, people on the road to recovery slide into their old ways. It could have been any one of his vices distracting him."

"Like alcohol, whores, or gambling," Keisha said.

"He hasn't been at the pub at all," Winona said. "The rumor is he's sober."

I considered the facts and our theories as I moved ideas around every which way, trying to connect the dots. Coming up blank, I sighed. "That might rule out drinking. I could check in with Lowalski about the gambling. I have a lesson coming up with Wowchoska, so I can also ask him if he's heard anything."

Keisha huffed. "You and your mobsters."

"They are nice guys," I said.

"Miranda, they're criminals," Lincoln reminded me.

"Yes. And so are three-quarters of the town council, the mayor, law enforcement, and most of the old money coal and lumber families."

"Miranda's right," said Winona.

Keisha and Lincoln's hunched shoulders indicated they were reconsidering their views on what constituted a criminal.

"What if Morrow set Stiles up?" Keisha asked.

"It's a possibility. But someone killed Morrow too. So it feels more like a case of mistaken identity." I propped onto my elbows with newfound energy. "Have any of you ever heard of Freida's in Greenport?"

"The whorehouse?" Keisha asked.

"Yes."

"I've heard of it," she said. "I don't know anything about it other than it's an old school brothel."

"I've heard of it too." Winona spasmed, and her elf ears came alive, flying from side to side like a helicopter in a hurricane. "All I know is, we are supposed to stay far away from it, or Grandma will beat us within inches of our lives."

I cut my gaze to Lincoln.

His chin jutted back in indignation. "I don't know anything about it. Alice would skin me alive, and those places are bad news."

The room was quiet, except for Keisha's fingernails tapping on an armrest and Spot's panting. Generators died, and light bulbs went dark due to the brain trust in The Bellmount Inn library sucking the power grid dry.

"I think there is something up with Timberlane. I don't trust the perv at all," said Keisha. "Remember he told us the holidays make him want to kill people?"

I chuckled. "Are you sure it isn't just that he is hitting on you?"

Winona pointed at Keisha. "You think horny equals guilt."

Keisha glared at Winona. "Horny men are the root of all evil. That, and dumb ass waitresses who have crushes on Neil Diamond and Barry Manilow."

"Keisha, not every man can look like Luther Vandross!" Winona snapped.

"Too bad." Keisha smiled and licked her lips.

I scratched at my itchy, blood-covered arms. "See what I put up with, Lincoln?"

A subtle smile tugged at my mentor's lips.

"Keisha, maybe you should follow Timberlane," Winona suggested. "I will follow Dinky, although I'm pretty sure he's innocent."

"Dinky?" Keisha asked.

"Yeah. Timberlane's friend. I told you all earlier

that I met him tonight. He stopped in the store to talk to Timberlane. He asked me out, and I said yes, so now I can spy on him. But he's innocent." Winona dreamily peered over our heads. "I can tell because he's super sweet."

Six eyes stared at her. Well, eight if you counted Spot. Make that ten, including Grandma Zoey. So much for Winona's crush on Tommy Little. I was certain Dinky had nothing to do with anything, but Winona needed an excuse to play detective and follow a man around.

"Dinky is taller than me, and he dresses so stylishly." Winona sighed before taking out her black notebook. "I learned a lot tonight."

"You had time to take notes?" Keisha asked.

"Of course," Winona said. "Unlike some people in this room, I take my job seriously."

"Your job is serving cheeseburgers to the town drunks," Keisha said.

Winona threw her head back in disgust, and her elf hat tumbled to the ground.

"So what did you learn?" I asked, diffusing the situation.

Winona propped her cap back on its perch and perused her notes. "We have a triple date coming up."

"Triple date?" Keisha's eyes narrowed.

"Yes, me and Dinky, Miranda and West—although that will be a disaster—and Keisha and Timberlane. Lincoln, you can come and bring Alice if you want."

"No way! I'm not going out with Timberlane. He's a pig!" bellowed Keisha.

Winona hemmed, hawed, and stuttered. "Um— well—I already said you would."

"You what?" Keisha jumped out of the wingback, her fists clenched.

Winona's cheeks reddened. "I figured you would go if you could ask him questions. Besides, you just said you think he's up to something."

Smoke nearly seeped from Keisha's normal-sized ears.

Lincoln chuckled. "I think I'm gonna pass on the dinner for now."

Despite Winona's skepticism and Keisha's horror, I thought it might be fun to go on a triple date if West was my partner. "But Timberlane just fired us."

Winona held up a finger. "He only fired you, Miranda. He thinks Keisha is sexy, and Dinky thinks I'm pretty, so the rest of us can keep working undercover. Plus, we are going to the Chinese restaurant in Greenport. It's gonna be great. The food is delicious. We can dress up and look pretty, and we can search for clues."

"I'm not going back to that department store ever again," Keisha emphatically declared.

Lincoln ran his hand through his beard. "Winona, I don't think so. Too much urine for my liking."

Winona's lips turned downward as she wrote in her journal. "I've been thinking, what if Greg Grainey's ghost came back from the dead and killed Morrow and Stiles?"

I held in my gasp. "Why would you bring up Greg Grainey's ghost?" Was he visiting Winona since finding out she had once crushed on him?

"Everyone knows that if you kill yourself, your ghost gets stuck on Earth because you are unshriven. Ghosts get angry when they can't eat, sleep, or touch their loved ones, so they start haunting houses and doing nasty things," Winona declared.

"Sweet sugarplums!" Winona and her crazy ability to throw theories about and almost hit on a truth. Although, if one tosses ten million basketballs, eventually, a pitch is bound to cross the end zone. Right?

"Winona, you're a fucking moron," Keisha said.

Winona Westinghouse would have died at Keisha's hands the same night she met Dinky, her dream man, if Aunt Edith, Russ, and Brad Gordon hadn't saved her by walking into the room when they did. My aunt carried a tray of coffee and raisin-filled cookies, and the doctor clutched the strap of his black bag.

"Were you guys just talking about Greg Grainey?" Aunt Edith asked.

"Yes," Keisha said. "The dingbat," she pointed at Winona, "thinks that Grainey's ghost has come back from the dead so that he can kill Santa Clauses."

Brad stopped short and stared at me.

I emitted a fake laugh and dismissed Winona's nonsense with the wave of my hand. "You guys just missed all of the fun. We are brainstorming silly theories." I tittered and gave Brad a look that said, *Don't worry. Greg hasn't murdered any Santas—yet.*

Brad nodded and pulled the blanket off of me. He gasped as he took in my shredded tights and bloody backside. "Edith, could you please get me some clean towels and warm water. Russ, could you find brighter lights and bring them in here. Winona, run upstairs and get Miranda clean underclothes and her robe, and then could you all excuse us for a couple of hours?"

Triple flippin' friggin' fudge! I wouldn't have my

chocolate chip pancakes or my whipped cream-covered bartender until the doctor removed the ornament shrapnel and pine splinters from my buttocks.

****

I was sound asleep on my velvet pallet when a handsome prince bestowed kisses across my lips. Too bad, my makeshift mattress was shorter than my five-three frame, and the kisses smelled like liver-flavored doggy chow.

Still, I experienced joy scratching behind the ears of His Royal Majesty with the lion-like mane as he vibrated with energy and adulation. Brad Gordon was asleep in the wingback. For the record, six-foot-two ex-college football players do not fit into Victorian chairs. God forbid the giant should spend an entire evening snoozing on one. Sleeping upright on dollhouse furniture had to be taking a toll on the saintly doctor.

When I moved, pain shot through me. Brad had left a bottle of painkillers on the end table. I forced myself to sit, fought with the childproof lid, then washed the medicine down with a sip of water. Finally, I laid my beaten body upon the settee and continued scratching Spot. Similar to the straw that broke the camel's back, my recent injuries seemed to be more than I could handle. My muscles, bones, and skin were in agony.

I was about to doze off when Brad's eyes opened. He stretched his legs, reached to the ceiling, and smiled.

I smiled back. "You slept in a chair, again? That can't be good for you."

"I had every intention of going home last night. I guess I was so tired I never made it. It looks like you didn't sleep in your bed, either."

"Nope. I'm stiff as a board," I said.

"Let me—"

Aunt Edith slid the pocket door open. "Bradley?" She scanned the room. "Did you sleep in the chair?"

"I'm sorry, Edith. I guess I was so tired I never made it home."

"My heavens. That had to be uncomfortable. I could have put you up in one of the guest rooms."

"Thanks. Although, I'm not sure I would have had the energy to make it up the stairs," Brad said.

Aunt Edith lovingly rubbed her hand over my forehead. "Thank goodness you're okay. You have company. I went upstairs to tell you, and you weren't in your room."

"Company?" The antique mantel clock read seven-thirty. Who could possibly be visiting so early on a Sunday morning?

"Weston is here asking for you," Aunt Edith said.

"West is here?" I pushed myself to a seated position.

Aunt Edith's gaze slid from me to Brad. "Should I show him in?"

"Yes! Of course." I scraped my fingers through my ringlets. It proved pointless because my hand got stuck, and it took a herculean-strength tug to free it.

Brad chuckled.

I gave up on combing and used my palms to scrunch and fluff.

"Weston," Aunt Edith called down the hallway. "I found her. She's in the library."

A second later, West peeked around Aunt Edith to take in me, then Brad. I was too busy smiling at West to witness Brad's reaction to the awkward moment. West wasn't blinking.

"I'm sorry I missed our date. I fell on a Christmas tree," I said.

West's frown consumed his face. "I know. Edith told me you're pretty banged up."

"Bradley, come to the kitchen when you're ready. Breakfast is sausage gravy, biscuits, and fresh fruit salad. Liam and Russ will join you," Aunt Edith said, alleviating some of the tension."

"Sounds delicious. I need to check out Miranda's injuries. Then I'll be in," Brad said.

"Weston, sausage and biscuits?" Aunt Edith asked.

West shook his head. "No, thanks. I have to be at work by eleven."

"Of course, he's staying. It isn't even eight yet, and we had a breakfast date planned for today." I nursed a sense of loss that West wasn't the one cooking it and that he wouldn't make love to me on top of the bar. Still, he was with me, and that was the next best thing. "Aunt Edith, could West and I have breakfast in the turret? I'm sore, and I think the window seat would be the most comfortable place for me to sit."

"Of course, honey," she said. "Brad, I know you want coffee. Coffee or tea for you, Weston?"

West hesitated. "Water."

"Westinghouse, could you give me ten minutes with my patient? I want to check her over, and then I will release her into your care. Just—"

"I know. Don't take her skydiving," West grumbled.

"Weston, join me in the kitchen." Aunt Edith motioned for him to follow. "You can help me fix your tray. By the time we're done, Bradley will have finished Miranda's examination."

West exited the library, and my aunt slid the door behind them.

"Westinghouse has it bad." Brad looked down at me. "Although, who can blame him?"

"Brad, I feel terrible. I've almost died, I've herniated my disk, I've broken my nose and had two concussions, and this is the worst I've ever felt."

He scratched his chin. "Well, it's cumulative. Even with my help and medicine, your body is working hard to heal. You're exhausted."

"You must really be tired, then."

"Part of the reason you might not be feeling well is I'm running low on energy. I have a limited supply, and I have to build it up. If I had infinite healing power, nobody in town would ever be sick."

"So I need to slow down on the klutzy accidents?" I forced a chuckle.

"Pretty much. I can give you a bit of help with the pain today. The rest will have to be good old scientific medicine."

"Are you sure?" I hated to take his energy, but I hurt so much.

"Yep. Edith's going to feed me well. That will help."

"Hey Brad, I was thinking. After you give me first aid, you should pet Spot. He has so much energy he vibrates. Maybe he could spare a bit, and you wouldn't feel so tired."

"Worth a try. What do you think, buddy?" Brad squatted and ruffled Spot's hair.

Spot wagged and gave a tiny woof.

"He says it's okay." I plopped my body down heavily.

Brad stood over me, his beautiful blues staring into my soul. "You can talk to animals?"

I didn't answer because my painkiller was kicking in, and my vision had begun to cloud.

"Roll over," Brad said.

The short couch, blanket, and robe made getting into my new position a challenge. For a moment, I felt self-conscious about my exposed backside. I recalled that the previous evening Winona had brought me my lavender silk panties and sighed in relief. Still, I wondered if I had any unattractive cellulite from my recent food frenzies.

Brad rearranged the blanket to protect my modesty, and then he began his gentle exploration. As his powerful energy filled me, I relaxed and forgot about everything, including my vanity.

"On your back," he said.

Although groggy, I rolled. His fingers trailed along my injured hip and thigh, and then they traveled up my arms to my face. I'm certain I dozed off. I'm uncertain if Brad leaned over and kissed me on the forehead while thinking, *Please take me back, sweetheart.*

I awoke with Brad and West hovering over me.

"Miranda." Brad's voice was far away. "Did you take one of these pills?" He held a blurry container in front of me.

It took my eyes a moment to focus. "Yes. Aren't those my pain pills?"

"Yeah, but I didn't know you had taken one, and I gave you other medicine."

A sprawled-out Sheltie caught my gaze.

"Is Spot okay? He isn't dead, is he?"

I crawled off the settee, plopped onto the floor,

wrapped my pup in my arms, and laid my head beside his. He looked at me, then flopped his chin onto the carpet and closed his eyes.

"Oh, Spot!" Although I wasn't watching the guys because I was worried about my comatose-acting fur baby, I took in bits and pieces of the conversation going on behind me.

"She's eatin' stars, Doc," West said. "What the hell ya give her?"

"She'll be okay after she eats something. I'll help you get her upstairs," Brad said.

West said something along the lines of "I don't need your help."

Brad lifted me from the floor. "Spot is fine, sweetheart. He just needs to sleep. I gave him a belly rub that seemed to make him tired."

Once I was standing, West wrapped his arm around my shoulder. "Come on, Shortcake." He guided me out of the library.

"Come on, Spot," I called.

Spot didn't move.

I'm not sure how long it took West to get me to the third floor but, I had to sit down at least once. He was sweating by the time we reached the landing and our strenuous climb temporarily cleared the fog from my brain.

West tucked me into the window seat and arranged my open robe to cover my exposed thighs. "So Doc calls you 'sweetheart?'"

"That's what he called me when we dated. Now he calls me Miranda. Except when he's saving my life, then he calls me 'sweetheart.'" It was a pretty stupid thing to say, but in my defense, I had a heavy-duty narcotic and a strong dose of energy painkiller in me.

West snorted.

I moved my lips around and slapped at my numb cheeks. "Are you jealous, Mr. Westinghouse?"

West snorted again. "I left our breakfast tray downstairs. I have to get it."

Sidetracked by my pets, he picked up my turtle and looked him in his little red eyes. "Hi, Princess Pickles with a Penis. How's it hanging?" He put the turtle down and taped Simon's cage. "Hiya, little fellow. Is the redhead bossing ya around? I know how ya feel. She bosses me around, too. Kiss me, West. Harder, West. Faster, West. Make me come, West."

"Weston!" Aunt Edith stood in the doorway, holding our tray.

I giggled at West's dirty talk and acted like a complete goofball, wiggling my fingers at my aunt.

West cleared his throat. "Sorry, Edith. I was joking around with the pets."

"Can I see you in the hallway, please?"

"West, you're in big trouble," I said between chuckles.

West gritted his teeth and groaned. "Edith, she's stoned out of her gourd on painkillers."

After West and Aunt Edith stepped into the hall, I reprimanded Simon. "Seriously, you hate me so much you would rather go live with West? F.Y.I., he will feed you mold."

I ignored Simon's nasty rebuttal, closed my eyes, and leaned against the window waiting for West's return.

A gentle kiss tasting of mint startled me. "Shortcake, let's get some food into you."

West sat beside me, fiddled with our breakfast, then lifted a fork full of biscuit to my mouth. I licked at it and nibbled. West finished the rest of my bite.

I smiled. "Isn't it beautiful?"

"Yeah." West grinned.

"The view of the town, West." My numb lips plastered themselves into a smile.

"Yeah. It's also beautiful." He held a cup of coffee to my mouth. "Drink."

I sipped, enjoying the intimacy of Weston Westinghouse the Third eating gravy and biscuits in my turret as he cared for me. I was living out a sweet cozy dream. Leaning back, I closed my eyes, and began a warm float as I drifted into sleep.

One of his arms wound around my shoulder, and the other gathered me from under my knees so that he could carry me to bed. The covers slid over me, and West's body weight settled onto the mattress.

The last thing I remember was his soft whistle as he thought sweet things and brushed out of control ringlets from my face.

Chapter 13

Wearing my favorite tweed suit and pearls, I knocked on the frame of Lincoln's office door. He ushered me in for our session and looked me over from head to toe.

"You look quite chipper for someone who wrestled with a twenty-foot evergreen less than seventy-two hours ago," he said.

I smiled and sat across from him.

"Tell me, how is keeping your shield in place going?" he asked.

Lincoln had taught me to embrace the sensation created when I focused my vision inward. Once I tapped into the feeling that puddled right behind my nose, I'd pull up on it until it landed above my eyebrows. His method kept me from absorbing others' thoughts, and it protected me from becoming immersed in energy footprints.

"I'm doing fairly well. I had issues holding onto it when I was on painkillers. I accidentally read some of Brad's thoughts and then some of West's. I also have problems if someone startles me or I'm not ready for their touch. Sergeant O'Sullivan blindsided me the other day, and I accidentally read his mind."

Lincoln ran his fingers through his beard. "I suspect those times might always be a challenge for you. The good news is you earned a ninety percent on your shield tests at our last session."

"Wow! That's great. But I think I need to stay away from narcotics." And energy medicine and kissing my sexy undercover sleuthing partner when I'm on stakeouts.

Lincoln laughed. "Probably a good idea. Now, let's talk about the constant injuries."

I cringed.

"Do you think you're working so hard to keep your filter in place that you aren't paying attention to your surroundings?"

I was pretty sure the chest wound was because I interrupted a murder. But had I slipped on the ice and had the slapstick episode with a humongous tree because I was concentrating on my shield? "Honestly, I don't know."

He wrote something in the notes he kept on our sessions.

"Lincoln, when I slipped on the ice and herniated my disk—"

He peered at me from under his glasses. "Miranda, I don't think you herniated a desk. If you had, it wouldn't have healed so soon."

I didn't want to out Brad without asking his permission. Taking in a breath, I summoned courage. "Lincoln, there's something about my injury that I haven't told you."

"I assume you had a liaison with Weston in the parking lot." Lincoln chuckled. "Nothing to be ashamed of."

"I probably was distracted by West, and it was icy, and I had on absurd shoes, but there's something else."

He studied me with his psychologist's scrutiny,

trying to read my mind while psychoanalyzing me. Good thing I adored him.

"Oh?"

I exhaled, then blurted out, "Greg Grainey was harassing me, and he threw West's keys across the parking lot. I went to pick them up, got frustrated, hit a patch of ice, and lost my balance." Hearing myself repeat the story solidified its insanity.

Lincoln put down his pen and, in slow, distinct words—as if he was talking to a child or an insane asylum patient—said, "Miranda, Greg died a few weeks ago."

I chewed on my bottom lip. "I know."

He took off his glasses, rubbed his eyes, then anchored them back onto his nose. "I think we got sidetracked from dealing with your post-traumatic stress disorder, and we need to get back to it. I know you feel guilty about what happened to Greg, and the ignorant masses in this town blame you, but it wasn't your fault."

"That's not it, Lincoln. I can see and talk to Greg's spirit energy. He is a pain in the butt, obsessed ghost. It isn't in my head. I assure you. I don't have post-traumatic stress disorder."

"Spirit energy?"

"I think it's somehow related to my telepathic abilities. I wonder if his energy is trapped in this plane, and it's so strong that I can see, hear, and feel him."

"Do you see other ghosts?" Lincoln asked.

"No. Only Greg. I have tried to talk to other people that have died, but I can't."

"Like your mother and grandmother?"

I nodded.

"And George Stiles and Joe Morrow?"

I nodded again.

"Interesting. Very interesting," Lincoln said.

"So, you believe me?"

"I'm considering all the possible reasons you think you are conversing with a dead man. Of course, one possible reason is your telepathic abilities."

I assumed the other "possible reasons" included PTSD, psychedelic mushrooms, or that I had finally sunk to the depths of bat-poop crazy.

"There is a psychic in Greenport that Greg communicates with. She claims to be able to read palms and tell fortunes, but that's a lie. Although she is a medium, and she can talk to the dead."

Lincoln's eyebrows practically landed in the line of his fuzzy white hair.

"Lincoln, there's another person in Bellmount who has energy abilities, but I don't feel at liberty to share his name with you without asking him if it's okay. Maybe you could also work with him to gather more information about humans that can harness energy?"

"A he?" Lincoln asked. "Wait! Back up. Is Greg's ghost here right now?" He looked around the room, staring into each of the corners.

"No. We had a pretty awful fight, and I told him to leave me alone."

Lincoln gave me his go-on eyes.

"This is kind of embarrassing." My cheeks burned. "Greg's obsessed with me. He thinks I'm one of his girlfriends and accuses me of shooting him. He keeps showing up in my bedroom in various states of dress and undress. And he is jealous of West and any other man who pays me the slightest bit of attention."

Lincoln winced. "He is in various states of dress and undress?"

I crinkled my nose in disgust. "Greg's energy is fashion-conscious and perverted. The same way he was in life."

"He's old enough to be your father." Lincoln closed his eyes for a moment and set two fingers on his temple. His lids lifted, and he sighed. "I don't have any idea what to say to that."

"I think Greg needs a therapist. Can you help him?"

Lincoln stood, turned his back to me, and looked out the window. "I'll talk to Bradley Gordon. His secret is safe with me, but I'm not up to treating an unscrupulous ghost."

I gasped. "But I didn't tell you it was Brad?"

He stared at the parking lot. "You didn't need to. Someone is patching you up quickly. I wasn't born yesterday. And the doctor is one hell of a man—larger than life."

"So, what do I do with a perverted poltergeist with an obsessive crush? I threw him out, but the truth is, he doesn't have many people to talk to. I think he's bored and lonely, and it seems he might be stuck in this form forever."

Lincoln faced me. "I feel no sympathy for the man. Perhaps you can take your concerns up with the medium."

"I've been thinking about doing that. Thanks for talking to me." I stood. "Lincoln, one more thing. Is there something in the water making men in Bellmount crazy? Men have never paid attention to me, and all of a sudden, they are acting like lovesick fools."

"It could be that you're giving off massive amounts of energy," he said.

"Really?"

Lincoln plopped into his swivel chair, picked up his pen, and leaned back. "I have no idea. It's just a guess. Although I'd say, it has more to do with the fact you are a lovely young woman. You are intelligent and bold, and you are new to town."

Lovely, intelligent, and bold? No way! I was a disheveled, walking disaster. Furthermore, had the distinguished Dr. Lincoln Harrison just referred to me as fresh meat?

"See you later, Lincoln. I have to teach my journalism class in a few minutes, and tonight, I'm attending a funeral."

Lincoln tapped his pen on his desk as he stared into space.

Chapter 14

I didn't attend George Stiles' funeral, although my aunt assured me it was a compassionate affair. Unfortunately, Joe Morrow's service was anything but.

Aunt Edith dressed in black, and I stayed in my gray suit and pearls. First, we stopped by Polly and Will's to pick up Winona. Then, we drove across town to pick up Keisha. Aunt Edith's adherence to etiquette and status on the town council meant she attended most funerals. I, on the other hand, was trying to bring justice to the man in the casket.

Aunt Edith pulled into the parking lot behind Konicki's and gave us a mini-lecture. "Girls, I know you are caught up in your investigation, but remember this is a solemn occasion. You know how your presence unsettles Pastor Smith, so avoid him. And Miranda, please don't hurt yourself."

Winona and I nodded in acquiescence. However, Keisha blurted out, "That ass of a pastor comes near me, and he is going down."

"Keisha Brown." Aunt Edith gave her a disapproving look.

"Keisha swallowed. "Yes, ma'am. I'll behave."

Abashed, my friends and I followed Aunt Edith onto the porch of the sprawling funeral home.

Konicki's was a three-story Victorian mansion. Its ornately carved door sat between four columns.

Although Mr. Konicki had painted the siding, wood, and gingerbread tan, the colorful stained-glass windows in various styles and sizes made the building a work of art. Porches surrounded both the first and second stories. Multiple sized gables adorned the third floor.

Upon entering, we met with the smell of fresh flowers. Spectacular arrangements of lilies, roses, and carnations sat in every available space. A distinguished gentleman in a suit shook hands with Aunt Edith and pointed us toward the room where Joe's viewing was in progress.

A couple of dozen people milled about. Aunt Edith excused herself and headed to the casket where an older woman and a young man stood. Winona followed at her heels. Keisha disappeared around a corner, leaving me alone.

Brad Gordon's height and powerful presence made him stand out in the room full of mourners. He wore a dark suit, a light purple shirt, a dark purple tie, and shoes shined to perfection. His eyes were so blue that a Kashmir sapphire paled in comparison. Although I was no longer in love with Brad, he stole my breath. I was a woman, after all, and God had created a perfect specimen when she molded Dr. Bradley Gordon. He waved. I melted—because I was a woman—not because I was in love. He walked my way.

"I love the suit, Dr. Albright." His dimples appeared.

"I love your purple tie, Dr. Gordon." I smiled back.

"Let me guess." He leaned close. "You are here investigating Joe Morrow's death."

My discreet answer was the most imperceptible of nods.

"Promise me you won't get hurt. As much as I love coming to your rescue, I hate to see you in pain," he said.

I winced as I recalled exposing my injured rear and my face plant on the carpet.

As if on cue, Brad asked, "How is Spot? I guess I took too much of his energy."

"Poor little guy. He was out of it until yesterday afternoon. Although so was I. I missed my second day of work this semester, and I had to cancel my reading lesson with my friend, Wochowska."

Brad stepped closer so that mourners could navigate around us.

"I earned a perfect attendance award in high school, and I only missed three days of class as an undergrad, and that was because I had the flu. I hate taking sick days."

"I'm sorry that you overdosed on painkillers, and I feel terrible about the mess up."

"Oh, Brad. You shouldn't feel bad about it. You have taken such good care of me. Given the circumstances, more than I deserve."

Brad cleared his throat, and his emotion-filled eyes pierced mine. "You deserve the world."

Once again, Brad Gordon left me speechless.

He put his hand on my shoulder. "I'm going to take off now before Jessica arrives. Stay safe, sweetheart."

A smiling Aunt Edith gawked as my handsome savior walked toward the exit. Had my aunt been twenty years younger and not had a live-in boyfriend, she may have eloped with Dr. Bradley Gordon in a heartbeat. I suspect my aunt vicariously lived her romantic fantasies through me.

Brad was two feet from the door when his ex-wife entered. Greg, dressed in a tailored suit, strutted beside his daughter.

Brad stood still as Jessica approached and placed her hand on his forearm. He nodded, then walked away.

She stared after him.

When Brad reached the exit, he turned and gave me a tiny wave and a warm smile.

I waved back.

A frowning Jessica Grainey caught the exchange. Followed by her wispy father, the Ice Queen clicked my way. She muttered, "slut," as she pushed past me on her way to the far corner where her mother, the mayor's wife, and Ian Patterson's wife posed.

Since the only man I had ever behaved wantonly with happened to be the younger Weston Westinghouse, I found her statement uncalled for and crude. I regretted my promise to behave.

As the four women in the corner pointed and whispered, Greg stopped beside me. *"I'm sorry. They are cruel. I have come to despise Louise. I don't know why I married her, and I hate the lot of biddies."*

I couldn't respond to Greg in a room full of people, so I sucked up my pride as two generations of Bellmount Bitches bad-mouthed me.

Aunt Edith caught sight of my predicament. She and Winona interspersed themselves among the group, halting whatever rumors the nasty women were cooking up.

"I love Jessica," Greg said, his voice soulful and sad. *"I want her to be better than her mother and better than I was. I spoiled her. I wish I had a do-over for my life."*

I tilted my head slightly, indicating he should follow me. Chattering away, he trailed behind as I searched for a private space. After traveling down a secluded hallway, I triple-checked to make sure we were alone.

"Does Jessica know you are—" I wasn't sure what word to use, although "here?" seemed to convey my meaning.

"No. I've been staying in the guest room at her house. She has no idea that I'm there. I try to talk to her and tell her I love her. I ask her to change her ways. Then I visit Gordon and beg him to give her another chance and help her be a better person." He shook his head. *"I feel helpless."*

My heart ached. "Greg, I'm sorry I pushed you away, but your tantrum seriously injured me."

He sighed. *"At first, you were just this sexy piece of ass playing hard to get, but after I died, you became my entire world. I don't want to share you with other men, especially Gordon. He's Jessica's. Or Westinghouse because he's an arrogant little shit who is too sexy for his own good. Or that damn cop. Bellmount isn't even his hometown. What if he takes you away?"*

I groaned. "I've been thinking, why don't we take a trip to visit Alina? We can go tomorrow when I get off work."

"A date?" Greg smiled mischievously.

"Not a romantic date, but a friend date."

"We'll see about that." He winked. *"Maybe a sexy little threesome?"*

I clenched my teeth and growled.

"No worries. No need to rush into it. I don't mind going slow."

"We aren't having a threesome. Don't be a pervert. Don't force me to push you away again."

"Fine," he said. *"I'll check in with Alina to see if she's free."*

Greg dissolved, and I headed back to the viewing. I still hadn't done any digging into Joe Morrow's death, and I needed to get a handle on the soap opera that was my life.

I nonchalantly slid into the room and took a seat diagonal from the casket. Aunt Edith and Winona remained nestled in the corner with the mean girls. Keisha had cornered Mayor Reynolds, and Pastor Smith stood between the woman and young man at the casket. Mike Stevens, the owner of the convenience store, quickly visited Joe, then departed.

Eventually, Keisha excused herself from her conversation and sat beside me."I was talking to Gene."

"Which one is Gene?"

"Our mayor. He's an ass, but it never hurts to be nice to him."

"Oh, I didn't know Reynolds's had a first name." I chuckled at my silly observation. "Who are the people with Smith?"

"That is Joe Morrow's sister and nephew,"

"Ah."

"They are his only surviving family."

Sadness overtook me until I concluded that a small family was better than no family. Besides, for a man who had lived most of his life on the edge, there was a good turnout at his funeral.

Greg reappeared and sat next to Keisha.

A hush settled over the room. A pink-haired, heavily made-up woman stood in the entranceway.

Although her black dress was modest, it didn't disguise her curves, and her hips swayed as her stilettos navigated the carpet. Freida from the Stevens Speed-mart parking lot pulled her shoulders back, lifted her chin, and glided across that room.

She approached Morrow's family. His nephew's bottom lip dropped, and his sister turned her back to the prostitute. Pastor Smith frowned and shook his head. Freida ignored her heartless dismissal, placed her hand in the casket, and stood by Joe Morrow. The nasty women in the corner—minus Winona and Aunt Edith—pointed and whispered. Aunt Edith approached, then slid her arm around the grieving woman.

When Freida turned to face her judgmental audience, there was no denying her tears. With her chin lifted, she embarked on her excruciating trek, halting in front of the mayor.

He frowned at her and motioned her on with a wrist flick.

Never one for impeccable timing, Shultz shuffled into the room.

I'd never seen the sheriff in street clothes, and he appeared even shorter and rounder in his suit. The jacket wasn't buttoned, his pant legs were about two inches too short, and his clip-on tie was crooked. He grabbed a tissue from a side table and handed it to Freida. She wiped at her eyes and left the room.

Had Shultz just behaved like a gentleman?

Shultz's squinty eyes settled on me, and he snorted in disgust. I'd been mistaken. The sheriff was still insect larvae droppings.

The previous hum of voices picked up, and the viewing went on as if most of the town hadn't just blackballed a distressed human.

"Who in the hell was that?" Keisha asked.

"I'll tell you later," I whispered.

Greg Grainey leaped from his chair. *"My wife is a fucking cunt!"*

Too bad I was the only one who heard the much-deserved pronouncement.

"That man that just started talking to Reynolds is Thomas Klinger." Keisha used a palm to cover her pointed finger. "He's the mayor of Greenport. I'm going to say hi."

Keisha's long, lean body sauntered to the men. Her sleek black pants, flowing tunic, and high heels were to die for. She carried herself like a queen, but it wasn't with the same iciness Jessica Grainey gave off. Keisha was all confidence and female power. Oh, what I wouldn't give to exude that air. She extended her hand to Mayor Klinger, and he took her palm in his.

"Hey, Crimson."

I kept my gaze on Keisha and the men she talked to.

"Alina's free tomorrow. I'm bored, so I'm going to try to get me some Romanian nookie. See you tomorrow around four."

I kept my yuck response nonverbal and remained inconspicuous.

My ghost kissed me on the top of my head and disintegrated.

Before leaving the room, the pastor announced that he would soon be saying a prayer in Joseph's honor and requested everyone take a seat. Winona and Keisha joined me. Aunt Edith found a spot across the aisle from us.

Keisha leaned close to whisper, "Reynolds is a son of a bitch. He just told me to keep my nose out of the investigation. I think he threatened my job. I informed him that he has no authority over me. Klinger heard the entire conversation."

"Shh," Winona said.

"Shush yourself, woman," Keisha said.

I needed my head examined if I continued to sit between my friends at somber occasions.

A few moments later, Pastor Smith returned and took his place beside the casket. "Praise be to God!" he called out, alerting everyone that he was about to start his prayer. He cleared his throat and let loose. "We have gathered together today to send our God-fearing Brother Joseph Morrow to the Lord's kingdom."

"Praise be to God," a couple of people called back.

Winona rummaged through her purse, took out her notebook, and started to draw.

"Joseph recently found the Lord and rid himself of the evils of the flesh. Women and wine went to the way-side because he found the answers he sought in our Lord. Like we learn in Galatians 5:19, 'The acts of the flesh are obvious: sexual immorality, impurity, and debauchery; idolatry and witchcraft; hatred, discord, jealousy, fits of rage, selfish ambition, dissensions, factions, and envy; drunkenness, orgies, and the like.' I warn you that those who live like this will not inherit the kingdom of God.'"

Only the arrogant Smith would take advantage of a man's death to remind impure souls to stay away from orgies.

With her expression intense and serious, Winona sketched a fist and an erect male organ.

I successfully stifled my giggles. Even from far away, I could see Aunt Edith wrestled with decorum as she worked to control her twitching facial muscles. I supposed her mirth was at Pastor Smith's absurd prayer since she wasn't privy to Winona's notes.

Keisha tapped on my arm, using her expressive eyes to guide my vision to Smith's shoe. A four-inch-long piece of toilet paper trailed behind him. Keisha's shoulders heaved, and her entire body shook as she folded both of her hands over her mouth.

My aunt shot me a don't-you-dare-laugh warning.

A muffled choking sound came from the seat beside me right before Keisha jumped up and dashed toward the exit.

Winona, unaware of the threatening brouhaha, concentrated on drawing a diagonal line through a mug of beer. She studied it and frowned.

Aunt Edith eyed the pastor's snowy white train. Her palm flew to her mouth, and her shoulders vibrated.

"Like Daniel, Joseph Morrow, 'resolved that he would not defile himself with the king's food or with the wine that he drank. Therefore, he asked the chief of the eunuchs to not allow him to defile himself.'"

"Winona leaned close. "What's a eunuch?"

My palm hit my mouth.

Aunt Edith's light tremble turned into a full-body convulsion. She stood, then crawled over the row of people seated to her left. When she reached the side aisle, she doubled over, grabbed her stomach, and headed to the exit.

In an effort to control my laughter, I dug my fingernails into my wrist.

Pastor Smith's final words rang out. "May Jesus

forgive Joseph for his wayward life and save him from the fiery pits of hell. In Joseph Morrow's memory, may you all avoid the sins of this earthly existence."

I leaped from my seat and sprinted to the exit. Beating the throng of mourners to the hallway just in time, I braced against a wall as my building boffola blew.

Aunt Edith and Keisha stood near the front door. Keisha wiped her watery eyes with a tissue. My aunt held her ribs and snorted. To the casual observer they appeared to be heartbroken mourners.

One of Joe's guests glared at Keisha as she turned her titter into a sneeze.

"Damn flower allergy." Keisha patted her nose. "Oh, these lilies," she called to a group preparing to disperse into the night.

Aunt Edith deserved an award for her performance. "Oh," she moaned. "I must give up those rich dinners." She rubbed her stomach and stumbled about.

Between their moments of theatrics, they continued to look at each other and snigger.

Outwardly I had pulled myself together, and hopefully appeared demure in my tweed and pearls. Inwardly I found my hunched-over aunt betraying her years of pristine etiquette to be hilarious.

Keisha pointed, and I turned.

Pastor Smith stood with Joe's sister and nephew. Winona Westinghouse, sweetheart that she was, tapped him on the shoulder and removed the piece of toilet paper from his shoe. He thanked her with a hideous scowl. She smiled warmly at him.

Winona hugged Joe's sister, patted his nephew on the shoulder, threw the paper into a nearby trash can, and walked toward us.

Aunt Edith, Keisha, and I slunk to the car; our shoulders slumped in shame.

"Oh, I'm so disappointed in myself," Aunt Edith said. "I behaved atrociously."

"Edith, I tried to tell you Smith would behave like a bastard," Keisha said.

In both Keisha and Aunt Edith's defense, Smith was a buffoon; his prayer was absurdly inappropriate, and he did have toilet tissue stuck to his black wingtip.

We climbed into the car, and Winona frantically looked around the back seat. "Oh, no, I forgot my notebook on my chair."

I needed to walk off my evening, and it was the least I could do for my kind-hearted friend. "I'll get it, Winona."

I hopped out of the car and moved as quickly as my black pumps allowed. The pastor, Joe's family, the undertaker, and Mayor Reynolds stood inside the front entrance. I passed by their scowls to enter the viewing room, where the sheriff stood by the casket.

"I will miss you, my friend," Shultz said to Joe.

My calf hit a chair, and a ting echoed in the now empty room. My number two enemy faced me.

"You," he grunted between clenched teeth.

His clip-on tie took that moment to fall into the casket. The ludicrous man reached for it, and there was a loud crash. The coffin flew in one direction, a deceased Joe flew in the other, and Shultz hit the ground.

Shultz's torso slumped against the casket, and his stubby legs stretched out in front of him, as if chirping birdies flitted about the sheriff's bulbous head, and black crosses seemed to appear over his eyes. Thank goodness, he had saved it! His right hand held that tie in the air in triumph. The casket, Joe, and Shultz may have been discombobulated, but the cheesy orange and yellow striped accessory remained an unscathed trophy.

"Fuck me up the ass!" Shultz sputtered.

I have no idea why I thought it a good idea to come to Shultz's aid. Maybe I had been addled by the kindness he had shown to Freida and the sadness he felt over Joe. Or, perhaps I had been poisoned by the fumes from his stale vegetable-soup-with-loads-of-onions stench. When my hand reached to help him, his lips curled into a sneer.

When I find him, I'm going to kill the mother fucker who did this to Joe. A typical demeaning Shultz-ism followed this semi-appropriate thought. *Damn, what a waste putting nice tits on the red-headed bitch!*

Since Shultz was having a tough night, I didn't want to prove him wrong, so bitch that I was; I let go of his forearm and enjoyed the satisfying sound of his whale blubber slapping the floor.

Pastor Smith, Mayor Reynolds, and Joe's sister entered the room.

"What the hell just happened?" Reynolds bellowed all sorts of colorful words as he took on the arduous task of helping the weeble wobble to his feet.

Shultz kind of clipped his tie into place and pointed at me. "The damn trouble-making girl pushed me into the casket. I've told her aunt to keep her on a leash, but she's still running around wreaking havoc."

"I wasn't anywhere near you when you made this mess, Shultz."

"Ms. Albright, leave the premises this instant,"

Smith demanded.

I stared Smith down. "This isn't your church. You have no authority here."

Joe Morrow's sister looked back and forth between her brother's askew corpse and his lopsided casket. "I would like you to leave, too."

"Fudge." I grabbed Winona's notebook, and stomped out of the funeral home with my cheeks on fire.

The most disturbing part of the evening was my realization that Shultz and I had a lot in common. We now ran neck-and-neck for the Clumsiest Fool in Bellmount Award.

****

We listened to the same compact disk play over and over for months. Not that Aunt Edith's 1970s rock tunes were hard on the ears, but I craved variety. Since Christmas was coming, I would make sure there was new music under the tree. I'd overheard my aunt mention that she had crushes on a few pop singers. However, the holiday was still a couple of weeks away, so on the way home from James Morrow's funeral, Winona and Aunt Edith once again harmonized about thunder when it rained.

Winona halted her performance. "Why don't we go to the pub for dessert? I can make everyone one of my pumpkin hot chocolates. It's yummy. Just ask Miranda. Plus, my mom baked one of her Black Forest cakes. It's this week's special."

"Yum," I said, not wanting to hurt Winona's feelings. Although she was great at baking and omelets, her hot drink concoctions were lacking. "But I can't tonight. I have to correct final essays before the end of the week, and I have to finish my lecture for tomorrow. My budget is due to Keisha, and I need to review the campus newspaper before it goes to print." My chest tightened, and I let out a long exhale. "I have hours of work ahead of me."

"I do love Polly's cakes," Aunt Edith said.

"Throw a little somepin' somepin' in my glass, and I'm in," Keisha said. "And, girlfriend, I'll help you with your budget over lunch tomorrow."

"Come on, Miranda. Please," Winona pleaded. "I'll have West put on a pot of coffee for you."

"Yum," I said again, thinking about West. "Okay. But I can't stay long."

The last time West and I had been together, I had been loopy on painkillers and had fallen asleep while he gently played with my hair. The prospect of sneaking into the storeroom for a kiss elicited tingles.

The girls and I chose a table in the corner. While Winona prepared our snack, I flitted to my handsome man.

West grinned at my approach. "Hiya, Doctor Shortcake. You got the sexy librarian thing goin' tonight."

"You have the sexy bartender thing going every night." I bit my lip.

West leaned across the bar and studied me with his heavy-lidded kissy-eyes.

From behind him, one of his regular barflies called, "Weston!"

"We're thirsty," the barfly's companion said.

The women could have been twins. Both had hair permed within inches of its life, and their clothing was scanty and cheap. One appeared prettier, but that was because she had taken the time to blend her make-up. I took no pride in my mean girl analysis. Although in my defense, they made a habit of flirting with my boyfriend. I regularly battled my green-eyed monster because women were always posing near the bar, making googly-eyes at West. Sometimes, he flirted back, saying it helped him earn better tips.

West rolled his eyes so that only I could see. He looked over his shoulder at them. "Be there in a sec, ladies." Then he focused his attention entirely on me.

"I was a naughty boy. I didn't return my books." He tilted his head from side to side. "I think I need punished, Miss Hotty Librarian."

I giggled. "That's the worst pick-up line I've ever heard, Mister Sexy Bartender."

"Yeah. Well, maybe you should punish me for it."

I giggled again. "West, I miss you, but I have so many papers to correct. I don't know if I'm even going to get to sleep tonight."

He pushed his bottom lip out and blinked his long lashes a half dozen times.

"Can you get off work Friday night?" I asked. "We can go to dinner and kiss for hours?"

"Mmm. That sounds fun. If I tell Pop I need time to take you out, he'll probably give me the entire night off. Maybe he'll even pay."

I held up crossed fingers. "Pop has always been good to me."

"I think he likes you more than he likes me."

"That's not true, Weston Westinghouse. You may be the most incorrigible man in the county, but everyone adores you. I, on the other hand, am a walking scandal."

"Yeah, but you're my scandal." He bopped my nose.

West's 'ladies' squirmed in their seats as they sent me nasty looks. I supposed they wanted both the alcohol and his attention. Either way, they needed to be patient because I wasn't finished. I grabbed West by the collar of his t-shirt and pulled him to me. Practically crawling onto the bar, I threaded my hands through his hair and shoved my tongue down his throat.

When I let go, West was panting.

"Damn," he said.

"Friday," I said.

I pranced to the table where my friends and aunt stared at me like I had forgotten to put on clothes. I sat down, eyed my treat, and drooled because Polly had adorned the decadent layers with chocolate shavings.

Winona contorted her mouth in disgust. "I couldn't ask West to make your coffee because you were sucking on his face."

Keisha's laugh came out as a snort.

Aunt Edith sighed.

I shoveled a planet-sized bite of cake into my mouth.

"Who was the woman that caused the commotion at the funeral?" Keisha asked.

I swallowed chocolate heaven. "That was Freida."

"Oh," Keisha said. "That's what the infamous Freida looks like."

"How do you know who she is?" my aunt asked.

I needed my head examined because I blurted out, "From my stakeout with Sergeant O'Sullivan."

Winona's fork hovered mid-scoop, and her mouth hung open.

Keisha choked on her wine. "What the hell, girl! Stakeout? You want to fill us in?"

"It was no big deal." I flicked my wrist. "We sat outside the Stevens Speed-mart and watched the comings and goings." I prepared to take another bite, but Keisha grabbed my cake, holding it ransom.

"And?" she asked.

I considered stabbing her hand with sharp prongs. "Well, a group of drunk college kids had a snack in the parking lot. Shultz showed up and dropped his hot dog down his shirt. Then Freida bought a cup of coffee and talked to Shultz. Now give me my cake."

"What was Frieda doing in Bellmount? I doubt she was here to buy coffee," Aunt Edith said.

I shrugged. "No idea. And Reynolds showed up and argued with Stevens, the owner. Then Stevens almost caught us spying."

"No shit," Keisha said.

"Almost?" Aunt Edith asked.

"Stevens got distracted by something." Like Sean and I making out in an unmarked police car trying to keep our cover.

"Anything else you haven't shared with us?" Keisha asked.

"Let's see." Desperate for chocolate, I spilled. "The first thing that happened was I heard three shots. Then I found George Stiles' corpse at the Speed-mart. Mason, my student, says the parking lot camera has been broken since summer, and nobody can explain why it hasn't been fixed. Sergeant O'Sullivan and I think George was shot somewhere else, and his corpse was moved to the Speed-mart. Stevens acted suspiciously." I left out that the accusation was from my ghost and that West and I had made passionate love to each other on Thanksgiving.

"I found George Stiles in the alley, and he said, 'help the girls', then I was shot by Santa and almost died. Brad found me and saved my life." No need to mention the doctor's ability to heal with magical energy.

"That psychotic elf, Peppermint, knew that George filled in for Joe at the community center party and that a strange man dressed in a costume lurked about the store." Confessing that I read Sean's mind and that he wanted to come into my turret and kiss me senseless sounded insane and arrogant. "Sergeant O'Sullivan and I think the intended target was Morrow and that Stiles was a case of mistaken identity."

A few sentences more, and I could have my dessert back. "Keisha thinks Timberlane is somehow involved, and Winona doesn't think Dinky has anything to do with it. Lincoln thinks I keep getting hurt because I'm not paying attention." No way was I admitting that I was extra clumsy because of concentrating on keeping a telepathic shield in place or that The Curse of the Redhead was causing a heap of trouble. "I think that's everything."

I forced a toothy grin.

"Oh. One more thing. Did you guys know Morrow was friends with Shultz?"

Winona shook her head and took out her notebook.

Aunt Edith's brow furrowed. "If you have lived in town long enough, you pretty much know everyone." She looked to the ceiling, contemplating something.

"No," Keisha said. "How did you find out?"

"When I went back to the funeral for Winona's

notebook, Shultz said, 'I will miss you, my friend,' right before he knocked the casket over."

Their "What?" was so loud everyone in the pub gawked.

"Shultz is such a buffoon that his tie fell into the casket. He tried to get it back and knocked the coffin over."

Keisha sat my cake in front of me. "He knocked the casket and the body onto the floor?" She rested her hand on her forehead.

"Yep," I said, my mouth full.

"No shit!" Keisha let out a half-choke, half-laugh. "Shultz is a royal ass!"

"At least nobody got hurt tonight," Aunt Edith said.

"Well, unless you count the damage done to Joe's corpse." I shivered.

"This night!" If my aunt was a religious woman, I supposed she would have taken that moment to make the sign of the cross.

"Aunt Edith, I can tell something else is on your mind. What is it?"

"I'm not sure, honey. Something about Morrow and Shultz's friendship. I can't pinpoint what I'm thinking."

Winona was conspicuously quiet, although she was making a lot of notations.

"I think Timberlane offed his Santa," Keisha said.

A theory hit me with the force of a flying asteroid, and I sat my fork down. "What if 'the girls' Joe referred to are a group of children or women at the community center?"

"Oh! Maybe we should go undercover to find out."

Winona bounced up and down in her seat. "They might need us to save them. We could be heroes. They could interview us on the news and give us Good Citizen Awards. You know, they do that sometimes. My Great Uncle Ralph got drunk and ran headfirst into a wasp nest. When he was trying to get away, he fell down a well. He got stuck there for an entire night. My Great Aunt Sally couldn't find him, and the chickens were really hungry."

Keisha gawked, and Aunt Edith pretended as if Winona hadn't just told the most nonsensical tale in the history of the world.

"Winona, is that the end of the story because I don't see what that has to do with being a hero or a good citizen?" I said.

Winona sat forward and looked each of us in the eyes before continuing. "Well, Mickey Unger found Uncle Ralph and yelled down to him—" She formed a megaphone and called into it, "'Don't worry Ralph, I'll take care of Sally and feed the chickens'".

"So, was Mickey Unger awarded the Good Citizen Award on the news for taking care of the chickens or for saving Uncle Ralph?" I asked.

"Neither. Mickey left Uncle Ralph in the well and had an affair with Aunt Sally, so she isn't my great aunt anymore."

Keisha slapped the table.

"Winona, who got the Good Citizen award?" I asked.

"Laverne, the chicken who saved Uncle Ralph."

"Please stop. I can't take it anymore." Keisha shook her head from side to side, her cheeks and lips violently vibrated, and her braids flung about, slapping at her face. Once she had shaken the confusion from her brain, she gulped her wine and pointed at Aunt Edith then me. "Don't either of you freaking ask how a chicken saved a drunk-as-a-skunk hick in a hole."

So much for Winona's passive note-taking and Keisha's pleasant mood.

Winona's cheeks turned crimson, and her shoulders slumped. "It's kind of sad because all of Uncle Ralph's chickens died. He said since Aunt Sally was a nagging bitch he was better off without her, but then no one reminded him to feed the chickens, and they starved."

"That is sad, but how did Laverne the chicken save Great Uncle Ralph?" I braced myself in case Keisha slapped me.

"Because she clucked so loud, Old Man Johnson came to the well and pulled Uncle Ralph out. Uncle Ralph was so proud he hung Laverne's award in the dining room between The Last Supper and his autographed picture of Jimmy Carter. Uncle Ralph likes Jesus and Jimmy and chickens."

Keisha groaned.

While licking icing off of my fork, I considered asking if maybe Old Man Johnson should have won the award but abstained. I had already pushed my luck, and I wasn't sure if I was more afraid of Keisha's wrath or Winona's answer.

"Maybe if you girls don't cause any damage or incur any injuries, you could do a tour of the Community Center." Liam, Tom, and Bradley all have memberships," suggested Aunt Edith.

The brain trust engaged in deep thought. I supposed we were considering which poor man we should choose to be our tour guide, or perhaps we were still stuck on Uncle Ralph's award-winning fowl and what she was doing beside a well.

West interrupted our scheming when he carried a cup of coffee and a bottle of wine to the table. "Just the way you like it, Shortcake. Figured it would give you a little boost to correct those papers." He set the cup in front of me, topped off Keisha's glass, and kissed his cousin on the top of her head.

"It's girls' night, West. Get lost." Winona swatted at him.

"Hi, Edith." He bestowed the most charming of smiles on my aunt.

"Hi, Weston," Aunt Edith said.

"Keisha, you're looking lovely, as always." West winked at her.

Keisha leaned back and swirled the wine in her glass as she looked West over. She raised an eyebrow in approval.

"Pop gave me Friday evening off, Shortcake."

Giddiness overtook me. "Yay!"

West put the chardonnay on the table. With his hands on either side of my head, he tilted it back, and kissed me. I hadn't yet kissed him from that particular angle. Perhaps it was that my blood had all pooled around my brain, but when Weston Westinghouse the Third let go of me, I was dizzy and gasping for air.

"Please excuse me. I've got to get back to work, ladies." He picked up the bottle and swaggered to his post.

Keisha watched his backside retreat."That boy has a fine ass."

"Eww!" Winona's bottom lip jutted out. "He got Friday off? I wanted off for my date."

Aunt Edith grabbed then chugged the rest of Keisha's wine. "All aboard, the taxi is leaving."

My aunt had reached her trauma limit for the evening and I had an interminable night of mediocre essays ahead of me.

Chapter 15

Greg Grainey sat in the front seat of The Tank, sorting through a pile of cassette tapes. His obnoxious grunts, groans, and four-letter utterances had to alert the universe to his displeasure. I have no idea if ghosts typically had an odor, but Greg had doused himself in some sort of psychic musk that burned my eyes.

A dabbed at the tear dripping down my cheek. "Greg, I think you put on too much poltergeist perfume." I chuckled at my humorous alliteration.

Greg snorted. "Country music?"

"That's West's cassette," I said

"I hate country music and Westinghouse."

After sighing at the absurdity of Greg going out of his way to pretend he wasn't from a small rural town, I reminded him to be nice.

"Folk-rock? Are you a stoned fraternity brother?" he bellowed.

"That's Tommy's."

"What the hell was Little doing in your car?"

"He's my friend," I snapped. "You're way too nosey."

He slammed the cassettes about in his attempt to find one that met with his artistic éclat. "What the hell? Seriously? This singer's a dweeb?"

"That's Winona's."

"Christ," he said.

Greg's theatrics had grown each day of his ghostly existence. Give him an old mansion, a rusted chain, and a flannel nightcap, and he'd have a new business. His tantrums and spectral shenanigans could have fueled the scariest of haunted houses, or entertained Broadway-bound spectators visiting historic haunted theatres.

"Any cheese with that whine?" I asked.

"*Pfft*. Riders of the Purple Sage. What the hell kind of music is that?" He held my novel on tape in the air.

"That's Zane Grey, a classic book."

Greg grumbled and used one of my lines against me. "Eyes. Road."

His nagging was because he was irritated, not because he cared if I drove dangerously. Greg's middle name was danger, after all.

"There's nothing here worth listening to, so why don't we talk about something interesting, like my cock," the filthy talking ghost said.

I grabbed a cassette and shoved it into The Tank's mouth. Unfortunately, lyrics referencing the hottest spot north of Havana crashed through the old speakers. I figured if I took the time to swap tapes, Greg might take advantage of the lull to fill me in on the "extraordinary adventures of his magnificent love stick."

"What good is owning this beast of a car if you're going to drive this slow?" Greg asked.

I turned the clanging down. "I'm driving the speed limit."

"Yeah, I know. Like I said, too damn slow."

I rolled my eyes.

"I told you we should have driven my convertible. My CD collection is as extensive as my conquests."

It was my turn to snort. "I've told you ten million times that I don't know how to drive a stick shift."

Greg drummed his hands on the dashboard. "I could have driven."

"You can't drive. What would I do if all of a sudden, you just faded away, or someone saw your car without a driver?"

"I don't give a fuck what people think. I'm dead," he said.

He had a point. However, I was still a live professor who was entirely too scandalous.

"People already think I'm crazy. And if anyone saw me in your car, they'd think I stole it. Your daughter and wife would like nothing more than to see me locked in a prison cell."

Greg was a master pouter and his spoiled brat energy filled the front seat of the largest car in the world.

"Greg, why don't you just enjoy the ride? Look at the scenery. Be happy we're friends and that we're spending the afternoon together."

"I do like the scenery," he said.

We rode the rest of the way in silence. I gazed at the road. Greg stared at me.

****

I pushed on the door beneath a sign that read *Madame's Brews and True Psychic Readings: Palms, Tarot, and Medium* and a dozen bells tinkled.

When Greg walked across the store to greet the lovely woman behind the counter, the craziest thing happened. He didn't slide or float. He pulled his shoulders back and strutted like the living playboy Greg Grainey. He wrapped Alina in an embrace, and his hands caressed her rear. She returned the gesture, her hands kneading his jeaned bottom.

I wrinkled my nose as his mouth swallowed hers. Although it was a disgusting display of public affection, I gawked because Greg didn't appear wispy.

After their groping session, Greg pulled from his lover's embrace to introduce us. "This is Crimson. Crimson, Alina."

"We know each other," Alina said in her nasally New York accent. She extended her bangled arm and brushed a strand of hair from my cheek.

"Hello, Alina," I said.

Alina and I had met a few weeks prior. I had told her I was searching for information about Suzy Smith's murder. Although it was the truth, I had also wanted to find a kindred spirit.

She held her chin high. "My dear, I think de last time we talked, you accused me of bein' a fraud."

"Well, you can't read palms or minds, and you aren't from Romania." I held my breath and waited for the rebuttal I knew was coming.

"Child's play. I speak to de dead, de greatest psychic gift of all." She lifted her chin even higher. "I may have been raised in Brooklyn, but my grandmother was from Romania."

Since he could save lives, Brad Gordon had trumped both Alina and me. But, in the case she could put a spell on me with one of her magic brews, have me haunted by a sociopath, or had a voodoo doll workshop somewhere on the premises, I decided to keep my opinion to myself.

Alina retrieved the spectacles that sat on a long wooden counter. She proped them on her nose and folded her arms across her torso. She may have been looking me over, but it didn't spare her a second of my scrutiny.

The forty-something Alina was lovely. All thick curly hair and big dark eyes. Her peasant blouse and floral skirt added to her mystical allure.

"Gregawhy, she's pale and much too young for you. Also, she's a bit top-heavy."

I covered my chest, and my face caught fire. "I'm in the room." I hated it when people talked about me like I wasn't standing three feet away.

"Yeah," Greg said. "I like those things."

I narrowed my eyes.

Alina laughed. "I suppose you do. She's beautiful, though."

"Still here." I waved my arms at them.

"Come."

Alina grabbed Greg's hand, and he grabbed mine. Greg's body took on a somewhat tangible form. I concluded it was a trick of the light in the dark stairwell. Linked like construction paper Christmas garland, the three of us climbed the stairs and entered a room I hadn't yet seen.

Alina lived above her store. A mint-colored kitchenette made up one end of the studio apartment, and her bed, nightstand, and dresser were strategically arranged at the other. A vase of fresh flowers sat atop a lace doily in the center of a cottage breakfast table. She had beautified a plain white lampshade using a fringed pink scarf, and a crocheted rosette blanket covered her mattress. Each of the granny squares showcased a 3D rose in various shades of pinks and reds.

A box containing jeweled bracelets and earrings

overflowed onto her dresser. Dozens of floral skirts, colorful blouses, and flowing dresses hung from an exposed metal clothes rack. I couldn't see her bathroom from my position, but I imagined it was as lacey and romantic as the rest of the apartment.

Her light and dreamy living area contrasted with the heavy velvets and gold tassels of her storefront and psychic quarters.

Of course Greg liked her. Her feminine playfulness met his masculine prowess head-on.

We sat in rod-iron chairs reminiscent of an ice cream shop I had visited when I was a child.

She poured two cups of tea. "Sugar and cream?"

"Both." I ran my finger over a hand-painted rose that decorated the delicate china cup she placed in front of me.

"I want a shot," said Greg, ruining girl tea time.

"Gregawhy!" Alina waved a finger back and forth and *tsk*ed. "You know it doesn't work that way, and it messes with your energy."

"Damn." He crossed his arms over his chest, leaned back in his tiny chair, and frowned. Meanwhile, he wavered back and forth between wispy lines and a more tangible, less flimsy form.

Alina sat out a plate of iced petit fours. An edible purple bow topped each bite-sized cake.

My mouth watered.

Alina caught me patting at drool and smiled. "Gregawhy said you wanna see me. Do you wish to speak to someone on de other side, or what?

"No. I want to talk to you about Gregory."

Greg puffed up his chest. "Told you, Alina, my Crimson's crazy about me."

I grunted. "Alina, it's his boundaries. He doesn't have any."

"Hey," Greg said. "I resent that remark."

Alina shushed him. "Go on, dear."

"My mentor is a psychology professor. He was a practicing therapist, and he's helping me deal with my energy issues. I asked him to work with Greg, but he suggested we come to you."

Greg's chin jutted back in indignation. "What the hell? I don't need a psychologist."

I stared Greg down. "Yes, you do. But there is no listing for ghost therapist in the yellow pages, so here we are."

Greg *harrumph*ed and squinted one eye. I supposed it was his theatrical way of telling me that he was too irritated to view me with both eyes.

"Anyway, he shows up when I'm on dates, and sometimes he lurks outside my shower. There are times I have to remind him to put on clothes. He's haunting my friends. The list of my concerns is pretty long."

"Like my cock." He grinned. "And tell the truth. I only harass your male friends, and you don't seem to mind when I haunt and torment your enemies."

"I kind of like it when he torments this obnoxious cop I hate. But still—" I waved my hands. "The rest is too much."

Alina's voice was stern. "A woman needs privacy, especially in her bathing chambers. Remember I have told you only to enter when invited."

"Shit." His head hung in shame, suggesting he also barged in on Alina whenever he felt like it.

"Greg, you can't keep showing up on my dates." I cut my gaze to the medium. "I have a boyfriend, and

Greg got so jealous he had a tantrum, and I fell and herniated a disk."

"Her boyfriend's a pain in my ass."

I gritted my teeth. "He has never done a thing to you!"

Greg squished up his handsome face. "He's a cock block with all that country boy charm. Plus, his hair is annoying."

Alina sipped her tea.

I had no response and lacked discipline, so I shoveled in one of the treats. "Mmm," I muttered before remembering that my orgasmic reaction to sweets tended to set off the deprived ghost.

My discretion was a bit late because Greg entered into one of his full-blown hangry fits.

"Alina, tell Crimson that fucking on a kitchen floor and making out in a parking lot isn't a date. A date involves a movie and dinner before the fuck!"

I stuck a finger in Greg's chest and poked him ten trillion times. "Alina, tell Greg that West and I are going to dinner tomorrow night. If you would also be so kind as to tell him that I don't want to send him away because I think he's bored and lonely. But if he doesn't start behaving—" I stopped stabbing to thumb over my shoulder. "I'll throw him out again."

Alina frowned and gave Greg a shrug that I interpreted as you haven't got a choice, buddy.

"Greg, maybe you need a hobby like playing cello, painting, or haunting some old house?" I said.

"I think de girl's correct. We might need to come up with a list of things for you to do."

"I've got things to do. I check on the store. I visit my daughter, and I beg my ex-son-in-law to take her back. I try to get in Crimson's pants." He used his flirty voice. "Sometimes I get in your pants." His snippy tone returned. "And I haunt people I don't like."

"Bad ghost," I chided. "Alina, another thing. He keeps accusing me of shooting him."

"Right through his heart," Alina said.

I groaned. Greg had gotten to her.

"I didn't, Alina, I swear."

"Metaphorically, you destroyed him. He thought you cared for him but instead, you trapped him and left him no way out."

"No," I shook my head. "He should have told the truth."

She clasped my hand. "He will pay for his mistake every second for eternity, long after our energy fades." Her other hand caressed Greg's knuckle

I took Greg's free hand in mine. "I'm sorry. I wish it had never happened. I'd do anything to take it back." My voice was all sad defeat.

Three seconds after my hand made contact with his, Greg's body completely changed.

"Sweet sugarplums!"

Alina's "Omigod," slurred into one word.

"Jesus Christ!" Greg shouted.

Greg Grainey appeared to be alive. His hand felt warm, and there was a soft peach hue to his previously pale skin. Alina gaped as understanding dawned. We took our hands off him at the same time. It took a moment, but eventually, he faded. He wasn't quite as filmy as usual, but almost. We put our hands on him, and he became life-like. We did this a few times, and then we alternated who touched him.

Alina's touch was more powerful than mine, and

when we both put our hands on him, his form became as real as ours.

"You're like a glowing firefly," I said.

"Yeah," he said. "I'm alive again."

"No, Gregawhy. Not alive but energized."

"Like Frankenstein's monster," I said.

Greg grunted. "What the fuck? I'm no ugly monster."

I chuckled. "Alina, what's going on?"

Alina poked at Greg's arm, then his cheek. "I've never seen anything like it. I suppose that together our energy is so powerful that we're animating him." She ran her fingers through his hair.

Greg popped from the chair. "Come on. I want to dance."

Alina's face lit up. She stood and wrapped an arm around his neck. He pulled her close, and they twirled around the apartment a few times. On their third pass, they stopped in front of me.

Greg held out his hand. "Come on, Crimson."

Like a lady at a grand ball, I extended my arm gracefully, and the three of us spun. Greg hummed a waltz as Alina and I giggled. Seeing Greg happy alleviated some of the guilt I carried. The burden lifted; I danced, laughed, and felt incredible joy. The three of us whirled and pirouetted until I became so cold I shivered and so sleepy it became painful to stand. Without even asking, I crawled under the pretty rose blanket and curled into a ball.

As I snuggled in that bed, I recalled the happy childhood memories of listening to my parents' soft conversations fade as I drifted off to sleep. I missed those safe, soothing moments so much I ached. For a brief time, I relived them in that lovely apartment as Alina and Greg's voices carried to me from the kitchen table.

"Thank you, Alina. This is the happiest I have felt in years," Greg said.

Her harsh voice sounded gentle. "Your company makes me happy too."

Greg's statement was akin to luxurious velvet. "Do you think the princess is okay? She looks so washed-out?"

"She'll be fine. She isn't a medium. Her energy doesn't work like mine. I think it took a lot from her."

"So, if we let her nap, she'll be okay?"

"Yes."

It became more difficult to distinguish their words as my body relaxed.

"She's a good girl, but this guilt will destroy her. Think of your Jessica. What would you do if a man tormented her de way you torment that poor girl?"

"I'd kill anyone who hurt either of them. I'd hunt the man down and…"

****

It was dark when Alina shook me awake. I panicked because the clock read seven thirty-three. I had at least a half-hour drive ahead of me and a lot of papers to correct.

Alina fed me a couple of her pretty cakes then sent us on our way, telling Greg that after I got home safely, he should come back for a visit. At the door, she slid a bag into my hand.

"A present for you." She kissed me on the cheek. "Chamomile tea, and don't wait for Gregawhy to bring you. Visit anytime. You and I will be good friends.

Okay?"

"Yes. Thank you, Alina." I hugged her

Greg beamed. "I knew my girls would get along."

I was almost out the door when Alina said, "Your mother wants you to know she loves you."

I faced her. "Do you know what happened to her?" I held my breath.

"No, she hasn't said."

"Can you ask her?"

"Dear, de dead come to me if they wanna talk, and I don't think she wants you to know."

"Will you try to find out if she comes to you again?"

She nodded.

"George Stiles and Joe Morrow? Have they been to you?"

Her expression clouded in confusion."No."

"Crimson's new mystery," Greg said.

"Ah." Alina wrapped Greg in her arms and kissed him passionately.

Greg and I walked to The Tank in silence.

We were on the road for almost ten minutes before he spoke.

"If anyone ever treated Jessica the way I've treated you, I would kill him. I won't ever hurt you again." Then Greg Grainey gave me the most sincere apology at his disposal—he sang to me.

"Mmm." Greg had the most exquisite singing voice I'd ever heard. "Another song," I begged.

Greg's voice as a human had been strong and melodic. His ghostly crooning was mesmerizing. He had a multi-leveled lilting timbre, like that of a siren calling sailors to shore.

"Greg, sing me a Christmas carol," I begged.

"Come they told me, Pa rum pum pum pum. A newborn king to see. Pa rum pum pum pum."

Greg's words lifted into the air and traveled toward the moon. I think a part of me followed after them. My eyes struggled to focus, and the road became blurry.

"Christ, Crimson!" Greg yelled.

Greg's frantic call brought me out of my dream-like state just in time. I swerved and barely avoided hitting an oncoming truck.

"Jesus, you were in the wrong lane."

It took me a moment to come around. For almost having smashed The Tank into an accordion, I remained surprisingly calm.

"Your voice is lovely and hypnotic. It's like a lullaby mixed with a drug. It made me sleepy."

"Shit," Greg said. "If I thought you might die and spend eternity with me, I'd let you run headfirst into a brick wall, but you'd probably go to heaven and leave me here in this hell by myself. So, don't you dare fall asleep at the wheel again."

"Try singing me an upbeat carol."

"Jingle bells, Jingle bells," he hollered in a voice akin to Tommy Little singing with a mouth full of marbles.

I chuckled, and we safely sang cheesy songs all the way to Bellmount.

****

I sat at my window seat and Spot rested his chin on my foot as I corrected the final papers of the semester.

"Hey, Crimson. It's your bedtime," Greg announced.

I rubbed my eyes and looked at the clock. I wasn't

finished, but the rest of the papers would have to wait. It was two a.m., and I had to be up in a few hours.

"Beep, beep!" I said.

Spot lifted his head and jumped off the window seat.

I gathered my papers into two stacks. Luckily the graded pile towered over the ungraded. I shoved them into my backpack.

"That's so gross." Greg cringed while staring at my green bag. "The blood is still on it."

I had no idea whose blood dotted the backpack since Greg and I had both bled out on it.

"I've scrubbed and scrubbed. I think it's permanently stained."

"You need a briefcase," he said.

"I need a briefcase, a cellular phone, a car that isn't single-handedly destroying the ozone layer, and according to your daughter, a new wardrobe."

Greg huffed in disgust. I was unsure if his reaction was due to my style sense or his daughter's snottiness.

I crawled under the covers. Spot hopped into bed, spun around two times, and settled into his c-shaped sleep position at the foot of my bed.

"Good night, everyone," I called to my turtle, rat, dog, and ghost. I switched off the blue swan-neck lamp and closed my eyes.

Greg sat at the window seat in my tower, looking out over his beloved Bellmount, as his hauntingly beautiful serenade ushered me into my dreams.

Chapter 16

Sean O'Sullivan was so far out of my league we didn't even reside in the same galaxy. When women used words such as "hot," "stud," and "testosterone-God" to describe the detective, it was in no way an understatement.

I would be remiss if I didn't point out that my ex-boyfriend, Bradley Gordon, the movie-star handsome physician, was also out of my league. Then there was the strangest phenomenon of all. Although Weston Westinghouse, the sexiest man in the solar system, had never been tied to any female, he had announced to an entire town that I was "his little Shortcake."

I had no delusions. I was Miranda Albright, the once chubby, silly-looking kid. I may have thinned out and discovered makeup, but I was still a nerdy bookworm with a quirky sense of humor that only I found hilarious.

The point being, I had no idea what was going on with the recent attention I was receiving or why the strawberry-blonde hunk was once again casually propped on the hood of The Tank. The only plausible explanation was that I was staring The Curse of the Redhead square in its mystifying ironic eyes. The problem was, according to Lincoln, reputable scientists, and the last of my common sense, curses didn't exist.

"Come on, Red. Hop in. We have places to go and

things to investigate," Sean said in the Sutton Hall parking lot as snow flurries landed on his tweed cap.

"I can't. I have a date tonight," I said.

"What time?"

"Five-thirty."

He checked his watch. "That gives us an hour-and–a-half."

I looked back and forth between my Tank and his undercover cop car.

"Come on. Hurry up, or you're going to be late for your date. You don't want to miss out on my big news." When I didn't move, he pointed at the passenger side door. "Tick tock. Tick tock."

Since I was curious about the "big news," I climbed into Sean's car ninety minutes before my much anticipated night with West. "Where are we going?"

Sean started his car, cleared his throat, and declared, "Shultz's house."

"What? No way!" I reached for the door handle, but the car was already in motion. "I don't want to catch Shultz cooties. Besides, I only have an hour because I need to get ready for my date."

"I heard you the first time. We'll be back in plenty of time, and don't worry, the cootie spray is in the glove compartment." He chuckled.

I groaned. "What's the big news, and why are we going to see Shultz?"

"We aren't going to see Shultz. We are keeping an eye on his house. He's currently locked up in the county jail for three murders."

I gasped as I flashed back to the funeral and divining Shultz's thoughts. "Did Shultz kill the guy who murdered Joe Morrow?"

Sean gazed at the road. "Allegedly. There's evidence Shultz killed a guy named Trenton Deckler. No evidence yet that Deckler killed Morrow or Stiles. Deckler is from Greenport and has a record a mile long."

"What evidence?"

"First of all, Shultz left a piece of his wardrobe at Deckler's apartment."

He must have sensed my confusion because he said, "He left a tie."

I slapped Sean's shoulder. "No way! Did the tie happen to be a cheap yellow and orange clip-on?"

Sean pulled up to a stop sign. He checked right and left before looking at me. "Yep. How did you know that, Nancy Drew?"

"How did you find out it was Shultz's tie?"

"The mayor of Bellmount identified it, and then the mayor of Greenport backed it up. How did you know about it, and why are you asking?"

"He wore the tie to Joe's funeral and was having trouble keeping it on."

Sean had one eye on the road and the other on me "Why do you have that funny look on your face?"

"That hideous tie seems to be bringing Shultz a heaping dose of bad luck. You said three murders. Do they think he also murdered George and Joe?"

"Back up," Sean said. "I was still filling you in on the evidence. It gets more incriminating. A gun matching the bullets pulled out of you, Joe, and George was found in Shultz's closet. There was also a Santa suit, a schedule for the community center party, and one of Timberlane's cards at Shultz's house."

"Wow. That's a lot of evidence. What about the

gun used to kill Deckler?"

"That was Shultz's police issued firearm, and a Greenport cop found it at Deckler's apartment beside the corpse."

"Does Shultz have an alibi?"

"Nope. He says he was home alone the evening of the first murder, working alone the morning of the second murder, and he was sitting outside Deckler's apartment the night of his murder. Shultz claims the last time he saw Deckler, he was alive. He doesn't have any idea how his gun got to the crime scene. He says he never entered Deckler's apartment and has no idea why the evidence was in his house. We're waiting for the fingerprints to come back on the gun in his closet. I doubt we'll find any on it, and we expect ballistics to be a match."

"Is Shultz claiming that while he was watching Deckler's residence, someone else snuck in and killed him?" I asked.

"Yep!" Sean parked three trailers away from Shultz's gray double wide and turned off the engine. His Optimum Optics sat on the dashboard untouched.

I stared at the odd little house on stilts. "I hate Shultz. If I could put a copperhead in his pillowcase, I would, but I know he wasn't the one who shot me. I would know his beady eyes anywhere. I also know he didn't kill Joe Morrow. I overheard him talking to Joe's corpse. He was pretty distraught and vowed to find the man who did."

Sean twisted to grab a folder from the backseat, then handed it to me. "Take a look at this. Recognize the guy?"

I slid a photo out and studied it. "No."

"Picture him in glasses and a Santa suit."

I double checked. "I don't recognize him. Do you think this is the guy who shot me?"

"Maybe. That's Trenton Deckler."

"It could be him. Honestly, I'm not sure. The sun was reflecting off the snow, so I didn't get a good look at him, plus I was scared." And my ghost was attacking him. "What are we watching for?"

"Someone. Anyone. Going in or out."

"Do you think that Deckler planted the evidence on Shultz and that Shultz killed him?"

"If I thought that, I wouldn't be sitting here right now because I'd have one dead killer and another murderer in custody."

"You think somebody else set him up?" I asked.

"The thing is, Shultz is a—"

"Buffoon, idiot, maggot poo," I said.

Sean laughed. "Pretty much. A serious screw-up. But even a fool like him wouldn't leave the weapon he killed someone with at the crime scene with fingerprints all over it."

"So you think this other guy committed the Santa murders, and then someone killed him and framed Shultz for it all?"

Sean nodded. "Yeah."

"How does a guy like Shultz become sheriff?" I asked.

"Probably his connection to the mayor."

I shivered at Reynolds's and Shultz's odd dynamic. "Do you think Timberlane has something to do with it? My friend Keisha Brown thinks he's guilty."

"No motive and he is alibied for every shooting. He spends long hours at the store, and a lot of employees saw him working."

"I assumed as much. What about Stevens, the owner of the Speed-mart? Something seems off with him."

Sean shook his head. "He was working at the convenience store at the time of Morrow and Deckler's murder."

"But not Stiles's murder?"

"Right," Sean said.

"Hmm," I said.

Sean interrupted my musings. "Are things still going well with you and the bartender?"

It took me a moment to focus on the change in conversation. "Yes. I'm crazy about him, and I have been since I was a kid. He kind of tormented me when I was little." I laughed. "I guess I'm a glutton for punishment. What about you? I find it hard to believe that you don't have a girlfriend."

"Not currently," Sean said.

"That seems odd. I mean—" I swallowed. "Well, look at you."

"Look at me? What does that mean?"

I blurted out, "You're handsome, and you smell good." What the heck? I chastised myself.

He chuckled. "Thanks. I guess." He exhaled. "I have an ex-wife."

"Oh."

"And an ex-fiancée."

"Oh," I said again. "Do you want to talk about it?"

He answered without hesitation. "They left me for similar reasons."

"What happened?"

"I was married for three years to a sweet

kindergarten teacher. Man, I loved her. I came home from work to find she had packed her bags and left. Two years later, I asked a professional ballerina to marry me. She performs with the Western Pennsylvania Ballet, and she took off with the lead choreographer. Both of my exes hated my job."

"I'm sorry. Do you get shot at, threatened, beat up, and humiliated a lot? Because I do." I emitted a sound that almost sounded like a laugh.

"No. I guess I'm not around enough because I travel over a couple of counties and work long hours. The work can get depressing as hell. I try not to let it get to me, but sometimes it does, and I can be moody. I suppose it makes me a difficult guy to love."

I kept my gaze on the house while Sean's singed my profile. "Why do you do the job then?"

"I guess I love it and hate it."

"I think I understand." I angled my body, and faced him. "You hate death and the disturbing violence, but you love bringing justice to families that have lost a loved one. The challenge of solving crimes gets you up every day and makes you fight through the tough times."

Sean stared into my eyes. "You get it, Red. I want to find a woman who isn't terrified that I won't return home every time I walk out the door. I'm thirty-four and not getting any younger. I'd like to find someone who understands how important my job is to me. I want to settle down."

"Sean, is that why you take me on stakeouts with you? Because I don't think cops are supposed to take civilians with them?"

"There's something about you. You don't seem

like the average civilian, and, somehow, I know you understand. Sometimes you seem more like a crime reporter than a college professor." He took a strand of my hair between his thumb and forefinger.

Because I'm a weirdo, telepath. "But I have a boyfriend."

He dropped my hair to press two fingers to his forehead. "Not to sound like an ass, but he seems wrong for you."

I considered telling Sean to go to H-E double toothpicks. "What makes you say that?"

"A few weeks ago, we watched him try to score with some college girl while he was waiting on us."

"He wasn't trying to score with her. He was trying to score with me."

Sean huffed. "He had a funny way of showing it."

"We have a long history. We've been annoying each other for over twenty years."

"He has been tormenting you since you were a toddler?"

"Tormenting isn't quite the right word. Teasing would be a more appropriate way to describe it. Don't worry. I get my fair share of shots in." A West-tingle hit my belly, leaving me breathless.

"He's a lucky son of a bitch," Sean said.

I flashed back to when I was dating Brad, and West had said, "Doc's a lucky son of a bitch."

Something was up. If I considered there was no such thing as curses, what else could it be? Perhaps it was Aunt Edith's cooking, I was putting on the pounds, and all the extra blubber was going straight to my cup size. I looked down at my freakishly large cleavage and sighed.

"What's wrong?" Sean asked.

"Nothing," I said. "I think it's time for me to go home."

"Just give me a few more minutes, Red. Something's up. I can feel it."

I'm not sure why my anxiety reached earthquake levels as I sat in the front seat of that cruiser. But a niggling nagging feeling told me "something was up," that I was in way over my head, and monumental troubles were headed my way.

****

West didn't answer when I knocked on his weather-beaten door. I checked the latch, and as usual, it wasn't locked. "Good grief. People need to secure their doors."

Murderers were overtaking the town, and inhabitants still thought they lived in the 1950s, where their next-door neighbor wore red cardigan sweaters and, without warning, broke into cheerful song. Certain that my late arrival caused me to miss West, I was about to leave when I heard heavy breathing.

"West," I called into the blackness. I detected a faint rustling, so I flipped on the overhead light.

West lay on his couch with the afghan pulled up to his chin. Wadded-up tissues littered his whiskey crate coffee table. A bottle of aspirin sat open, and a bag of cough drops had spilled onto the floor. West's breathing was labored, and he was sound asleep.

"Poor baby," I said.

West stirred and his eyes opened. "Hi, beautiful," he rasped.

"You're sick, sweetie."

"Just have a little cold. Sorry, I fell asleep. We

have dinner reservations. Let's go?"

I molded myself into the tiny space the curve of his hip left free and settled the back of my hand on his sweaty forehead. "You aren't going anywhere. You're burning up."

He frowned. "I'm fine."

"You most certainly are not. You are staying home tonight."

He grinned at me and croaked, "Wanna fool around?" right before an *achoo* exploded and liquid spurted from his nose.

I handed him a tissue. "As soon as you are better."

"Karma's a bitch!" His bottom lip stuck out.

"What?"

"I lied and told people I was sick so that I could run off with you. Now I really am sick."

"I think you might be catching my curse."

"Your curse?" *Achoo!*

"The Curse of the Redhead the evil witch put on me when I moved to Bellmount that makes me find corpses, and get hurt. It also makes you think you like me, and prevents me from being able to curl up in your lap and kiss you to death."

He grinned. "You can still kiss me. Come here." He was about to pull me to him but halted mid-reach to blow his nose.

I scrunched up my own.

"Am I gross?" he asked.

"Still super sexy. I just don't want to catch whatever you have. If I do, we'll have to wait for me to get better, and it will be even longer before we can kiss."

"Damn." He grunted.

I moved to the chair. "I'm sorry, I'm late. I was on a stakeout."

"With Winona and Keisha?"

"No. Sergeant O'Sullivan."

"O'Sullivan?"

"Yes," I said.

"What the hell? Why?"

"Get this! Shultz is in jail for murdering three people."

"What the hell?" *Achoo!* "Who?"

"George Stiles, Joe Morrow, some guy named Deckler—and for shooting me. I hate him, but he didn't shoot me, and I know he didn't murder Joe Morrow. Did you know they were friends?"

West raised a brow. "I didn't know Shultz had friends."

I chuckled. "Shultz was his usual buffoon self, and he knocked Joe's casket over at the funeral."

West grimaced. "No shit."

"Seriously, and when I was helping him up, I read his mind. He didn't kill Joe, but he wants to kill the guy who did. I suspect he didn't kill George either, but he might have killed Deckler, a low-life criminal from Greenport. Although maybe he was set up." I stared at the black television screen in thought.

West interrupted my reflections. "So, you did your little—" A wiggly hand motion above his head indicated my telepathy— "on Shultz?"

"Yep." I drummed my fingers on the arm of the chair.

"Earth to Shortcake. Can we get back to O'Sullivan taking you on a stakeout?"

"Okay," I said with a heaping dose of hesitancy.

"You know I support you using your superpowers to help solve crimes." West blew his nose. "But the detective is behaving unprofessionally. I think he's trying to get in your pants."

West's comment annoyed me and sounded like it was coming out of Greg's mouth. Although, if a relationship and getting in my pants were related, Sean had indicated an interest.

"Nobody is getting into my pants but you, Mr. Westinghouse, but not until you get better, so let's get you to bed. Come on."

"Really," he said, his voice so scratchy I could barely understand him.

"Really. Come on, you snotty sex god."

He groaned with each movement, making it obvious that his muscles ached. Once he was upright, he wrapped his arm around my shoulder and leaned his body weight on me. "Officer Hunky know about your superpowers?"

"No. Just you, Brad, and Lincoln."

Achoo! "Doc knows?"

"Come on, sweetie." I wrapped my arm around him and led him across the room to the bed. "Where are your pajamas?"

He grinned. "I sleep in my birthday suit."

"Of course you do." While helping him out of his shirt, I caught sight of his chiseled torso and gasped.

The all-knowing gleam in West's eyes indicated he knew the power he had over me. "Wanna fuck?" he asked right before he sneezed in my hair.

I ran to the bathroom, rinsed my face in the sink, and then returned to help him finish undressing. Once he was supine, I pulled the covers over him.

"I'm sorry, Shortcake. I'm hideous right now."

"Never," I said. "You would be handsome even if you were covered in bloody boils."

He snuggled into his nest. "You're a peach."

I held up a finger to indicate I would be right back. Then I raced around the apartment, gathering up his water, cough drops, and tissues. I arranged them on the nightstand, took off my shoes, and picked up the book that I was curious about.

"You're reading *A Clockwork Orange*?"

"Yeah. You look surprised. I'm not a Neanderthal."

I brushed a strand of hair from his eye. "I never said you were. I think you are the smartest, sexiest man I've ever met. Brawn and brains."

Even though he was feverish, West's grin knocked the wind out of me. "Better to fuck you with."

My finger lingered on his cheek, gently stroking. Oh, how I adored his playful sense of humor. "Do you want me to read to you for a little while?"

"Yeah." He gave the most imperceptible of nods. "Could you turn off the overhead light? It's too bright for my headache. There's a flashlight in there." He pointed to his nightstand.

I opened the drawer.

"It will be like camping." He gave me one of his adorable lopsided smirks that made me mushy.

I turned off the ceiling light then crawled into bed beside him. I switched on the flashlight and aimed it at the book in my lap. Our "camping" served as a reminder that West and I were both seriously lacking in material possessions.

"You need a table lamp," I said.

"Nah. I got my flashlight."

I supposed Weston Westinghouse the Third had his flashlight, and his eclectic apartment, and the happiest disposition of anyone I had ever met, especially since it appeared I no longer annoyed him. I opened the book to where a folded-up tissue was being used as a bookmark and read.

Fifteen minutes later, West was one of Mr. Sandman's casualties. I read a little longer because I didn't want our date to end. Eventually, I studied his handsome face in the glow of the flashlight. His bright red nose did nothing to detract from his appeal, and he resembled a slumbering angel. I wanted to wake him and whisper sweet sentiments into his ear for an eternity.

I brushed the hair from his forehead and started to tell him a secret. "West, I think I lo... Please don't break my heart."

I marked our place with the flimsy marker, then placed the book on his nightstand. I put on my shoes, turned off the flashlight, and then confiscated it—I'd return it later. After locking the door behind me, I turned on the flashlight, and searched the dark for attackers. Finding none, I sprinted up the hill to the inn.

I gasped for air by the time I reached the front porch. "Good grief!"

Even Aunt Edith left her home unlocked. And holy moly, was I in bad shape.

I kissed Spot then entered the kitchen where my aunt was baking.

"Hi, Miranda. I thought you had your big date with Weston this evening," she said.

"Hi, Aunt Edith. West has a nasty cold, maybe the

flu. Could you teach me how to make your homemade chicken soup with dumplings tomorrow?"

"Of course. I have all the ingredients."

"He probably needs some medicine and a thermometer. I'll go to the drugstore in the morning as soon as it opens," I said.

"Grab some vitamin C, tea, and honey. We'll make up a basket for him. I'll bake him chocolate chip cookies. You should learn to make them because they're his favorite."

Lucky for me, my aunt was the most thoughtful woman in the world, and we would assemble the greatest care package of all time.

I put down the flashlight and sat at the table. "Why don't people in Bellmount lock their doors?"

"I guess people feel safe here. We have a low crime rate."

"There have been four murders since August, and someone shot me."

She stopped forming dough balls to gape. "Four? I only know of three."

"Technically, the one was in Greenport. Sean told me about it. A criminal named Trenton Deckler."

"Yes," she said. "I just heard about that." She slid the sticky bun batter she had prepared into the refrigerator. "I suppose Bear County is changing."

I sighed then used my index finger to dig into the little circles on the olive-green gadget. After saying hello, I waited for Mrs. Little to track down Tommy.

According to Tommy, I could speak at breakneck speed when on a mission since it took me less than three seconds to say, "Hi, Tommy, It's Randa. I need to get in shape. I can't even run up the hill out front anymore. Can you take me to the Community Center right now, and can Keisha and Winona come? One more thing, do you mind if I ask around about George and Joe while I'm there?"

I dialed my best friend. "Hi Keisha, it's Miranda. I'm getting fat, and I need to work out. Tommy is taking us to his gym. Put on something comfortable, bring a flashlight, and meet me in front of the inn in fifteen minutes. Also, I'm super hungry for a Speedmart dog and a cherry Slurpicy. Oh, can you drive?"

I phoned the pub.

"Hey Winona. I noticed you guys aren't busy tonight. Can you get off work and meet me in front of the inn in fifteen minutes? Make sure you bring your notebook."

Aunt Edith gave me one of her what-are-you-up-to-looks.

Shrugging, I flashed her a cheesy grin. Then I ran upstairs and changed into black leggings and a black t-shirt. After emptying my blood-pack, I exchanged my papers and books for a black sweatshirt, West's flashlight, a loaded Princess, and twenty dollars from my cellular phone fund. My dream of owning the super cool Radio World contraption wasn't meant to be.

I fed Princess Pickles and Simon a snack then sprinted down the stairs and waited on the front porch for my friends.

My fingers remained crossed as I hopped about, trying to stay warm.

If Keisha had to test out the speed of her sneakers in a back alley, I was one dead redhead.

Chapter 17

Sandwiched between Winona's healthy down-on-the-farm, six-foot frame and Keisha's five-foot-nine-inch regal elegance, I studied our reflections in the locker room mirror. Winona wore her waitress uniform of black pants, a white t-shirt, sneakers, gold earrings, and a ponytail. Keisha had on a blue and purple two-piece leotard, scrunchy socks, and high tops. She had pulled her cornrowed hair into a high ponytail and looked like the 1989 Aerobic Fitness Champion of the Universe. I was envious of my beautiful friends because I had incorrigible hair and looked like a pregnant cat burglar.

I pulled my t-shirt over my belly and frowned. "I'm getting fat!"

"Nuh-uh. You just have big boobs," Winona said.

"Men like large-chested women, don't they?" It was a stupid question, but I needed to understand my strange effect on the male species.

"Duh." Keisha admired her hind end in the mirror. "And you're built like a brick shit house."

"Do you guys think I'm getting bigger?" I pointed to my bosom.

"No. Same as always," Winona said.

Keisha shrugged. "Like I said, a five-foot-three brick shit house." Her eyes widened. "Wait a minute! You aren't pregnant, are you?"

"What?" I had a moment of panic before remembering that I had my period a few days prior. "I knew it. I'm getting so fat, I look pregnant?"

"Grandma Westinghouse would skin West alive," Winona said. "You two better use protection."

My cheeks became the color of a ripe cherry tomato. No need to explain to them that due to a comedy of errors, West and I hadn't been intimate since the morning of the shooting. First of all, it was none of their business. Second, the realization saddened me. And third, they wouldn't believe me anyway.

"Maybe you are pregnant. You've been tired lately," Winona said.

I settled my hands on my hips and let loose. "I'm tired because I have suffered multiple concussions, been shot in the chest, fallen on the ice, and been attacked by a killer Christmas tree. Plus, I'm overeating because my aunt is a great cook, and I spend too much time sitting on my rump correcting essays. I need to get in shape." I poked Winona in her shoulder with each syllable. "I'm not pregnant! I'm fat!"

"Then let's do this shit!" Keisha declared.

Winona and I followed the fitness queen into the aerobic studio at the Bear County Community Center.

Somehow the three of us convinced Tommy Little to join a class of twenty women. He looked out of place in his red sweatpants and gray t-shirt. With a sweeping arm, he beckoned us to the back row.

"Hi Keisha. Wow, you look great. Like a pro," Tommy said.

Her ponytail of braids swung about as she acknowledged Tommy's compliment with a quick pose.

"Hi, Winona. Hi, Rand—"

The music blared, and a chipper voice called out, "Let's go, people. One, two, three, four, five, six, seven, eight. Get those knees up. Move it, ladies and gentlemen."

My brain refused to connect to my legs, and my knees fought back in passive indignation.

Our instructor, Ms. Perkypants, skipped to the back of the room to scream in my face. "Come on, girl. Don't be lazy. Lift those knees."

My body finally moved. However, I didn't enjoy the feel of it one single bit.

The second time Winona stepped on Keisha's foot, Keisha relocated to the front row, where she imitated the moves with precision and grace. Showoff!

"Single, single, double!" called out Perkypants.

"Augh," I said.

"Shit. Oops. Sorry." Tommy body-slammed me from the right.

"I think I've got it," Winona hollered right before she elbowed me in the nose.

After twenty minutes of a waterboarding style of torture, Perkypants bellowed, "Grab a drink of water, then get those buns of steel ready for more."

More? Was she serious?

Keisha didn't require H20 to be an aerobic wonder. Winona, Tommy, and I left a smelly trail of sweat from the studio to the water fountain. The other women in class daintily sipped at the water bottles they had brought with them.

"This is fun! I'm doing good," said the delusional waitress

"I like the instructor. She's cute and has a lot of energy," said the hormonal park ranger.

Nicki Pascarella

I said, "Grrr."

"Miranda, are you sure you aren't pregnant? You're grumpy," Winona said.

Tommy finished guzzling from the water fountain and wiped his chin. "What?"

"I'm not pregnant! I'm fat!" I mumbled as I marched back to class.

Things went from bad to worse when my cousin pressed his face against the dance studio window, waved his hands about to get our attention, then doubled over in laughter. I think he was more amused at Tommy's performance than my lack of coordination. Still, my mood regressed at warp speed. Liam needed to make up his mind! One minute he was a snooty accountant, wearing fancy suits, nagging me, and acting all prim with his debutante girlfriend. The next he was an immature twelve-year-old.

Liam beckoned to someone in the hallway as Perkypants called out, "Grapevine right."

Winona crisscrossed to the left, knocked me into Tommy, and Brad Gordon's face appeared in the window.

I grunted.

Even though I was no longer in love with Brad, he was too handsome to watch me make a fool of myself. Liam pointed at Tommy, and Tommy shot him a middle finger. Brad's subtle grin signified his amusement.

Clad in a turquoise sports bra, Gina Schuster popped up between Brad and Liam. My cousin rested his hand on her shoulder, and the three of them watched Tommy Little, Winona Westinghouse, and I run into each other—over and over again.

216

Eventually, they tired of our humiliating performance and walked away.

Eventually, the annoying music stopped.

Eventually, the sunshiney drill sergeant stopped screaming in my face.

Finally, I stomped out of the studio.

"I'm not going on a diet, and I'm not doing that ever again," I called over my shoulder as I pounded down the hall to the Director of Special Activities' office.

I would have to be pudgy for the time being. I also intended to be grumpy every time someone tried to take away my cookies, make me work out, or referenced the nonexistent fetus in my uterus.

****

Tommy introduced us to the graying, blue-eyed Ms. White. She invited the four of us into her office. There weren't enough seats, so Tommy and Winona stood behind Keisha and me.

"Tom is a wonderful asset. He is invaluable in setting up our summer camps." The activities director gave Tommy a goofy smile.

I cringed because she resembled his mother and was eyeing him like a chocolate brownie with fudge icing and sprinkles.

When she finished showering Tommy with moony eyes, she asked, "What can I do for you?"

"I'm a professor at Bellmount College, and our campus newspaper is doing a story on Joe Morrow. I understand he was a volunteer Santa here?" I lied.

Keisha extended her hand. "I'm the Assistant to the Dean."

"I'm Detective Westinghouse." Winona flashed

Ms. White one of her toothy grins.

Somehow, Keisha refrained from slapping Winona.

"A detective? Wow," Ms. White said.

Winona pulled her shoulders back. Her eyes got smaller, her cheeks widened, and her teeth grew in size.

I shook off my Winona-annoyance. "Ms. White, I understand Joe was to be the Santa at one of your events."

"He was scheduled to hand out presents and pose for pictures at our annual party for indigent children. He called two hours before the event to say he had an emergency he needed to tend to. He said another man would fill in. I was worried, but George Stiles came in his place and did a wonderful job."

"Do you have any idea what the emergency was?" I asked.

Ms. White shook her head. "No. I never asked."

"Anything unusual you can tell us about the party?" I asked.

"Like what?"

"Any strange people about? Did George mention anything concerning? Did he say why he was filling in?"

"Not that I can recall. But I have a problem. This coming week we have our special needs Christmas party and our Alcoholics Anonymous holiday meeting. I scheduled Joe to volunteer at both, so now I don't have a Santa." She batted her eyes at Tommy.

Tommy's knee banged into the back of my chair.

"Ohh. Ohh." Winona raised her hand as if she was in elementary school. "My cousin Clive goes to AA, and my cousin Cindi has special needs. Plus, I know a guy with a Santa suit. He has a beard—"

I continued to glower over my shoulder as Tommy's right hand clamped Winona's mouth shut.

Since Tommy had the impending Winona situation under control, I focused my attention forward. "I'll have one of my reporters contact you to follow up." I stood and extended my hand. "Thank you for your time, Ms. White."

"What about the guy with the Santa suit?" asked the desperate special events coordinator.

I shrugged, grabbed Winona, and dragged her to the locker room so that we could retrieve our jackets.

"Well, that was useless," Keisha said as we headed toward the parking lot.

Keisha was right. I had sweated for nothing, and now I would have to get Liza Smith, my star reporter, to do an article on Joe Morrow. At least Lincoln wouldn't have to murder Winona in her sleep for volunteering him.

"Hey Randa," Tommy said. "You know my dad sometimes hears gossip on his postal route."

"Has he heard something?" I asked.

"I don't know if it's true, but Mrs. Silva told him that Mr. Clifton heard that Joe was at the bakery with Lily Anne Stevens and that Gerty Bowers thinks they were having an affair."

I drew a mental diagram to connect the gossip dots.

"Lily Anne? The real estate agent?" Winona asked.

"Yeah. Lily Anne, Mike Stevens's wife," said Tommy.

I grabbed Tommy's arm. "Could 'help the girls' have been a reference to Lily Anne and a daughter?"

"Their daughter graduated from college last year," he said.

"They also have a son at the college," Winona added.

I let go of Tommy but remained contemplative as we tramped across the parking lot. Was Joe Morrow having an affair with Mike Stevens's wife? Were the girls Lily Anne and her daughter? Would Stevens have Morrow murdered and left in front of his store? Hmmm. That seemed unwise.

One thing I knew for sure, Shultz's unjust accusation was getting in my way of taking him down legitimately, so we needed to amp up the speed of the investigation. When it dawned on me that I wouldn't have had to torture myself with the stupid workout class if Tommy had provided me with his information upfront, it added to my lousy mood.

It was eight-twenty when I halted in the middle of the parking lot. "Let's get dinner at the Speed-mart. I'm buying."

"This the hotdog and Slurpicy craving you were telling me about?" Keisha asked.

I nodded, then congratulated myself for my surprisingly resilient attitude concerning my dining choice. After all, I had settled on convenience food when I was supposed to be at a fancy restaurant with my handsome boyfriend.

"I thought you wanted to lose weight," Winona said.

My jaw clenched, and I growled, "I would like to spy on Stevens for a few minutes."

"Oh," Winona said.

"Thanks, Randa, but I'm going to pass," Tommy said. "Trisha, the aerobics instructor, invited me out for a spinach smoothie."

I didn't even try to temper my gag.

On our ride to dinner, I expected Winona to pine away and get teary-eyed. She didn't. She was completely unfazed by Tommy's proclamation.

Keisha, on the other hand, looked as though someone had just peed in her fancy gym bag.

****

Winona compared nutritional values on snack bags while Keisha leaned against the freezer, sipping a pink Slurpicy.

Not only was I aching for West's kisses, I was also sweaty, chunky, and hungry. I piled a third layer of nacho cheese onto my hot dog, hoping it might take the edge off my irritation.

Even though I hadn't yet paid for my mess on a bun, I bit into it. The goo dripped down my chin. Once again, I realized that Shultz and I seemed to have a lot in common. I grabbed a napkin and attempted to clean myself. It was pointless since it smashed the cheese into the cotton fibers of my shirt. I moaned.

"What are you after?" Keisha lifted her chin toward Stevens, who stood behind the counter, watching a woman in a red bathing suit run across the television screen.

The three of us had tried numerous times to engage Stevens in conversation, but the show he watched consumed him.

"No way we are going to tear his attention away from her," Keisha said.

I assumed Keisha referenced the large-chested woman sprinting along the beach. It was no wonder his wife might have been having an affair.

"Hey, Mike," Winona called. "How's Lily Anne?"

Mike Stevens fixated on the screen. "Fine."

"She sold any houses lately?"

Winona just might redeem herself before the night was through.

Mike glanced at Winona. "Her business is slow. Some big company out of Pittsburg keeps screwing up her deals." He returned to his gawking.

I filed the 'big company out of Pittsburgh" away so I could fill my aunt in. I wondered if this might be E.R. Development. If so, besides being a thorn to the town council, Tommy, Liam, and Timberlane, the mystery business also seemed to be causing Lily Anne Stevens grief.

"Is your student working tonight?" Winona called to me.

"No." I chomped down on fake meat. I had every intention of paying for my hotdog. I wasn't a thief. I just wanted to have something in my belly before I made a mess all over the store.

"You know, these chips are unhealthy," Winona said.

Now that she had one workout under her belt, Winona was a health and fitness expert.

I took my last bite and washed it down with a sip of icy heaven. It was time to commence Operation Slurpicy. I kept my eyes on Stevens as I poured my drink onto the floor.

Keisha watched with fascination.

The distressed waitress gasped at the edible puddle of liquid. "Miranda, what are you doing?"

I put my index finger to my lips to let her know she needed to be quiet. She clamped her lips closed.

I carefully sat on the floor beside the drink. My

caution proved pointless because my pants soaked up the pink ice. "Eek!!" I stretched out my legs and got into character, exhaled, then went for it. "Oh my. I fell."

Stevens didn't look up from his television show.

"Oh my. I slipped and hurt myself," I yelled.

Stevens remained hypnotized by the lady in red.

Keisha stomped to the counter. "Jesus Christ. What's wrong with you? My friend just fell and hurt herself. We'll sue your ass."

Stevens shook himself from his fantasy and came out from behind the counter to study the disaster. "What happened?"

"I fell," I said.

"I can see that. Can you get up?"

"I need you to help me?"

"Are you Mason's college professor?" he asked.

I didn't answer because I was withholding that thought until we had skin-to-skin contact. "Can you help me? Please?"

Winona leaped to my side. "I'll help you."

I adored Winona, but my mood had become too sour to be in her presence for much longer. "No, I don't want you to hurt your back."

"My dad says I'm as strong as a Russian musk ox," she proudly declared. "I won't hurt my back."

I clenched my jaw. "I would like him to help me." I pointed at Stevens.

Winona's cheeks grew red. She frowned and looked at the ground.

I'd behaved like a hideous friend, but I needed to touch Stevens, and playing touchy-feely across the counter would have been creepy.

Finally, he leaned over, grasped my hand, and pulled me to my feet.

"I was the one who was here with Mason and discovered George Stiles," I said.

"Yeah. I know. I remember." He thought about mopping the sticky floor.

I held onto his forearm and fell into him. He steadied me as I clutched at him. "I was shot the same day as Joe Morrow."

Stevens' brain went into overdrive. *Damn. Poor Joe. It isn't fair. He was getting his life together. I hope they catch the guy soon.* Then his thoughts shifted gears. *Shit, I know that hair. She was in the car making out with the guy across the street that I thought might be snooping.*

"I recognize your hair. You're the chick who—"

I let go of him. "I need to get going. I'm late." I tossed the twenty dollars at him. "Keep the change. Winona, Keisha, hurry up! We're going to be late!" I raced out the door and jumped into the car.

My friends followed.

"What the hell was that?" asked Keisha as she climbed into the driver's seat.

"We have another place to check out, and it's getting late."

Keisha started her car. "Which way am I going?"

"Go out of the parking lot and make a left. Drive along the river."

I wiped a bead of sweat from my brow. That had been close. My kiss with Sean had been innocent, but I doubted anyone else would see it that way. Operation Slurpicy hadn't been a total waste. I now knew Stevens hadn't killed Joe Morrow.

Now to figure out who had.

****

I visited the Elmwood Trailer Park for the second time in one day. We drove along the river and passed by the town center, then the college campus, to get there. The neighborhood contained about three dozen trailers, and although well maintained, was poorly lit. Keisha parked her car eight trailers away. I grabbed my blood-pack and flashlight, and the three of us traipsed in the dark to Shultz's front porch.

I wriggled the latch on the sheriff's door. "Are you kidding? Is he the only person in the entire county who locks his house?"

"Maybe he locked up before he got his ass locked up." Keisha chuckled.

"Figures," I whispered. "Don't either of you know how to jimmy a lock?"

Winona shuffled her feet and looked about nervously. "Are you sure we should be doing this?"

"We definitely should not be doing this," I replied.

"If you're going to be a chicken shit, we can take you home," Keisha told Winona.

"I don't want to go home," Winona said. "But I don't want to go to jail either. My mom will beat me if I get arrested."

Keisha used a hip to nudge me to the side then took her turn fiddling with the lock. "We won't get arrested. Shultz is the only one who would cart us off to jail, and he's already there."

Where was Greg when I needed him? An industrial-grade safe couldn't keep him out. He had finally started to diversify his schedule at the same time I could have used his assistance.

Keisha peered over her shoulder at us. "Hey, dingbat. Don't you have any stories about great-great-great-uncles with pet unicorns who knew how to pick locks?"

"For Pete's sake, nobody in my family ever had a pet unicorn," Winona said.

Keisha grumbled something under her breath as she continued jiggling the knob.

"But my Grandma Westinghouse used to lock my Grandpa Westinghouse out of the house every Saturday," Winona declared.

"I can't believe I have sunk so low as to ask," Keisha said. "What did he do when it happened?"

"He had this homemade still in the woods outback. He liked to drink right out of the copper flute. Then, he would try to kiss Grandma, saying they needed more kids. Grandma told him they had too many kids already, and he should keep his whiskey-pecker in his pants."

I grimaced. The man I was crazy about had probably descended from moonshine and a "whiskey-pecker."

"Not why he got locked out. What did he do when he got locked out?" Keisha asked.

"Oh," Winona said. "He climbed in through the kitchen window above the sink and kissed her anyway. I guess Grandma always forgot to lock that one. I think that's why there are so many Westinghouses."

A meaningful glance passed between Keisha and me. We simultaneously leaped down the front porch steps to search for the kitchen.

"Hey, where are you two going?" Winona called after us.

By the time Winona caught up, Keisha and I were standing under a single-hung window that was the perfect size and placement to scream I don't need to be secured.

"It's so high. Why did he put his house on stilts?" I asked.

"Cause he's a hick," Keisha said.

Winona nodded in agreement.

"Meaning?" I still wasn't privy to all of the nuisances of being a bumpkin from the boondocks.

"Meaning he enjoys the smell of feral cats and angry skunks," Keisha said.

"They get in your barn, too." Winona shuddered. "Yuck! Putting your house up high can keep them out."

"Hell, no. It gives them a place to live," Keisha said. "They get under there and piss and ejaculate and do all kinds of foul shit."

Winona stiffened. "Keisha, you don't know what you are talking about. You should just go back to Pittsburgh."

"*You* don't know what you are talking about. I lived on Nanna's farm until I was a teenager."

I fought an urge to stomp my foot. "Shh, you two. I'm sorry I asked. If you don't stop your bickering, someone will hear us."

Winona looked at the ground and softly said, "Plus, this area floods. Being off the ground keeps the water out."

"Yeah. That too," Keisha conceded.

I sighed then studied our dilemma, concluding that if Winona lifted her arms into the air, she could reach the bottom of the window.

"Winona, maybe if Keisha and I give you a boost,

you can crawl inside."

"Oh, no way," Winona said. "You can't lift me, and I won't fit. That window is small. You're tiny, Miranda. You have to do it."

"I thought I was fat," I grumbled.

"I keep telling you; you aren't fat!" Winona said.

"For once, the dingbat is correct," Keisha said. "You got some kind of nutty thing going on in your brain. You look the same as always—mini brick shit house."

Winona bent low. "Come on, Miranda. Climb onto my shoulders."

"No way!" I said.

"I'm as strong as—"

"We know a Ukrainian cow," Keisha said.

Winona traded her hunched-over position for an upright stance. "No, Keisha, a Russian musk ox." She bent low again. "Help Miranda climb onto me."

I slid my blood-pack over my shoulders, shoved West's flashlight into the waistband of my pants, and wrapped my legs around the back of Winona's neck. As she straightened, Keisha arranged me on her shoulders.

Since I was excited, my "Got it. Got it," came out as a chant.

"Ouch! You're on my hair," Winona shouted.

I attempted to move her ponytail from under my bottom.

"Ouch," she yelled right before she toppled over.

Unfortunately, six feet of Eastern European bovine-ness landed on top of me.

"Ouch," Winona said when her elbow gutted me.

"Freaking fudge," I said moments after her head knocked the wind out of me.

"Are you guys okay?" Keisha asked.

Winona popped up and bounced on her toes. "I'm fine. I never get hurt. Are you okay, Miranda?"

Although I wasn't one hundred percent certain how I was, I said, "I think so."

They each grabbed a hand and pulled me onto my feet.

I shook off my mashing and wiped at the gunk on my butt. I guess a more accurate description would be that I finger-painted myself with the mud from Shultz's yard.

Keisha laced her fingers together. "Miranda, use my hands as a step, and then, Dingbat, push her from behind."

I stepped, Winona hoisted, and then the freakishly strong woman threw me face first into the siding.

I backed up. "Ouch." I rubbed my nose and blinked a few times to make sure I was alive. "How close to the window was I?"

"About two feet short," Keisha said.

"But I'm only two feet short standing here."

"Yeah." Keisha stared at the glass casing with contempt.

"Weren't either of you a cheerleader?" I asked.

"I was cool. I was a majorette," Keisha said.

"Oh, me too. I loved my baton," Winona said.

"I wore this short skirt and these sexy-ass white boots." Keisha swung her hips back and forth in a little dance.

"Me too," said Winona. "I also had a hat with a big white plume. It was so pretty."

"It wasn't Uncle Leo's pet canary, was it?" Keisha asked.

Winona narrowed her eyes. "I don't have an Uncle Leo."

Keisha sniggered.

"And you should stop teasing me about tragic things."

I wasn't in the mood to find out what was tragic about Winona's band front feathers. We needed to get into Shultz's house, and we were making a lot of noise.

"Come on, guys. Concentrate," I said.

"*Pfft,*" Keisha sputtered.

"After it caught on fire, it wasn't pretty. It was black and frizzy, and it smelled like Grandma Westinghouse's ashtray," Winona said.

I ignored Winona, but Keisha was horrified. "The fool that let you have a fire baton needs strapped to a gridiron."

"No one let me have a fire baton, Keisha. Grandma Westinghouse loved my performance, so she hugged me, and her cigarette caught it on fire. I ran around with flames shooting out the top of my head until my mom grabbed my hat and rolled on it. I was lucky. None of my hair burnt or anything. I was sad, though, because my plume was ugly, and everyone laughed at me."

Keisha palmed her forehead.

I couldn't decide between rubbing my brow and giggling. I ended up jumping because from out of nowhere, Keisha broke into song.

"La, la, la, boom." She danced about as her pretend baton twirled through the air.

"Blah, blah, blah. Laaaa!" sang Winona in a loud whisper as she marched across the sheriff's backyard. She spun in a circle and grabbed at something—I guess it was her shiny pretend baton that hurtled toward her.

It must have landed in her hand precisely because she bowed.

"Boom, boom, bam!" Keisha bellowed and kicked her leg into the air while Winona's vocal cymbals clanged! Their song crescendoed. They spun in unison, posed, and yelled, "Ta-da."

"Good grief." I rubbed my brow. "You two will wake up the entire neighborhood!"

"Jeeze, Miranda. You're a party pooper," Winona informed me.

"Yea," Keisha said. "Do you need to get laid?"

I grunted because Keisha had hit the nail on the head. However, I would never admit it. "Cheerleaders are probably more helpful than majorettes at breaking and entering." However, I wasn't brave enough to say it loud enough for Keisha to hear.

At last, they quieted, and the three of us thought until an idea hit me.

"Lunge like this." I demonstrated by taking a massive step to the side. I positioned the two of them so that I could put one foot on each of their thighs.

Keisha held me while Winona boosted.

I reached and touched the target. "Got it."

I grabbed hold of the bottom of the frame and pushed. It moved. They held onto me as I forced the window up. I gripped the edge and attempted to hoist myself through. Unfortunately, I had the upper body strength of two-week-old pudding. I grunted and groaned as they nudged me from underneath.

Lesson learned. Maybe I did need the gym.

Keisha counted. "One, two, three."

They heaved, and I pulled. My torso almost propelled through the open window. My legs waved about as I precariously teetered upside down, half in, half out, of my archenemy's house.

There were giggles from below.

"You okay, Miranda?" my ex-friends called.

I scooted my body over the metal casing and fell face first onto something soft. I grasped my flashlight and switched it on. Much to my horror, I wasn't in the kitchen. I was in the middle of Shultz's bed.

"Eww! Yuck!" I panicked and crawled off. I took a moment—or ten—to jump up and down and remove the Shultz cooties.

Being careful to touch his mattress and blankets with only my sneakers, I stomped onto the bed and peeked outside. The moonlight illuminated two faces and reflected off four wide eyes.

I formed my thumb and index finger into a circle and held it for them to see. "I'm okay. Meet me at the front door," I called in a restrained whisper.

The flashlight had been a smart move. I wouldn't have been able to navigate the path down the hall to the entrance without it. Keisha and Winona waited on the porch until I ushered them in and closed the door.

"What are we looking for?" Keisha asked.

"Anything that connects Shultz to Morrow, Deckler, Timberlane, or the Stevens family. The cops found a gun, a Santa suit, and other things they think somebody planted. We are looking for photos, letters, messages." I paused. "Also, look for anything that links Shultz to the brothel in Greenport.

"Aye, aye, captain." Winona saluted. "But I don't have a flashlight."

The universe turned upside down.

"You can share mine." Keisha tapped Winona on

the lips. "But keep your mouth shut."

The earth had righted itself.

Keisha and Winona rummaged around on a desk in the living area. I routed through the kitchen drawers. I found batteries, a shot glass, a pinnacle deck, a dozen pencils, a superhero figurine, and cough drops.

"Nothing," I said, right before a bright light shot through the kitchen window.

I jumped. Winona whimpered, and Keisha yelled, "Shit!"

"This is the state police. Come out with your hands up and remain on the porch!"

"What should we do?" Winona hopped up and down, waving her arms in the air.

"Quick! Jump out the back window!" Keisha's escape was thwarted when she met with a panicked wall of Winona Westinghouse.

I secured my blood-pack on my shoulder and slowly walked to the entrance. I held my hands high and exited first. A spotlight prevented me from making out more than a human shape standing in the street.

"Red?"

"Sean? It's Miranda. Please don't shoot us."

"Miller, put your gun down," Sean said.

When the light dimmed, I discerned that two cars had parked in front of the trailer. Sean held a bullhorn in his hand. Miller shielded himself with his car door and aimed a gun at my head.

"Keep your hands where I can see them," Miller called.

He didn't need to ask me twice. I wasn't moving.

"For Christ's sake, Miller. Put your gun down," Sean said. "Stay there, ladies. I'm coming up."

Miller disappeared into his front seat as Sean walked forward.

"Explain!" Sean demanded when he reached the landing.

"Please don't arrest me, Sergeant O'Sullivan. My mom will ground me," Winona said.

"Aren't you thirty-five?"

Winona pulled her shoulders back. "I'm only thirty-two."

Sean shook his head. "Want to fill me in?"

"Someone shot my friend here." Keisha thumbed toward me. "It appears as though you need assistance finding out who did it."

I considered Sean an ally. It was hard to say for sure because of my Weston obsession, but perhaps if I hadn't been crazy about the bartender, I might have given Sean the chance he requested. And given my affinity for a detective who tried to solve crimes, I cringed at Keisha's insult.

Sean glared at me. "I thought you had a date tonight."

I cleared my throat. "I did. West has the flu."

"Did you find anything in there?" He inclined his chin toward the door.

"Nothing."

Keisha frowned. "Not a damn thing."

Winona shrugged and looked guilty.

"Where's The Tank?" Sean asked.

"I drove," Keisha said.

"Ms. Brown, I'll have Detective Miller follow you home. Ms. Westinghouse, I'll give you and Nancy Drew a lift. Then the three of you will climb into your beds and thank your lucky stars that you weren't shot or arrested. Next time I catch any of you somewhere where you shouldn't be, I will cuff you and take you into the station myself." He leaned forward so that his face was inches from mine. "Any questions?"

Keisha was speechless.

Winona shook her head violently.

I thought about the contents of my blood-pack and winced. I was tired of begging Shultz to complete the paperwork for me to carry a firearm. When he got out of prison, I was going to bombard him with annoying, relentless requests.

The three of us followed the scent of fresh bergamot and citrus down the front stoop.

"Hey, you wanna follow Ms. Brown home?" Sean asked his partner.

A second later, the blaring police sirens charging toward us alerted us there was a change in plans.

Miller sniffed in the direction of the noise. "I called it in. The municipal cops are on their way."

"Are we going to be arrested?" Winona asked.

Sean sighed. "Looks like it."

Two police cars skidded to a stop and parked at cattywampus angles as Elmwood residents exited their doublewides to watch the show. While everyone was distracted by the arrival of more law enforcement agents, I slid my bag off my shoulder, shoved West's flashlight into the front pocket, and grabbed Sean's arm.

"Help me. Please." I did my best to calm my shaking. "Take my backpack. Don't let anyone see it."

"Shit!" Sean shoved it into the back of his car as Shultz's minions handcuffed the crying waitress, then wrangled with the feisty assistant to the dean.

I held my upturned wrists in front of me. There had to be a way out of our situation. Unfortunately, I had no idea what it was.

****

The officer who escorted us into our grand chalet didn't think it necessary to do a strip search on three "harmless" women. However, we were booked, fingerprinted, and given phone calls.

I was too embarrassed to call Aunt Edith, Winona was terrified to call her parents, and Keisha didn't want to scare her grandmother. West was sick. Liam would freak out, and Tommy was on a date with Perkypants. In case one of Shultz's toadies murdered us in our sleep, we called Lincoln so that someone knew where we were. I found it slightly insulting that Lincoln wasn't surprised by our predicament.

Both of the cells at the Bellmount Municipal Police station contained a cot covered in plastic. Unlike the movies I had seen as a child, there wasn't a toilet in the middle of the cell, and no one had graffitied slashes of day counts on the walls. The municipal jail was a holding place for drunks and brawlers. Trespassers were few and far between because western Pennsylvanians owned arsenals. Breaking and entering resulted in an angry gun owner blowing a hole in your torso.

Anyone locked up for any length of time was transported to the county jail in Greenport. A precedent hadn't been established for breaking into the sheriff's home while he was detained. Making matters more confusing, no Bellmount sheriff had ever been accused of three counts of murder and one count of attempted murder. The bumbling officers were flustered and had no idea what to do with us.

Winona, Keisha, and I shared a cell. Wilkes, the town drunk, had passed out in the other. Winona had her head in Keisha's lap, and Keisha gently ran her fingers through Winona's hair.

I stopped banging on the bars to say, "The good thing is, we didn't steal. They would throw the book at us if we pilfered something."

Winona sat up and wiped at her tears. "Miranda," she whispered. "Come here."

I sat beside her.

"I kind of stole something." She opened her jacket and reached into the front of her pants.

I held my breath as she removed a book.

"Everything okay, ladies?" an officer called.

We jumped and Winona shoved the book under her shirt and pulled her jacket closed.

I balked when I recognized the man. Unfortunately, I had gotten him into trouble a few months prior when I snuck into the Suzy Smith crime scene.

"Hi, Doug." Winona smiled at him through her tears.

"Hi, Winona." He blushed. "How are your parents?"

"They're good," she said. "But they're going to kill me."

He looked at his shiny black shoes. "That would suck."

"Do you guys know each other?" I asked.

What a stupid question. Of course, they knew each other. Everyone knew everyone in Bellmount.

"We went to high school together," Kline said.

"Where is Sergeant O'Sullivan?" I asked.

"No idea, Dr. Albright. Do you want to talk to his partner?"

It was probably safer to take my chances with the man who seemed gentle and may have forgiven me for getting him into trouble. Besides, I suspected he had a thing for Winona.

"No. I can talk to you. Are we getting out of here tonight? My boyfriend is sick, and I need to check on him."

"Miranda is West's girlfriend," Winona said.

"No way, a girl finally trapped Weston the Third."

I bristled but held my tongue. No use picking a fight with a cop while in a jail cell.

"Are formal charges being brought against us?" Keisha asked.

Kline studied Winona, frowned, then called down the hallway, "Miller, Hayes, can you guys come back here?"

The unexpected holler caused Wilkes to roll over.

I grimaced because I didn't want to wake the drunk man. He was notorious for mooning pets and people while under the influence.

The young cop who had booked us, along with Detective Miller, strolled toward the cell.

"The ladies are asking about formal charges," Kline said.

The young Hayes inclined his chin toward me. "Man, Shultz hates you. He'll want to press charges, and trespassing is a serious offense."

Winona whimpered again.

"Are we going before the magistrate?" Keisha asked.

"Not until morning." Miller faced the officers. "I'm

heading home. You guys need something else?"

"Nope. Night shift is coming on soon," Hayes said.

"Are we stuck here overnight?" Keisha asked.

"Yep," Hayes said.

"Could I get a snack? I'm hungry. My dinner was cut short." Since she was still irritated over our hasty exit from the Speed-mart, Keisha glared at me.

Hayes leaned against the bars. A nasally twang oozed from him. "Snacks? This ain't a fancy inn."

"I'll find you something to munch on," Kline, the good cop, said.

Hayes sucked on his cheek and slurped. "Unless you ladies want to see vagrant ass, you might want to keep it down."

The three of us sat quietly.

Kline returned a few minutes later with a bag of peanuts, a package of sandwich cookies, and three drinks.

"Will this work?" He slid the food through the bars.

"Thanks," we said.

He smiled at Winona.

The cops returned to the lobby, leaving us alone. We huddled together with our snacks and Winona's contraband, a 1957 Bellmount High School yearbook.

"Why did you take it?" Keisha twisted the top of a cookie and scraped the cream with her teeth.

Winona's shoulders slumped. "We were talking about being majorettes, and I wanted to see what they looked like in 1957. Plus, Miranda said, find pictures."

I supposed I had told her to find pictures, and it turned out to be a valuable acquisition since looking at the band photos entertained the ex-majorettes during our confinement.

We combed through the pages and found Greg Grainey's old football photo. A heaviness settled over us at the sight of his handsome image.

I turned the page to find a young Aunt Edith wearing a black drape and pearls. I tapped the photo. "This is my aunt's freshman picture."

"That's Liam's dad." Winona pointed to a photo of my Uncle Liam.

I didn't recognize him. He had died in a car accident when I was a toddler, and my memories of him had faded.

"He was handsome. Just like Liam," Keisha said.

Winona and I nodded.

"Are your parents in there?" Keisha asked Winona.

"No." My mom went to Lakeside, and my dad is older." Winona flipped the page. "Hey. It's Shultz, Stevens, and Morrow."

The three smiling men stood arm in arm in front of the school. The caption read *The Three Musketeers*. The Three Stooges might have been more appropriate.

"Well, now we know Shultz, Morrow, and Stevens have a past," Keisha said. "I bet that is what Edith tried to recall the other night at the pub when we were talking."

I kissed Winona on the top of her ponytailed head. "Great job!"

She beamed.

"Maybe we should take turns sleeping," Keisha said.

"You two go first," I suggested.

Winona stretched out on her side, and Keisha scrunched up tight next to her. I sat on the floor, cuddled under my coat, and leaned against the bars. I was a fabulous sentry. I passed out immediately.

"Hey, Red," a voice whispered, waking me.

It took me a moment to remember where I was. "Sean?"

He squatted down on the other side of the bars so that we were beside each other. "I went to the county jail to talk to Shultz, and he is going to say you had permission to be in his house. You will be out of here by breakfast."

I rubbed my eyes, thinking it might clear the confusion from my brain. It didn't help. "Why would Shultz do that? He detests me."

"Oh, he's pissed, and it took some bribing. But I told him, you know he didn't shoot you, and you want to figure out who framed him. Since he's a dick, he's letting you sit in jail overnight before he says anything. I couldn't talk him out of that."

"What do you have to give him?"

"I promised to find the responsible parties and get him out of there."

"Sean, why is Shultz locked up if you don't think he's guilty?"

Sean's lips twisted. "All of the evidence is pointing to him. Besides, whoever framed him might be careless and easier to catch if it looks like we are giving up on the investigation, and Shultz is out of the picture."

I nodded. "Do you have my backpack?"

"Yep. It's safe, but we need to have a little talk about the contents."

I cringed, then deflected. "You searched a lady's private bag?"

He huffed. "That lady is sitting in jail for

trespassing, and I'm saving her ass."

I bit my lip.

"No. I didn't search it. I'll stop by the inn tomorrow afternoon and give it to you."

My shoulders, that moments before lined up with my cheeks, fell into place. "So, we are definitely getting out of here by tomorrow morning? Shultz won't change his mind last minute?"

"He isn't going to change his mind. It's in his best interest to let your little indiscretion go so we can concentrate on finding the murderer."

Shultz's mercy seemed too good to be true. However, the scuzzball planned to let us sweat it out overnight.

"I feel terrible. I got my friends into trouble." I pointed to the snoozing women on the cot.

"They're big girls. They know right from wrong. But you have to start thinking before you drag people into your schemes."

"*Humph*! Says the senior homicide detective who takes citizens on stakeouts."

"Let me go get that backpack right now." Sean grabbed the bars to hoist himself upright.

I reached through them to grab his forearm. "No! I'm sorry."

He laughed. "I'm teasing. It's safe. I'll see you tomorrow."

Relief flooded over me.

He reached his other hand through the bar and ruffled my hair. "You got me all goofy, girl."

"I'm sorry, Sean. I think there is some kind of weird curse messing with your brain."

He leaned close. "Curse? Nah. It's your damn

perseverance. I like that in a woman."

I'm not sure why the heavenly smelling detective didn't find my post-workout, nacho cheese, earthy odor offensive. If the look in his eyes was any indication, he found it appealing.

I tried not to bat my eyelashes when I said, "Thank you, Sean."

Sean O'Sullivan stood, smiled down at me, then left me sitting on the floor of the Bellmount Municipal Police station.

Wilkes stirred and looked at me through his inebriated haze.

"Dang, curse of the redhead!" I brazenly told the lush.

The town drunk didn't want to talk. He wiped the drool from his chin and rolled over to face the wall.

I wrapped my arms around my torso and burrowed inside my jacket.

It was going to be a long night.

Chapter 18

I awoke with the sleeve of my jacket wrapped around my neck and Winona's sneaker kicking me in the face. Keisha was sound asleep on the floor, and Wilkes, the town drunk, eyeballed us.

I moaned, moved Winona's foot away from my nose, and rolled to face the wall. I didn't want to be mooned and was afraid eye contact might encourage the derelict to pull down his pants. A sickening stench permeated the twin cells. Wilkes's body odor had mingled with the smell of three unshowered workout queens. The unholy malodor proved my point. The devil had invented aerobic dance classes.

The snoring from the cell next to us indicated Wilkes had fallen back to sleep. Thank goodness, because a bare-bottomed geriatric sighting after a night in the slammer was more than I could handle. Unfortunately, a loud conversation coming from the front lobby alerted me that Aunt Edith, Russ, and Polly were in the police station.

"Winona," I whispered, tapping her thigh. "Your mom is here. So are my aunt and Russ."

Winona wiped the sleep from her eyes, and the two of us concentrated on the heated conversation.

Anger infused Polly's voice. "There's no way my daughter broke into the sheriff's house. Winona has never broken the law or gotten herself into any kind of trouble. She knows I would beat her."

Mumble, mumble, mumble, went a voice I couldn't quite place.

"If you mistreated those girls, you will be hearing from my attorney," Aunt Edith said.

The empty soda cans and cookie wrapper might make the mistreated girls' case hard to prove.

Mumble. Mumble.

"Why weren't we notified? Didn't they each receive their phone calls?" asked my aunt.

I cringed.

Russ's voice carried to the stinky cell blocks loud and clear. "Zimmerman, you better have your fucking ducks in a row."

Recognition dawned. I had met the gangly man when I'd been to the station to confront Shultz about a false parking ticket.

Keisha had insisted she trade places with me sometime before daybreak. Russ's bellow awakened her, and from her supine position on the dirty floor, she stared up at us.

I held my finger to my lips then cupped my palm to my ear, indicating she should remain silent and listen.

"Is my granddaughter okay? You better have treated her well. You know she's a good girl. I'm sure she didn't do anything wrong."

"Nanna," Keisha mouthed before dropping her head into her hands.

"Troublemaking redhead," said Zimmerman. Mumble, mumble.

"Let's place the blame where it belongs—an inept police force and a corrupt sheriff," exclaimed Russ.

"Agreed," said Nanna Brown.

I winced. Although Russ was correct, we weren't innocent. We had broken into the sheriff's house, and in his defense, he was going to cover for us. Besides, if Russ upset Zimmerman with his insults, the three of us might be imprisoned forever.

The phone rang, halting the conversation.

"Hello. Bellmount sheriff's office. Deputy Zimmerman speaking... Are you sure, sheriff? We caught them red-handed... You gave them permission?... Okay. Their rides are here. Bye."

Muffled voices made the rest of the conversation impossible to understand. Once the chatter subsided, Zimmerman strutted down the hall toward us. Keisha, Winona, and I stood at attention as he slid the bars open.

"Ladies, your rides are here."

Heads hanging, we left our cell of shame.

I jumped when Zimmerman bellowed, "God damn it, Wilkes. Pull up your pants."

Walking arm-in-arm, Winona and I knew better than to turn around.

"Christ! That ass is nothing to show off, old man. If you have any pride, you might want to keep that cratered moon in the dark," Keisha bellowed.

Although I giggled, by the time I reached the lobby, my overwhelming remorse had returned, and I struggled to meet my aunt's gaze.

Zimmerman faced our gang, put his hands on his belt, and thrust his hips forward. "Ladies, you owe the sheriff a heaping dose of gratitude for not pressing charges, or you would have ended up locked up at County. He is claiming he told you to water his plants while he was gone." He smirked. "Dr. Albright, Shultz also said he didn't want to have to spend time in the same building as you." Although his comment wasn't funny, Zimmerman chuckled "You know, Sergeant O'Sullivan also had a hand in getting the three of you out of this mess."

"Douglas Kline was very nice to us," Winona said. "He made sure we had snacks and pop and checked on us a lot. He should get a raise or a certificate or something."

Zimmerman looked the three of us over, his eyes taking on a lecherous quality. "I bet Kline was a regular maître d'."

Russ narrowed his eyes and stepped toward the gloating cop.

Zimmerman scrambled backward. Smart move on his part because waves of dangerous fury radiated from Russ.

Feeling like an incorrigible child escorted out of the principal's office, I kept my exasperation tucked inside as the seven of us walked out of jail.

Before we parted ways, I sincerely apologized. "Polly, Nanna Brown, I'm sorry. It was my fault. I dragged Keisha and Winona into this mess."

"Don't be ridiculous, little one," Nanna Brown said. "If someone had shot me and I had almost died, I'd be kicking ass and taking names trying to figure out who did it."

I wrapped an arm around Keisha's grandmother. "If you would like another granddaughter, I'm available."

Nanna kissed my cheek. "I always have room for Keisha's friends."

The heaviness of my situation faded at her kind

words. When I climbed into the backseat of my aunt's car, she faced me.

"What were you thinking, breaking into a house? You could have been shot."

"I'm sorry, Aunt—"

"Where in the hell is your gun?" Russ asked, his voice gruff.

"Sergeant O'Sullivan has it. It's safe."

Aunt Edith glared at me. "Why is the detective covering for you?"

"I don't know," I said sheepishly.

"Try again," my aunt said.

I cleared my throat. "I think Sean likes me."

"You should have called. Your aunt knew you were up to something, and she worried for the entire night. She even woke West up looking for you. The boy had a fever, and he spent the night fretting. Then we called Tom Little, Liam, then Doc. They told us the last time they saw the three of you was at the gym. We called Keisha's grandmother sometime after midnight, and she was beside herself. Thank goodness Lincoln called us early this morning."

My stomach churned. I tried to rationalize my poor decision by convincing myself it wasn't worth worrying them when I wasn't sure they'd even notice I was missing.

"To top it all off, your aunt had to set out a continental breakfast this morning. You know she feels guilty about things like that."

"Miranda," Aunt Edith said. "I can't claim to understand what you've been through. I imagine being shot was terrifying, but I think you need to consider what your obsession with these murders is doing to your friends and family."

"You're correct, Aunt Edith," I said.

"On the way home, we'll stop by the drug store and pick up a few things for West. We have a busy afternoon ahead of us. Remember, you have your chicken and dumplings cooking lesson. You can visit with West for a while and apologize for scaring him to death. Then you can help prepare tonight's pot roast because Lincoln and Alice are coming for dinner. You also need to let Tom, Bradley, and Liam know you are okay."

I stared out the window as we passed by the businesses on the main street. Besides calling Liam, Tommy, and Brad to confess my arrest, the day sounded wonderful.

"That sounds like a very nice day, Aunt Edith."

The back of my aunt's head bobbed. "I asked Lincoln if he could find a few minutes after dessert to talk with you about how you are coping with your mother's death."

I stopped looking out the side window to stare straight ahead. A sucker punch of monumental proportions smashed me in the chest.

"Yeah," Russ said. "Next time you go to jail, I need to know right away so I can get you out. Now, I'm probably going to have to kick Zimmerman's smart ass, and if Shultz doesn't sign your paperwork to carry that damn gun, I'll need to break every one of his stubby fingers." Russ faced me. "And, you need to convince that detective to return your gun immediately."

I'd keep Russ apprised of my arrests, and I would retrieve Princess, but I had no intention of talking to Lincoln about my mother's death.

****

After my brief incarceration, Aunt Edith and I spent the rest of the morning in the inn's kitchen. Even as a child, I loved the cherry blossom wallpaper and the red gingham curtains and tablecloth. The wainscot paneling, red Formica countertops, and pine floors added to the charm. Copper pots hung from the ceiling, and farmhouse decorations adorned the wooden shelves. The rest of the inn was elegant Victorian, but the country kitchen was the cozy hub where our family gathered.

By early afternoon we were ready to put together West's care package. It included homemade chicken and dumpling soup and a dozen chocolate chip cookies that I had helped make. We added pumpkin muffins, cough drops, a thermometer, vitamin C drops, tissues, vapor rub, and a *Wheels and Motorcycles International* magazine. Aunt Edith stuck a big blue bow on top, and I walked it down the hill.

West's door was once again unlocked, and he was sound asleep. I put the soup in his mini-fridge and left the basket on his newly repaired counter before trudging back to the inn.

Sean O'Sullivan had not returned my blood-pack.

Aunt Edith granted me a short reprieve, so I made a quick trip to the campus health center, where the nurse practitioner prescribed a green packet of monthly pills.

I spent the early afternoon Christmas shopping. After my brawl with the live Christmas tree, I still wasn't welcome at Lightsingers, so I did my gift buying at the town's four-store pseudo-mall. I returned home and wrapped my purchases.

My blood-pack was nowhere to be seen.

I spent the late afternoon preparing for our guests. I was in charge of chopping up the potatoes and carrots, polishing the silver, and setting the table in the guest parlor. The gold-rimmed green china embellished with purple and blue flowers and the crystal goblets sparkled under the chandelier.

Lincoln arrived five minutes before the hour. He donned a brightly colored sweater, and his wife, Alice, wore a classy emerald dress and pearls. After dinner, Aunt Edith closed the sliding pocket door, locking me away with Lincoln. I searched the room, my gaze settling on Grandma Zoey's portrait above the fireplace.

Lincoln cleared his throat to get my attention. "Miranda, your aunt, would like you to talk about your mother's death."

"Lincoln, we went to the Speed-mart last night, and I read Stevens's mind. He didn't kill Morrow. Shultz didn't kill Morrow either. So who did?"

Lincoln furrowed his brow. "I have no idea, but Keisha thinks it was Timberlane."

"That's because Timberlane keeps hitting on her. Keisha doesn't like to be hit on."

He chuckled.

"Sergeant O'Sullivan has my backpack. My gun is in it, and he hasn't brought it back yet. He will get himself fired because of his absurd crush. What the heck is going on? He says he likes my determination. What does that even mean? I think it is this stupid curse."

"It means he likes your determination," Lincoln said. "And I told you before, curses aren't real."

"There is also no such thing as psychics or ghosts, and since I have proof they both exist, maybe we should investigate and see if there is some sort of curse that makes handsome men fall for nerdy women. Although I don't want to remove the spell from West."

Lincoln ran his fingers through his beard. "Can we talk about your mother?"

"Do you think we can remove the curse from Brad and Sean but leave it on West? Is that unethical? It seems like some annoying aerobics instructor lifted it from Tommy." I snorted. "This girl is annoying. She has way too much energy."

Lincoln rubbed his forehead. "You have a lot of energy."

Even though I had great respect for my mentor, I glared at him. "I hope you aren't comparing me to Perkypants. She is Satan's evil aerobics adjunct."

Lincoln studied me with his inquisitive psychologist's eyes. "It sounds like you might be jealous that Tom has found a new girl?"

"What?" I pulled my shoulders back. "Absolutely not. I just don't like aerobics, and I hate that I'm gaining weight."

Lincoln slapped his palms to his thighs then stood. "On that note, let's go get some more pie."

I popped off the settee. "Yum! Pie!"

We returned to the dinner table, where Lincoln flashed my aunt a thumbs up. Who knew my mentor was capable of such deception? I adored him even more at that moment.

Aunt Edith bowed her head in thanks.

I sighed and piled whipped cream on two slices of pecan pie. Lincoln and I ate while we listened to Aunt Edith, Russ, and Alice talk about nostalgic holiday memories.

After the Harrisons left, I called Sean. He didn't pick up.

I walked down the hill to check on West. His apartment was dark, so I turned on his overhead light to discover him snoozing away. I kissed him on the forehead, and he stirred.

"Hiya, Shortcake."

"Hi, West," I whispered. "How are you feeling?"

"Good now that you're here. Thanks for the cookies and soup. They were delicious. I'll eat the muffins tomorrow."

His appetite was back, and his voice didn't sound as nasally, but his nose was still gooey, and there were dark circles under his eyes.

I brushed a wavy strand of hair from his forehead. "I'm sorry I worried you."

"Heard you were in the clinker." His laugh turned into a cough.

"Who told you?"

"Aunt Polly was here this morning, and Winona checked on me this afternoon. I think it's hysterical, although you do worry the crap out of me."

I gently rubbed his forearm as I studied his handsome face. "Want me to read to you?"

"Sure, grab my flashlight."

I grimaced and swallowed. I didn't want to admit to West that his flashlight was in my blood-pack beside Princess, and they had disappeared with a hunky cop who had proclaimed a crush.

"I'd rather smooth vapor rub on your chest."

"Sure." He rolled onto his side and faced me.

I grabbed the menthol and climbed into bed beside him. Concentrating on his skin beneath my fingers, I stared into his eyes.

Eventually, his breath evened out, his lids slid closed, and his lips curved into a contented smile.

"I can come back tomorrow and spend the afternoon with you," I said.

"That'd be grea…" West's voice trailed off as he drifted to sleep.

I laid beside him, wanting nothing more than to spend the night, but I had to find my gun. Eventually, I crawled out of bed, locked up his apartment, and searched the dark for marauders. Finding none, I half-heartedly sprinted up the hill.

I stopped in the kitchen and checked the message board. Sean hadn't called, so I had returned home for nothing. Spot and I climbed the stairs to the third floor.

Greg sat at the window seat, looking out over the town. He turned at my entrance. "You didn't spend the night with Westinghouse last night, so where have you been?"

"Jail. Where've you been?"

He grabbed his ribs and chortled.

I glared and tapped my foot on the carpeting until he finished guffawing like a fool.

"I'm working on a project. Did they finally lock you up for shooting me?"

I scowled at him. "I thought we weren't doing that anymore."

"Oops. That's right. I forgot. So why were you in jail?"

I sat beside him and looked out over the town. Twinkling colored lights lit up the view.

"Winona, Keisha, and I broke into Shultz's house and got caught. I could have used your help picking the lock."

"No shit. Was he there?"

"No. He's being detained in the county jail. Sergeant O'Sullivan believes someone planted evidence making it look like he committed this rash of murders."

"What kind of evidence?" Greg asked.

"The murder weapon, a Santa suit, Shultz's tie, and a few other items that attached him to the Community Center."

Greg's eyes clouded with confusion. "His tie?"

"You remember that cheap tie he had on at Morrow's funeral?"

"Yeah. It was fucking ugly. Everyone stared at it."

"And it kept falling off." I stopped talking to allow my idea to percolate, and when it boiled over, I leaped from my seat. "Greg, everyone at the funeral noticed that tie. It stole the show!"

Greg nodded in agreement.

I held an index finger high. "So, if someone wanted to frame Shultz, a lot of people saw him wearing that hideous thing."

"Sure," Greg said, his gaze intense.

"Which means—"

"That whoever framed him had to know what a spectacle that tie was."

"Which means whoever did it was at the funeral," I said.

I grabbed a pen and a notepad, and we listed everyone at Konicki's.

"Do you know Freida, the prostitute?" I asked.

Greg's nose wrinkled in disgust. "Never needed a whore."

I grunted, then became contemplative. Under what

pretense could I visit Freida's brothel and do a reading on her? I couldn't imagine any of the men in my life taking me except Greg, and I wasn't sure I wanted to hear his commentary concerning my questionable idea. I had gotten Keisha and Winona into enough trouble for the time being. Would Aunt Edith take me? Russ? Dumb idea! I would have to keep thinking about it, but going by myself sometime in the next twenty-four hours was becoming more and more likely.

Greg interrupted my reverie. "What are you thinking?"

"What is this project you're working on?"

Greg dismissed my question with a wave of his hand. "It's kind of personal."

My inner alarm dinged. "Who are you haunting?"

"Don't worry yourself. How about I sing you to sleep?"

"Okay. Let me change first." I jabbed my finger into his filmy chest. "Stay out of my bathroom while I'm getting into my pajamas."

He raised his palms to the ceiling as if to say, Who me? "Fine. I'm behaving now."

I tried not to roll my eyes, then closed the bathroom door and repeatedly checked over my shoulder as I readied myself for sleep.

A few minutes before midnight, Spot curled up at the foot of the bed, Simon stopped his incessant running, Princess Pickles hunkered down in his shell, I pulled my blankets up to my chin, and Greg sang us to sleep with a lovely lullaby.

Chapter 19

Covered in goose pimples, I parked in front of the pub. I sprinted up the stairs, knocked once, and then opened West's door.

He lounged on his couch with his feet propped on his whiskey crate. His new motorcycle magazine sat on his lap, and he looked healthy and rested.

"Hello there, my little jailbird," he said.

With my hand on my chest, I panted. "Doggone steps. Are you feeling better?"

"One-hundred percent. Must have been a forty-eight-hour bug."

"Good. Then help me unload my car."

West grinned, and my heart flip-flopped.

I beckoned with curling fingers. "Hurry. Come help."

He put down the magazine but didn't move from his spot. "Patience, Shortcake. You need to learn patience."

I also needed to increase my cardiovascular fitness, and West needed to help me, so I didn't croak on his landing. "Hurry up!"

He laughed, shoved his feet into his sneakers, and joined me at the door. Before following me down the stairs, he grasped my face between his hands and kissed me. It was hard to focus with West's tongue in my mouth, but I refused to allow the distraction. We could make out as soon as my car was empty.

Two trips and ten minutes later, my breathing had stabilized, and boxes and bags littered his apartment.

"What's all this?" West asked.

"I have our afternoon planned."

"Does this plan include me getting in your pants?"

"West!" My cheeks burned. The truth was, I was only partially indignant because I was thoroughly intrigued by the concept.

West picked up a long thin box. "Is this a Christmas tree?"

I grinned.

"Cool!" He retrieved a pocketknife from his nightstand, sliced the box open, and pulled out a pre-assembled four-foot tree.

"Let's put it over here." I directed him to a spot beside his makeshift entertainment center.

He twisted the base into place and set the decoration upright. I fluffed up the branches, and he helped me hang a string of colored lights.

"I figured you like blinky."

His eyes twinkled. "You figured correctly."

After unpacking glass bulbs and silver bows, he plopped himself in his chair. "Shortcake, I wanna watch you hang them?"

"Oh, no. You don't want to help me? Are you still feeling sick?"

"I feel great. I just wanna watch you," he said in his sexy voice.

My girl parts got gushy, and I cast him a coquettish over-the-shoulder smile. "If you want."

My voyeur propped up his feet, put his hands behind his head, and leaned back. His lips parted and his breathing became heavy as he watched me from beneath heavy lids.

I hummed a Christmas tune as I busied myself with the task. I placed three wrapped gifts under the tree. Then removed a shiny star from the packaging and positioned it at the highest point. Once it was perfect, I stood back and admired my handiwork.

"Do you like it?" I asked.

"Yeah. It's the best Christmas Tree I've ever seen."

It was a miniature plastic variety store knick-knack adorned in bargain bin decorations, but the faraway look in his eyes indicated he was sincere. I also adored the cheap garnishment since it was our first tree.

He stared at the presents. "Are those for me?"

"Yes."

He bit his bottom lip. "What ya get me?"

"You have to wait. You can open them after your family holiday party." My shoulders did a flirty up and down dance. "That is if I'm your date."

West stalked across the room toward the packages. "Tell me now. What ya get me?"

I pushed him away, and we ended up wrestling. He grabbed me and tossed me onto the couch. I half-heartedly fought him off.

"West, stop!" I giggled as his hands traversed my body.

He licked at my lips. "Why?"

I moaned, then attempted to muster discipline. It was an almost impossible endeavor since West had a drug-like effect on me. "Because I got us lunch."

"Food!" He crawled off of me and sniffed the air in search of something to eat.

What a blow to my ego. A hoagie had too easily

replaced fondling me.

It took all of my discipline to unpack, then arrange a large roast beef sub and a soda pop, a small turkey sub and iced tea, two chocolate chip cookies, and a large bag of potato chips. We sat on the couch, ate our meal, stared at our tree, and talked about life.

"So, you wanna be my date for the party?" he asked.

"Yes!" I sang out with embarrassing enthusiasm.

He planted a peck on my forehead before devouring his sandwich.

"West, if you didn't bartend at the pub, what would your dream job be?"

His brow furrowed in thought. "I'd like to cook. Not burgers and fries, but gourmet food. Why? Does it bother you that I'm a bartender?"

"I love that you bartend because I get to stare at you and eat mozzarella sticks while you work."

"Gluttonous girl!" He kissed my nose. "I'd also love to race mountain bikes professionally. How about you? What if you weren't a professor?"

"I've wanted to be a professor since I was four. But it might be fun to write fiction. Or, maybe Winona, Keisha, and I could be fulltime detectives."

We laughed at the absurdity of the last statement.

"Your superpower thingy? He wiggled his fingers over his head. "Can you control it?"

"Not until recently. Lincoln's been working with me, and now I can most of the time. Sometimes I mess up if I'm tired, overstimulated, or surprised, and the filter I use can exhaust me."

He rested his chin on his fingers. "Tell me about this filter."

"Think of putting a piece of paper between two cheap refrigerator magnets." I demonstrated this by placing one hand over the other. "I'm one magnet. The person I'm touching is the other. The paper is like my filter. It keeps the magnets from sticking."

He looked toward the ceiling and nodded. "Makes sense. Can you do anything else?"

"You mean like move objects, bring things back from the dead, blow things up with my mind power?"

His eyes got big. "Yeah, like that. It would be totally sexy if you could blow things up!"

I giggled. "No other superpowers." I wrinkled my nose. "Wait. I can do one other thing, but it's related."

He encouraged me with go-on eyes.

Stalling, I sipped my soda, nibbled on a cookie, looked around the room, then sighed. "There are these things called psychic footprints. They are left behind after tragic events. I can sense and find them. That's how I solved Suzy Smith's murder."

"Holy shit!"

"Does it freak you out?"

"Still processing, but I don't think so 'cause I still want you to be my girl and to be my date for the party."

I threw my hands in the air. "Yay!"

There had been enough crazy revelations for one day, so I didn't bring up my obsessed perverted dead sidekick.

West sipped his soda. "So exactly how long have you been into me?"

"Since I was four, and you tricked me into eating that worm. It's embarrassing to confess since you weren't into me until the curse hit you."

"The curse?"

"The curse of the redhead that made you like me because why else would you want to date me?"

West put his food down to ruffle my hair. "Then I've been cursed on and off since I was six, and you ate that worm for me."

"Ewww. Gross!" I gagged. "But West, you have always been cool. I was nerdy and looked like a chubby cartoon character. You threw bugs on me and knocked me into the dirt."

"That was when I was little. I didn't master the art of flirting until I was eleven." He bonked my nose with his finger. "I have always liked how nerdy you are."

I playfully slapped his shoulder. "I also recall a few bug showers in my teen years."

"I had to fight Little for your attention. I was desperate."

Although he seemed sincere, I struggled to process his admission. "Do you miss all your other girls?"

He raised a brow.

"You aren't dating other girls. Just me? Right?" I held my breath.

"Just you, Shortcake. You exhaust me. I'm too damn tired to miss other women."

"Good," I said. "I will keep being a pain in the butt, so you only have enough energy for me."

He ran a finger over my cheek. "I'd like that." He wrapped the rest of his sandwich into its foil and tossed it onto the coffee table. "You know what Sunday afternoons are for, don't you?"

"Football."

"Only if you don't have a hot chick to kiss. If you've got a hot chick, Sunday afternoons are for making out."

I ran my hand over his forearm and batted my eyelashes. "Do you have a hot chick?"

"Yeah. Hot as hell."

He held my face in his hands and rubbed his thumb over my mouth. My aching lips lunged for his.

"Sundays are for going slow. Really slow. Like this."

His fingers threaded through my ringlets, and he gently pulled on my hair as his face languidly moved toward mine. When our lips touched, he lingered, and my body melted. His tongue slid into my mouth, and he set our leisurely pace. If I got excited or moved quickly, he slowed me down.

"Like this, love," he whispered in a voice akin to decadent chocolate-covered strawberries.

Eventually, he broke from our kisses to study my lips.

I struggled to form words. "Slow is so nice."

"Mmm. Yes, and Sunday afternoons are also perfect for my favorite game, What Do You Like?"

I focused my foggy lust-filled eyes. "What Do You Like?"

"Yeah," he said. "You tell me something you like, and I have to do it. Then I'll tell you something I like, and you have to do it. The only thing is, you can't cheat and use your superpowers."

"West, I never read your mind anymore unless I ask you first."

"Really?"

"Really," I said.

"I'm relieved, and that's probably a good thing. My mind doesn't always behave."

"Do you have inappropriate thoughts?" I asked

between chuckles.

"My brain is full of imbecilic immature junior high things. But when I'm around you, they turn into filthy lustful things. You wouldn't want to know about them."

Oh, how wrong he was with his last statement.

"I'm ready. Let's play," I said.

"You go first."

I curled my legs underneath me."I like it when you whisper in my ear."

He gathered my hair and tossed it over my shoulder.

I scrunched closer and tilted my ear towards his mouth.

"Pineapple."

I had no idea why he was whispering about tropical fruit, but his breath on my ear and his soft drawl were super duper sexy.

"Rubber baby buggy bumpers," he whispered.

"Huh?" I pulled back to study him.

His eyes gleamed with amusement.

I pushed on his shoulder, knowing my indignant response would only encourage his gamesomeness. "Let me try." I blew into his ear. "The British are coming."

"Oh, baby." He fanned himself and his lips cupped my ear. "She sells seashells down by the seashore."

I could barely contain my joy as I leaned close. "The rain in Spain stays mainly on the plain." I giggled.

He softly cooed, "Miranda, oh, Miranda. Wrap me in your beautiful hair, your soft hands, and your warm thighs."

I stopped laughing.

"Miranda," he purred. "Let me kiss your nose, your

freckles, your neck."

I was a mass of beating heart and boneless limbs by the time my poet recited his last line.

"My love, let me taste your sweet lips, your full breasts, your pretty pussy."

My body melted. "Oh, God, West."

"Are you wet?" he asked between kisses.

"Yes." I held his ear to my lips. "West, you make me happy."

He wrapped a wayward ringlet around his finger. "Now, it's my turn." He leaned close and nibbled on my ear. "I like it when you crawl into my bed."

I left his embrace to climb onto the mattress. "My turn again." I tossed him my best seductive smile as I lounged on his pillows. "I like it when you take off your shirt."

Standing tall, he positioned himself at the foot of the bed, and his gaze seared my skin. He lifted his shirt over his head and tossed it to the ground.

His jeans rode low on his narrow waist showcasing the V line where his hips met his pelvis. His bicep muscles popped, and his chest begged to be caressed. He was five feet, eleven inches of chiseled perfection. The curse wasn't a burden on my end since West was an Adonis, and he was about to make love to me.

"You're so handsome. I'm so—"

"Beautiful. The most beautiful woman in Bellmount, and I like it when you take off your panties."

I would have set him straight about inflating my aesthetic status, but I was busy sliding out of my leggings and underwear. Naked from the waist down, I leaned against his headboard.

"Let me see," he said.

"No. It's my turn."

The sensual West, who made demands and love like a magical art, replaced the silly, fun-loving West.

His pitch dropped to an octave that resonated in my core. "Let me see."

I opened my thighs for a second, then snapped them closed.

"No. Open wide and let me see."

I did as he commanded

He swallowed. "Fuck."

He fell onto all fours and crawled across the mattress toward me. I met him halfway. He grabbed the bottom of my sweater. I lifted my hands over my head, and he tugged my top off. I unhooked my bra, and he flung it into the corner, then his lips brushed my left breast.

"Shit!"

My filter crashed.

Damn. It scarred her perfect skin. What would I have done if she had died? I couldn't have survived without her. I think I—

I pulled my filter into place. "It's just a scar, and I didn't die, so you don't have to be without me."

West bristled and backed up.

I reached for him, but I wasn't fast enough. Weston Westinghouse the Third leaped from the bed and sought refuge from his freakish girlfriend behind a locked bathroom door.

My mind whirled following West's brusque retreat. I knocked on the bathroom door. "Sweetie, are you okay?"

"Yeah."

"Can I come in?"

The lock clicked. "No"

I ran my index finger in a small circle above the doorknob. "Do you have a stomach bug?"

"No."

"Was the roast beef bad?"

"I need a few minutes," he said.

Since West's abrupt departure left my body and heart aching, I ran my palm over the wooden door searching for his energy. "Please tell me what's wrong?"

"I said I need a few minutes."

My heart shattered into sharp shards.

Pushing my back against the door, I slid to the floor. Wrapping my arms around my body didn't keep me warm, although it symbolically shielded the world from my hideous "superpower."

I'm unsure how long I sat there, naked and pathetic. Eventually, the door gave and I braced myself so that I didn't fall as it opened.

West stepped around me. He still wore his jeans and socks, and his hair was more tousled than when he had left my embrace. He whistled as he strolled across the room to the dresser. Bending low, he grabbed a navy sweatshirt, and pulled it over his head. He opened the top drawer, and slid on a pair of work gloves.

I hugged my arms tighter as the jagged edges of my heart sliced at me.

West finally looked at me, and his eyes widened. "Christ!" He pulled me to standing, set me on the end of his bed, wrapped the afghan around my shoulders, and gathered my scattered clothes. "You're shivering. Let's get you dressed."

I stared into space as my bra swung back and forth between his outstretched fingers.

Realizing I had no intention of touching it, he slid the blanket down so that he could slip the straps over my shoulders. He struggled to put the cups into place and couldn't clasp the back since his fingers were under work gloves. After fumbling for a bit, he gave up, slid my bra off, and tossed it into the corner.

I quivered.

He knelt in front of me and attempted to wriggle my underwear over my hips. Again, he gave up and tossed my panties in the same direction as my bra.

He sighed. "Look, you have to help me. We need to get you dressed."

He anchored my feet into the bottom of my leggings. I remained motionless for a few more seconds. When I gathered the will to stand, he pulled my pants up, and I plopped down. He pulled my sweater over my head, and his gloved fingers awkwardly fought to remove my hair from the collar. Before he conceded that battle, he managed to get my arms into the sleeves.

"Let's talk," he said, sitting beside me.

I suspect his clumsy gloved hand meant to pull another strand of hair from under my sweater. Instead, it knocked into my chin, and rage replaced my zombie-like state.

I jumped from the bed, huffed to my shoes, and shoved my feet into them.

"Where are you going?" he asked.

I opened his front door and slammed it behind me. By the time I reached the last step, West was behind me.

"Wait!" he called. He hovered on one foot, while putting a sneaker on the other.

Grunting, I tramped across the parking lot.

He caught up to me, grabbed me, and forced me to face him.

"Damn it! We need to talk!"

"Why?"

The rough fabric reached for my cheek and slapped at my face.

Even though I knew it was an accident, I was furious. I grabbed the glove, pulled it off, and threw it across the parking lot.

I growled like a psychopath before tackling the hill.

"I'm sorry you heard my thoughts. But you broke your promise."

I faced him. "It was an accident. You scared me when you yelled. I'm sorry my stupid breast is ugly now. And I'm sorry I'm such a freak that you have to hide in your bathroom and wear gloves to touch me." I stared into his wild eyes. "I'd take the pain of getting shot again over the way you just made me feel. I'd take the beatings and the falls and all of the humiliation I've experienced since I came to this town not to have lived these last ten minutes."

He touched my cheek. "What about the other things?"

"What do you mean?"

"The other things I thought?"

"I have no idea what you are talking about." I turned my back to him and trudged up the steep incline.

I didn't stop until I reached the front of the inn. I stopped short and moaned. Keisha and Sean's cars were parked in the driveway and I wasn't in the mood to talk to anyone. On top of that, my ugly car was still at the pub, and my stupid keys were in West's apartment.

West stood in the same place I had left him. My anger instantly faded, and I ached to run to him. I fought my urge since the curse had broken, and he thought me bizarre. I knew the time would come, but I hadn't expected it to come at the high price of West treating me with disgust and disdain.

Swallowing my tears, I mentally prepared to retrieve my gun.

****

I found my visitors in the kitchen with Aunt Edith. A large tray of iced sugar cookies consumed the center of the table. Sean leaned against the counter, half a cookie in his hand, the other half puffing up his cheeks, and my blood-pack was on the floor beside him. Keisha sat slumped over, and Aunt Edith rubbed her back.

"Keisha, what's wrong?" I asked.

She looked up at me with red-rimmed eyes.

"Is Nanna okay?" I asked

"Nanna is fine," Aunt Edith said. "Why don't you and Sergeant O'Sullivan talk in the library? Keisha and I will wait here."

I reached for my blood-pack but wasn't fast enough. Sean pulled it out from under me, and tossed it over his shoulder. He grabbed another treat and headed to the kitchen door. I reached for the sweets out of habit, realized I wasn't hungry, and followed him.

By the time we got to the library, his cookie was gone. With barely any effort, he slid the heavy oak door open. "We need to talk."

I followed him into the room.

He pushed the door closed then stared at my

braless torso. When he didn't say anything, I crossed my arms across my chest.

"I thought you were stopping by yesterday. I waited all day for you to bring me my bag."

He clenched his jaw so tightly that a blue vein popped out on his neck. "I was busy. You want to explain the contents?"

"I always carry gloves, a book, and a couple of dollars. Although, I spent all of my money on a hot dog."

He tapped his foot dramatically.

"I was afraid I might get cold, so I brought an extra sweatshirt, and I borrowed West's flashlight. I think that's everything."

"*Pfft.* Your boyfriend's flashlight?"

"Yes. I don't have one, so I borrowed his." I suspected the issue Sean had with the flashlight wasn't that I had one, but that it belonged to West. The two of them were fast becoming adversaries. "Oh, and my lipstick was in the front pocket."

He raised his scarred eyebrow."That's hardly everything."

I pulled my shoulders back. "So I guess you searched it?"

"Yes. I needed to know what in the hell you didn't want me to see and what I protected. I assumed you had confiscated some inconsequential piece of evidence, not that you had a concealed firearm."

I lifted my chin. "It's not my fault. Shultz won't sign my paperwork. And, what do you mean inconsequential? Are you insinuating I'm too inept to know a valuable clue from a useless distraction?"

Sean stepped close and bent forward. He put his

handsome Roman nose two inches from my freckled one. If it weren't for the waves of fury vibrating off of him, I would have thought he intended to push me up against the wall and kiss me senseless. Not that I would have let him because I was never kissing a man again.

"You're not a detective or a cop. You and a firearm equal disaster. I'm done covering for you. Keep out of my investigation. Got it? Far away! If you come near it again, I will lock you up myself." He pushed the door open, and it slammed into its pocket. He glared at me from over his shoulder before leaving.

What in the heck had just happened? I sat on the settee for a few moments and pulled myself together. All I needed was for Bradley Gordon to show up and punch me in the face.

"Be careful what you wish for, right?" I asked Grandma Zoey. "I liked it better when men were dopey with desire." I pouted to the kitchen.

Aunt Edith rubbed Keisha's shoulders while I slammed my butt into a chair.

"What's wrong, Keisha?"

"Dean Johnson called me today," she said, her voice soft and defeated.

"On a Sunday?"

"Yes. I got into trouble for being arrested Friday night. He said that he was disappointed in me, and if I interfered with the investigation again, he would fire me."

Aunt Edith closed her eyes and let out a pained puff.

"Can he do that?" I asked.

"I don't know. I worked hard, and it took me years to prove myself. I love my job, and I don't want to lose it."

"Did you stand up for yourself and tell him off?" My best friend and the woman I admired would never kowtow to a man with a bad toupee.

"Of course not. He isn't Michealson or some witless son of a bitch. He's my boss and one of the few people I admire."

I rested my hand on hers. "But Dean Johnson can't wipe his butt without your help, Keisha."

She collapsed her upper body onto the table, whimpered, then sat up. "Well, apparently he thinks he can."

"How can you be in trouble, and I'm not?" I asked.

"I think you're in trouble, too. He plans to tell you to stay out of the investigation, and if you don't, he'll put a letter of insubordination in your file."

"How does he know about the arrest?" I asked. "It wasn't in the newspaper since the police dismissed the charges, correct?"

Keisha shrugged.

"No. At least not yet," said Aunt Edith.

"Sean is upset too. Someone must have complained about us," I said.

"Shultz?" Keisha asked.

"Maybe. But if Shultz wanted to punish us, he would have pressed charges. Who else would want to get us into trouble with the dean?" I asked.

"Mayor Reynolds dislikes you a lot," Aunt Edith said.

"Do you think it was him?" I asked.

Aunt Edith looked thoughtful. "It was someone who found out about Friday night, so I assume someone in the know. We haven't had a town council meeting since the arrest, so I doubt it was Jessica Grainey, Ian Patterson, or Pastor Smith. Bradley would never do anything to hurt you. And Reynolds knows everything that goes on at that station."

"Do you think it was Stevens because we were spying on him?" Keisha asked.

"I don't think Stevens would be privy to the arrest information," Aunt Edith said.

"Wait! Stevens is friends with Shultz. Maybe Shultz told him."

Seconds later, I shook my head because that wasn't it. Stevens didn't wield enough power to upset Sean or Dean Johnson.

"I bet it was Timberlane," Keisha said. "And Winona set me up on that damn date with him this week."

"I don't think it's Timberlane. How would he have found out?" I suppressed my glare since Kiesha was already distraught. "Aunt Edith, what should we do?"

"I suspect that neither of you is in trouble and that the dean is bluffing because someone is putting pressure on him. You have your union protection, and I think if you both lay low, it will blow over."

"Does that mean I shouldn't talk to Freida in Greenport?" I asked.

Keisha glowered at me as if I was growing horns. "What the hell, Miranda? The prostitute?"

"It means laying low, honey. Just do your job and hang out with West. No talking to anyone. Sergeant O'Sullivan is a good cop. Let him do his job," said my aunt.

Something burned my eyes.

"Could you please excuse me? I need to use the

restroom."

They both nodded. I picked my bag up by the strap and an "*Achoo!*" exploded from me.

"Oh, no," Aunt Edith said.

"*Achoo!*" I grabbed a tissue on the counter, blew my nose, and verbal diarrhea followed. "Sean is furious at me. Keisha and I are having our jobs threatened because I dragged her into my mess. You and Russ are disappointed in me, and I spent a night in jail." I blew my nose again. "West and I had a terrible fight. I don't think he likes me anymore. My heart hurts so much I can't breathe." I grabbed a handful of tissues to pat at my watery eyes and snotty nose. "Aunt Edith, I don't feel well."

Keisha held up her fingers in the shape of a cross, letting me know I was to stay away.

Aunt Edith placed the back of her hand on my forehead. "You're burning up. Get to bed. I'll see Keisha out and make you some tea with honey."

"And, I miss my mom," I whispered to Spot as he followed me up the stairs, where I laid on my bed and cried and sneezed until the early dawn.

Chapter 20

A half-hour in the shower did nothing to clear the mucus from my brain, and no amount of make-up disguised my red-rimmed eyes. Aunt Edith insisted I stay home from work. However, since it was the final week of the semester, a sick day was out of the question.

I didn't have an appetite, so I drank half a glass of orange juice and called it breakfast. I tucked Princess into my dresser and filled my blood-pack with tissues, cough drops, and aspirin. Then I left the cozy inn to brave the cold flurries. I had prepared to walk down the hill to retrieve my car, but someone had parked it in the driveway. Upon further inspection, I found my keys on the passenger seat with a note reading, *Shortcake, let's talk. West.*

I folded the painful, precious note in half and stowed it in my glove compartment. I sat in the front seat and reflected. The previous day had been crappier than the time Pastor Smith's goons beat me to a pulp. It was even worse than the day I was shot. It wasn't as bad as my mother's death or the day Greg Grainey died. However, it was the third-worst day of my life.

I called Pat Grimwood from my office phone. The arrest hadn't come across his wire and his editor had squelched his latest article about the Santa murders. Someone important was covering up the incident, rendering Pat voiceless. It seemed our release from jail had been another attempt to gloss over the crime spree.

My second phone call was to confirm my lesson with Wochowska. I asked him if he would look into a few things. We cut our conversation short because as the morning wore on, my sore throat worsened.

I planned to prepare my students for finals, but my garbled voice prevented them from understanding me. I changed tactics forgoing my lecture to write notes on the chalkboard, and I looked so hideous that even John Gibbons didn't rib me.

After my pathetic excuse for a lesson, I headed to the new journalism office. Keisha had recently secured us a room in the basement of Sutton Hall. The space didn't have a window, but it did boast an empty kitchenette, a large worktable, a cast-off sofa, two computers, and an outdated printer.

Liza Smith perched on a chair as Michael Dunlap handed her index cards to tack onto the wall-sized bulletin board.

"The office is coming along. You two are doing a great job," I said.

"We're planning the first edition for next semester," Liza said as Michael extended a hand to help her down. Once we were eye-level, she did a double-take. "Dr. Albright, you look awful. You should go home."

"You look terrible," Michael said.

I popped a cough drop into my mouth and grabbed a drink of water from the kitchenette. "Liza, I need you to write about Joe Morrow, the murdered volunteer Santa. Play up the human interest aspect and talk about his twelve-step rehabilitation."

Liza's lips twisted. "Dean Johnson was just here. He told me we are not to run any stories related to the Santa murders because"—in an attempt to imitate the dean, she scowled and attempted a stern voice—"Individuals in this town are impeding the investigation."

I wiped a bead of sweat from my forehead.

"Do you have a fever?" Michael asked.

"I'm not sure," I said, right before the floor shifted up then down.

"I'm assuming you want me to ignore the dean and write the story anyway," Liza said.

"What? No. I don't want you to get into trouble."

"But I'm a reporter. I do my homework and write a factual article no matter whose feathers I ruffle, correct?" Liza asked.

When I didn't answer, Michael said, "Those were your exact words our first day of class, Dr. Albright."

I plopped onto the sofa. "Boy, I'm hot."

After retrieving ice and a towel from the kitchenette, Liza assembled a cold compress, and Michael handed me my glass of water.

It killed me to go against the code I had instilled in my reporters, but I was in over my head. Perhaps if West hadn't broken my heart and my brain wasn't on fire from fever, I would have come to a different conclusion.

"Liza, drop any stories that have to do with the Santa murders. We need to lay low and do what Dean Johnson says."

"But Dr. Albright—"

"I'm serious about this. No stories about anything to do with the murders or anyone involved in them, for now. *Achoo!* See you both in journalism class tomorrow."

"There's no way you'll be in class. You'll be in bed," Michael said.

"I'll see you tomorrow. Remember, lay low." I coughed, blew my nose, and closed the door behind me.

I held onto the wall and staggered to my office. I opened the door to find the dean in my swivel chair.

"Hello, Dean Johnson."

"You look like hell."

I wiped my nose. "I'm okay. It's just a little cold." And an apoplectic boss, and a broken heart, and a mess of a life.

"We need to discuss your arrest and your interference with police investigations."

"Sir, with all due respect, I almost died, and the man who shot me is getting away with it. As much as I dislike the sheriff, they have the wrong man locked up. Besides, the charges were dropped."

Johnson was the grand champion of intimidating scowls.

"We pride ourselves on our upstanding institution. We hold our staff to high academic and moral standards. If you want to remain employed by the college, you will knock off the nonsense and apply yourself to your teaching. The first time you disregard my directive, you will be looking at insubordination. You don't want to even think about a second offense."

"I am devoted to my job. I'm just—"

"Go home and get some sleep."

"Can you tell me, did someone complain about us? Is that why Keisha and I are in trouble?"

He snorted. "Don't test me. If you continue to drag

Ms. Brown into your messes, you'll be looking at more than a letter of insubordination." With that, he got up from my desk, stomped to the door, and slammed it shut.

Three things were obvious. There was no way he planned to fire Keisha. Someone had told him to keep us out of the investigation, and he had no qualms about getting rid of me.

I had too much to do to go home. So I tweaked my final exam, then headed to the library to meet Wochowska for his reading lesson. He towered over the circulation desk as he talked to the eyelash-fluttering librarian.

"Hi, Wochowska. Hi, Betsy," I said before blowing my nose.

Wochowski winced. "Dr. Miranda, you look terrible. We could have rescheduled."

"I canceled our last two lessons. I didn't want to let you down."

He motioned for me to follow him to an isolated corner.

"I looked into those things for you. Lowalski says as far as he knows, Morrow wasn't gambling anymore, although he was hanging out at a whorehouse in Greenport," he whispered.

"Freida's," I said

"Yep. But the rumor is Morrow wasn't messing around with Freida either."

"What was he doing there if he wasn't using her services or gambling?"

"Lowalski says he doesn't know. He also says I'm not allowed to take you there."

I hacked and leaned against a bookshelf to keep

upright. "How did he know I wanted to meet her?"

Wowchoska backed up and raised an eyebrow. "Lowalski's exact words were, 'Wochowska, if that curious little professor asks you to take her to the whorehouse, you tell her no. This is out of control, and if she gets hurt, it's your ass!'"

"*Achoo!* Does he know anything?"

Wochowska shook his head. "I don't think so. He said too many people have died, his little redhead got hurt, and he doesn't want to be anywhere near this when the pissed-off homicide detective blows."

"Sergeant O'Sullivan?"

"Yep. He's going rogue."

"In what way?" I asked.

"I'm not sure. That's all Lowalski told me."

A pursed-lipped Betsy glared at us as we walked toward her desk.

"Dr. Albright, you need to go home because you are probably contagious and infecting everyone you come near." She studied at her new beau with lovey-dovey eyes. "I hope you didn't get Lester sick."

That was the moment it hit me. In an attempt to do the right thing for my students, I had been self-centered and exposed everyone to my West flu.

I hung my head in shame. "I'm sorry. I think I'll go home and rest. Both of you have a great holiday."

As I drove to the inn, I accepted defeat. Once home, I crawled into bed, where I spent the next thirty-six hours in an odd-dream-like state.

I had disjointed memories of Greg singing to me, and Aunt Edith woke me a few times to force-feed me water. I'm pretty sure Doctor Brad came to check on me, and I sent him away.

Also, West visited me and ran a cold washcloth over my forehead—although that might have been a wishful dream.

Chapter 21

Being careful not to spill my hot chocolate, I climbed the winding staircase, planning to curl up on my window seat with a book. Warm air blew from the furnace grates, the Christmas tree lights cast a soft glow in the foyer, electric candles lit every window, and the citrusy smell of pine that wafted through the air was an olfactory reminder of the season.

My pajama pockets held a couple of doggy biscuits, and Spot trotted at my heels. We were halfway up the first flight when the front door opened.

"Hello!" Winona called.

I balanced my full cup so that I could turn.

"Hi, Wino—"

Not only had Winona entered, so had West and a tall man wearing a checkerboard jacket and a thin black tie. The stranger's dark hair spiked into the air on top and hung down past his shoulders in the back. My ears caught fire because the odd-looking man and West gawked at my purple and pink kitty pjs. To add insult to injury, a lime green banana clip held the strands I had tossed onto the top of my head in place, creating a less than flattering Medusa look.

Winona contorted her face. "Miranda, Are you still sick? You're not dressing like that, are you? You look kind of…"

West tilted his chin to the side. "She's blowing us

off, Einstein. Let's go."

Since heartbreak, illness, and finals consumed my thoughts, I had forgotten about our triple date.

"I feel fine, I just lost track of time. Give me ten minutes. Winona, take the guys to the library and pour them a glass of wine."

I attempted to sprint up the stairs but my chocolate kept splashing down my arm. Once in my room, I set the cup on my dresser and called to my menagerie, "What should I wear?"

The turtle, the rat, and the Sheltie were no help when it came to date fashion. At least the pup joined me at the closet door.

I stared into my closet. "You have to do this."

My dilemma was layered. I couldn't back out on Winona because she was beyond excited for her big date. Keisha would never forgive me if I stranded her with the dingbat, the checkerboarded DJ, and the department store pervert. Besides, no way was Weston Westinghouse getting off easy. He was taking me on a date, I would look pretty, I would pout, and he would put up with it.

"Augh! Augh! Augh!" I cried.

Spot and I hopped about. Spot provided moral support. I acted like a crazy woman.

Finally, I settled on my short black skirt, a cowl neck lavender sweater, black nylons, and high heels. I took my hair out of the glow-in-the-dark clip and tried to finger comb. Since my ringlets were obstinate, I threw in the towel and pulled a few strands into a diamond clip. I coated my lashes with mascara, my lids with shadow and liner, and my lips with ruby gunk. I sniffed my underarms, gagged, and tried not to leave streaks on my sweater as I rubbed antiperspirant into my skin. After dowsing myself in perfume, I grabbed my blood-pack, and headed down the stairs.

Spot followed, sneezing up a storm.

When I entered the library, Winona's date gawked at my chest. Aunt Edith and Russ had joined my guests, and everyone but West had a glass of wine.

"Sorry," I said.

"You look pretty," Winona said.

"You look beautiful too."

Winona wore a sleek black dress that flattered her curvy figure and her make-up highlighted her pretty eyes. She had pulled her shoulder-length dirty blonde hair into a twist, and precisely placed tendrils framed her face.

Winona beamed before hugging my aunt.

"Have fun, girls." Aunt Edith's eyes sparkled.

West and the checkerboard shook hands with Russ.

West intervened as I slid an arm into my tweed dress coat.

"No. I'm fine." I nudged his hand away.

Aunt Edith glared at the dismissal of West's chivalry. She hated when I shot holes in the young lady etiquette she had instilled in me. I handed West my coat and begrudgingly let him hold the shoulders as I shoved my other arm in. Aunt Edith gave me a chin down in approval.

I turned on my stilettos then stomped out the door and across the front walk to Dinky's black sedan. West and I sat in the back, silently staring out our windows as Winona chattered from the front seat.

"Richard, Miranda is the youngest teacher at the college. She is super smart. Her students love her. We are like private detectives in our spare time."

I gaped at Winona's profile.

West let out a "*Pfft*" before I could.

I secretly joked about our sleuthing endeavors, but Winona telling people we were detectives humiliated me. Besides, I could balk at Winona's pronouncement, but I would not permit West to make skeptical utterances. I glowered at him.

"Miranda and West, Richard is a DJ at the radio station. Isn't that super cool? That's why the guys call him Dinky."

"And why he looks like Adam Ant," West whispered.

I ignored West because I had no idea what he was talking about, and I was setting my you mean nothing to me precedent for the evening.

I also had no idea how Richard, Dinky, and DJ were related. "Should I call you Richard or Dinky?"

"Dinky works," the goofy man said.

"I'm the only person who calls him Richard," Winona said. "Richard, West is my favorite cousin. We grew up together. He's good at sports, climbing things, and cooking. He has a motorcycle and a mountain bike. I think bikes are dangerous, so I hope he doesn't kill himself."

West wriggled in his seat, as my heart pounded at my chest. Although angry at West for humiliating me, it would destroy me if he ever got hurt.

"This is West and Miranda's first date. Isn't that cool?"

West and I faced each other. Was he also thinking, Holy crap, our first date? Did our stolen kisses and passionate lovemaking not count?

I sighed. I'd given West my heart and body, and he had found me so unappealing that he couldn't touch me without gloves. There we were sitting beside each other on what should be a romantic evening, and I was so hurt and angry that I couldn't talk to him.

Winona's blabbing faded into the background as West and I studied each other.

He leaned toward me and said, "You look beautiful."

A cream-colored sweater peeked out from under his ski jacket. He was clean-shaven, but his hair was its usual seductive mess. Aftershave floated through the air and my traitorous insides screamed *We Want West*. I closed my eyes and bit my lip as a tickle in my girl parts left me breathless.

West reached for my hand. "I'm so sorry."

I pulled away.

He rubbed his palm on his thigh. "Did you get my note?"

Sitting forward, I called into the front seat, "So, Dinky, tell me what it's like to work at the radio station. Do you have a favorite type of music?"

****

Keisha and Timberlane sat at a round table in the center of the Chinese Restaurant. Timberlane consumed Keisha's space, and her shoulders clenched her chin. She gave us an ear full about being late and her colorful expletives livened up the rebuke.

Since it was my fault we were tardy, I sucked it up and accepted my reprimand. I slipped my arm out of my coat and was about to pull out the other when West reached over to help. I pushed his hand away and he blanched.

"Keisha, it's no big deal. Miranda just lost track of time," Winona said.

West snorted. "Yeah, because tonight was important to her."

I tossed a dirty look in West's direction and dramatically slammed myself into my seat.

West hung his jacket on the back of his chair. "Be careful, darling. Doc isn't here to patch up your ass tonight if you get hurt." He sat down and smiled like he hadn't just said something hideous.

"Good thing I didn't bring Princess." I stared West down. "Because the doctor isn't here to patch up your behind either."

Keisha's gaze lifted to the ceiling, and she shook her head violently.

The waiter arranged a plate of spring rolls in the center of the table. Keisha and Timberlane had already placed their orders. I didn't catch what Winona and Dinky requested. West asked for water, wonton soup, and extra spicy beef lo mein. I ordered chicken fried rice, coconut pudding, and a cup of coffee.

"I'll have to make a fresh pot," our waiter said.

"Good idea. It's less of a pain in the ass for you to make her coffee now, so she doesn't—" West lifted a cupped hand to his mouth, tilted his head back, and gulped as if he was doing a shot. "I have to cart her ass around when she gets drunk. And nobody wants that. She is a foul-mouthed horny drunk."

Spittle flew from my mouth. "He's one to talk since he is foul-mouthed and horny as a rule."

West gathered the knives and handed them to the waiter. "You might want to take all the sharp objects. She has a habit of injuring herself. That way, she gets to spend time with her doctor boyfriend."

Everyone, including the waiter, gasped, and I slammed my spring roll onto my plate. The glasses and silverware clinked, and my appetizer sailed across the restaurant, hitting an innocent man in the back of the head.

"Holy donkey balls," Dinky said.

"She's sorry," Keisha said to the man when he turned to see who had beaned him in the noggin with fried cabbage.

I blushed while simultaneously gritting my teeth. "I'm sorry."

The man acknowledged my apology with a forced smile, then faced his date.

"What the hell? Both of you need to settle down," Keisha said.

"I tried to tell you guys that you were all wrong for each other," Winona said. "You didn't listen, and now you're ruining my special night."

Winona's comment was more than I could bear. It was a million times worse than any of the insults that West and I hurdled at each other because we were behaving like hurt children. Winona's comment rang true.

I stood. "Excuse me. I need some fresh air." I grabbed my coat and threw my blood-pack over my shoulder.

West's voice carried to me as I headed to the exit. "Winona, that was a shitty thing to say."

The main street of Greenport would have been charming, except the air was cold, the streets were slushy, and I was in a snit. The holiday storefronts, and the evergreen wreaths adorned with red bows that hung from streetlamps, did nothing to improve my mood. I donned my coat as I decided which way to travel. Then my heels splashed in the muck while I vented to the air that I hated Weston Westinghouse the Third.

West called to me.

I stopped walking, closed my eyes and listened.

"Wait up."

I extended my stride as wide as possible in my impractical shoes and headed away from him and down a side street.

"Damn it. Stop for a second." West caught up to me. "This is ridiculous."

I faced him and let loose. "What part? The part that you would rather wear gloves than deal with my telepathy? Or the part where you find me so unattractive that you would rather lock yourself in your bathroom than touch me?"

"Stop it. That isn't true. If you would just talk to me—"

"*Talk* to you?" Since people were on the sidewalk, I kept my hysterical voice at a volume that didn't create a scene. "So, you can pretend like you have feelings for me then humiliate me?"

"How many ways can I say I'm sorry?" He rubbed his forehead. "You're making me crazy. I think I'm losing my mind every time I get near you."

"Then don't come near me." I huffed and stomped.

He chased me down. "Listen. I know you have been through a lot, but so have I. I thought you had died. Don't you get that? The rumor was you were fatally shot."

"Rumor. I'm quite alive."

"Doc's right. You get hurt every time you come

near me. I want to protect you, and I can't, and he's always there to pick up the pieces."

"If you haven't noticed, West, I get hurt all of the time, no matter who is near me, and he is a doctor. He treats the injured." I ached to tell him that a manipulative ghost had planted the absurd idea in Brad's head.

"I waited for you all night. I didn't know where you were. I sat there with the fucking whipped cream and chocolate chips, wondering if you had finally gotten yourself killed. Do you know what that's like?"

"You are making excuses because you're a chicken," I said.

He shook his head and let out a snort. For a moment, I thought he might walk away. Instead, he caressed my cheek.

"When I saw the scar, I behaved like a chicken shit. But not for the reasons you think."

West's honest and raw comment tugged at my heart. I was about to ask him to help me understand his reasons for crushing me like an insect on a picnic table when a blinking sign caught my attention.

"Sweet sugarplums! What a crazy coincidence. Freida's Massage and Fantasy?" I stepped around him and headed toward the brightly painted building. "I need a massage."

"Wait!" West lunged in front of me. "That isn't a massage parlor. It's a whorehouse."

"How would you know that?" Maybe there was an accusatory tone to my voice. Or perhaps he thought me difficult since I was undaunted by his warning and continued on my mission.

He grunted. "I would tell you to go to hell if I

wasn't such a gentleman."

Our five seconds of romantically staring into each other's eyes had passed.

"A gentleman. Huh! I'm sure you have patronized it a few times over the years." I *clonk*ed up the steps.

There were daggers in West's eyes. "You don't need a whorehouse when you have women eating out of your hand."

I dismissed him with a wave. "That's right. When you have women begging you to sleep with them, you can laugh at them and send them home without their underwear."

West grabbed my shoulder and spun me to face him. "Enough. I didn't laugh at you, and you have proven your point. I was an ass. Now, let's go."

"I'm not trying to prove a point to you, Mr. Westinghouse. If you will excuse me, I'm trying to find a murderer." I knocked his hands away and clasped the doorknob.

Freida's brothel was housed in a Victorian mansion that, despite its beautiful architecture, lacked the sophistication of The Bellmount Inn. It wasn't just that the building tilted slightly to the left; it still might have been magnificent if the pink and purple gingerbread lattice hadn't cried out for a fresh coat of paint, and if the light above the front door hadn't been psychedelic red. And then there was the blinking sex sign that hung on the weather-beaten gable.

A statue of a nude golden woman greeted us. A four-foot high arrangement of fake flowers stood beside her, and the red and gold textured paper in the foyer peeled at the seams.

West followed me through the festooned red velvet

draperies that led to the parlor. Two red couches and half a dozen burgundy chairs decorated the room.

He stopped in his tracks and stared at a wall-sized mural painted in the Rubenesque style. A woman stretched her body out wantonly on a pile of Ottoman Empire pillows. The long hair cascading over her breasts didn't hide her nipples, and she tucked her pale hand into the dark hair that covered her most intimate area. The suggestiveness of the painting and the memories of my debacle with West rattled me. I had a second of lust replaced by eons of shame. West's gaze settled on me for a moment before returning to the painting.

A tall man with a shaved head stood behind a bar that looked like a scene out of an old cowboy movie. He nodded at something Freida said. The woman's teased pink hair formed a towering bouffant. Two older men sipped at drinks, and three scantily clad women perched about the room. Everyone looked up from their drinks to stare.

I shook off my paranoia and approached the lovely woman. "Hello, Frieda."

Her painted lips turned upward, and her blue eyes twinkled from under exotic false lashes. Bountiful curves were packed into her spandex dress, making her look like a turquoise sausage. Her voice carried a sensual echo, making me think of red silk blowing in the wind.

"Hello, beautiful. Can I help you?"

"I want a massage." I cringed, since my voice sounded like a child's next to hers.

"Shit," West said.

She came out from behind the bar to run her hand

over West's cheek. "A couple's massage?"

I may have hated Weston Westinghouse at that moment, but I didn't want a pink-haired hooker rubbing herself all over him.

"Just me," I said.

She wrapped one of my ringlets around her finger. "How fun."

West moaned.

She focused on West. "What do you want, handsome?"

"To go home."

"Oh my." She ran her hand under his jacket. "Relax, sexy."

"Yeah. Relax," I said as I envied the pink-tipped nails that caressed his clothed body.

West's unblinking eyes consumed his face.

"How much for just me?" I asked.

"For an hour, give or take, and with that body—" She eyed me up and down. "I'd lean toward the give." She smiled. "Fifty. Cash. Upfront."

I reached into the pocket of my blood-pack for my wallet. Thank goodness I had sixty dollars on me. I counted out fifty and placed it into her hand. Unfortunately, I had once again dipped into my cellular phone fund.

"Shit." West removed a wallet from his back pocket. He handed her a wad of bills. "Both of us."

"Would you like a drink first?" she asked.

"No, thank you," I said.

"Hell, yes," West said. "The strongest thing you've got."

The bald man slid a shot across the bar.

West slammed five dollars down, chugged, and

shook his head from side to side. West, the man who never imbibed, was in search of liquid courage. To be fair, we were in a somewhat unsettling situation.

Freida smiled seductively. "Come."

West and I followed her up the gaudy stairwell of shiny golds and brilliant reds and then down an all gold hallway. Freida ushered us into the last room on the left. She switched on the light, and purple damask walls, a satin comforter, black pillows and a round mattress screamed, EROTIC!

Black curtains hung from the ceiling above the headboard, and an upholstered chair with gold legs faced the bed. Thick drapes obscured the windows, promising secrecy and discretion.

"Make yourselves at home." Freida kissed me on the cheek and ran her fingers through West's hair. "You two are beautiful," she purred in her silky voice. "Let me go get the lucky girls." She closed the door, locking us in the fantasy room.

"Lucky girls?" I sat on the end of the bed.

"Ew! Ew! Ew! What the hell? Don't sit on it. Do you want crabs, lice, and a venereal disease?"

"Said the man who has slept with half the county." As soon as I muttered it, I wanted nothing more than to take it back.

West's jaw clenched. "What will you do if this place gets raided and Edith and Pop have to bail us out of jail? Of course, everyone will blame me. 'It must have been Westinghouse the scoundrel's idea because it couldn't be the sweet Miranda's fault.'"

"You're such a chicken." Cramming my hands under my armpits, I flapped my wings. "*Bok! Bok! Bok!*" I chirped and hopped around like an insane fool, clucking wildly as West's angry gaze seared me. I was lucky he didn't turn me into a big old bucket of fried chicken.

Knock. Knock.

West and I stopped arguing to gawk at two women. A pretty girl with shiny black hair, and an even shinier black eye, looked to be in her early twenties. The other was tall and solid with short spiky magenta hair. A heavy eye shadow mask surrounded her eyes. She was in her mid-thirties and was sexy, in a terrifying way.

Madame Shiny wrapped her arms around West. He peeled her fingers off and backed away. "I'm just watching."

Both women slunk toward me.

"Let's get you undressed, darling." Madame Spiky said to me. She faced West. "You must love sucking on her sexy tits, and I bet she has a sweet pussy?"

I backed away and held up a palm to halt her. "Wait. I thought Freida was taking care of us."

"She thought you would prefer us. I like you." Madame Spiky inclined her chin toward me. Then she pointed at West. "And Tia likes him. I promise we'll take good care of you."

Madame Spiky grabbed my hair and pulled me to her. I rolled my head to the side to avoid her lips. She caught me on the cheek the first time but nailed my lips the second.

West hissed.

Madame Shiny came around behind me and looped her arm around my waist. Unfortunately, I had become the meat in a hooker sandwich.

"Oh shit," West said. This time his expletive was more out of fascination than disgust. He plopped himself onto the germ chair. His eyes went wide, his lips parted, and his jaw hovered a millimeter above the floor. The fool almost drowned in his own saliva.

I fought to break free from the girls and put distance between us. "I thought I paid for Freida."

"Fine." Madame Spiky headed toward the door, and Madame Shiny followed.

Before they departed, they ogled West. He tracked their backsides as the door closed behind them.

"Ew!" he said again once we were alone. "I hope to hell you know what you're doing. The walls are so thin you can hear the fucking next door."

I listened for one minute, cringed, then blocked it out. "You didn't look like you thought they were *ewww* when you were staring at their butts."

"Hey, Shortcake." West's eyes were tiny slits, and the truth was, his crazed angry look was seriously sexy. "You jealous of the hookers you insisted upon?"

I glowered at him. "*Bok! Bok! Bok!*"

"I swear to God, when we get out of this mess, you're going to pay dearly. Starting with my fifty-five dollars."

"A cheap chicken," I said.

West chased me. I ducked and weaved, flapped my wings, and half leaped, half crawled across the bed to get away from him. Of course, there was no way the klutzy Professor Albright in heels could evade the athletic Weston the Third. West caught me in a headlock and rubbed his fist into the top of my head.

I was enthusiastically chirping, "*Bok! Bok!*" and West was wholeheartedly yelling "Noogie!" when Frieda entered.

She stopped short and frowned. "What kind of

freaky shit are you two into? I have limits."

West laughed and I gasped.

I broke free and pulled my shoulders back. "I'm not freaky. He's just a huge jerk."

"You cops?" she asked.

"Hardly," West said.

"He's a scoundrel who bartends on the side," I said.

"No. I'm a bartender who has a soft spot for women. And she's a sexy, pain-in-the-ass college professor who makes me want to bash my head into a wall."

"Aww. You think I'm sexy?" I bit my lip and fluttered my lashes.

West's eyes narrowed. "Shortcake, how in the hell do you not know that I think you're the sexiest woman I've ever met?"

My heart flipped, flopped, then missed a few beats.

Freida sighed. "You two need a therapist, not a *ménage a trois*."

I filed away West's confession. "I need a massage. My back hurts, and he won't take care of it for me."

West's eyeballs about popped out of their sockets. Maybe he thought massage was code for sex, and I had called his prowess into question in front of a sexpert.

Of course, I simply needed a lady of the evening to rub her hands on my bare skin so I could get a reading. I slid out of my coat then closed my eyes as the truth dawned on me. I needed to remove my sweater.

I concentrated on blocking out the noise from the neighboring room. "On the bed?"

"Wherever you like," she said.

The sound that came out of West was some sort of

howl-like vibrating cry.

I slid my sweater off and covered my torso with my arms. "I just want a back massage."

I faced the end of the bed because I needed to see West. Suddenly, I was terrified and glad he was with me. I couldn't have accomplished my goal at Freida's with anyone but him. I laid down. My bra, skirt, nylons, and panties were all still in place, but I was shirtless and staring into his eyes.

Freida kneaded my neck. "Please join us, handsome."

West sat forward and swallowed. His gaze locked with mine, and I had a moment of mushy brain as I fantasized about him walking across the room and entwining his tongue with mine. I moaned, felt shame, then refocused.

"I told my friend Joe Morrow my back was hurting, and he recommended you," I said.

What the hell! She stopped rubbing and removed her hands.

I looked over my shoulder. "Keep massaging."

She hesitated before dropping her palm on my back.

"Joe spoke highly of you," I said.

Damn, I miss him. He treated me like a queen.

"You know he discovered Jesus. I heard him testify once. It was so inspiring." I had found Joe's confession to be shocking and scandalous and not inspiring in the least. "Joe said he gave up gambling, liquor, and messing around. But he said you were different. He still liked you."

Since I had told four truths and only three lies, I didn't feel too heinous. Maybe I could still get on

Santa's nice list? *Pfft*! Who was I kidding?

Once again, she removed her hands.

"Massage, please," I said.

Her fingers rested on my back. "If you are looking for dirt on Joe, you won't get it from me. He was on the straight and narrow. He wasn't fucking around anymore."

Freida passed the lie detector with flying colors.

There was a knock at the door, and Spiky entered. "Freida, I'm sorry. He's here again and demanding to see you.

"Tell him I'm with someone," Freida said.

Spiky swished across the room and whispered into Freida's ear. I heard every detail as I divined Freida's thoughts.

I popped up.

West stared at my chest.

"I have to go," Freida said. "Megan will take over."

I pulled my sweater on. "Great massage. I feel better." I clutched my coat, grabbed West's arm, and chased after Freida.

"Freida," I called down the hallway.

She stood silent, her back to me.

"Joe died in my arms. He asked me to help you."

She faced me.

"I'm Miranda. I know you are afraid of Bellmount's mayor and that he is downstairs demanding you. Please help us get out of here without him seeing us, and I'll do whatever I can to help you. Send me a message at The Bellmount Inn."

Freida herded us back into the purple room. "Are you the woman from the alley the reporter wrote about?"

I nodded.

"Stay here. Megan will sneak you out." She reached into the front of her dress, dug for a wad of money, and handed it to me.

"Keep it," I said.

West shook his head violently.

"Cheap," I mouthed at him.

Freida closed the door, leaving me alone with West.

Erotic, erotic, erotic, the purple walls softly taunted.

"You wanna fill me in on what just happened?" he asked.

I scrunched up my nose.

"I'm assuming this entire farce was so you could do some mind-reading. I'm just now realizing that the whore orgy would have been safer than whatever other shit you have yourself wrapped up in."

Erotic! called the round bed.

I ran my hand over the satin comforter attempting to focus. "I think Mayor Reynolds had three men killed, and he is forcing Freida to have sex with him. I just don't know why."

"Maybe he's extorting Freida, telling her he'll have her closed down unless she pays him. Then he is getting a little—" His fist pumped. "*Ee-ee, ee-ee* on the side. Freida confided in Morrow, and Morrow threatened Reynolds. The mayor contracted Deckler to kill Morrow, but since Stiles was filling in for Morrow at the kiddie party, he accidentally killed him. Reynolds is such a bastard he also killed his hired gun. It seems Scrooge doesn't want Christmas to come this year."

"West! I bet that's it. Have you been studying my investigation?"

"Yeah. I'm tired of you using me for my body. I'm not just a love machine. I have brains too." He winked at me, and the angry lines in his face softened.

Erroootic! The black curtains over the bed sang.

"So how do Stevens, Dinky, and Timberlane fit in?"

He grinned. "Shortcake, I'm not gonna solve your entire mystery for you."

"Good grief." I rolled my eyes at his comment although my traitorous girl parts tickled.

"Timberlane? Who knows? Probably nothing. But if he thinks he's gonna fuck with Keisha, he's dumber than a stump. And I'll tell you what, if Dinky, the dick of a DJ, hurts Winona, he's gonna be dickless."

Erotic!!! screamed the gold and black chair.

Something niggled inside my panties and I ached to grab West and kiss him in that erotic bordello. For a moment, I thought he might toss me onto that erotic bed in that scandalous erotic room.

Neither of us would ever know because Madame Megan, with the magenta hair and kinky mask, opened the door.

"Come on, hurry!" she called before she guided us down the red and gold staircase and out the door.

****

"Where the hell have you two been?" Keisha asked. "One of you owes me for dinner." She pointed at our bagged meals that sat in front of a frowning Winona.

West picked up the bill and studied it. "Yikes."

"Cheap," I mouthed to him before subtly flapping

my arms.

West hid his mouth behind his hand so that only I could see his tongue curling suggestively. Then he retrieved his wallet and flashed me a five.

I showed him a ten, and he grimaced.

I forced my shoulders back and bravely faced my best friend. "About the bill, Keisha…"

Keisha's face contorted into a Quasimodo-like mask and Dinky called out, "Donkey slobber shit fucks!"

There was a silver lining to my strange evening. I wasn't going to have to join Timberlane and Dinky for a triple date ever again!

****

West held my hand as we giggled on the ride home from our disastrous dinner, and neither one of us wore gloves. Then he had Dinky drop him off at the inn. We were still laughing when he walked me to the front door.

He sat our bagged Chinese food on a porch table then filled my personal space. "I ended up having a hell of a good time."

Concentrating became difficult with his cologne enveloping me. "Me too."

"I guess maybe I should stop by Keisha's place tomorrow and pay her back."

"Don't worry. I'll take care of it. It was kind of my fault that we didn't have enough money to pay for dinner."

West smiled, then bonked my nose. "One hundred percent your fault."

I moved a smidge closer to his warmth.

"This week sucked," he said.

"The worst," I agreed.

He positioned himself so that we were less than an inch apart. "Seeing you hurt and angry and then seeing you that sick about killed me."

"You saw me sick?"

"Yeah. I came and sat with you before work. I figured since I already had whatever it was, I was immune."

"You did sit with me? I thought it was a dream."

"I even read to you from the girly book that was in your backpack," confessed the man who loved soap operas.

Warmth surged through me. "Thank you, West."

I reached for the door handle, and West grabbed me. He spun me to face him and pulled my body to his. Seconds later, his hands were in my hair, and his lips were on mine.

My fingers threaded through his soft waves, and my aching hips pressed into his.

A click distracted us, the front door opened, and Russ gawked.

"Oh, sorry. I heard something out here and came to check."

My cheeks became habanera-style hot, as West remained cool as a chilled cucumber.

"Just saying good night to my girl," West declared.

"Okay, then. Good night." Russ closed the door giving us back our privacy.

West laughed and clutched my waist.

"Yikes. Embarrassing," I said.

"Nah. Just a little bit of harmless making out." West was all shining eyes and humongous grin.

I looked up at him through my eyelashes. "West, I

hate my telepathy. I'm ashamed of it. But I can't help it. It's who I am."

"I know." He kissed my nose. "If I could take back how I made you feel, I would. It's just— Look, I'm not very good at expressing my emotions and, I didn't know how much of my thoughts you'd heard."

What hadn't he wanted me to hear?

"I don't wanna talk about it anymore. I wanna do this." He kissed me.

"So, I'm ashamed of who I am, and you can't express emotions. Where does that leave us?"

"It leaves us standing on your front porch, making out." He leaned down for another kiss.

My body craved him, and I wanted to make love to West right there in the front yard.

"I think it means we should hold hands and go slow," he said.

"Slow," I said, thinking of our previous sexy game and preparing for what I hoped would be a sensual lingering kiss.

He pulled back. "I meant, I need to help you deal with your superpowers, and you need to help me deal with my fear of getting emotionally close to someone."

"Oh."

"Don't look so sad. We're gonna figure it out together, and that's a good thing." He caressed my cheek then put his lips beside my ear. "I have to tell you a secret."

A pleasant tingle coursed through me at the prospect of having secrets with West. "What?"

"You're the first girl I've ever cared about enough to feel jealousy, and I hate the feeling."

"Jealousy? Over me?"

"I'm crazy jealous of other men when it comes to you."

"You are?"

"Be careful, Shortcake. What if your face gets stuck like that?"

I smiled and tried to relax my forehead.

"Doc makes me lose my mind. I want to punch that damn detective's teeth in, and if Little doesn't stop sniffing around you, I might have to slap him silly."

"You shouldn't be jealous of anyone. You're the only person I want to kiss." I pulled his face to mine.

"Good because I'd strangle anyone who touched you."

I rolled my eyes. The fabulous Weston battling the green-eyed monster over the nerdy girl he had once convinced to eat worms and jump off bridges. Preposterous!

"You have no idea how beautiful you are, do you?" he said, his voice gentle.

"I think the curse of the redhead is back."

"I have it bad, and I don't want it to go away. Now, hold my hand, and everything will be okay."

Weston Westinghouse the Third clasped my palm in his and kissed me good-night until stars shot through my body.

Perhaps, my date wasn't a disaster after all.

Chapter 22

Life was looking up. The winter holiday had arrived, I had slept in, and the night before, West had kissed me senseless. I was also one step closer to discovering who had shot me because I now knew that Mayor Reynolds was involved in the murder spree.

Knowing that my silencing wasn't personal brought me some peace. It appeared that anyone who asked anything about the crime received a scolding. I wasn't sure how all of the puzzle pieces fit together, but I knew I hadn't been singled out. I also knew that West would never divulge my brothel sleuthing secret, so I shouldn't find myself in additional trouble with Dean Johnson.

Spot shifted positions and left the end of the bed to curl up on the pillow beside me. I scratched his ears and told him my secrets.

"West is crazy about me. What do you think about that?"

Spot barked.

"Hey, guys," I called to the rat and the turtle, encouraging them to join our powwow. "I might be wrong about this curse thing. It seems West thinks I'm beautiful, and our childhood was as special to him as it was to me. I think Brad is drawn to me because we share an energy ability. Maybe Sean does like that I am relentless. As usual, Lincoln is correct. It seems as though curses don't exist. Comments? Anyone?"

Spot was the only animal paying attention, and his tail wagged like a flag in the wind.

I concluded West didn't think I was chunking up, so I could enjoy a few more cookies.

Since it was the Christmas break, I had the luxury of staying under my warm covers as I organized my life. I had finished most of my gift shopping: purchasing toys for the animals, pretty journals for Winona and Keisha, fancy pen sets for Liam and Lincoln, CDs and perfume for Aunt Edith, and baseball hats for Russ and Tommy. West's presents were under his tree. I had a new sweater and a book for my dad.

The only people I had left were Greg and Brad. What to give a ghost for Christmas? Maybe I could get a new cassette and play it the next time we had an errand to run. I needed a spectacular idea for Brad. He had saved my life and taken care of me the past month. And according to Aunt Edith, I had not treated him well while I was ill.

"What should I get for my friend Brad?" I asked my pets.

Spot licked my cheek.

"Oh, that's a good idea, boy. Although I'm not sure if I have enough money."

****

I arrived at Brad's office, carrying a nine-week-old black puppy. The white patch around his nose and bright blue eyes made the bundle especially precious. Theresa Kane, AKA Nurse Nasty, from the hospital, scowled from behind the reception desk. Usually, a sweet older lady with blue hair and rosy cheeks occupied the seat.

"Hello, Nurse Kane," I said.

She glared at me, then the puppy. "You can't bring an animal into the office."

"This is Dr. Gordon's puppy."

"As far as I know, Dr. Gordon doesn't have pets. If he did, I wouldn't have agreed to come here and organize this mess for him." She looked around at the "mess." "He is upstairs in his apartment, and you can't take that thing up there."

The nurse was certifiable. Brad kept both his office and his apartment immaculate.

"Brad is expecting me," I lied. I walked past the glowering woman and climbed the stairs to his second-floor abode.

I knocked, and Brad's muffled voice called out.

Unfortunately, Nurse Nasty clomped up the stairs behind me. My heartbeat tripled. I let myself into his apartment, then leaned against the door and breathed.

"Miranda?" Brad said, his eyes huge.

My eyes widened a second after his because he wore pants and socks and was in the process of swinging a flannel shirt over his shoulders. I caught sight of his muscular chest and gasped.

"Sorry, Brad." Even though I looked away, I peeked from the corner of my eye.

He strolled toward me as his fingers fiddled with buttons. "Who do we have here?" He stroked the ball of fluff in my arms.

Brad was four buttons short of having himself clothed, and his dark hair stood in the air. His gaze focused on the puppy and his face lit with joy.

Dang! Brad was handsome in flannel.

"Merry Christmas," I said.

Knock. Knock.

"Fudge." I secured the puppy in Brad's safe arms. "It's Nurse Nasty."

"Let her in," Brad said as he cooed at the baby.

Although I shook my head vehemently, I opened the door to the pinched-faced ogre.

"Hi Theresa," Brad said. "Do you need something?"

"I told the girl that she couldn't bring that filthy animal up here, but she didn't listen." The grumpy nurse glared at the darling furball and smiled.

Both doctor and puppy had black hair and stunning blue eyes, and the adorable animal looked miniature against Brad's massive chest.

She fought with her quivering lips as she forced them to turn downward.

"I've got it, Theresa. Thanks for your help. You can head out today, and I'll see you next week."

"Are you sure, Dr. Gordon? I don't mind staying late today. You might get some phone calls. The flu is knocking people down, and someone might need to clean up after that creature." She pointed at the puppy. Her lips twisted into a grimace, but her eyes shone with joy.

"You go home and enjoy your weekend. I've got it," he said.

The door closed, and my body relaxed. "Did you hire her as your new receptionist?"

"No. My new nurse. But she thinks she is the receptionist, the doctor, and the queen of the castle."

I chuckled.

"How does Spot like his new brother?" Brad asked.

"He isn't my puppy. I got him for you. Merry

Christmas," I said again.

Brad's eyes glimmered, his smile widened, and his dimples deepened. "Mine?"

"Yes. Thank you for saving my life, for taking care of me, for understanding how I feel about West, and for checking on me when I had the flu. I understand I wasn't very gracious when you came to treat me. I'm sorry. I was out of it. I don't remember much."

"He's the cutest thing I've ever seen. I don't know what to say."

"Say you can keep him. I got him at the humane society. I'm not sure what breed he is, but they said he might have some black Lab in him, and he is probably going to get big."

"Of course, I can keep him. He's the best present I've ever received. I bet he's a Lab-husky mix."

"What about Nurse Nasty?"

Brad chuckled. "Under all that grumbling, she's a sweetie."

I narrowed my eyes and scrunched up my face until it hurt.

"She loved him. I could tell." Brad held his puppy up so that they stared into each other's eyes. "Little fellow, I'm going to call you Night."

"You could call him Knight with a K-N like he is a knight in shining armor."

When Brad and I had dated, I considered him to be my knight in shining armor.

"I love it. Knight it is," Brad said.

Knight licked Brad on the lips, and the mountain of a man giggled.

I handed Brad a brown bag of puppy food and a blue leash that I had stashed in my coat pocket. "Mix this with whatever you decide to feed him for a couple of days. Stop at Lou Romano's pet store across the street. You can pick out the brand you want and choose a dog dish. It's all paid for."

Brad removed a piece of food from the bag, held it to Knight's nose, and the little guy gobbled it up.

"Ah," I murmured, enchanted by cuteness overload. I was about to leave when I recalled I hadn't yet filled Brad in. "One more thing. I swear I didn't tell Lincoln about your abilities. But he has been helping me, and he knows about you. If you ever want to confide anything to him, you can."

"Dr. Harrison at the college?" Brad asked.

"Yes."

He thought for a moment. "I may take him up on that."

"Have a great holiday. I have to get going." I reached for the doorknob.

"Wait, Miranda."

I faced the gorgeous man and his wriggling companion. They both stared at me with puppy dog eyes.

"Are things still going well with Westinghouse?"

"Yes. Wonderful."

The puppy continued to squirm, so Brad set the chubby ball on the floor, and he half-hopped, half-ran toward the bedroom.

Brad watched the bounding fluff. "I better go get him."

So that the renegade pup didn't sprint past us and fall down the steps, I cracked the door and slid into the hall. "Bye, Brad. I know you two will love each other."

He smiled at me one last time before chasing down

his present.

I paused outside his door. A dog was a serious commitment. Had I done the right thing? Of course, I had. The puppy was perfect for Brad.

Shaking off my doubts, I tip-toed down the stairs, praying that Nasty Nurse Kane had left for the day.

****

When I returned from Brad's, Freida's powder blue car sat in the driveway. I found her holding a cup of tea in the library. Aunt Edith, Winona, and Spot gathered around her. A string of drool dripped down Winona's chin as she eyed a tray of iced cookies. My misguided friend had not yet abandoned her recent health food kick.

Freida wore black pants, a red blouse, a black linen jacket, and four-inch heels. Her nails and lips matched her bouffant. Most women couldn't pull off pink hair, but somehow Freida did, and it added a certain *je ne sais quoi.*

"Hello, Freida," I said.

"Hello, Miranda. Your aunt and Winona have been keeping me company. I hope it's okay that I came."

"Yes. Of course. I'm glad you did."

"I thought maybe we could talk about the thing you mentioned last night during your visit," Freida said.

Winona's gaze traveled from the cookies to me, and her chin dropped to the floor. Aunt Edith stared me down, raising an eyebrow. Their reaction probably had more to do with defying my instructions to "lay low" than visiting a prostitute.

I sat on the settee beside Freida. She put down her teacup and folded her hands into her lap.

Feeling the need to provide some context to Aunt

Edith, I declared, "West and I walked past Freida's business last night and stopped in."

Winona gaped. "West isn't allowed there. Grandma Westinghouse will kill him!"

"Don't worry. We were just investigating."

"That is where you guys disappeared to. We thought you were fighting or—" Winona's gaze met Aunt Edith's and she clamped her lips shut. However, a moment later, words exploded from her. "Keisha's really mad, but I knew you and West weren't really—"

"Freida, you can talk freely in front of all three of us," Aunt Edith said.

"We will do our best to help you. I know the mayor is tormenting you, and Joe was trying to protect you. I just don't understand why," I said

"I don't want anyone else to get hurt, and I'm terrified." Freida bit her lip.

"I'm not sure what the two of you have gotten yourselves into." Aunt Edith motioned back and forth between Freida and me. "But Miranda has already been hurt."

"Miranda almost died." Winona picked up a cookie and gnawed the head off a Santa.

I settled my hand on Frieda's forearm. "Tell us everything. We can't help you until we understand." I'm unsure if it was ethical now that she trusted me, but I dropped my shield and listened in on her thoughts.

Freida studied the ceiling and let out a long exhale. "Gene Reynolds became my client about two years ago. About nine months ago, he started demanding my services even if I was with someone else."

I didn't even try to hide my gag. Did the poor woman have to sleep with Shultz too? There wasn't enough money in the world!

"Then about six months ago, he threatened to destroy my business if I didn't do what he said. He even refused to pay for my services."

"You poor thing," Aunt Edith said.

Winona swallowed Santa's beard. "What about his wife?" She grabbed a Christmas tree-shaped cookie. *Chomp*! *Chomp*!

Repulsion over sex with Reynolds consumed Freida. My skin crawled. I removed my hand from her arm.

"How was he going to destroy your business?" Aunt Edith asked.

"Each time I don't do what he says, he raises the rent on the building. When I do what he wants, he lowers it."

"Changing the rent can't be legal," I said.

"No. But neither is running a brothel. So my hands are tied."

"How is he raising it? Don't you have a lease?" Aunt Edith asked. "Does he know the person who owns the building?"

Freida shook her head. "He owns the building."

The missing puzzle piece hit my brain with a *thunk*. "Wait a minute. Does E.R. Development own it?"

Freida nodded.

"Is Gene short for Eugene? Is E.R. Eugene Reynolds?" I asked.

"Good Lord. Reynolds owns E.R. Development?" Aunt Edith brought her hand to her temple and closed her eyes for a moment. "The mayor is the one trying to buy up all of the property in the county? He's using his position to profit on real estate deals?"

Freida nodded again.

"How is he getting away with this?" Aunt Edith asked. "It would be one thing if he were transparent, but he's doing it under an anonymous company and using unethical business tactics. How deep does this go?"

"There's more." Freida wrung her hands. "At first, I thought it was because Gene was obsessed with me. I have known for a while that I had to get out from under him. The truth is, I didn't know how, and he scares me to death. So, I went to Joe who had a friend from high school named Mike Stevens. Mike's wife is a real estate agent, and she said she could help me find my own place."

"Was Joe with you and Lily Anne Stevens the night George Stiles filled in for him? Is that why he needed a last-minute replacement?" I asked.

"Yes. Lily Anne had a piece of property we needed to move quickly on. The thing is, E.R's attorney offered so much money, I couldn't match it. Lily Anne had no idea because it happened behind her back. Gene, the son of a bitch, isn't using the building for anything. He plans to let it sit vacant for the time being."

"The rumor was that Lily and Joe might be having an affair, but if they weren't, then why leave George's body in front of the Speed-mart?" I asked.

"It's all so crazy," Freida said. "I didn't think anything of George Stiles being murdered, except that it was sad. Then a few days later, Joe died. When I found out you were the girl shot in the alley, I got a funny feeling that Gene was involved and that the deaths were connected."

"I think they mistook George for Joe," I said.

"Which means someone, probably Reynolds, knew Joe's schedule but didn't know about the last-minute change. But, I still don't understand why he would leave the body in front of the Speed-mart if Mike Stevens wasn't involved."

"I have a theory," Freida said. "I think when Reynolds accidentally killed George, he left him in front of the Speed-mart to send a message. He must have thought Stevens knew something. But at that time, Stevens didn't know a thing. His wife was innocently trying to sell me a building. Of course, after the killer dropped off the body and someone interfered with the cameras, I think he realized someone was fucking with him. The only problem with my theory is Gene would never have mistaken George for Joe, not even in costume. He knew Joe like the back of his hand."

"I think Reynolds hired a guy named Deckler to murder Joe," I said

"That piece of shit conman. I've heard stories about him. Dirty deeds done dirt cheap." Even when she swore, Freida's voice held a lovely timbre.

"So Reynolds killed his hired hitman, then framed the sheriff?" Aunt Edith asked.

Freida raised her eyes to the ceiling as if to say, Oh, dear lord! "Joe, the sheriff, and Stevens have been friends since they were boys. I know Joe never confided my troubles to them, but Shultz was investigating Joe's death on his own. He must have been getting too close, and Gene wanted to shut him up."

"I found a picture of the three of them together in an old yearbook." Winona puffed up her chest. "I knew they were somehow connected. I'm a pretty good detective."

"And the mayor knew that tie stood out at the funeral," I said.

"Shultz is an easy target. He's enough of a screw-up that nobody would give his involvement a second thought," Aunt Edith said. "The plan was foiled because Miranda was accidentally shot in the crossfire, and Sergeant O'Sullivan is nobody's fool."

"And, the mayor is the only one with enough power to threaten the sergeant, the newspaper, and the college." Winona proudly tapped her noggin. "And he made it look like it was because he was worried about the reputation of the town during hunting season. *Pfft*."

"It's all coming together. The thing is—" Freida sighed. "The mayor's started to ask for some of the other girls, and he's getting rough with them. I can hear him through the walls. My job is dealing with horny men, and he's beyond depraved."

"Don't you have a pimp who can beat him up?" Winona asked.

Freida gawked at Winona.

Winona shrugged. "I thought prostitutes had pimps. They do on TV."

Freida performed the shake-Winona-from-my-brain-movement. "At first, I thought he was a perverted piece of shit who had fallen for me, but now I think he's a murderer. I don't think Gene is even doing this for the money. He craves power. I'm afraid for my life and the rest of the girls' safety. He'll be in again tonight, and every time he walks through the door, I'm more afraid. He has to know I suspect him of killing Joe. I worry about Mike and Lily Anne. They have kids."

"Sean can help," I said.

"Is that the handsome detective who's been snooping around?" Frieda asked. "Because I think he's making Gene paranoid. He said something along the lines of, 'I thought they were sending the confused old guy.'"

I *harrumph*ed. "The mayor thought that Miller would investigate, and he would get away with everything. He should be paranoid because Sergeant O'Sullivan will get to the bottom of this."

Freida held up a palm. "If we go to the police, they'll raid my place and shut it down."

"Freida, if we don't go to the sergeant for help, more people might die. Maybe even you, or one of your girls. I saw Reynolds and Stevens arguing in front of the store. Stevens and his family may be in danger," I said.

She let out a long, pained breath.

"I know Sean won't shut you down. He isn't that kind of guy. He just wants to find the murderer," I said.

"Please stay for lunch." Aunt Edith grasped Freida's hand. "It will give Miranda a chance to call Sergeant O'Sullivan and work out a plan to help you. Reynolds needs to be stopped. You can't live in fear, and he can't continue this reign of terror."

I left Aunt Edith, Freida, and Winona in the library to seek out the kitchen phone. The sergeant detective answered on the third ring.

"Sean, how quickly can you get to the inn?" I asked.

"Give me forty minutes," he said.

I hung up, grabbed a piece of paper from Aunt Edith's message board, wrote down my plan, and studied it. It would work. I knew I could do it.

All I had to do was convince an angry rogue cop with a fading crush that I was the woman for the job.

Chapter 23

Keisha and Winona spent the early evening "hooker-ing me up." Keisha painted my nails blood red, glued false lashes onto my lids, added a thick layer of liquid eyeliner, and colored me in with bright green shadow. Winona piled my hair under a net and shoved an old Marilyn Monroe Halloween wig onto my head.

They wrangled me into a red thrift shop dress that was eighty sizes too small. I finished my disguise with a pair of Polly's too-large 1972 platform heels. Once dressed, I turned in a circle.

"Damn, you look skanky," Keisha said.

Winona cringed.

I studied my image in the mirror as I awkwardly posed. "I'll call you guys first thing tomorrow morning and let you know how it goes."

"What are you talking about? We're going with you," Keisha said.

"I'm sorry. You can't. It's official police business. It took everything I had to convince Sean to let me do this. Shultz and Miller will be there, and they'd flip if I brought my friends."

"Shultz?" Keisha asked.

"He and Freida are part of the sting."

"Wow!" Keisha said.

"Frieda is super sweet, Keisha. Just because she's a prostitute doesn't make her a bad person," Winona said.

Keisha glowered. "What the hell is wrong with you? Did Polly drop you on your head, or did the umbilical cord wrap around your neck in the birthing chamber?"

"It's true. It doesn't make Freida a bad person. Tell her, Miranda."

Keisha pursed her lips, and her head bobbled from side to side. "I never said she was a bad person. Although to be clear, I did insinuate that you are a dingbat."

So much for the compassion and friendship that had blossomed between them the night of our arrest.

I groaned. "Sean isn't sure if the warrant is going to come through in time, so the entire thing is—" I waved a hand. "Up in the air."

"Is it dangerous?" Winona asked.

Keisha rolled her eyes. "Of course it's dangerous. Miranda is posing as a prostitute with a murderer who likes to beat on women."

Winona's face lit up at the mention of dangerous espionage. "Is the hunky detective going to tape a wire to you and listen in? Did you know that when they pull the wire off you, it pulls your chest hair out?" She shivered. "And if a bad guy finds it, he might kill you right then and there. Criminals yell things like, 'You son-of-a-bitch, is this a wire?' right before they axe you." She cut a line across her neck and stuck out her tongue. "Ack! So, you have to be careful."

"I don't have chest hair," I said. "And they are going to put some kind of listening device in the room."

Winona clapped. "Like a British secret agent. You're so lucky. Oh my gosh, maybe they will put a bug in your lipstick? They can do that, you know?"

"According to your cheesy detective shows?" Keisha asked.

Winona put her hands on her hips. "At least I learn things that help us, unlike your stupid daytime stories, Keisha. West watches them too. They make you dumb."

Keisha stuck her index finger in Winona's face. "You wanna talk about dumb?"

"Focus," I demanded. "Anyway, one device will be behind a lamp. The other will be behind a bottle of schnapps."

"Although, if they do put a bug in your lipstick, can you confiscate it for me?" Keisha asked. "I could tape that perverted store manager and nail him to the wall."

"They aren't bugging my makeup!" I squawked.

My friends, crestfallen over the disappointing spy paraphernalia, wore twin frowny faces.

I exhaled and lowered my voice. "I'm sorry. I wish you guys could come. Please don't worry. I know I can get Reynolds to talk, but Sean isn't convinced." I hugged Winona first, and she clung to me like I was dying.

Then Keisha stared into my eyes like she was sending her firstborn to college. I pressed the money I owed for the Chinese dinner debacle into the palm of her hand.

"Oh, Miranda," Keisha said. "I don't care about the money. I just want you to be safe."

I pretended not to notice her wet eyes. "I need a few moments to meditate. So, if you could give me some time alone, I'll call you both tomorrow morning," I promised.

For the next ten minutes, they performed every stalling action imaginable. Finally, I nudged them into the hallway and closed the door behind them.

Earlier in the afternoon, I had purloined Aunt Edith's sewing kit. I lifted the bottom of my short dress and wound a piece of elastic around my thigh. Using the strip like a ruler, I cut and measured two more pieces. I reinforced the stitches as I sewed them into three garters. Then I studied my reflection.

I hated to mess with my disguise, but I had no choice. I couldn't hide anything under the too-tight dress. I rooted through my closet and found an out-of-style puffy black skirt circa 1983. Using pinking shears, I cut it so that it hit right below my thigh. I found my favorite knit green jersey, hesitated, then sliced the bottom off.

I did a quick hemline stitch and cut the shirt's neck to show cleavage. My legs, stomach, and the line of my bosom were exposed, but the top of my hips hid under a fabric puff. It was the perfect outfit to show skin while hiding contraband. Ensuring the safety was on, I tucked Princess into my homemade thigh holster.

"Damn, you look like a tramp," Greg said from behind me.

I jumped. "Like a prostitute?"

"Like a slutty street urchin," he said.

I winced since a slutty street urchin wasn't the look I was going for. "I'm going undercover tonight. We are arresting Mayor Reynolds."

"What for?"

"He hired Trenton Deckler to kill Joe Morrow. Trenton accidentally killed George Stiles and shot me. Since Deckler screwed up, Reynolds killed him. At least, that's our theory."

"So, why are you dressed like that?"

"Reynolds likes to exert control over prostitutes. He owns the building Freida's business is in and is holding her hostage. He also owns E.R. Development, the company he's convincing the town council to sell the green lot outside of town to. I'm going to get him to admit what he has done. If the warrant comes through in time, we'll get it on tape."

"Holy shit!" Greg said.

"You might want to talk to your daughter about vetoing the sale. She's on the wrong side of this right now."

Greg's eyes lost their sparkle. "I wish I could talk to her."

I did an internal forehead slap at my *faux pas* as I jumped up and down. Greg gawked as my cleavage bounced.

I shot him my don't-go-there look. "I'm making sure Princess doesn't fall out."

"Where is she?"

"I made a thigh holster."

"Is the safety on?"

"Yes," I said.

"Christ, Crimson. This plan sounds dangerous. Not to mention you'll probably shoot your foot off. I'm going to cancel my show and go with you."

"No, you aren't. I'll be fine. Sean will be with me."

Greg raised an eyebrow.

"So will Shultz and Miller."

"Those two imbeciles don't exactly make me think you're going to be safe."

"There will be a ton of cops there. Please don't

cancel your plans. Although I am curious about this project that has occupied you these last few days."

He waved a dismissive hand. "It's nothing."

"Then tell me."

"Nah."

"Not only am I going into a dangerous situation, but I'll be worried about what mischief you are up to."

He sighed. "Fine. I've been singing."

"And?"

"You told me I should find a hobby and that my voice was magical. So I got a job."

I peered into his ghostly soul.

He grunted. "I discovered that my singing helps to ease the pain of people who are leaving this world and moving on."

"You mean you are comforting people who are dying?"

"Yeah," he said.

"Oh, Greg! That is the most beautiful thing I've ever heard." I grabbed his filmy hand and squeezed.

"I knew you would make a big deal out of it. That's why I didn't want to tell you."

"I think it's wonderful!"

"Yeah, I'm a fucking saint. Just don't be one of those dying people tonight. And don't shoot anyone else." He kissed me on the forehead and diffused.

After retrieving a small jewelry box from my dresser, I clasped a rose gold necklace into place. Spot joined me at the mirror as I studied my image. The only things I recognized were Spot, my eyes, and a diamond gun charm that Greg gave me before he died.

"I can do this," I told the dog, the rat, the turtle, and my terrified image as it stared back at me.

****

West's breath hitched, and his gaze tracked me as I clicked across the room to take a seat at the end of the bar. I slid out of my dress coat and gave him my best seductive smile.

"Hey, sexy lady. I have a big bed upstairs," he said.

Sass accompanied my disguise. I fluttered my sticky eyelashes and attempted dirty talk. "It isn't a big bed I'm after."

"No problem, I've got a lot of big things."

My head flew back, my wig bobbled, and I laughed. "Like a big ego."

"Among other things." He grinned. "You picking our sexy game tonight? I wanna play."

I used my curling index finger to motion his ear to my mouth.

"Shh. I'm undercover."

"Under the covers in my big bed with my big—"

"West." I swatted at his shoulder. "I'm serious. Keep it down."

"So that's why Winona needed the night off?"

I perused the room. "No. She must be with Dinky."

West's brow furrowed. "Are you going undercover with Keisha?"

I leaned close and shushed him. "With the police."

West backed up, studied my face, tilted his head to the side, and let expletives fly. Opening the kitchen door a crack, he called, "Aunt Polly, you gotta come out here and cover." He came around from behind the bar, placed his hand on my forearm, and escorted me to the storeroom. Once we were alone, his jaw clenched. "Start at the beginning."

Suddenly, I wasn't feeling well. I knew West might

worry, but I hadn't expected him to be angry.

"Freida came to see me today," I said.

"What did she have to say?"

"Your theories about the Santa murders are right on."

"I suppose there's more," he said.

"Have you heard of E.R. Development?"

West looked to the ceiling and thought. "No."

"It's the company that has been buying up property this past year. They put a bid on the green land outside of town, and Reynolds has been trying to get the town council to accept the offer."

"Yeah. My dad and uncle have been bitchin' about it. Little told me if they develop that land, it will pollute the reservoir."

"Exactly. That is what I heard too. Anyway, Reynolds set up some sort of anonymous company called E.R. Development, and he is manipulating the council into selling him that land."

West's eyes narrowed.

"I think he bought the building Lightsingers is in. He might be trying to put them out of business so he can build a mall. And he bought the building the brothel is in. He has been threatening to close Freida down unless she does what he wants. From what Liam has said, this E.R. company has purchased a lot of properties, and no one knows Reynolds is behind it."

West rubbed his temple and grunted.

"Reynolds tries to cover up every criminal thing that happens. He even interfered with the Smith murder investigation. I thought it was because he wanted to keep the town's reputation untarnished. Here, he's keeping people from looking too closely at him."

"I've never trusted him," West said.

"Those bruises on Tia, Freida's girl, are because he has started beating on them."

Understanding dawned in West's eyes. "Shit. Please tell me you aren't dressed like a prostitute because you are involved in a sting at the whorehouse."

I bit my lip.

"Don't they have some female cop who can do it?"

I ran my finger along West's jaw.

"Don't," he said, taking my hand off his face. "Don't try to distract me."

"I'll be fine. Sergeant O'Sullivan is working with homicide, the mayor of Greenport, and the Bellmount police force. There will be at least a half dozen law enforcement agents there." I didn't inform West that Miller and Shultz would also be there since that wouldn't bring him comfort.

"Please don't do this," he begged. "Ever since you walked back into my life, all I do is worry. Every day it's something else."

"Look," I said, caressing his cheek. "I'm a freak. I never fit in, and I never understood why I was different. But using my telepathy to help solve crimes means there is an important reason that I'm like this."

"You aren't a freak," he said.

Instead of arguing with him, I closed my eyes and composed my thoughts. "My telepathy will allow me to manipulate Reynolds. There will be listening devices in the rooms, and the cops are going to keep me safe."

West kicked at something invisible. "I didn't think O'Sullivan knew about your abilities."

"He doesn't."

"I don't understand. Then why is he letting you do

this?"

"Reynolds has killed three people. He's beating on women and creating an empire, and he is getting away with it. And West," I held his face so that he had no choice but to look into my eyes. "I almost died because he has some sort of maniacal power issue. I have to do this."

"I understand, and I'm proud of how brave you are, but I hate worrying, and every time you get hurt, I..." His voice trailed off.

"You know how you call my telepathy my superpower?"

"Yeah."

"Just think of me as a superhero, and I help save those poor women."

His jaw relaxed.

"Maybe I'll even help save the entire town from an evil villain."

"With that body—" he looked me over from head to toe. "You're Sexy Woman." He ran his finger over my charm. "Hey, that looks like the gun you tried to kill me with." He chuckled.

As usual, West's corny sense of humor made me giggle. I wrapped my arms around his neck and pulled his lips to mine. His hands circled my waist, and we held each other until it was time for me to go.

Arm in arm, we strolled into the main room, where I grabbed my coat.

"Aunt Polly, I'm sorry. Emergency. You have to cover. I'll explain later," he called.

West followed me to my car, where he climbed into the driver's seat. Confused, I sat in the passenger's seat.

"Key me." He held out his palm.

"What are you doing?" I asked.

"Driving you to the chicken ranch."

"Huh?"

He chuckled and bonked my nose. "It's another name for a whorehouse."

I stared at him.

"Never mind. I'm driving you to Greenport."

"West, you can't go in. The police won't let you near the place."

"Who says I'm going in? I'm just giving my girl a ride to her hooker-gig so she can save the world from an evil villain." He grinned. "I've always wanted to say that."

I poked his shoulder. "You have not."

"Nope. You're correct. Never wanted to use "my" and "girl" in the same sentence until I met you."

I kissed him and handed him the keys.

West started the engine.

Chapter 24

My confidence diminished two seconds after entering Freida's establishment because her nose crinkled as if I were smelly cheese. I lifted my underarm to sniff and inhaled deodorant and perfume.

She escorted me upstairs to the room where Sean's crew had set up surveillance equipment.

"The warrant came through," Sean said, right before his jaw hit the floor.

Miller shook his head in horror, and Shultz frowned. Sean's gawk dissipated as he doubled over and laughed until he nearly hyperventilated. By the time the sergeant pulled himself together, I was both irritated and ready to go home.

"You look like a cross between a drag queen and a bag lady," Sean informed me.

Freida nudged me to her bedroom, where we argued about a cantaloupe-colored spandex dress.

"Redheads can't wear orange," I insisted.

"You're platinum blond right now," she said.

I grimaced then violently shook my head. It wasn't the shade of the tight dress that had me concerned.

She held up a black skirt and an elegant cream-colored blouse.

"I can't wear that," I said.

"What's wrong with this?" She waved the outfit beneath my nose. "It's lovely, unlike that thing you have on."

It was lovely, but I didn't want my weapon to bulge from beneath a skin-tight skirt.

I lifted my chin. "I'm self-conscious about my rear."

She spun me around to check out my backside. "Well, last night you had a cute little ass, but today that rag makes it look huge."

I grunted. "I know I'm getting fat. Why is everyone lying to me?"

She grunted back. "You have an adorable little body, but in that outfit, you look like my grandmother the day she decided she wanted to screw the eighty-year-old butcher."

Winona, Keisha, and Greg hadn't appreciated my disguise, and Sean had almost wet himself in laughter. Why hadn't West told me how horrible I looked? He had even called me "sexy."

Freida rummaged through her closet. "How about this?" She handed me a blue dress and turned her back.

I disrobed and slipped the garment over my head. Sapphire silk draped perfectly to expose the rim of my cleavage. The cut tapered in to kiss my waist and hips, then flowed out, landing above my knee. I twirled, and the luxurious skirt swirled with me.

Freida crawled around on the floor of her closet. Her arm popped up, producing a pair of black stilettos. I removed Polly's clunky platforms and slid into Freida's slim pumps.

She exchanged my Halloween wig for long frosted waves. "It's my Farrah look." She shoved bobby pins into my scalp to secure the hairpiece. After placing me at her vanity, she wiped away and reapplied my makeup. Finally, Freida stood back and smiled. "There, much better." She walked me to her full-length mirror.

"Oh, I look like a movie star." I spun again.

"Gene won't be able to resist you." She grasped my hand. "Thank you. Most women in this backward county treat me like I have a disease. You, your aunt, and your friend were kind. And you are brave."

"My aunt is the most amazing woman in the world, and Winona is a sweetheart. Half the women in this town don't like me either." I forced a smile. "Thanks, but I'm not brave. I'm faking it. I'm terrified."

She kissed my cheek.

"Freida, if you can get out from under Reynolds and buy your own building, why don't you start another business?"

"I'm not sure what else I could do."

"Maybe a fashion boutique where you help women feel beautiful. You could choose their outfits and do makeovers."

Her pretty eyes twinkled. "You think people would come to me?"

"Are you kidding? Look at me." I used sweeping hands to showcase my enhanced look.

Freida pranced like a peacock as we made our way back to the cops. Miller raised an eyebrow in appreciation. My skin crawled at Shultz's grin.

Sean's lips parted. His tongue appeared, and he let out a moan. Then he tested my wig by tugging on it. "Perfect," he said. "But you're shaking."

"I'm terrified."

With his palms on my shoulders, he looked down at me. "You don't have to do this."

"Yes, I do. I know I can get him to talk. It is power

he wants, so I will hand it to him on a silver platter."

Sean escorted me into the hallway. "Remember, stay near the devices. At the bar, it's behind the schnapps, and while in the room, keep as close to the lamp as you can. You can't let him drag you anywhere else, and limit the amount of time in the hallway and on the stairs. If you talk loud enough, we can hear you in the room next door. Don't distort your voice. That could alert him that something's up."

I nodded.

He motioned to the wall. "Paper-thin."

I nodded again.

I followed him to the stairwell, where he whispered, "I'm sorry about my temper. I was frustrated when I visited you the other day. But I knew it was Reynolds, and I wanted you to stay away so you didn't get hurt."

Too terrified to respond, I bobbed my head in understanding.

"You can't carry that gun in your backpack anymore. Okay?"

"Okay." My thigh didn't count as a backpack.

Sean leaned in for a kiss. He smelled so good, and I was so scared that I froze for a moment before pulling away.

It was his turn to nod.

My archenemy and the disgrace entered the hallway, and Sean stepped back.

"Ready?" Miller asked.

I shivered. Miller and Shultz were my protectors. Would I be okay? I studied Sean's face one last time before descending the stairs.

You are going to be okay. Sean will keep you safe,

and you are brave, I assured myself as I stepped onto the first floor landing.

I exhaled then swung my hips as I strolled to the bar where Eli, the tall bartender, and Freida waited for me. I spied the bottle of schnapps then sat on a stool, willing my breath to slow.

A scantily clad stocky female officer from the Greenport force lounged on one of the couches as two cops stationed outside turned the evening's customers away.

Freida tapped on my thigh and pointed.

Kline sat in the corner disguised in a curly blond wig and a handlebar mustache. He made eye contact before disappearing through the velvet draperies.

Two minutes later, I followed Freida's shocked gaze.

Two women and a man entered from the foyer. The tall, dark-skinned woman wore a silver pants suit and a long blonde wig. The big-boned woman wore a purple boa, sunglasses, and a beach hat. My boyfriend hadn't even bothered to disguise himself.

"Freida! What are they doing here? How did they get in?"

She shrugged.

A sheepish Kline trailed behind them. Winona had to have bamboozled him into admitting them. Unless West had threatened him, or Keisha had terrified him?

Kline gave us a thumbs up. That might be the last time the infatuated officer used the digit because when Sean found out what he had done, he would rip every one of the officer's fingers off.

My unlikely backup crew posed on the settee at the far end of the room.

I shot West an evil eye.

He pulled Keisha onto his lap and hid his face behind platinum strands.

Although the clock said it had been twenty minutes, the room stood still for what seemed an eternity.

Kline stuck his index finger in the air and pointed toward the front door.

My heart missed a beat, then pounded like a bass drum on fire.

Reynolds entered wearing a black fedora. His coat collar concealed his chin. He didn't look suspicious in the least.

West's eyes peeked out from under Keisha's fake hair, and Winona ducked behind her boa.

Freida's shaking arm leaned on the bar as the bartender nervously set a glass of whiskey on the counter.

Nope, nothing odd going on at all.

"Well, who do we have here?" Reynolds gaped at my bosom.

I fought a gag. It had been pointless to beg Sean to include me in the operation because I couldn't do it. I stared into Freida's sad eyes, remembered how they brightened at the mention of freedom and a fashion boutique and received a bolt of courage.

"I'm Farrah," I said.

Freida's eyes sparkled, and the hint of a smile tugged at her lips.

Reynolds picked up the whiskey and sipped while I motioned for my drink. Sean had instructed me to get Reynolds to drink as much as possible early on. I, on the other hand, was drinking a sparkling apple juice that looked like wine. The bartender filled my glass, and I downed it. Chugging apple juice was more challenging than I expected. I liked applesauce, apple pie, and apple dumplings. But apple juice—two words—baby urine.

"Another," I said.

The mayor gulped. "Make that two." He pointed to his empty glass.

He was a piece of cake.

"Farrah's my new girl," Freida said.

Ignoring the absurd trio in the corner, I glanced at the putrid Reynolds through false lashes. "My first night.".

"Really?" Reynolds asked.

Freida answered for me. "She's learning the ropes. I'm not putting her on the floor yet."

Reynolds's grin made me ill.

He ran a finger over my shoulder. "I'll show her the ropes."

Freida put a shaking hand on her hip. "No!"

He bristled. "Why the hell not?"

I used the line I had practiced. "I haven't had a john yet."

His chest expanded. "I'm going to be your first."

He was putty in our hands.

Freida followed the script. "Absolutely not."

Meanwhile Eli and I plied the creep full of booze.

"Do I need to remind you who is in charge?" Reynolds asked while using his sleeve as a napkin.

Freida was one heck of an actress. She lifted her chin, and pursed her lips.

Reynolds did three shots in less than five minutes. Sean had told me to aim for five in ten minutes. Anymore, and he would be too drunk to talk, any less, and he wouldn't be loose-lipped enough to blab.

I dangled the glass in front of him and smiled.

He clasped it in his bloated fingers. Then, without taking a sip, he discarded it on the counter and shot Freida an intimidating glower.

I bit my lip and thought. I picked up his glass, waited until he made eye contact, then licked the rim.

Yuck! Yuck! Yuck! On so many levels—Yuck!

It worked. Reynolds clasped the glass, licked where my tongue had been, tilted his head back, and the liquid disappeared down his throat.

One more to go, then all I had to do was get him upstairs and make him think he had been in control the entire time.

"Come on." He reached for my arm.

"Another drink?" I asked.

"No, I'm good," he said.

I grabbed the bottle from Eli's hand. Winona and Keisha grabbed West and held him on the settee. Gene Reynolds grabbed my arm and dragged me up the velvet wallpapered stairwell of Freida's house of ill repute.

****

I led a stout middle-aged man who smelled like two-day-old seafood into a red room. He removed his coat and hat. I cringed at the spare tire above his waist and the lousy dye job atop his head. I stood in front of the gold lamp and attempted a seductive pose with the whiskey bottle.

"Are you a virgin?" Mayor Reynolds asked.

"Do you want me to be?"

He answered with a firm, "Yes."

I swung the bottle back and forth and pushed my

hip out in what I hoped was a provocative stance. "Let's have another drink."

He sat on the edge of the bed.

I brought the whiskey to my lips and pretended to take a swig. The brief encounter with my skin burned. I handed the flask to him, and he gulped. We repeated the back-and-forth dance with the golden bottle three more times.

"Are you nervous?" he asked.

"A little." I hoped I was a convincing actress because "a lot" would have been a more accurate answer. "I'm a virgin, and you seem like an important man." I did one thousand eyelash flutters in one second.

"I am," he said.

I giggled. "I like that my first time is with a powerful man."

"Then you will enjoy this." He held the bottle in one hand and pulled my waist to him with the other.

What if I puked all over him?

I lightly pushed him onto the red bed and then knelt before him, keeping one hand on his bare wrist. "Are you a lawyer?"

He touched the swell of my bosom. "No."

I tapped a finger to my cheek. "Are you a doctor?"

"No."

"I know! You are a politician," I said.

"Yes." He clonked the bottle on the floor and played with a strand of my fake hair. "Have you ever given a politician a blow job?" His other hand searched for his zipper.

There was a touch of humor in his disgusting question. He was so drunk he couldn't find his zipper.

"How powerful are you?" I asked in my best airhead voice.

"The most powerful man in the county." He continued to search for the elusive zipper.

Placing my hand on his allowed me to divine that he wanted to brag about himself.

"Tell me more, Mr. Politician."

"I'm a mayor; I'm rich; I fuck who I want, and I own this county," he slurred.

"Rich? Do you own property?"

"I own thisss building you work in. The biggest department store in western Pennsylvania. Four restaurantsss." He blinked, and both of his hands fell limply to his side.

I caressed his hand. "Tell me more."

"I'm mayor of the town over, and the damn town councilsss so dumb they don't know I'm tricking them into selling me everything." He moved his head forward and back as he struggled to focus his gaze.

He wanted me to tell him he was sexy, so I did.

"Smart men are sexy."

Reynolds wanted to tell me that he had outsmarted the cops, but he wasn't sure if he could trust me. He decided he would tell me and then shut me up by threatening me and shoving his body parts into my mouth. He thought maybe I was the kind of girl who got turned on by bad boys. Perhaps he was in for a night of crazy sex and I would do filthy things to him. He wondered if he might get to force me to do those things. Finally, he asked himself why he felt woozy and drunk.

He was a depraved hideous human.

"Tell me more, Mr. Sexy Mayor," I said. "I want to be a special friend to you."

"The local sheriff's such a stupid asssss. I framed him for three crimessss I committed, and he got locked in prisssson. I even got his replacement all picked out."

"Oh, Mr. Mayor," I cooed. "You outsmarted everyone, and no one will ever know. So sexy!"

"Yessss. I hired a guy to get rid of a troublemaker, and then I got rid of him, too. Did 'im in myself."

Bingo! We had our confession.

"Time to fuck, my little Farrah." He reached for me.

I stood, but before I could step away, he grabbed me, pushed me onto the bed, and climbed on top of me.

I pounded on his chest. "Get off of me!"

Although he was uncoordinated from drink, he was strong. While his body weight held me down, his hands slid under my dress, grabbing at the waist of my underwear.

I wriggled with all my might and clasped at his groping hands.

"What the hell is this?" he asked.

I made one last-ditch effort to push him off of me. Unfortunately, the elastic gave before I could get away.

"Sean!" I called just as Reynolds pulled Princess from under my dress.

Reynolds held her in the air. "A gun?"

I rolled out from under him and jumped off the bed.

He fought with coordination as he tried to talk, stand, and point the gun at me. "You a vice cop?"

I exhaled. "No."

The gun shook in his trembling hand. He ripped the wig and the net from my head, and ringlets tumbled. It took his drunk eyes time to focus. "Edith Marshall's niece. I should 'ave known."

The door flew open, and both Reynolds and I jumped. I expected Sean to barge in and save me. However, that didn't happen.

"You piece of shit," Mike Stevens yelled. "I know you killed Joe! I know you canceled the guy that was supposed to fix the security camera so you could skulk around my place spying on me, and then you left the body to scare my wife. You son of a bitch!"

"Please, Mayor Reynolds. Put down the gun," I begged.

Stevens's gaze landed on the bejeweled weapon and he froze.

Reynolds's outstretched arm continued to quake, and the gun swayed from side to side.

Stevens studied the wavering mayor and then let out a disturbing laugh. "You mother fucker, you're drunk." He stepped toward us.

I knew with every fiber of my being that Reynolds intended to use the gun since I had just been privy to his thoughts. I'm unsure if I directed my "No! Please don't" to the drunk man with the flailing weapon or the angry skeptic charging towards his death.

Bang! Bang!

Stevens collapsed.

I closed my eyes and prayed.

****

It took an eternity for the cops to enter the room and aim their guns at Reynolds. I hadn't wanted Greg Grainey to die. However, I wanted pieces of Reynolds' brain to splatter against the wall. Instead, he dropped my gun onto the bed and lifted his hands above his head.

Sean motioned for me to move from the center of the fray.

Terrified, I followed his instructions precisely.

Mike Stevens sat propped against the wall, his hand covering his bloody shoulder. Officer Kline stepped into the hall to call for an ambulance. Shultz's gun remained on the mayor, Miller hung out like he was on a Jamaican vacation.

Sean read Reynolds his Miranda rights—no pun intended. "Keep your hands up and turn around slowly. That's good. Now hands behind your head."

I bent to check on Stevens as a worried West appeared in the doorway.

"Shortcake," he called.

Miller returned from his retirement cruise to bar West's entrance with an outstretched palm. "How in the hell did you get up here?"

Kline looked at his feet.

West pushed past the men and wrapped me in his arms.

"I'm okay," I murmured.

"Thank God." He kissed the top of my head and held me so tightly I thought he might squeeze my insides out of my ears.

Shivering, I held onto him and soaked up his body heat.

"*Humph,*" the bleeding Stevens said. "I got it all wrong. I thought since you two were making out in that car in front of my store, you were the item." He pointed to Sean, then me.

I gasped.

West backed up, looked at me, then Sean. "Shit!" he said. His head hung forward as he left the room.

I followed him. "West, let me explain."

The color had drained from West's face.

I frantically reached for him. "That isn't what happened."

"Did you make out with O'Sullivan?"

"Yes. But—"

Sean stepped into the hall and pointed at West. "Hey, you need to get out of here, now!"

Perhaps West Westinghouse was pale because Sean O'Sullivan had absorbed the color from everything in that hallway. Sean's face was fire engine red, with patches of purple and blue here and there. He pointed at me.

"And Albright, don't you fucking go anywhere."

"I can't do this relationship shit. I tried, but it hurts too damn much," West said before walking away from me.

****

The drive to the state police headquarters in Greenport was the longest, loneliest ten minutes of my life. I needed West, and if I couldn't have him, I required Keisha and Winona. However, Kline escorted them back to Bellmount. Therefore, I was companionless and ashamed as I made the horrible trek across Greenport dry-heaving to the memory of Reynold's touches.

When I entered the station, I received accolades, high fives, and pats on the back from everyone I passed.

"We got him."

"You were amazing!"

"Reynolds's is going to jail for a very long time."

"That piece of shit's career and life are finished."

The praise came from everyone but Sean. The fire

in his eyes incinerated me as he grumbled, "Jesus Christ. How in the hell did you get the gun in the room?"

I fired back. "Why did it take you so long to get to me?"

Waves of heat radiated from him. "Because I heard him find your damn gun, and we couldn't very well barge in there and have him blow your head off. Or worse, one of our heads!"

I sought out a bathroom stall and remained there until someone knocked on the door.

"Are you okay?" the station receptionist asked. "Sergeant O'Sullivan is looking for you. I think they need you in Lieutenant Kramer's office."

I swiped at my tears with toilet paper."I'm fine."

The receptionist escorted me to a room where I sat with Sean, Miller, and an intimidating woman named Lieutenant Bonnie Kramer. Kramer asked the same questions in numerous ways. Then came the one I dreaded.

"Dr. Albright, does the gun that Mayor Gene Reynolds used to shoot Mike Stevens belong to you?"

"Yes," I said.

"How did it get to the scene?"

My shoulders slumped "I carried it in under my dress."

Miller muttered "*Pfft.*"

Sean drummed his fingers on the table.

Not only had I lost my boyfriend, but I was going to jail. Sean couldn't protect me this time, and we both knew it.

"Was this part of the operation as discussed with Sergeant O'Sullivan and Detective Miller?" Kramer asked.

There was a knock on the door, and Shultz's bulbous head appeared. "Hey, Lieutenant, I just got word from the hospital that Mike Stevens is going to be okay. I also wanted to make sure everyone's aware that Dr. Albright's paperwork to carry her gun is in order. I have it in my office back in Bellmount."

Had Shultz been watching from one of those mirrored rooms?

He sniffed at something. "I'll let you get back to it." He closed the door.

Shultz, my nemesis and enemy had just saved my hide. Although, by securing Reynold's confession, I had also saved his.

The lines in Sean's face never softened, but his shoulders relaxed.

I remained a jumble of nerves because the questions continued for another hour. Before I left my inquisition, I asked, "Are you closing down Freida's business?"

The lieutenant shrugged. "As far as I know, there weren't any vice cops there tonight." She glared at Sean. "Although, it seems I wasn't apprised of everything ahead of time."

For the time being, Freida was safe. Although it seemed Sean was in all kinds of trouble. To be fair, I had informed him I wasn't worth the messes I caused—numerous times—and he hadn't heeded the warnings. Still, guilt surged through me.

Shultz slept in a chair outside the lieutenant's office. He folded his hands across his chest and propped his head against the wall.

I stopped in front of him.

He opened his eyes and grunted. "Thanks."

I forced myself to say, "You too."

"You're still a pain in my ass," he said.

"You're still maggot poo," I said.

He narrowed his beady little eyes. "That's Sheriff Maggot Poo to you, young lady." His lips curled into a sneer, and his bloated jowls quivered.

Chapter 25

Winona had pined away, convinced that she wouldn't have a date for the Westinghouse holiday party, but there she was, on the makeshift dance floor, surrounded by merrymakers and twirling in Dinky's arms. Polly and Will slow-danced beside Aunt Edith and Russ. Tommy's eyes were bright, and his grin humongous as he escorted Trisha, the aerobics instructor, around the floor. Liam and Gina needed waltzing lessons because they used their lips instead of their legs to dance. Yuck!

At least three dozen Westinghouses, and a dozen more of their friends, had driven in from the farthest reaches of the county to celebrate. Willa, Winona's sister, visited from Pittsburgh. Grandma Westinghouse wore her matriarchal crown with panache. Her hair was teased. Her lipstick was red. Her cigarette hung from her mouth and her hazel-colored eyes took in everything.

Weston Westinghouse the Third wore a smile that caused a painful ache that started in my toes, flowed through every one of my veins, then exploded behind my overtaxed heart.

Only three people in that room weren't enjoying themselves—Pop, Keisha, and me.

Keisha waved to West, then leaned close. "That smile is fake. He's as miserable as we are."

"You know what's so ironic? Winona thought she was the one who wouldn't have a date. She thought you and I would have multiple dates," I said.

Keisha snorted.

"I miss West so much I can't breathe."

"I know." She clasped my hand. "It will get easier. Maybe you should get back together with Bradley."

I exhaled. "Brad is perfect, but he isn't my soul mate."

Keisha smiled and waved to Tommy. "I don't like that Trisha girl. You're correct. She's too perky!"

I kept my amusement inside of me for two reasons. First, I wanted to prove how miserable I was. Second, I didn't want Keisha to know that I had discovered she had feelings for Tommy. It was pointless since she would deny them.

"I'm going to go say hi to West. Do you want anything to drink?"

"Sure," she said. "Grab me a glass of wine and a brownie."

West sat at a table with his country bumpkin relatives, mussing his cousin Cindi's hair.

I approached and sheepishly said, "Hello."

A table of Westinghouses greeted me.

"Hi, West," I said.

He looked me over from head to toe and gave me a lopsided grin. "Glad you came, Doctor Shortcake."

I clamped my mouth shut and didn't mention that Keisha, Winona, and Aunt Edith had forced me.

"Hi, Miranda," tiny Cindi Westinghouse said, her tongue slightly protruding through her toothy grin.

"Hi, Cindi. The last time I saw you, we played dolls." She had been almost thirteen at the time, and I had helped Aunt Edith look after her.

"I'm not a baby anymore." Her grin was so wide it knocked at her thick-lensed glasses.

"No. You are a grown woman now. How old are you?"

"I'm twenty. When I'm twenty-one, I can work at the inn. Edith says I'll be a good worker."

West ruffled her hair again.

She giggled. "I'm grade-ating soon."

"You're graduating? That's great," I said.

"Miranda, I will call you Doctor Shortcake, like Weston," Cindi declared.

Cindi had a slight speech impediment, so I tilted my ear to hear her over the music and surrounding conversations.

"Doctor Shortcake, I think you're pretty. I'm a detective. And West loves you."

Gasps filled the room. How adorable. Cindi Westinghouse made her rakish cousin blush.

"Cindi Lou, are you making up stories again?" West asked.

Cindi shook her head so hard her glasses wobbled. "I don't make up stories except about ghosts because ghosts aren't real."

It was my turn to gasp. "Well, have a great time, everyone. I have to get my friend a glass of wine and some dessert." I turned, swallowed, and composed myself.

I poured Keisha's wine and perused the dessert table as someone behind me said, "Hi, Red."

"Sean, what are you doing here?"

"I have a Christmas present for you. I stopped at the inn first, but you weren't there, so I assumed you were here." He handed me an unwrapped box. "It isn't anything big. Just something I thought you'd get a kick out of."

"I've wanted to talk to you," I said. "I'm sorry about the gun and that I got you into trouble. It's just... I've almost died a couple of times. Anyway, I was an idiot, and I'm sorry."

"I didn't get into too much trouble, and I'm over my tantrum. You have a knack for worrying me, pissing me off, and making me lose my mind with desi—" He stopped talking at West's approach.

West squared off against Sean with tense shoulders and clenched fists. "Hey, Sergeant. I'm not sure how you missed it because it's huge, but there's a sign on the front door that says Closed For A Private Party."

"I'm not staying. I wanted to give Miranda something before I left town. I don't suppose I'll be back too often unless she continues to stumble over corpses." He chuckled. "Although I do love Edith's cookies."

Fire shot from the normally laid-back West's eyes.

The hot-tempered Sean remained unusually calm and relaxed. "Bartender, I need to talk to you for a minute."

"Oh?" West's eyebrow raised, and his eye spasmed.

"Privately," Sean said.

West worked his jaw back and forth—back and forth. "I'm busy with my friends and family."

"It will just take a minute. It's pretty important."

West motioned for Sean to follow.

My stomach dropped as they disappeared down the back hallway. What could they possibly have to talk about?

I headed to my table.

"What's going on?" Keisha asked.

"I don't know," I said.

"Where's my wine?"

"I don't know."

"My brownie?"

"Sorry, I forgot it."

I stared at the hallway, waiting for the men to return.

"What's in the box?" Keisha asked.

I gently shook the gift in my hand. "I don't know."

"For crying out loud, open it."

I lifted the lid to discover a child's plastic detective badge. Although embarrassed by private investigator jokes, I thought it cute, so I pinned it to my sweater.

About five minutes later, Sean entered and strolled to our table.

"Hi, Ms. Brown," he said.

"Sergeant." She winked at him.

I showcased my badge with a sweeping arm gesture. "I love it."

Sean chuckled. Will you walk me to my car?"

"Sure. If you tell me what was so important that you had to talk to West privately."

The second the door closed behind us, he said, "I tried to talk some sense into him. I think things will be okay between the two of you once he calms down. Although I can't say the same thing for his wrist or the wall."

I cringed.

We strolled to the cop car parked in the no-parking zone.

Sean opened the automobile door. "I think he'll be out here any second. But if he doesn't get his head out of his ass, I'm only forty minutes away."

A bark distracted me. I bent low and held out my arms. "Knight!"

A tiny black fluff ball ran to me and licked my lips.

I gazed upward. "Hi Brad. Out for a walk?"

Just then, the door behind me opened.

"Told you." Sean inclined his chin toward the man behind me and lifted one muscular leg into his car.

"Miranda, I'm done pretending. You need to know, I love you," Dr. Bradley Gordon blurted out in front of an audience as his puppy kissed me.

"Wow, I didn't expect that one. Welcome to 1990, Red," Sean O'Sullivan said right before he placed his other leg into his car, closed the door, and started the engine.

From behind me, West simply sputtered, "Shit!"

Epilogue

Mid-January brought Bellmount's second official blizzard of the season. Liam could have made it to his apartment if he had wanted to walk. Instead, he asked, "Mom, can you put me up for the weekend?"

Aunt Edith practically wept with joy. She packed ham and cheese sandwiches, a tin of leftover Christmas cookies, a jar of homemade pickles, plates, napkins, and a bag of corn chips into her picnic basket. Russ handed Liam a six-pack of beer. Then Liam and I bundled up and held onto each other as we chortled and slid down the big hill.

We passed by the *Closed Due To Inclement Weather* sign taped to the pub's front door and made our way up the side stairs. Liam knocked. West answered, and his eyes lit up. Unfortunately, he wasn't looking at me.

He grabbed the basket and rummaged through it. "I'm gonna marry Edith."

Tommy was upon us in an instant. He grabbed the six-pack. "I'm gonna marry Russ."

I removed my boots and set them by the front door. Then I laid my hat and coat on West's bed alongside the guys' winter gear. Since I was cold, I kept my gloves on.

West had neatly arranged the Christmas presents I had given him. A copper lamp and a hard copy of *Zen and the Art of Motorcycle Maintenance* sat on the nightstand beside his flashlight. A brass W marked the page he was on. I ran my gloved finger over the embossed lettering on the book. My heart ached, recalling the note I had written inside*: West, with all my heart. Forever, Your Shortcake.*

I plopped into the center of the couch as the guys fixed their snacks. Usually a chowhound, I was too nervous to eat. I missed West so much that I had spent large amounts of time struggling to breathe, and this was the first time I had seen him since the unfortunate holiday party.

So what if our relationship had been a disaster, and no one else thought we made a good couple? Who cared if West was a big chicken who was jealous that I had kissed one man and another had proclaimed his love for me? West was my soulmate, and somehow I would prove it to him. I was relentless, obsessed, and stubborn, after all. Weston Westinghouse the Third had no idea that he had released a red tornado the first time he kissed me.

Liam, his plate of food in hand, sat beside me. "I was thinking next month we could do a movie night at my place, and I could invite Gina."

I balked.

"Great idea," Tommy said. "I could invite Trisha."

I fought the urge to clutch at my heart.

"No way," said West. "No skirts at movie night."

"Randa's a skirt," Tommy pointed out.

"No, Miranda's a shortcake, not a skirt."

I wasn't thrilled with the negative female connotation, but no way did I want a Bellmount Bitch and Perkypants at movie night. "I agree with West. No girls. I don't count."

"I agree with big-ears and pretty-boy. I think we need more skirts," Greg said as he tried to squeeze in between Tommy and me. He didn't fit, so he pushed on Tommy with all of his ghostly strength.

Tommy swatted at the air. "I think there's a fly in here."

"In the winter?" West said. "I don't think so."

"True," Tommy said as he batted at Greg's ethereal form.

Greg snorted in disgust, gave up, and propped himself on the arm of the couch.

"Fine, movie night is just for guys and Shortcake. I'll host a dinner party at my place for Valentine's. All four of us come, and if anyone wants to bring a date, they can," Liam said.

"What about me?" Greg asked.

"Great idea," said Tommy.

West and I both groaned.

West excused himself to the kitchen and brought back two glasses of water. He handed me one and sipped at the other before picking up the remote. "Who's ready for the movie?"

"Me," Greg yelled, raising his hand into the air.

"What are you smiling at?" West asked.

I bit my lip. "I guess I'm just happy to be with my friends."

Greg grinned.

West scratched his head, pressed play, and we stared at the television screen. Five minutes into the old movie about a down-and-out boxer, West pressed pause.

Groans from the peanut gallery echoed off the

wooden walls.

"Turn it on, Westinghouse," Liam yelled.

"Movie! Movie! Movie!" Tommy chanted.

A projectile corn chip hit West in the head.

"What the hell? Who's throwing food?" West asked.

"Not I," Tommy and Liam said in chorus.

West picked the chip up and glared at me.

"I didn't throw anything," I said.

Greg chuckled, and I shot him a dirty look.

After depositing the snack into the trash, West grabbed the afghan off his bed. He carried it back to the couch and tossed it into the air over top of me. When it landed, he tucked it around me. "You looked cold."

I held the blanket to my nose and breathed in West's scent. "Not anymore. Now I'm warm and almost perfect."

West's eyes softened. "Me too," he said. "Almost."

Then he strolled to his chair and pressed play.

www.ingramcontent.com/pod-product-compliance
Lightning Source LLC
Chambersburg PA
CBHW051130030726
47504CB00004B/791